Praise for
NOT HER DAUGHTER

"A cleverly constructed novel that will have you questioning everything you believe about right or wrong. Frey skillfully tangles you up in these two women's lives and never lets up on the tension all the way until the dramatic conclusion. A remarkable portrayal of motherhood, in all its beautiful glory and heart-wrenching despair."
—*New York Times* bestselling author Chevy Stevens

"In *Not Her Daughter,* Frey pulls off a difficult task: balancing a nail-biting plot with a thought-provoking question—is a crime committed with the best intentions still a crime? A chilling, powerful tale of love and sacrifice, of truth and perception, *Not Her Daughter* will make you miss your bedtime, guaranteed. A stunning debut."
—Kimberly Belle, internationally bestselling author of
The Marriage Lie

"A deft and beautifully written examination of taboo maternal fantasies: Can a kidnapping ever be justified? Can motherhood be undone? Engrossing and suspenseful, Frey writes her characters with depth and compassion, challenging readers to question their own codes of ethics."   —Zoje Stage, author of *Baby Teeth*

not her daughter

Rea Frey

St. Martin's Paperbacks

For the girl with the red bow . . .
I still remember you.

This is a work of fiction. All of the characters, organizations, and events portrayed in this novel are either products of the author's imagination or are used fictitiously.

Published in the United States by St. Martin's Paperbacks, an imprint of St. Martin's Publishing Group

NOT HER DAUGHTER

Copyright © 2018 by Rea Frey.

All rights reserved.

For information, address St. Martin's Publishing Group, 120 Broadway, New York, NY 10271.

www.stmartins.com

ISBN: 978-1-250-20957-3

Our books may be purchased in bulk for promotional, educational, or business use. Please contact your local bookseller or the Macmillan Corporate and Premium Sales Department at 1-800-221-7945, ext. 5442, or by e-mail at MacmillanSpecialMarkets@macmillan.com.

Printed in the United States of America

St. Martin's Griffin edition / August 2018
St. Martin's Paperbacks edition / July 2019

10   9   8   7   6   5   4   3   2   1

acknowledgments

Books are a precarious thing, and this one is no exception.

To my incredible, enthusiastic, tireless agent, Rachel Beck, who *makes shit happen*; to my steadfast editor, Alexandra Sehulster, whose instincts, passion, collaboration, and insight have made this a better book; to the sales force at St. Martin's Press and everyone at the audio team: Mary Beth Roche, Robert Allen, Kathryn Carroll, Laura Wilson, Samantha Beerman, and Brisa Robinson; to the publicity team: Staci Burt, Brant Janeway, and Jordan Hanley; to my copy editor, Karen Richardson, and cover designer, Lesley Worrell.

To Crystal Patriarche of BookSparks, who made me bust my ass to raise enough money through freelance projects to afford you; to the writers I worship who provided blurbs; to Francesca Vannucci, who taught me that Instagram isn't all shameless selfies and internet trolls; to my Nashville writing group: Brad, Cassidy, Deana, Cheryl, Betsy, and Pam. Finding you was magic. Your writing is magic. You all inspire me to be better. To Kyle and Johnny, two men who have brawn *and* brains. Your enthusiasm, belief, humor, and friendship have made all the difference.

To my village of women (and one man): April, Dena, Helena, Jess, Amanda, Jenn, Nikki, Lauren, and Jeremy. Mothering is hard. Writing a book while mothering, wifing, working, and adulting is harder. You ladies (and gentleman) have let me talk, laugh, obsess, and provide playtime for my child when I went into zombie writing mode. I couldn't do this parenthood thing without you.

To Jessica Zweig, my female soul mate. Working with you has made me a better writer, human, and friend.

To my family, who is awesome, to writers who never give up, to my husband, who was my first reader, is my everyday PIC, and very best friend; to my daughter, who makes me understand the thin line between love and sanity, protectiveness and throwing myself off a cliff. You are my greatest story.

And lastly, to my readers: you are in the business of making dreams come true. Here's to the next one.

I love her
and that's the beginning and end
of everything.

—*F. SCOTT FITZGERALD*

sarah

during

I grip her hand. Dirt clings to her small palm and makes caked half-moons under her nails. I squeeze her against my side, a shield against the drizzle. Her red bow bobs as we move faster down the road. Even here, I can't escape the rain.

Don't stop moving.

My heart pirouettes and shoots a melodic thump to the center of my forehead—usually a precursor to a massive headache—but this, *this* is all nerves. My legs slice forward uncertainly, both of us moving toward our new destination.

She peers up at me, eyebrows pinched, her left cheek bloated and red. She opens her mouth, closes it. Without thinking, I adjust the umbrella and scoop her up, wrapping her spindly legs around my waist. Her shins dangle around my middle, which makes it difficult to walk.

A few more steps and we will be there. A few more steps and I can figure out what I'm doing, where I'm going, what I've just done.

We cross the threshold into the small, sparse, barren lobby. I lower the umbrella and tug her higher on my hip. I walk across the slick marble entryway, my shoes squeaking on the checked floor. My fingers hover over her red bow and her swollen cheek, concealing both in case anyone is bothering to look. I move to the bank of elevators, pressing a scratched, gold button. I tap my foot. I pull the girl higher. Her sour breath sweeps across my neck. With caution, I glance over my shoulder. My stomach roils—a warning.

The doors open. An elderly couple file out before we step in. I hit "4"—the top floor of this boutique hotel—and finally, carefully, ease the girl down.

It is only then that she looks at me—really looks at me—before shuffling back against the shiny, mirrored wall. I resist the urge to tell her to be careful against the glass.

"Where's my mommy?" she whispers, so that I have to lean in to hear.

"She's . . ." I hear the question and consider my answers. Her mother is at home. Her mother is searching. Her mother had her chance. I straighten. "She's at your house, remember?" I can see the question on Emma's face—*shouldn't I be with her, then?*—but we reach the floor and exit. I fish my key card from my wallet, my eyes on Emma, who has the pace of a child who's in no rush.

I tap the key to the lock, see the green light, and hear the soft click as I push the heavy door back on its hinges. We slip into darkness. It is humid, the air thick with the stench of cleaning products. I flip on the light and assess the tidy room. She stands a few feet from me, her breath punching the silence.

"Are you okay? Are you hungry?"

She turns. Her red bow quivers on top of her brown hair. She shakes her head no. Her eyes fill with tears. I need to shut this down, but I'm not sure what to say or how to handle this. We are practically strangers.

"Is Mommy looking for me?" She speaks louder than before, with more conviction.

I want to tell her to forget about her mother—that wherever that wretched woman looks, she won't find us. "I'm not sure, sweetheart."

I move past her and shove my clothes back into my bag, fighting the urge to run out of here as fast as I can. I probably have an hour, maybe more, before this town is turned upside down.

I walk over to her, unclip the red bow from her hair, and drop it into my bag.

The first piece of evidence.

"We have to go now," I say. "Will you come with me?"

She nods and swipes the edge of her palm up and across her nostrils, wincing as her fingertips flick against her tender cheek. I already paid for the night—in cash—but we are leaving. The room will sit here, empty, hot, and scrubbed clean by housekeeping.

I grab her hand as we head for the door again. Emma walks a few steps behind and kicks at the carpet, dragging the fingers of her left hand across the floral wallpaper, as though she is combing through water. I press the elevator button and scan the hallway. A few doors open and close, but no one joins us. The elevator opens. Empty. A sign? A small gift? I call to her—easy now—and she steps on again.

"Do you want to push the button?" I motion to the "1," but she shakes her head and shies away from me. I stab the button and wait for the doors to close. We lower, floor by floor, one step closer to freedom.

I drown the panic, tamp it down as best as I can. I don't know what I'm doing or what I've done, but I have to keep moving. I have to get home. And I have to take Emma—sweet, unsuspecting Emma—with me. She is my responsibility now, and I will do everything I can to protect her. I am rewriting her story, altering her memories, shifting her shitty childhood into clean chunks: *before, during, after. Then, now, someday.*

I take a quaking breath and wait. The elevator bumps to the first floor. A beat. The doors slide open. We step through.

We move on.

before

I opened my eyes.

It was a full minute before I registered Ethan was not beside me, his arms scooped under my ribs, as if preparing to roll me onto the floor. He never had morning breath—a lucky trait that left him brazen with a.m. kisses. Every morning, I would self-consciously extricate myself from his tangle of limbs to brush my teeth and slap on deodorant.

I had to get out of this condo before the daily reminders started: the lack of coffee, the stillness of the bedroom, the quiet, solo dressing, the crisp sheets on the right side of the bed. He was in our favorite café. He was on the muddy, green trails. He was on the TriMet, the MAX Light Rail, waiting outside the NW patisserie with a scone and a smile. The memory of him was everywhere.

People broke up every day. People lost people. People went through actual tragedies beyond the sad girl-meets-boy-boy-breaks-girl's-heart tale. I had to get on with it already.

Despite the millions of things I missed about him, what I missed the most, at the moment, was his coffee. He'd bought me a Chemex for my birthday, and despite never drinking coffee himself, he'd researched, bloomed, and whittled the brewing time to a swift science.

"Would you look at this?"

I'd scoot beside him, our elbows bumping, as I inhaled the rich dark chocolate and woodsy smells of whatever local brew he'd bought. "What?"

"There are like three bubbles in this. This coffee is shit." He'd palm the bag, poring over every detail, as if he'd missed something the $17.99 price tag had disguised. When he got a good bag and the bubbles exploded like soapsuds, he'd slap the countertop as if he'd won some sort of coffee competition. I loved this about him, loved that he had a personal investment in perfecting something that mattered to me, not him. I felt so lucky then, wrapped firmly in what I believed to be It. The One. Forever. There wasn't a world in which we didn't exist together.

Now that there was, I didn't know if I wanted to be a part of it.

I pulled up to the loft at 9:00 A.M. and rode the elevator to the seventh floor, running my eyes over the company logo: TACK, Teach. Activate. Create. Know. Ethan had carved the sign from walnut and helped bolt it to the wall almost three years ago.

"Morning, boss lady." Madison greeted me at the front desk.

"Morning. Busy yet?"

"Oh, you know." She walked around the desk to take my things. "Always. Do you want coffee first?"

I nodded, entered my office, and walked straight to the windows—my favorite feature—and pressed my fingers against the cool glass. It was raining, something

I hardly ever noticed anymore, mostly because it was always raining.

When I moved to Portland, I used to think it was just something people said—*it rains all the time!*—but it did rain as much as they said. Misty, ropy rain that saturated your hair and clothes just enough to be annoying. My hair was perpetually in a state of frizz, which meant I kept it knotted high on my head, in a bun, rammed with endless bobby pins. Ethan used to find the pins everywhere: in the couch cushions, on the floor, in the sheets. He'd open them up and create little uses for them, like scraping earwax from his ear—much to my horror—and pitting a whole bowlful of cherries, thanks to a video he saw on YouTube.

I fingered my skeleton-key necklace and flicked the metal around and around, thinking of all I had on the docket over the next few weeks. I was rolling out to Ethiopia and Senegal—two places I hadn't yet been for TACK. We had new products to implement in each country, and who better than the CEO to bring the children their educational kits?

TACK had started small, like most things: digital activity books personalized to children's interests. Kids or parents filled out questionnaires of their ages, favorite toys, subjects, and activities, and I crafted personalized stories to help them learn. Their parents would send photos of their children's beloved toys, pets, and a headshot, so they could become the stars in their own adventures. The activity books had gone viral in a matter of months; I'd been urged to make actual kits, though I wanted to stay in the digital space to keep costs down. Eventually, I'd tinkered with the idea of personalized kits specified to cultural interests, instead of age group. It had caught on so strongly internationally that I had three buyers desperate to purchase my business. They called once a week with offers that made my mind twitch with the possibility of complete financial freedom, but I wasn't there yet. I was still obsessed with my business and wanted to stay focused on both global and domestic growth.

Madison interrupted my train of thought with a giant mug of coffee. "Got the last of Travis's homemade almond milk."

"Perfect. Thank you." I gripped the hot mug and took a long sip.

Madison brought up her iPad and divulged all the recent orders, my travel itinerary, and what products had a few issues we were tweaking. "Brad and team have already started working out the kinks, so don't panic. Seriously. They're handling it." Madison gnawed at her bottom lip. She knew me well; if there were issues, I liked to take care of them myself. I'd been called a control freak, even panic-prone when problems flared, but I was learning to delegate.

"Fine." I gave her a reassuring smile. "I trust them. Next on the agenda?" I straightened in my chair and spun around to face the floor-to-ceiling windows. The wheels squealed in protest, and I flinched. The drizzle had already ceased and a slice of sun was threatening to spill through the clouds.

"That's really all in terms of the next forty-eight hours or so." Madison pulled a can of WD-40 out of my bottom desk drawer and sprayed the wheels. She wiped her hands and glanced at her watch, a nervous tic, because I was so obsessed with being punctual. "You have a meeting with Travis at eleven, which gives you almost two hours." Her Prada heels clacked toward the door. "Open or closed?"

"Closed, please."

The next two hours evaporated over a sea of unanswered

emails and preparations for my trip. On my third coffee refill, I took a break and pulled up a new browser. I had removed Facebook from my phone, but it still taunted me on my computer. *What was he doing? Was he seeing someone? What new pieces was he selling in the shop?* The not knowing ran its sharp fingernail underneath my skin.

"Don't do it, Walker. Don't." My stomach clenched. Who was I kidding? Every time I went online, I thought of him first. Every scroll through my news feed, I hoped to see him. Every time my phone dinged, I secretly prayed he was texting, calling, or sending me an email.

I perused my own page first and then my friends' news feeds, noticing one of the latest quizzes: "What Celebrity Do You Look Most Like?" I clicked it, let Facebook pull my personal photos and details, and then, voilà! There it was: *Congratulations! You are a classic, timeless beauty. Your celebrity lookalike is Anne Hathaway!* I scrutinized the photo of Anne and the one of me. There was a strong resemblance. We were both tall, pale with dark hair, and had large doe eyes. Ethan used to tell me I had bedroom eyes. That I looked the most beautiful just in from a run or when I had scrubbed my face free of makeup. Anne and I also had the same pouty, full lips. But where she was thin, I was athletic, more of a runner's body to her natural willowy frame. I closed the window, opting not to post it for all my digital audience to see.

I'd eaten up Ethan's compliments, hanging my entire life on them. What did that say about me, even now, crunching numbers, pushing objects into factories to be made for children, when I knew so little about my own life without a man in it? Ethan had filled a void for me, obviously, and so did my career. Now, it was as though all my hopes of a normal life—marriage, babies, a traditional home, family vacations—had been extinguished.

"Sarah?" Madison stuffed her head into the sliver of space from the cracked door. "Travis is ready."

"Be right there." I hovered over the small *x* to close the window. I wished he'd blocked me the moment we broke up, but Ethan wasn't that type of guy. He also wouldn't want to flaunt anything in my face if he were in a new relationship, but it wouldn't even dawn on him that I would be looking at his page. I'd gotten better—checking just once a week at most—but still. We were approaching the six-month mark post-breakup without even a casual run-in at any of our favorite places.

I took a breath and typed in Ethan's name. A photo of him popped up on his timeline—posted three days ago—his face pink from sun, his smile genuine, his arms wrapped around the shoulders of a woman.

I leaned closer, ripping her features apart. The way her bottom lip sagged slightly to the left. The curve of her petite nostrils. Her insanely arched eyebrows, which looked overly plucked. Her beautiful blond hair, piled in a topknot that caught the light of the sun. Her smile, and his, which revealed a relationship I didn't want to know about.

I closed my laptop and brought it to my meeting with Travis, slipping back into work mode. I finished the rest of the day in a blaze of tasks, meetings, and preparations, as though not thinking of Ethan would somehow ease the knot in my stomach and bring him back to me.

When I looked up again, it was dark. I blinked from my computer haze, stared at the twinkling lights, and soaked in the city sounds that gathered outside the glass in a blast of horns, sirens, and the occasional screech of tires on wet pavement. I gathered my things and locked up, taking the elevator back to the ground floor.

I knew why I couldn't shake the thought of Ethan today—it was our anniversary. It pained me to think what
we might have planned; how we would spend the night
trying to outdo each other with gestures and gifts. Even
when we weren't celebrating, Ethan and I would meet near
his furniture shop after work, pick a brewery at random,
and talk about our successes and failures for the day.
Sometimes, we'd slip into Powell's, making out in random
book stalls, before picking one book to purchase for each
other. No matter how long we'd been together, it was still
a thrill to see him after a long day at the office. It felt
like dating. It *always* felt like dating. Now, the city gave
me comfort as I walked toward home and smiled at the
people just beginning their night.

In my condo, after I changed into pajamas, ordered
takeout, and drank too many glasses of wine, my cell rang.

"Hi, Dad. Right on time."

"Am I that predictable?"

"Yes. You're like the news. Except less depressing."

He chuckled, which reminded me of sandpaper against
gritty wood. All the years of crying had left his voice
weaker than it should have been.

"So, what's up?"

"Just want to see what my favorite daughter is doing."

"That joke never gets old." I stretched and stifled a
yawn. "Just traveling the world, working myself toward an
early retirement. You?"

"Oh, you know . . ." A shuffle of papers filled the silence, perhaps the collection of bills he kept neatly stacked
by the telephone, or the daily newspaper, folded into thirds.
"Busy too."

We both knew that *busy* meant spending nights on the
couch or occasionally taking a walk around his neighborhood. My father no longer worked long hours, or very

much. His zest for sales had waned with his zest for life. He lived the simplest way one could, his mortgage wiped clean from a Christmas present after my second year in business. The only real expenses in his life were utilities, the upkeep for his beloved Mustang, and whiskey. I checked the time, knowing he was probably a third of a handle in.

"I want to come see you soon, okay? I've just got a big trip coming up, but then I can come visit for a few days. How does that sound? Or you can always come here . . ." It was the same suggestion I made every time he called. *Come to Portland. Get out of your comfort zone.*

"I can't get away anytime soon, but I'd love it if you could make it here." His tone shifted. "I thought since you and Ethan broke up, you'd visit a bit more."

"Well, you know, I've got a business to run, Dad." The defensiveness sliced across the line, and I immediately retracted it. "Sorry. You know what I mean. It's just filling all my time."

He didn't respond, but I could feel him nodding on the other end. Filling time had been his entire life's work after my mother. He was an expert at it. We both were.

"Well, kiddo, I hope to see you soon."

"Me too, Dad. Love you."

"Love you too. Be safe."

I hung up, no more satisfied than before he'd called. Every time the phone rang, I expected something to be different: for him to go overboard with his last drink, to have a wild night out and get arrested, to commit sloppy suicide, to tell me he'd met someone. But the years passed in the same linear pattern, only my successes dictating the difference between yesterday and today. Despite all of my efforts to improve his life, nothing ever changed.

My flight for Ethiopia left Thursday. I'd told Madison to book the cheapest flight, not realizing that cheap meant indirect. I was flying from PDX to Calgary. Then from Calgary, I'd head to Toronto, and after an interminable lay-over, I'd finally descend into Addis Ababa after a twenty-eight-hour flight. It wasn't the first time I'd done it, but as I looked at my ticket, I realized it would be the first time I wasn't in first class.

I edged through the security line and plucked a gray bin from the pile, shoving my shoes and computer into separate containers. I hated this part, how cumbersome travel had become, how invasive. I organized my bag on the belt, mentally running through my to-do list when I touched down in Ethiopia.

Once, Ethan and I had talked about adopting a girl from Ethiopia due to the extreme local sex trafficking—how our daughter would wear her heritage like a badge, how we'd visit her native country, make authentic Ethiopian cuisine, and expose her to all sorts of cultures and customs. Was he ever serious about any of it, about me? Did I somehow miss some giant, obvious sign?

I shook my head. I was always looking for signs. A bit superstitious, I made constant deals with myself, as though these deals would culminate in some life-changing event: *If there are five babies on the plane, it won't crash. If I just say yes to this client, I'll get into* Forbes. *If the light turns green when I count to three, I won't complain for the rest of the day. If I don't eat dessert today, I can have Mexican tomorrow.*

I yawned and waited for the people beside me to get situated and keep the line going by pushing their bins into the machine. My mind was already somewhere else—on a huge, generic coffee and the gossipy magazine I'd buy—when I saw her.

Something inside me wrenched. A little girl, not more than five or six, stood in a red dress with shiny sequins attached to a full skirt that swished when she moved. A red bow perched on her mousy brown ponytail. Slippers that could have been a match for Dorothy's in *The Wizard of Oz* hugged compact, white feet. She looked like Christmas. I watched her with a smile on my lips and felt, foolishly, like I recognized her; she was so familiar, she could have been my very own.

"Emma, stop! What are you doing? I said *stop it*!"

To my right, a short, overweight woman in a navy shirt and tight jeans was yelling at her daughter. Her face bloomed with angry red sores (acne? eczema? rosacea?), and she exhaled as she adjusted an exhausted-looking toddler on her hip. Behind her stood the girl in red. She stepped forward, shoes sparkling, but her mother shoved her out of the way, as if she were an attacker on the street and not her own flesh and blood. The girl stumbled back, and I instinctively reached out to catch her.

The father stood beside them, lean and pasty, oblivious to what his wife had just done. He was busy shooting off a text, then pocketed his phone. Their bags spilled around their feet. The mother struggled to lift a suitcase onto the conveyor belt while still holding the toddler, and the dad grabbed the same bag in an attempt to help.

"That's my arm! What are you doing?"

"I was just helping you. Jesus."

"Let go of my arm, Richard." The woman stared accusingly at my bins. "We don't have any bins. Now we're not going to make our flight because we have no bins."

"Well, what do you want me to do about the bins, Amy? Invent more bins?"

"I don't know. Just stop talking. Stop saying *bins* like that! For the love of God, just please, please, please, stop talking." Amy turned, her pocked jaw pulsing as she clenched her teeth. "Emma, I said stop it. What is wrong with you?" The girl was rocking back and forth on her heels, reaching for her mother's fingers. Every time the mother knocked her fingers away, Emma would come back and touch a different part of her mother's body: her waist, her elbow, her hips. Her small cuticles were chewed and bloody, and I noticed a faded bruise on the girl's left wrist.

"Do you even want to try and make this flight, Richard?"

"Oh, stop right there. Don't even try and blame me. This is your fault and you know it."

"What's my fault? The line? Not having bins? Not getting the kids out the door on time? This is an important day for me—"

"Yes, all of that. Your fault. Not mine."

"You're an asshole."

"*You're* an asshole."

"Excuse me?"

He lifted his flimsy arms in surrender. "I'm just saying."

They slopped the rest of their luggage on the belt and snatched a fresh stack of bins brought over by a worker. "Emma, go!" Emma was busy adjusting her parents' gray bin, her brain having made the connection that they had turned it a different way from everyone else's. "Stop touching that and go!" The mother reached one thick palm, fingers flexed, and pushed into the thin crease between the girl's shoulder blades, forcing her arms to flap like wings. She continued to shove the little girl through the X-ray machine, where an airport guard motioned them over to have the mother's hands swiped.

I stepped through the full-body scanner, my arms held above my head as they searched my body for hidden weapons. While I waited for confirmation that I wasn't smuggling anything illegal, I saw Emma reach for her brother's toes. Her mother wrenched her fingers backward, prying them free. She turned her back to the girl, but Emma clutched her sore hand and jumped up and down in an attempt to get her mother's attention. The woman fussed with the toddler and snapped at the dad. And the girl, truly unable to get her mother to notice, finally gave up and stared off into space, disconnected, her hand folded protectively in the skirt of her red dress.

On the other side, I collected my belongings and looked at the guards, who were too busy directing, swiping, and yawning to notice. I waited for someone to acknowledge the mother's aggressive behavior, while my boots and laptop sagged in my fingers.

I remembered so much about my mother then, the way she always walked ahead of me in parking lots, at the grocery store, or even crossing the street. I never knew if she was embarrassed by me or if she simply didn't care. I always trailed behind her as an afterthought, trying to pepper her with compliments: "Mama, you look so beautiful today. Mama, I love your hair. Mama, I love that skirt."

She would sigh in disgust and insist the only reason I was saying those things was because I was afraid of getting in trouble and not because I meant them. I could never do anything right, and it's something I recognized in this little girl now, as she dragged her feet, kicked at the airport carpet, and waited for someone to just pay her some attention.

Having worked with children for years, I knew parents had off days. I knew the airport was the definition of family stress. I knew how little beings could take hold of your psyche and ravage you. I knew there were rare breaks and little explanation as to how they could suddenly, without warning, push you to the edge and shift you from pleasant to monstrous. I knew all of that, but seeing this out-

right act of cruelty for no apparent reason made me want
to punch this woman in the face.

I moved out of the way, zipped my boots, and replaced
my computer in my bag. I walked past the foursome, the
dad busy pulling their bags from the conveyor belt. I
slowed even more as I passed, my fingers so close I could
touch the girl's head. "I like your red bow," I said. The
three of them turned, the baby's reflexes not yet up to par
with his family's. In that moment, Emma's face relaxed
back into a little girl's, and she began to smile. "It's so
pretty," I said. I kept walking, not looking back, trying to
shake these people from my conscience.

After waiting in a line that snaked around the Starbucks
kiosk, the brain fog disappeared as I took my first hurried
sip. I bought a few magazines to go along with my novel,
checked to make sure the flight wasn't delayed, and let myself sink into ridiculous celebrity gossip. Halfway through
my coffee and an article about Hollywood women caught
on camera without makeup, I looked up. There, at the gate
to the left of mine, stood the couple. Arguing.

"Go!" Amy pushed Emma. She snagged her red shoe
on the carpet and pitched forward, skidding to a stop on
her knees and elbows.

The mother, rolling her eyes, hoisted the baby higher
and jerked Emma up by her elbow. I watched the red
splotches erupt on her arm, splotches that would later
bruise and turn purple. Emma pulled herself up and rubbed
her sore elbow and carpet-burned knees.

The couple harrumphed about and sat in chairs on
the other side of the gate. They moved around each other
with such agitation, it was as though someone were on the
verge of detonating. Only Emma, the victim in all of this,
seemed unruffled, humming and playing with her shoes,
while her mother sighed so loudly, you could hear it across

the terminal. She bounced the baby up and down until he looked sick.

I flipped through the glossy magazine pages, my mind fixated on the girl. I checked my phone. Still thirty minutes to board. As though on cue, the mother grabbed Emma by the wrist and started yanking her to the bathroom. Emma half-walked, half-ran behind her as the woman balanced the baby on one side and her daughter on the other. I waited a few beats, shouldered my carry-on bag, and followed.

Emma's red shoes swung back and forth under one stall, her mother and brother at the end of the shotgun space, a dirty diaper being ripped off and shoved to the side of the fold-out changing table.

"Emma, hurry up."

"Okay, Mama."

I eyed the stalls—mostly empty—and ducked into one. The tops of the girl's shoes strained to touch the ground. She kicked the front of the toilet with her dainty heels and hummed, which made me smile. After some maneuvering with the toilet paper dispenser, Emma flushed.

"Come into this stall. I need to go too. Watch Robert. Make sure he doesn't hit his head or touch anything. I cannot afford for either one of you to get sick right now."

They piled into the handicap stall on the end, the family's shoes shuffling and shifting against the dirty tile. I flushed and prepared to exit, then stopped.

"Watch out for his foot, Emma! You almost stepped on him."

"No, I didn't."

"Yes, you did." The little boy began to cry, and I could hear the mother struggling to pee and handle her two children. "Can you—Jesus, *get* him, Emma! He's falling! Get out of the way!" A loud bang rattled the stall, and then Emma's voice morphed into a whine.

"Listen to me right this instant, young lady! I have had it with you today, do you hear me? Stop this dramatic behavior, or we are going to cancel our trip. Do you understand?"

I leaned over the sink and started washing my hands. The door swung open and slammed against the wall. Emma's face was red, her bow askew, her breath coming in shudders. I scanned her body for physical wounds but just saw the tears. "Are you okay, sweetheart?"

The mother jerked her head at me, jowls quivering. "Emma Grace, stop talking to strangers and wash your hands."

We all washed our hands, and I locked eyes with the mother. She had sad eyes, as if her whole life were a lie. She looked away first, and I watched them go, hoisting my carry-on higher, unsure of what to do. A woman moved to the sink beside me and pumped the soap a few times.

"Did you hear any of that? Or did I just imagine it?"

The woman, older, tattooed, shook her head and rinsed her hands. "I heard it, but hey, it's not your child, right? What can you do?"

What could I do? Report her to airport officials? Child Protective Services? Even I wasn't that idiotic to think an incident in an airport bathroom stall under stressful conditions would warrant anything other than a mother's right to scold—or possibly spank—her own child. I nodded at the woman and returned to the concourse, waiting for my group to board. I busied myself with my magazine, but I could still hear the mom, could see her pushing and pulling her daughter like an unwanted puppy on a fraying leash.

When it was time to board, I waited for them to call my seat. At the next gate, the family was lining up for their own flight, all of us going our separate ways.

I glanced once more at Emma, who looked almost glassy-eyed, her mother bumping her from behind to move faster, walk faster, *go* faster. A few heads swiveled as the family corralled at the boarding line, obviously surprised at the woman's brash behavior and the girl's tear-stained face.

I handed over my paper ticket—I refused to use my phone for any sort of travel in case of technological malfunctions—and craned my neck to the left to see Emma, waiting behind her mother to board a big steel bird and go to who knows where. Home? A vacation? Boarding school? I strained to see the destination listed on the board with her flight number, but couldn't quite make it out.

I kept sight of her as long as I could before turning back toward my own gate, the temperature shifting as I walked closer toward the open mouth of the plane. But I couldn't get that red bow out of my mind, or the girl's eyes, or her sore elbow, or the loud bang, or her mother's crusted, hateful face.

I couldn't forget Emma.

I couldn't forget.

during

My fingers tremble as I struggle to unlock the car doors, wedging open the back and then the driver's side.

Emma peeks inside, high on her toes like a ballerina. "Where's the car seat?"

I shove my bag into the back and look at her. "The what?"

"The car seat. Where is it?" A perfectly normal question under circumstances that are anything but.

I eye the naked backseat. "Oh shit." The keys dangle by my side as Emma inhales.

"You said *shit*," she whispers.

"I did. I did say *shit*. You're right. I didn't mean to. It's just . . . I don't have a car seat." I look around, feeling time closing in. I prime my ears for police sirens. Beads of sweat cluster at my hairline. "Let's just buckle you in really well and then we'll figure it out, okay?" She nods as I help her up into the Tahoe, moving her behind the passenger seat so I can see her better while driving. I get in, hit the locks, locate the child lock, and press that too. "Okay. Think, think. It's going to be okay."

"Who are you talking to?"

I crane around to look at Emma, hope buzzing in my chest like a small swarm of bees. *She is here, in my car! I did it! She's safe!* I soften my jaw until my face feels like putty and manage to mold my lips into a flimsy smile. "I'm just being silly and talking to myself."

"What's okay?"

"Everything's okay. Is your seatbelt tight?" She nods. I throw the car into drive and release the parking brake. Before stepping on the gas, I punch in the directions to home. Longview is only an hour from my condo—probably too close for comfort. Should I take her somewhere else? The directions appear, and I follow the robotic voice. We drive in silence, Emma occasionally sniffling from the back. "Are you sick or anything, Emma? Do you have a cold?"

She wipes her nose with her palm and shakes her head no.

"Just stuffy?"

She nods, and her lips work into a small, chapped frown.

"Are you thirsty?" I dig into my bag for bottled water—courtesy of the hotel—and pass it back to her. She takes it, unscrews the lid, and drinks. The crackle of plastic fills the car as she guzzles the last drops of water and squeezes out all the bottle's air.

We continue to drive, the radio on low so I can hear the directions. My hands stutter on the wheel as I grasp the reality of my actions. *I could be arrested. I could go to jail for the rest of my life. What the fuck am I doing? What have I actually done?* I shake away the worry, instead focusing on the task in front of me: *Get home. Get her safe.*

The hour lengthens as we bump into traffic at the edge of the city. I live in north Portland. It is a short commute downtown on most days, and right now, I wish I lived in a bungalow tucked behind a towering privacy fence and a bank of endless trees.

I wait for Emma to say something, but she stays silent,

her eyes absorbing the sights as they pass by, her fingers gathered in her lap, working over her dress like it's a dishrag. We pull up to my midrise, and I park on the street. I unbuckle my seatbelt and look at her.

"Do you live here?"

I clear my throat. "I do live here. I thought we could eat some food and rest for a bit. Is that okay?"

"Do you have toys?"

"You know what? Yes, actually. I have something even better than toys. Want to see?" I silently thank the gods above for the extra inventory of boxes I keep in my utility closet. She unbuckles her belt and opens the door, almost spilling onto the pavement.

I offer my hand and she grabs it, her fingers tacky and warm. We walk toward the door. I fumble with the keys and locate the key fob to swipe us both in. We ride the elevator up to the fifth floor. I unlock my door as quickly as I can, suddenly wishing for a dog or cat so Emma would be entertained. I drop my bag, release her hand, and bolt the door behind me. "There."

She turns. "There what?"

"No, nothing. Just there. Here. We're here." I sound ridiculous, but I have to keep calm, keep her calm. I look at her face. The outline of her mother's handprint runs across her jaw and looks like it has a pulse. "Does your cheek hurt?"

Emma lifts her hand and touches the forming bruise. "Uh-huh."

I rummage in the freezer and grab a bag of peas. "Are you hungry?"

Emma shifts in the front hall. "Do you have mac and cheese?"

I offer her the bag.

"I don't want peas."

"No, sweetie, not to eat. For your face. Here, like this." I press the peas to her cheek, and she bucks. "I know it's cold, but it will get better after a few minutes. Here, let me grab something to make it less cold." I tear a few paper towels from the roll, rewrap the peas, and hand it back to her. She moves it on and off her face, the crunch of frozen veggies competing with the frenzy of my heart.

"I think . . ." I scour the cabinets and find an old box of brown rice noodles. I scan my fridge and spot a half-eaten block of Fontina cheese and a small carton of whole milk. "I think I can whip up some mac and cheese. Would you like to play or watch TV?"

"Watch TV." She looks around. "Do you have kids?"

"I don't."

"I have a baby brother."

"You do? I bet that's fun."

"Where's the TV?"

I lead her to the living room and pull the shades. She hands me the remote from the coffee table. I don't even know what channels are the kid channels, or if I have them. What if a picture of Emma flashes on the nightly news? What if my phone squeals with an AMBER Alert? What if the police are already looking for her? I scroll through the channels until I find Disney Junior. "Is this okay?"

She nods and sits on the couch.

"Do you need to go to the bathroom?"

"No." She pulls her legs underneath her and fixates on the television. The bag of peas moves on and off her face.

"Okay. I'll make dinner."

I move to the kitchen and squeeze the edge of the countertop. *Just breathe.* I want to call Lisa, but I can't fathom what she would say. I don't want to drag anyone into this as an unwilling accomplice, especially my best friend. I just want to give Emma a break, even a small one.

I busy myself with the task at hand—dinner—hoping she will eat this slightly altered version of a comforting childhood staple. I slop her noodles into a bowl, realizing I have nothing kid-friendly: no plastic cups, no bottles, no miniature silverware. No premeditation.

I offer Emma her food, and she takes it, her eyes still on the TV. She lifts the spoon to her lips and immediately drops it, the hot metal clanging against the porcelain edge of the bowl.

"Sorry, honey. It's hot. Just blow on it."

She does as she is told, tenderly taking another bite and then another. She makes a face as she tucks in, but hunger overcomes the strange taste, and she devours the entire bowl, licking her spoon, never breaking eye contact from the cartoon or the commercials. She emits a fat sigh when done, the bowl resting against the stained, wilted fabric of her red dress.

"Do you want anything else?"

"Do you got juice?"

"I actually don't have juice. Is water okay?"

She nods. I grab a small glass and sit beside her on the couch while she drinks, looking around my condo. My eyes rest on my phone. I walk to it and key in the password. Should I take a video? Explain what happened? Why I did what I did? Maybe I could capture Emma confessing to how horrible her mother is.

I find my voice memos and hit *record*. I grab the remote and turn the television off, positioning my body to face hers.

Her glassy eyes blink and then focus. "Where'd the show go?"

"It's still there. I just wanted to talk to you about a few things, if that's okay? Then we can watch more cartoons."

She stares into her water glass. I have no idea who this

little person is. I know she is wondering where her mommy is. And growing up with my own complicated mother-daughter relationship, I understand exactly why.

"So, Emma. Do you remember seeing me at the airport a few months ago? I told you how much I liked your pretty red bow?"

She tilts her head to the side.

"That's okay if you don't. But I saw you. At the airport several months back. And I saw your mom being tough on you. With her words. And her hands."

Emma shrugs. "That's just Mama."

"What's just Mama?"

She scratches her nose and looks around the condo, as if just realizing where she is. "Do you have those toys?"

I'm losing her. "Yes. I do. But it's really important that I just . . . understand a little bit about your mommy and daddy first, okay? And then we can play."

"What?"

"What do I want to understand?"

She nods.

"Oh. Well, I guess I just want to know if you feel safe at home."

"I don't know."

"Okay, how about this? I'm going to ask you something, and I want you to be completely honest with me. And you won't get into trouble, I promise. No one is getting mad about anything here. Okay?"

"Okay."

"Does your mommy hurt you?"

She squirms and looks at the blank TV. "When I'm bad."

The statement hangs in the air, loaded. I wait for her to

say more but she doesn't. I click off the voice memos. "All right. Playtime?"

She smiles—a flicker—and I lead her to the closet and remove a kit for kindergarteners. "How old are you?"

She holds up all the fingers of her right hand.

"Five? What a big girl! That's how old I thought you were. These are for kids just your age. Want to see?"

I spread out the contents on the floor, watching as she takes the time to play with each one. She is meticulous in her movements and examines each individual object before moving on to the next.

"Mama does hurt me."

The confession comes out of nowhere, and my chest heaves with the new information. "How does that make you feel?"

"Bad. She says I'm bad all the time."

"Do you think you're bad all the time?"

"I don't know. I don't think so."

"Are you afraid of her?"

"Sometimes."

"Does your daddy hurt you too?"

"No. He doesn't know Mama hurts me."

I swallow. "What do you mean?"

She shrugs. "She never does it when he's around."

"Have you told your daddy this?"

"Mama said not to tell."

"Why?"

"Because I'd get in trouble."

I calculate all the ways to tell her it's okay; that it's not her fault. That her mother's actions are not about her. That she has the right to be loved. "Emma, you know when mommies and daddies get super-tired or frustrated, they shouldn't hurt you, right?"

"She doesn't always hurt me. But she *always* yells." Emma fits a puzzle piece into a cube and moves on. "Like every day."

Well, that decides it.

"I'm so sorry, Emma. That must be very hard." I stand and head to the bedroom, grabbing my duffel from the top shelf. My suitcase is still in the back of the car. I start throwing in more items: underwear, hiking boots, scarves, tampons. My hands shake so violently, I can barely grip my toiletries, my clothes, or my five extra pairs of folded socks.

I sit on the edge of the bed. I could drop her off at a police station and report what she just told me. But the protectiveness I feel over her already . . . I'm not willing to let her go.

I have a choice to make, and it is an irreparable one. I'm either all in or all out. I step back into the hall and listen to the babble of play in the next room. I stare at her red, swollen cheek. I filter through everything I've seen between her and her mother. What am I willing to live with?

And then I know. I know exactly where I'm going to take her, and the exact store I can purchase everything we need. I know where we will sleep and wake up, and that no one will be looking for her where we are going. It's a long shot, a stupid shot, but it's my only one.

I call Madison and tell her my father and I have the flu. They think I have been visiting my father the last few days. My little knot of employees are germaphobes, steering clear if someone so much as sneezes. It will buy me time—not a lot, but enough to come up with something better—some long-term excuse that will not leave my company in ruins and my employees suspicious. But there's too much to do now.

I must get Emma to come with me somewhere else, to a place that is not her home, with a person who is not her mother.

I just hope I don't run out of time.

before

The day before my mother walked out, she made me pancakes.

I always helped her make the batter, eagerly scraping a chair to the Formica countertops and waiting for her instructions to pour flour, sugar, and cinnamon into the eggs and milk. She'd let me handle the wooden spoon and spin the dough until it was sticky and wet. It happened so rarely that I immediately dropped whatever I was doing when she offered. I'd learned long ago to stop asking for pancakes—if I wanted them, *she* would offer—so I was surprised and delighted when she suggested it.

She dusted the flour from my nose, kissed the top of my head, and pulled me close. In those startling, rare moments, I was filled with something like love. We ate our pancakes while my father slept—a redundant Saturday habit—as it was the one day my dad could sleep in. My mother let me have extra maple syrup that morning and had even warmed it on the stove and sprinkled blueberries and a few chocolate chips on top of my stack.

I should have known something was wrong; she was being too nice. There'd been no arguments, raised voices, or muttering about how hard her life was, how disastrous the house was, how unorganized the closets, how it all wasn't fair that this was her life. How she needed to be alone, to be her own person; how she needed to shake her family loose to live the life she was actually meant for.

Her love came in waves. When she was happy, everyone felt it. When she was sad, I would often hide in my room with a book, because everything was wrong and nothing my father or I did could change it.

I ate my pancakes, sure to chew with my mouth closed, while she sipped her coffee and stared at our brown patch of backyard.

"Do you ever feel that you're living someone else's life?"

I paused, just as I was lifting a forkful of fluffy pancakes to my mouth. My lips were blue, I was pretty sure, and I had just been on the verge of asking my mother if I looked like a Smurf. Instead, I chewed, swallowed, and pretended to give it some thought, though I had absolutely no idea what she was talking about.

If I said yes, I understood, she'd tell me I was a kid and couldn't possibly understand. If I said no, I didn't, she'd tell me to grow up and face reality. So I said nothing and waited for the ramifications to pour down, but they didn't. After a few moments, she smiled at me, asked me if I wanted another pancake, and then actually stood and got me one.

I held my breath, wondering what was coming next, but she returned with a huge pancake poised on the spatula and deposited it on my plate with a soft plop. "A treat for my treat," she said. Her eyes were far too glassy. Her fingers were twitching around the utensil. I could hear the frenzy in her voice—my dad had taught me that word, had tried to sugarcoat it for what it was, but it meant a shift was coming—into anger, annoyance, abuse, or absence—so I hurriedly thanked her, ate it, and asked if I could go outside and play.

She told me yes—she didn't make a negative comment about our pathetic excuse of a backyard, the noisy neighbors, or how the Midwest was the most uncreative, regular, normal area in all of America. She just said *yes*.

Before I eased out the back door, I ran to her, slid my arms around her slim waist, and squeezed. She did not hug me back, but she let me stay there for a full thirty seconds, laughed, and then told me to go play.

As I bounded out the back door and crunched over the hot, stale grass, I made a wish right then and there that if there was a God, to please let things stay just like this. For just a little bit longer. For just one more day, at least.

My mother went out with friends that night, as she usually did on Saturdays. Her group consisted of random strangers and neighbors, though tonight were a few of my favorites: Peggy with the big boobs, Arthur with the combover, and Suzanne with the limp. My dad was never invited on these outings, and I was glad. There wasn't much of a budget for babysitting, as my mom constantly reminded him, so he stayed home with me.

We fried fish and potatoes and watched a movie together, curled up like parentheses on the couch. My mother often called us sloths when she'd come back, smelling of cigarettes and booze, but she was always so beautiful that I would will myself awake, hoping she would hug me, or tell me she liked my pajamas. But instead, she often just excused herself to the bedroom, where she'd take two sleeping pills and pass out until midday Sunday.

My father and I waited for her to come home. The hours dragged by, and I was tired, but I wanted to see her before bed. I hadn't told him about the pancakes that morning, hoarding that delicious secret for myself. At midnight, my dad lifted me off the couch, letting me forgo brushing my teeth, and deposited me in bed.

"Where's Elaine?" My mother had given me strict instructions at age six to call her Elaine. She did not want to be called *Mom, Mama, Mommy,* or the more formal *Mother,* and eager to please, I retrained my brain to call her by her first name. I slipped up often in those early months, but I was eight now, and it was practically ingrained.

"I don't know, pumpkin. She's not home yet. I'm sure she's just having fun with her friends." He looked sad when he said it, and looking back, I wondered if he knew, or suspected, but he just kissed the top of my head and let me go to sleep.

The next morning, I pinched the dark green crust from the corners of my eyes and smacked them off my comforter. I yawned—my breath sour—and went to pee and brush my teeth. The house was quiet, and I wondered if I had woken up too early. Or too late. I peeked in my parents' room. My dad's side was rumpled. My mother's was not.

Panic wound itself around my skin, but I told myself to relax, that maybe she'd slept on the couch or just stayed out all night. But the truth was this: my father and I had spent my entire young life waiting for something bad to happen. Elaine had never wanted children, a well-known fact she discussed every chance she got. I was an accident. I ruined her acting career. I changed everything.

My father had worked the last eight years trying to pick up the slack so she wouldn't have to do much of anything. He'd convinced her to keep the baby—I'll never know how—but being raised knowing you weren't wanted was something I wouldn't wish on any kid.

I was suddenly breathless as I ran to the kitchen. I shrieked as I saw my father sitting at the kitchen table, his hands folded in his lap, staring blankly out the window. I stood next to him to see what he was seeing. Maybe it was a deer or a rabbit, or maybe it was snowing in August?—but there was nothing of interest. I placed my hand on my father's shoulder, since he hadn't budged when I'd screamed, and shook him.

"Dad . . . Daddy?" I was scared, and I didn't know why. But I knew something was different in this house.

He turned, as if his entire body were made of drying cement, and looked at me with eyes that were broken, glazed, and defeated.

"Where's Elaine?" It was the same thing I'd asked last night, but this morning, it seemed it would have an entirely different meaning.

"She's gone." It came out hoarse, and I waited for him to continue.

"Gone where? Like, still out with her friends?"

My father began to wail then—crying so hard, he gripped my shoulders, pulled me into him, and squeezed me until I thought I would break. But I didn't dare pull back. "Oh God, Oh God, Sarah. Oh God. What am I going to do now? What am I going to *do* without her?"

He said *I,* not *we,* as though I wasn't even a factor, as though I had been written off as the reason for my mother's departure. He didn't say that, would never say that, but from that day on, I felt it. I was the problem. I'd always been the problem. He would have made a trade for her, and we both knew it.

I waited for him to stop crying before pulling away. "How do you know she's gone, Daddy? Maybe she just stayed out with her friends?"

He took me by the hand, shaking his head like a mad-man, and ushered me to their bedroom. "There. Look."

I gazed into the contents of their bedroom: at the bed, the walls, and the dresser, looking for clues of any sort. "What?"

"There, there, there! In the closet, in the bathroom, the car! Gone. All of it. She took everything she could get her hands on. I don't know if she came in the night or not. I'm . . . I was asleep. I was asleep! I just can't believe this is happening to me."

I spun around in a circle, hunting for signs, and went to her closet. They shared a small one, my mother claiming at least two-thirds. Her hangers, cloth-covered and plush, were mostly full, but a few were bare, while my father's cheap standard wires were covered in button-downs and T-shirts. I shut the door and went to the bathroom to in-spect her drawers. Her makeup and perfumes were gone, her jewelry too. Her stash of cigarettes, her stockings, her high heels . . . I ran to the garage and tripped on something that ripped into the flesh of my heel. I sat down and cra-dled my foot, trying not to scream. I had to keep it together for my father. I looked down for the offending object and saw it—my mother's favorite necklace: her skeleton key on a thin, silver chain.

My mother was a possessive, materialistic woman, so I put together a stash of her most prized possessions on the days and nights she didn't come home: lipsticks, high heels, pendants, scarves. I would play with them all day, pressing my DNA into them, and then put them back exactly the way they'd been so she'd never know I had touched them. I just wanted to know the woman I should have already known but didn't; I just wanted to covet what she coveted.

It would destroy my father to see her favorite piece of jewelry abandoned like this. I greedily plucked the necklace from the gap in the wooden planks and stuffed it in the pocket of my pajamas. I wanted it. She'd never let me touch it before, and I couldn't wait to slip it around my neck.

I went outside and saw the old oil spot from her Beetle. Her car was gone. She'd taken most of her favorite things. Was there a note somewhere?

I sat down on the steps and waited for all of this to come together in my head.

My mother had taken her things. She'd made me pancakes yesterday. She'd kissed me—twice!—and gone out like normal last night. But she'd never come home, and now my father thought she'd left him and wasn't coming back again.

I stabbed the skeleton key in the dirt and drew pictures: a cat's face, a small house, an ice-cream cone, a star. It was hot—even early morning in August the sun was still brutal—and pondered what all of this meant.

Was she never coming back again? Would we not experience the mood swings, the terror, the instability of never knowing what side of her we would get? I covered my mouth with my hands and let out a muffled scream. I pulled myself off the stoop and began running around the side of my house and to the front, grinning until my cheeks hurt, feeling a lightness I'd never known.

The source of all my problems had vanished. I'd asked for her to stay nice, and instead, the universe had simply plucked her out of it, doing me a bigger favor by taking her away from me. I would never have to please an unreasonable person again. I would never have to deal with one of her mood swings, or bags of ice on sore wounds, or justifying her bizarre and cruel behavior just to get on with my day. My father could move on with his life. He could be happy. We could be happy without her.

I collapsed on the dewy grass and began making grass angels—a ridiculous movement that would have received a gallon of ridicule if my mother had been outside with me—and I continued to move my arms in that lazy pattern, up and down, up and down, as if I could fly right out of my body, zip up to the heavens, and thank them personally.

during

She does not sleep. Her eyelids stretch wide, as if pulled back with tape. She blinks in small bursts as the lights from other cars filter in and out of the windows. I have little explanation for where we are going or why. I just keep telling her to be patient. To wait.

A few hours outside of Portland, I begin to relax. I find the Walmart I've been to a million times, and we park in the middle of two SUVs as I prepare myself for what to say. I turn to her, so wired in the backseat, metrical in her jumpiness, as my eyes search for people who can see she's not in a car seat, even with the Tahoe's tinted windows. I see her lower lip quiver. Her face begins to fold in on itself, and every part of me wants to hug her, but I'm afraid she'll scream.

"Oh sweetie, hey. Please don't cry. Everything is going to be okay. Look at me." I reach one hand into the darkness and touch her knee, which is covered with blond peach fuzz and crusted scabs. Her body begins to shake with sobs, and I am so sorry I am causing her more worry, more pain, more fear.

"Hey, Emma. Can you look at me for just one second? Please? It's important that you hear this." I think about bribing her with a toy—*please stop crying, and you can have any toy you want!*—but I'm not that impatient. She opens her mouth and an anguished wail comes out, and I can't help myself—I look around for suspicious eyes in the parking lot—but it is late at night, and no one is watching.

I wait until she takes a few breaths, and then I rub her knee again, as if that's helping. "I promise I'm here to help you. I just want to . . ." *What*? I dig deep, thinking of all the different ways I've ever connected to children from other countries, children whose languages I don't speak, children who go without, entitled children who think the TACK kits are boring. But I've never had to deal with a child in a situation like this. "Hey, Emma. Do you have a favorite toy at home?"

She brightens a fraction, and I think I'm on to something. "I bet you do, right? Do you have something that makes you feel better, that helps you calm down when you're scared?"

"Like a lovey?"

"What's a lovey?"

"It's a toy we bring to school to help us nap."

"Yes. Like a lovey. Do you have a favorite?"

She nods and hiccups. "Share Bear."

"A Care Bear?"

"Share Bear. She's . . . *eekup* . . . she's one of the, those Care Bears. Daddy got her for me."

"You know what? We are going to go in here and get you another Share Bear. I know it won't be your exact Share Bear, but it will be close enough, okay? Would that make you feel a little bit better?"

She nods. "But I'm not scared."

"You're not?"

"No."

"Then why are you crying?"

"Because."

"Because why?"

"Because I'm afraid what Mommy is going to do to me since I ran away from her. She's going to be so mad at me, I don't know what she'll do." She cries as she says it, until snot is dripping into her mouth.

"Oh, you sweet little girl. Listen to me." I move to the backseat, unbuckle her seatbelt, and she jumps into my arms. I hold her there, shushing her as she cries. "Your mommy is not going to do anything or be angry at all, okay? I promise. You are with me for a reason. Do you know what that reason is?"

She shakes her head and squeezes tighter.

"I am here to keep you happy and safe. That is my only job. Doesn't that sound like a fun job?"

She shrugs.

"And you know what else comes with that job? Getting you all kinds of fun things in this store to help you stay happy. But it's been so long since I've had to shop for kid stuff, I don't even know what to get! Do you think you could help me find the right things you need? And maybe we can get you some fun toys too? For being such a brave girl?"

She pulls back, wipes her eyes, and nods, the idea of new toys starting to make sense in her brain. I take the hem of my shirt and gingerly blot her tears. I flip on the interior light and study her face, which is turning purple along her cheek and jaw. I dig in my bag and find some cover-up. "Do you know what this is?"

"No."

"Well, this is some magic medicine for your face that is going to help it not hurt so much. Can I?" I untwist the cap and shake some into my fingers. "Can I tap some of this on your cheek? And if it hurts, you can just tell me to stop, okay?" I begin to blend—lightly—and swipe until the purple turns to pink and then a beige that is one shade too dark for her skin. "Is that okay? Does that hurt?"

"No, it's okay."

I place my hands on her shoulders and gently squeeze. "I just want you to relax and have fun. To have a summer vacation. Does that sound okay?" I think about lying. About telling her that her parents told me to take her on a trip, that I'm her new babysitter, a nanny, or a new teacher from her school. But I cannot lie to this child. I make a decision right here, in this car, that I will not lie to her about anything.

"What's a summer cation?" She hiccups again, saying it wrong, but she's not pulling away from me.

"You've never taken a summer vacation before? Well, we are going to have to do so many fun things, then. Do you think you're up for a little adventure?"

She nods. There is almost a smile, and I think we are going to be okay—at least initially—if we can get far enough out of town. I know this is not some movie or book—there are real consequences here—and I'm trying to be careful not to push too much too soon. We will get the necessities we need. I will pay in cash. We will keep driving.

The soft wash of the moon hangs high in the sky. It is late and well past a child's normal bedtime, but we only have twenty-four hours max to get as far from Washington as possible—before the authorities are alerted and the real investigation unfolds. To people who see us, she will go from being a disgruntled child to a *missing* child, and if anyone makes the connection while she's in my care, it's all over before it's even begun.

I ease her out of the car and kneel down to her level, parking lot rocks imprinting into the flesh of my knees. I smooth the hair from her face, which is hot and damp from tears, and arrange it over her left cheek, just in case. "Are you ready to go buy some fun toys?"

"Can I also get a doll? And some new clothes?"

"Of course. Though I know how much you love your red dress."

She looks down at herself and fingers a sequin. "Mommy always makes me wear this."

"Why is that?"

She shrugs. "Because I don't have a lot of clothes. She says it's easier this way."

"Well, I think it will be fun to get some new clothes. Don't you?"

She nods but does not make any move to come with me into the store. Only time will make her trust me, but I'm not sure we have any. I don't know what I was expecting— for her to simply come with me, not ask questions, and not miss home? No child is wired like that, even the unhappy ones. I should know.

I ask if I can hold her hand. She lets me, and then we are walking toward the big, bold lights of the store, our first public appearance as Sarah Walker and the Missing Girl.

We enter the automatic doors. The chill of the store lifts the hair on my arms and makes every sense crack with caution. I pick her up and deposit her in a cart, struggling to get her legs through the slots. She begins kicking her heels against it, like we've done this a million times.

Emma is here, in my bright blue cart, and I'm shopping for items to keep her for days, weeks, or even months. As I push the cart, Emma locks eyes with mine. Her tiny lips shift into a tentative smile. I smile back and feel something come loose in my chest.

As we go through the aisles, I ask her simple questions: *Are you allergic to anything? Peanuts? Dairy? Wheat? Do you take any regular medicine? Do you get head-*

aches? Do you get earaches? Do you have a cough? Do you have asthma? She spouts off a series of no's until it becomes like a game, and then I ask her silly questions: *Do you have three heads? Do you have bananas for arms? Do you have a monkey's butt?* And Emma starts to laugh, a sweet, innocent giggle that burrows deep into my bones.

It is late, and there are only a few workers aimlessly wandering about, the squawk of their walkie-talkies mingling with squeaky carts. I lead her into the dressing room, abandoning our supplies, and quickly change her into a set of new clothes. I rip off the tags and pocket them to give the cashier, and then ball her red dress to stuff into my purse.

"Why are you doing that?"

"I thought you might be tired of being in those clothes. I'm going to wash your pretty red dress for you, okay?"

"Okay."

We continue on through the aisles in a dizzying loop of our list—clothes, shoes, panties, wipes, first-aid kit, disposable cell phone, batteries, LeapFrog, games, snacks, toiletries, vitamins, socks, emergency pull-ups, books, Share Bear, Barbies, Legos. I keep pushing her from aisle to aisle, my eyes trained for anyone who gives us a lingering glance, hoping and praying that we can just get back in the car and keep driving before the alert hits out here, before "a few hours away from home" turns into an actual kidnapping.

At the car seat aisle, I waver. Is she too old for a car seat? Too heavy? I look at her gangly limbs sticking out of the shopping cart. She has sharp elbows and knees, high cheekbones and a pointy chin. I read the weight limit for each seat. "Emma, do you sit in a car seat or a booster seat?"

She shrugs. "Both. One for Daddy's car and one for Mommy's."

I wheel her to where the scales are and shake one loose from its box. Emma watches me with interest, as I lift her up and out of the cart, step on the scale until I see a zero, and place her on it. She stands still as the numbers whir and then stop at 40.8.

I take her back to the seats. Which is safer? I decide on a Graco booster seat with a back. For as many miles as we are driving, I want to be safe.

The cashier makes small talk at the register—*is it her birthday? are we moving? my, what a lucky girl to get all this new stuff!*—and my heartbeat rattles my throat as I try to keep her talking about anything other than the child in my cart.

The cashier is young, a gum chewer, sprinkled with tattoos and way too bored with her job to follow AMBER Alerts. In my nervousness, I forget to give her the tags to pay for Emma's clothes. I hesitate once she gives me the total, but pay for all of our objects with cash, and push Emma into the night, a cool sweat having drenched my T-shirt.

"Well, kiddo, you've got a lot of good stuff here."

Emma looks behind her in the cart brimming with plastic bags. "*All* this stuff is for me?"

I nod. "Well, who else would it be for, silly?"

"Really?" She claps her hands together, bounces in the seat, and smiles. "Thank you! I don't know what to play with first."

"You can play with whatever you want." I lift her out of the cart and into the car, and that's the moment I know: no matter what part of my conscience exists, what part of me understands right from wrong, I will do whatever it takes to keep this little girl safe.

That's what I'm going with: my intention to keep her safe. In spite of the facts, in spite of what I've done. Because it feels right. Being with Emma feels right.

It's the only thing I trust.

before

"Why are we doing this again?"

"Because it's important to maintain local relationships," Brad said, first adjusting his new readers and then his snakeskin belt.

While Travis was my right-hand man and Madison my left, Brad was my entire torso. Nothing happened without his approval. He was my creative director, my negotiator, and my designer. I was lucky to snag him from a top branding agency down the street. I promised him endless PTO and that I would buy him whatever software he needed for the duration of his career.

He pressed his hands to his hips and moved his pelvis forward with an exaggerated sigh. "Longview is in Washington but it's close. It's like two miles from Kelso, which has that awesome rustic street market you love so much. Remember? We went to it last year and you kept going on and on about what a cute town it was? And then we ate sushi and stayed at the Hudson Manor Inn?"

"God, that sushi was so good. But that was Kelso, not Longview. Who the hell goes to Longview?"

"We go to Longview. You can practically walk to Kelso," he exclaimed, slapping his folder against the desk. "When did you become such a location snob?"

"I'm not a snob. Honestly, I'm just exhausted. I'm still trying to finish up all the orders from the trip and create an entire new line of kits." I knew all the reasons why this was a good business move for us, positioning ourselves in new territory, but my schedule had been so packed since my overseas trip that I just wanted to hole up in my office and focus on nothing but digital.

"Would you like for us to just go, then?"

"No, I'll go. It's important. I was just hoping for an easy week."

He snorted, and Madison busied herself with looking at her phone. "When have you ever had an easy week?"

"Point taken. It's fine. Really. I just don't know why we're going somewhere so small, when Portland has like fifty million Montessori schools."

"Because they requested us. In Longview. Which is where we are going in about"—he flicked his wrist and adjusted his wooden watch, a thank-you gift I'd gotten him last Christmas—"twenty minutes." He leaned over the paper on my desk, running his finger across a line of text until he spotted the name. "Montessori Children's House. If someone requests your presence, you show up."

"See? You had to look at the itinerary because even you couldn't remember the name of where we're going."

"Listen, boss lady, it will be a quick zip down and back. This is our chance to get into Montessoris. Which, as you know, could be huge for us. And I'll also make sure from now on we only go to the cool ones with the crazy high budgets."

"Aren't all Montessoris cool? Isn't that the whole point?"

"I mean in cool *places*, smart-ass. And just think. Once we get into Montessoris, the Waldorf schools are next!"

I laughed. "You know I'm just giving you a hard time,

right? I like to put your negotiating skills to the test before we try and land a deal."

"How'd I do?"

"You passed."

Madison scurried around, packing things for the road trip. Her ears were primed, but she knew to stay out of our banter.

"And you are seriously the only one I will let get away with calling me a smart-ass. You know that, right?"

"Yeah, yeah," he said. "You love it." He placed the papers and his computer in his designer messenger bag and draped it over one shoulder. "Are we ready now?"

"Almost. Give me five minutes to wrap up a few things."

I finished some lingering emails while shoving files into my bag. At the front desk, Madison, Brad, and I waved to Travis, who was busy taking calls and responding to order requests from overseas clients.

We promised to bring him back some fun Washington souvenirs and all mouthed goodbye as we headed to pack the TACK van. We counted and re-counted our kits and then piled in.

I glanced at my pitch notes as we bumped onto the highway. I knew the challenges with Montessori—they had a very specific set of learning criteria. They believed in certain methods, work cycles, and building blocks to advancement. I wanted to show how we could be a complement to the method and not a deviation.

We hit rush hour about thirty minutes outside our destination. "Any back roads we can take?"

"If you know something Google Maps doesn't, then by all means," Brad snapped, his eyes on the road. He took the business of driving more seriously than anyone I'd ever met: no texting, no listening to loud music, barely talking.

He hated the stress, but he always insisted on driving to every location.

I smirked at Madison, and she raised her eyebrows. "Sensitive, sensitive man," I murmured.

"Really, Sarah? You're going to bust my chops right now? I'm driving."

"You *are*? I hadn't noticed how white your knuckles are, or that you're sitting about two inches from the steering wheel, Grandma."

"Actually, I think my grandmother sits farther back than that," Madison added.

"All right, assholes, seriously." He exhaled, sitting up even straighter, hands at ten and two.

"You know, I actually read somewhere that your hands are supposed to be at eleven and three to be the safest—"

"Get out! Both of you. Out of the car right now."

"I don't know why you always insist on driving if you hate to drive!"

"Because I don't trust anyone else to get us there on time. Isn't that obvious?"

Madison and I laughed and helped him navigate. We knew when to push, but we also knew that Brad had a limit, and he was quickly approaching it. We pulled up to the school two minutes early, and I stared at the small ranch house with the bright red door. "Wait. This is it? Are we sure?" Across the street sat a church, but other than these two businesses, the only other buildings were the houses that dotted the busy street in a straight row.

"This is it." Brad groaned as he stacked ten kits high and set them on the cart to wheel inside.

Madison and I helped arrange the kits, counting once more before checking in at the front office and locating the room for the pitch. Children of varying ages clustered around, ignoring the teacher's instructions to sit and wait. We introduced ourselves and dove into the usual question-and-answer portion to get the kids interested before letting them explore the products.

Despite all my busyness and constant traveling, I loved the pitch. I had created every single product, from concept to completion, obsessively researching, testing, and prototyping. Watching the children squeal with happiness brought me immense joy.

Madison stayed after to chat with the teacher, as she was the best salesperson on our team. If she didn't snag the deal, Brad would be the closer. Once the deal was done, I'd go over logistics: price, delivery, and a possible subscription service. I snapped photographs and told them I was taking a lap around to check out the school. I liked to grab as many photos as I could to showcase our location diversity on the site.

I decided to walk up the street, wondering if a coffee shop or juice bar was nearby. I passed house after house, feeling my legs loosen and my body wake up.

"Ahhhhhhhhhh!"

I stopped. The sound of a child's shriek pierced the morning like a siren. I slapped a hand to my chest and looked left and right, unable to locate where the scream had come from. I heard a loud bang and then another scream. I ran a few steps forward, my eyes scanning a row of three similar houses. I looked for movement, a sign. Another scream. Something.

I stood rooted to the spot, a few cars passing by on their morning errands or commutes to work. I couldn't see movement from any of the houses. Had I imagined it? Misinterpreted it? It hadn't sounded like a playful shout.

"Sarah!"

I turned. Brad was running down the sidewalk, gasping. "There you are. Come on. We need you."

"Sorry, I was just exploring." I trotted up to him.

"I can't believe you made me run."

"It won't kill you." I turned the camera over in my hands. "I just heard the craziest scream."

"Because I just screamed your name."

"No," I shook my head and pulled the camera strap from my neck. "It sounded . . . pained. It sounded like a child."

"Probably just one of the kids outside. Which is where we're going."

We moved back to the school and down the short hall to the back door. I could see the kids in one of the classrooms diving into our kits, while the teachers happily observed. Outside, an inventive playground fanned across the yard. There was a climbing wall, a garden, a rock oasis with a little stream, and even outdoor cubbies for rain boots, umbrellas, and backpacks.

"This is amazing."

"Right? Told you Longview wouldn't be bad." Brad bumped his bony shoulder into mine.

It was outside playtime for a few classrooms. Kids shoveled sand, dug dirt, held hands, and sang songs with no melody. Brad had brought a box of kits to set up on a picnic table, and there was a mad scramble of tiny feet as he announced it.

I scanned the grounds for a teacher and walked over. "Hi. I'm here with TACK. We just gave a presentation in classroom B."

"Yes. Wonderful products."

"Thank you. Would it be possible if I snapped a few photos of the facility and the kids exploring the kits? Your director already has the release forms in case any children want to be included in the photos."

"Be my guest."

I thanked her, crouched, and angled the camera to catch some interesting shots of the children playing with the products, shots that would make viewers on our site want to know more and hopefully encourage other Montessoris to be involved too.

"Hey, let me take over the role of photog, lady," Madison said, reaching for the camera. "The director wants to talk to you. Big orders heading our way."

I unloaded the camera and located the director, who was talking to Brad. I smoothed my hair and crunched over the gravel to where she stood. "Rachel? Would you like to talk?"

Her hand rested on Brad's arm, and they were both laughing. She fixed her gaze on me, her eyes watering from laughter. "Oh sure, sure, Sarah. You've got a gem here with this one."

"Don't I know it," I said. "He's special."

Brad blushed. "Oh stop. But go on. But stop."

He stepped aside as we discussed business. Forty minutes later, the deal was done, orders were complete, and we were back in the car, packed and looking for lunch.

"So, all in all, not a bad day, right?" Brad asked, much more relaxed in the passenger seat with Madison behind the wheel. He was always adamant about driving to locations but never took the initiative on the way back.

"Yes, Brad. You were right." I rolled my eyes playfully and flipped through the photographs, deciding which, if any, I wanted to post on social media and to the site. I'd have to wait for the parents' final approval first, as I never wanted to post—

"Holy fuck."

"What?" Madison looked at me in the rearview as Brad turned to ask the same thing.

"Did you forget something?"

"I—no. I didn't. I just remembered something I forgot to do. No worries. Sorry."

"Now who's the drama queen?" Brad asked, sliding his sunglasses higher on his nose.

My fingers shook on the shutter button as I looked down, enlarging the photo of the little girl in the sand-box. There were three shots: one from the back, the side, and the front. The red bow fluttered in the photo in various angles, as though it were a little bird taking flight. It could be any young girl, except it wasn't. Those sad gray eyes, that downturned mouth—it was *her*. It was Emma. Did she wear the red bow like some sort of safety blanket? Was that really her? I looked again, knowing with 100 percent certainty it was. The closer I looked, the more it appeared she was even in the same dress.

"I'm . . . you know what, guys?"

"What?"

What? What could I say? *Stop the car? Go back?* "Nothing. Sorry. I'm just frazzled. Totally forgot about a project. Can we just head straight back to town?"

I wanted to go back to the school. I wanted to talk to Emma, her parents, or her teachers. It couldn't be a coincidence that she was there, and that I was there too. That her face was on my camera, sitting here in my lap.

"What project?"

"Yeah, we know about *all* the projects," Madison added. "And it's not like you to turn down food."

"Just drive, please. I need to get back."

We rode the rest of the way without speaking, my eyes fixed on the three photographs, studying her every angle, the shape of her face, the tip of her nose, those eyes, that bow.

How long had it been? Two or three months since I last saw her? Why was she wearing the same outfit? I struggled to see her shoes, but her legs were folded and buried behind her in the sand. There were no other kids in the shot—just Emma.

I wanted to ask Madison why she'd taken three shots of her, if she'd seen something that had made her focus solely on this little girl.

As we neared the office, I was already looking up hotels in Kelso. I had to know if what I saw that day in the airport was a fluke or the real thing. If her mother was a monster or just having a bad day; if that little girl needed someone to stand up for her. To help.

I didn't even know what that help would look like—I wasn't a social worker or a child psychologist, after all—and this wasn't some bad Lifetime movie where I could make her parents see the errors of their ways. This was a real child in real life with real consequences. I knew I didn't have any right to inject myself into her life, but I had to know she'd be okay. Somehow. Some way.

during

I load up the Tahoe and fasten my bike onto the rear bike rack. Ethan and I used to ride weekly, tackling the rainy streets and avoiding streetcars with as much precision as Tour de France cyclists. I'd become a bit of an expert, a city pro, but I wasn't ever off my guard. I knew how easy it was to hit a pothole, let your mind wander, have a car make an illegal turn, and then down you'd tumble, tearing skin, shattering bones, and sawing the ends of your teeth against unforgiving concrete.

I get an oil change for the Tahoe, have the tires rotated, and get my fluids topped off. I take out cash from two ATMs on two separate days and then opt for cash back whenever the option arises at the grocery store. My pockets are stuffed with green, my suitcase packed. I have always been a person who likes to pay in cash, to keep up with numbers and bills. But I'm putting thought into this, which is dangerous, which should tell me something, but I don't yet know what. *I just want to see for myself. Do a little stakeout. Gather some information. It's all innocent. It's no big deal. I'm doing nothing wrong.*

I tell the office I am going to visit my father, who lives in a remote city in Washington, in a small house that hasn't been updated in at least fifteen years. I'll just be gone for a bit; nothing to worry about. I'll have my computer with me to tend to business as usual.

Madison, Travis, and Brad practically push me out the door. They think it's my job in life to revive him. What they don't understand is that if he doesn't want reviving, he won't be revived. Heartbreak will do that to you, even decades later. Having lost Ethan, I can actually empathize with him, but I am not going to end up in a sad house, on a saggy couch, drinking myself to death. I am not my father.

I tie up loose ends with impending orders, future sales, and go for a run before loading up the car. I don't know what I'm doing. Am I so bored or distraught that I am inventing something to occupy my time?

I've given the boutique hotel in Kelso a fake name. I'm paying in cash and purchased a store-bought Visa card to hold my reservation. I hope they won't ask to see my ID; if they do, I will present it and pay cash anyway. I'll smile sweetly and tell them the reservation is for my sister, and she's coming soon, but I'm surprising her! And paying for it. How lovely! I know how to pour on the charm—thanks to TACK—and I will play my part appropriately.

The hour drive goes fast, but my room is ready early. I leave my bike, helmet, and shoes in the car. I inspect my room—cute double beds with antique bedspreads, mismatched nightstands, a rotary phone, a gilded mirror—and head into town, hoping to find food. The hotel is close to the school, but I tell myself I'm simply a tourist stopping through.

I find a sandwich shop, grab a turkey club, bag of chips, and wash them down with a fresh-squeezed lemonade. I go for a walk, instantly regretting the greasy chips, and pull up the map to check out Longview. It's less than half a mile away. I want to go there now, but I want the timing to be right. I want to arrive before dismissal and scope out who picks Emma up from school. I don't know if I will be more obvious on a bike or on foot, but I'm going for the bike. With my hair tucked in a helmet and an androgynous jersey, hopefully no one will give me a second thought.

I check my watch when I return to the hotel. It's two. I know from our prior visit that dismissal is at three-thirty, and I have no way of knowing if Emma stays for aftercare.

I decide to throw on my bike clothes under my dress and walk to my car, which is parked on the street. I get in, remove my dress, and pop my keys and cell phone into my back pocket. I slip on my shoes and loosen my bike from the rack, positioning my water bottle in its holder, wedging on my helmet, and looking at the directions one more time before clipping in. It's a short ride, but the urgency takes hold. I just want to see her again. I want to get to her. I want to know she's okay.

Minutes later, I'm circling the school, thankful for the nice weather. It's eerily silent except for the children's voices that rise and fall from the playground. I think again about the child's scream I heard—how piercing it was, how anguished.

I cycle down the block, taking inventory of the houses, and wonder if Emma lives close or far. What if she lives thirty minutes from here? I won't ever be able to keep up on a bike. At three I decide to grab an espresso at a café I find three blocks from the school. I thank the owner, not wanting to draw too much attention to myself, and down the shot before racing back. I can't quite see into the back of the school without waltzing right up to the privacy fence and trying to peer through the cracks. I think about going through the woods and wading my way through the shrubbery and trees, but I don't want to be seen.

Cars start lining up in front of the school at three-fifteen.

There seems to be a decent order for child retrieval, as cars idle, music blasts, and parents jabber away on their cell phones. I pedal across the street and unclip, crouching down as though examining my back tire.

I keep my eyes alert, searching for Emma or her mother, but I don't see them. What if this is all a mistake? What if the girl in the photograph *isn't* Emma?

Three-thirty comes and goes. There's no Emma and no mom. No praying mantis of a father. No baby brother. I wait until four-thirty, circling the block, wondering every time I go around if I've somehow missed her.

When five comes, I've had enough. The espresso has left me jittery and hungry; I cycle back to the hotel as fast as I can, eager to beat rush hour, eager to figure out if what I'm doing is crazy, if I've imagined everything, if I need to go back home to my life in Portland and forget about this little girl for good.

Once I'm off my bike and back in the room, I call Madison to get a daily update. She answers on the first ring.

"How's your dad?" She's fumbling with something in the background, and I pull the phone away from my ear.

"He's . . . fine. You know, the same as always." I'm disgruntled, frustrated, and unsure of my next move. It's not yet dark, and I want to walk by the school one more time, combing through the neighborhood to see if I missed something.

I've already been on the Montessori Facebook page. You can't see the posts unless you're invited to the page, and I'm not a parent and don't want to request access. I've googled "Emma Grace," "Amy," and "Longview" and come up with nothing.

"Earth to Sarah. Did you hear me?"

"What? Sorry. My dad was asking me something. What did you say?"

"Oh, I said the research came back from both Ethiopia and Senegal. All rave reviews from both, except a few little snags in Senegal." She pores over the notes, and I switch back to work, giving her suggestions on what to say, outlining actionable tasks for Travis tomorrow.

"When are you coming back? Not that there's any rush," she adds. "You should be with your dad."

"I'm not sure yet. Hopefully, it will be just a quick visit. Thanks for holding down the fort while I'm gone."

We hang up, and I shower and head down to the bar. I can have a drink, a meal, and go to bed, or I can walk through the neighborhood and try to find some clue I missed. I decide food can wait and set out on foot, noticing several neighbors out walking their dogs, enjoying the budding summer heat.

I wave, smile, and insert my earbuds. I turn the corner by the school, making my way down the block like I did last time, where I heard the scream. Dogs bark. Tricycles tinkle while runners pound the pavement. A few bikers even huff an "on your left" as they whiz by.

I'm pleased to see there's a pulse here; it makes me feel good to know Emma doesn't live in a hole somewhere, kept from the pleasant hum of suburban life.

I walk down the block and around it, seeing no signs of the little girl or her family. It's getting dark. I'm starving. Inflamed clouds loom overhead. I circle back toward the hotel.

My nerves gather in a bundle at my willingness to stay and dig myself deeper into a self-made mystery. But there's a reason I can't let this little girl go. Not until I know she's safe.

I'll try again tomorrow, I think. I'll give it one more day.

I wake early and throw on my bike clothes from yesterday before grabbing a muffin and coffee downstairs. I clip in and hurry toward the school, thinking I have a better chance at drop-off than pickup. I'm going to see her today. I have to.

I glance at my watch: It's seven-thirty. Per the hours on the website, drop-off is officially at eight, so I have plenty of time. I circle the block a few more times, hoping I'm not becoming a bit of a distraction, when I see a few families walking their children toward the school. None of them look like Amy, though a few of the little girls give me pause. I see no red bow and hear no angry mothers. I keep riding.

By eight, I'm bored and tired of riding the same few blocks. I could have easily missed her going in. Maybe she's sick? It takes everything I have not to just go into the school, tell them I am following up on TACK business, and find her. But that would present its own handful of obvious problems.

I decide to make one more round. I'm pedaling down the same block, heading away from the school, when I hear a shriek. The same shriek I heard on my first visit. The same anguished cry. My stomach lurches as I slam on my brakes and look around, unclipping one foot and leaning to the side. My heart is in my throat. I wait, but there's nothing.

Cars speed by, impatiently ballooning out to make room for the stalled cyclist on the side of the road. I don't know whether to keep going or not; I want to know where that cry is coming from.

I decide to keep riding, to keep making my rounds, when I hear a voice so memorable, I want to scream. "Come on right this minute. You're already late."

It's coming from the house to my right, a small green cottage with a van parked in the driveway. The yard is unkempt, and I can hear footsteps approaching on the gravel from behind the house. And then there's Emma's mother, just as red-faced, pulling a toddling little boy by the hand. Where is she?

I don't see the dad. I cycle a little farther and stop, positioning my small mirror to see them behind me. The mother is hoisting the toddler up into the van. I see the top half of her disappear into the back, her lower half swaying left and right in an attempt to buckle him in. She slams the door with the force of ten men and stalks behind the house. Elevated voices merge with the traffic, and then she is coming back again, struggling to pull herself up and into the van. Her tires screech as she reverses into the street, like she's trying to get away from something. She barrels down the road, and I pray a child or dog doesn't decide, at that very moment, to dash across the street.

Her vehicle continues to shoot through the neighborhood with a sense of urgency. She speeds through the school zone, the crossing guard puffing her whistle and wagging her arms. Is Amy frustrated with her day already? Is she just running late? Is she a woman agitated by life?

I pedal back to their house, wondering where Emma is, when she appears in her driveway, shuffling through the gravel, to see where her mom went.

Her red bow ripples. Her ruby shoes halt. She is just as beautiful as I remember, and the maternal instincts I feel toward this stranger continue to surprise me. I am shocked by the audacity of it—this mother leaving her child—until I see the dad round the corner, yelling for Emma to come back right this instant, or else.

I wonder what the "or else" could be. Will I see it? The hope of him not being an asshole quickly extinguishes; I feel relief and disturbance at his presence. I'm glad Emma isn't on her own, standing in the chalky gravel, watching her mother drive away, and yet I want her to be. I want blatant evidence that she is not cared for, so I can . . . what?

I'm afraid of the answer to that question.

I begin to move on the opposite side of the street, keeping sight of that signature red bow in my small mirror. He tugs on her arm and tells her to hurry up, to come on. He drops her backpack at her feet. The bottom sags as she shrugs the weathered straps onto her shoulders. They begin walking toward the school, which is no more than a few blocks. He doesn't hold her hand, and it's clear she doesn't expect him to.

I am reminded of my own mother then, the way she would sometimes extend her right hand back if we were walking together, fingers stiff, as if she were a track star and I was supposed to pass her the baton for the last leg of the race. She never looked back, and if I didn't trot up to retrieve her offering, she would snatch away her fingers, emit an agitated huff, and walk faster.   .

Once, I'd stopped to tie my shoes at a flea market and lost sight of her completely. I knew by then to find a respectable-looking adult—no creepy mustaches, preferably no men, and no one homeless—and eventually Elaine would come back, impatience ravaging her features, as if I'd been the one to leave her.

I can see the same agitation in this family, how they run hot and cold, as if programmed by faucets. The way Emma skitters to a stop at the end of the driveway and how her mother just peels away anyway, unconcerned. The way the father barks after his daughter and she comes running, as if her parents' entire experience of Emma isn't about Emma at all: it's about *them*. These are the actions of a family who doesn't think anyone is watching.

But I am watching.

Now Emma weaves dangerously close to the edge of the sidewalk. There is an intake of breath as I stop my bike and dismount, again squatting down to check for a fake flat. I know that if Emma is to accidentally walk into traffic, everything would shift. The father and mother would band together and re-create their history with their daughter, as if they lived a happy, normal life, but they would have gotten away with it: being shitty parents.

She runs right up the steps to the front of the school. She doesn't wave goodbye to her father. He doesn't pat her on the head and tell her to have a good day. He's busy looking at his phone, bringing it to his ear and raising his hands in an obvious early-morning confrontation. I watch a teacher usher her inside and shake her head.

I decide to keep riding, satisfied that I've seen her, that she exists, that her parents are still awful, and she's still here. She's still the girl with the pretty red bow in the same red dress. The girl I first saw in the airport. The girl who rocketed back into my life when I was just starting to forget her.

I move faster, checking both ways at stop signs before braking near the hotel. I dismount, remove my helmet, and slug the rest of my water.

A mother and her three girls enter the hotel with their bright pink roller bags, giggling about something. I smile and wipe the sweat from my chin. I used to be in a state of constant envy of other young girls with their mothers, laughing, shopping, or stopping at the corner parlor to lick double scoops of ice cream. The way those mothers looked at their daughters—with tolerance, love, and patience—I could never recognize in my own. My mother only revealed annoyance, exhaustion, and intolerance. Even though I said so little and stayed so small, it didn't matter. The way I exhaled, sat, ate, looked . . . it was all one giant trigger for her. I was a mouth breather, a huncher, a sloppy chewer, a tomboy with ratty hair and chapped lips. I spent my entire childhood feeling small, scared, and lonely.

Did Emma?

I knock the question from my brain again—*so what if she does?*—but I can't shake the sight of her, the demeanor of her. It is like being taken back twenty-five years. The way Emma looks, the way her mother treats her. I recognize myself in her, and I want to help.

I work a decision over in my head and straddle the line between danger and necessity as I pop my bike back into the Tahoe. My legs are wobbly with nerves. I unstrap my shoes and toss them in the car. I know it's time to go home, that I should check out of the hotel and drive straight back to the office. Because now I've seen her again. I did what I set out to do.

But there's one question that cuts across the rest and keeps me rooted to the spot: *What if she needs to be rescued?*

before

Ethan strapped the canoe on top of his truck.

"Are you sure that thing's secure?"

He looked at me, fake annoyance in his voice. "You know, I have done this before." He motioned to the canoe on the roof. "Hence, why I have a canoe."

I lifted my hands in surrender before loading our cooler and thermoses into the front cab. "I'm just saying. I don't want it to fall and impale some innocent driver."

Ethan tightened the last strap and tapped the canoe twice. "Well, there was that one time someone lost a head, but that wasn't my fault."

"Someone should really tell you your jokes aren't funny."

"Oh, my wife tells me all the time."

"Good one."

We slammed the doors and were on the open road in minutes, heading to Cannon Beach for an afternoon excursion. My heart was still rippling with pleasure at the sound of the word *wife* coming from his lips. Yes, it was a joke, and it was not about me, but that's where we were headed. Someday, I would be Mrs. Ethan Turner. I could feel it.

I watched the landscape zip by, thinking of all the people tucked in these remotely built houses, mowing their yards, drinking coffee by bay windows, and scribbling out their to-do lists for the day. Some of them were born and raised locals; some were transplants. Others were just passing through. It always amazed me how you moved to new cities, cracked open all the yummy secrets of a foreign place, and fit virtual strangers into your life like sticks of gum in a pack. You fell in love; you made friendships; you created babies; you shaped careers. Often, you moved and started all over again, leaving pieces of yourself everywhere you went.

"What are you thinking about over there, Walker?"

We'd only been together for seven months, but I knew. I knew this was *it*, the way people knew they preferred chocolate over raspberry, or voted Democrat or Republican. He was the one. I looked at him and smiled. He was too easy on the eyes. I couldn't keep my thoughts from perpetually drifting to sex. I'd called Lisa in a panic after we'd first officially started dating—I'd asked him out after I wandered into his furniture shop—and told her we couldn't stop having sex.

"And?"

"Well, I don't know. Isn't that bad or something? We can't possibly keep this up, can we? It's making my brain all . . . fuzzy."

"Oh, please. Get married, pop out a few babies, and you won't even know what sex is."

"But you and Tom still have sex."

"Rarely. Because when we are both faced with a night of sleep or having sex, we choose sleep every time. No-brainer."

"Oh, please. Nothing is better than sex."

"Except uninterrupted sleep."

I couldn't imagine a life where I'd choose to sleep next to Ethan instead of with Ethan.

"Charlotte, stop it this instant, or I'm taking your train away. Do you understand me?" Her voice was muffled. "Sorry. Tiny terrorists at work. Are you using protection?"

"Like condoms?"

"Yes, like condoms, Ms. Au Naturel. Because I know you're not on birth control."

"Yes . . . most of the time."

"I give you three months before you're knocked up."

"I am not getting pregnant. We aren't ready for kids yet. We're not even engaged!"

Lisa snorted. "Everyone isn't ready for kids until they end up pregnant. Then you have no choice."

"We are being careful. I promise."

"Uh-huh." Lisa shuffled something. A door shut. "There. Temporary privacy. This is the thing. This is new. It's exciting. You think it's never going to change, but it will. One day, you'll look at him, and your stomach won't flip. You'll be thinking of the laundry you have to do when he's on top of you. And pretty soon, with the demands of everything, sex just isn't as mandatory as everyone thinks it is. Marriage is about so much more than sex. Tom's penis could literally fall off tomorrow, and I'd be fine with that, because he fulfills me in other ways."

"How sweet."

"No, I'm just saying that you can live without constant sex. But you absolutely cannot live without sleep."

I hoped to never understand her point; I wanted sex, sleep, romance, and happiness. I knew Ethan and I would be different. We'd have well-behaved children, travel the world, get 8.5 hours of sleep every night, have sex five times per week, and still run our businesses. We wouldn't become those exhausted, bickering, boring parents who only talked about the logistics of their days and got annoyed every time someone farted, got a cold, or forgot to take the trash out.

"Hello in there? Are you stroking out?" Ethan glanced at me.

I laughed. "Sorry." I uncapped my thermos and took a swig of coffee. "Daydreaming."

"About?"

I wiggled my eyebrows. "I'll never tell."

"Is it something kinky?" He squeezed my knee, and a tingle throttled through my stomach.

"No. I was actually thinking about our future."

"Are we naked in it?"

Ethan hit a pothole and my thermos tipped, spilling hot coffee on my thighs. "Shit, that's hot!" I swept the liquid from my legs, holding the thermos up high. I screwed on the lid and looked for a towel to mop up the mess. "Do we not have a towel in here?"

"Take the wheel."

"What? I'm dealing with third-degree thigh burns over here."

Ethan rolled his eyes. "Just take the wheel, drama queen." With one hand on my thermos and the other steadying the wheel, Ethan removed his T-shirt and threw it at me. It covered my face and landed in my coffee-drenched lap.

"I'm not using your T-shirt. What will you canoe in?"

"I brought another one. It's in my bag. Just use it."

I sniffed the shirt before lowering it to my lap, and Ethan groaned.

"Pathetic how obvious you are in your affections for me."

"I'm this affectionate to all my suitors."

This was our running joke—trying to convince the

other that we weren't that important, when we were entirely each other's world, and we knew it. I dabbed at the coffee and spread the red T-shirt across my lap.

"So, you were saying? Naked future?"

I swatted him on the arm. "No, not a naked future. Just, you know, the future."

"And what do you see?"

I stared at the rows of trees whipping by, the empty road ahead of us, the warmth of our bodies bouncing on the leather seats. "I just see . . . us. Together. Happy. What do you see?"

He smiled, his obliques flexing like fingers against his ribs. "I see the same thing. But in my version, you are most definitely naked."

I rolled my eyes. "Men. Always the same."

"What?"

"Always after the same thing, I mean."

"Hey, you know me better than that. I want your heart and your body."

"Yeah, yeah." I took another hesitant sip from my thermos. The warmth spread through my entire body, down to my fingers and toes. Here I was, with the love of my life, heading for a fun weekend. Life didn't get better than this. It couldn't.

We arrived at Cannon Beach in no time, after a few CDs and easy conversation. We unpacked the canoe, lowering it to the rocky, sandy earth. It seemed we weren't the only couple who had this in mind: men, women, children, and dogs dotted the beach. We smiled at the strangers, fitting our canoe among the pack, and worked our arms over the next few hours, paddling to rocky bluffs, watching birds dip in and out of the water to claw at fish, their talons primed. The muscles in Ethan's chest and shoulders contracted with every stroke. When sweat beaded my brow, he insisted I rest and eat my sandwich while he paddled.

We decided to stay over in a camping area not far from the beach. He'd brought his small tent and a few sleeping bags. I finger-brushed my teeth and helped him erect the tent and build a small fire. I loved camping. It always reminded me of the good days with my father, both of us giggling and struggling to put up our cheap, flimsy tents.

We crawled into our bags outside the tent, watched the stars, and talked about life. I knew Ethan had such a vastly different upbringing than I did. He was the product of a solid family who expected great things. I hadn't met them yet—Ethan didn't bring women home, but we had already arranged a dinner with all of us in two weeks—and I was excited to get to know the people who had raised him.

We pulled our sleeping bags in the tent when the temperature dropped and snuggled against each other. He fell asleep instantly, twitching beside me, while I concentrated on the hum of nature and the hard earth beneath my spine.

The next morning, we rose early and headed back, making a stop at Ethan's to take showers and get some proper breakfast. He lived downtown next to all our favorite haunts. I showered first because we both couldn't fit in the narrow stand-up. As I threw on my clothes, I emptied his duffel, pawing through the remains of our trip. I laughed at all the extra tools and clothing he'd brought, always over-prepared for any situation. He'd packed two pairs of tube socks and an extra for me. I smiled as I lifted them from his bag, folding them neatly to put away, but one was lumpy and hard. I fished deep into the wool and hooked my fingers around something velvety and firm. I immediately removed my hand and glanced nervously at the bathroom.

It couldn't be.

The excitement crackled through my entire body. I didn't want to look. I didn't want to ruin the surprise, but what if it wasn't a ring, and I was waiting for something that might never happen? Which would be worse?

I heard the water turn off and stuffed all Ethan's belongings back into his bag. I ran to the living room, turned on the television, and curled up on the sofa, as though asleep. My heartbeat vibrated my teeth. A thousand questions threatened my resolve. *When did he do it? Where did he go? How had he gotten my ring size?* I didn't wear rings—didn't even know what size my own ring finger was—but I knew Ethan well enough to know he was capable of figuring things out. *Did he talk to Lisa? Did Lisa know about this? Did the team? Was it a wooden ring? Did he make it himself? Was he planning to do it soon? Why did he have it with him on the trip?*

Ethan walked into the room, and I challenged my lids to stop fluttering. He kissed me on the eyebrow and brushed the hair from my face.

"Hey, Sarah. Sarah?" He rubbed my back, and I pretended to stir awake, looking at him as though I'd forgotten where I was.

"Sorry. I guess I fell asleep for a second."

"Don't apologize. Do you want to just make something here instead? We don't have to go out."

I pulled him on top of me and kissed his neck, working my mouth up to his earlobe. "No, let's go out. I'd love to get some breakfast with you."

He pulled me off the couch, and I reveled in the secret I now had to keep from him. Part of me was disappointed that I knew, but part of me felt immense relief. He loved me as much as I loved him. Now, it was all about the timing.

Five years, six months, and two days. That's how long I'd waited. And still no ring. Not for the first time, I was absolutely kicking myself for not having opened the box. It obviously hadn't been a ring, but he'd never given me anything remotely the same size as that box. Had that been a present for another woman? His mother? Had I been fooling myself all these years? Was he living some sort of double life?

I sat upright in bed and flung Ethan's arm to the side. I was angry this morning; I could feel it in my joints, which ached from a tough workout and too much sugar the day before. I padded to the bathroom and slammed the door. I washed my face, brushed my teeth, and stomped to the kitchen, grinding the coffee instead of waiting for him to do it.

In all these years, nothing had changed. He still slept over like we were casual daters, but he kept his place and would never leave his belongings at my house. He liked the autonomy, and most times, I did too, but not this long. This long was too long. I wanted the ultimate commitment, the merging of our lives.

I'd never been one of those girls who needed to get married or to have any validation when it came to men. *You love me? Great! I love you too. Let's love each other until we don't.* But once you met the guy who wouldn't give you all the things you thought you didn't want? It's all you wanted.

Every birthday and anniversary, the excitement built. *How would he do it? Where would we live? Would we have children immediately (hello, post-thirty egg decline!) or take our time?* We'd both traveled so much in our separate lives and as a couple, I knew we were ready to just slow down, set some roots, and grow. It was time.

The years slipped by. Our businesses grew. Looking forward to the unknown became a game and then a slow, resentful drip. Every day he didn't propose was one where I grew angrier, some bitter, calcified version of myself.

"Hey. Why all the noise, stompy?"

Ethan ran one hand over his recently shaved head. It was the first time he'd had no hair—due to his recent obsession with triathlons—and I couldn't stop running my fingers over it. Even now, as angry as I was, I wanted that fuzzy feeling against my palms.

"I'm just pissy."

"Work?" He moved over to where I was shaking the coffee grounds into the Chemex filter and took over.

"See? This is what I'm talking about."

"What? What is what you're talking about?"

"This." I motioned to the filter. "You do everything better than I do. You fix things when they're broken. You build tables from fucking tree branches. You make my coffee. And what's the point if none of this is guaranteed?"

"Wait, what? What are you talking about?"

"Us! I'm talking about us. I never wanted to be this girl, just so you know. This is important to know."

"What girl?" He motioned to the bedroom. "What happened from the time we went to bed until now?"

"The girl who always needs something, who isn't just happy with what she has or the way things are. Look." I leaned against the countertop and crossed my arms. "I don't need proof that you love me, because I know you do. But I want proof, and I hate myself for wanting it. And I hate you a little for making me want it." I wanted to mention the ring box. I wanted to know the truth about what I'd found all those years ago. But what if the truth was something else entirely?

He set the beaker down and came to me, arms

outstretched. I attempted to push him away, but I couldn't. I collapsed into his warm chest and gripped his bare back, turning my head so I could hear the rush of blood whooshing through his sternum. "It just sucks. I don't know why you don't want to marry me. I want you too much. I love you too much. It's exhausting." Silence filled my kitchen. I waited for him to say something or to reassure me. His heart began to pound against my cheek.

"Who says I don't want to marry you?"

I pulled away, my face incredulous. "Are you kidding? How about almost six years of not getting engaged?"

"Since when are you so obsessed with getting engaged?"

"Since you haven't proposed. Since nothing has changed. You either know or you don't know, right? Isn't that what everyone says?"

He pulled away from me completely. "Well, that's your opinion. That's not a fact."

"Oh really? The facts aren't in the actions—or in your case, the *in*actions?"

"Sarah, we've talked about this. That's just your opinion. And it's just not been the right—"

"Oh, please. Don't talk about it not being the 'right time'—see? Look at me! I'm even that asshole who uses air quotes. Who am I?" I dropped my fingers and squeezed them into fists. "Screw the right time. Seriously. It's all just such a bullshit excuse. If everyone waited for the right time, no one would ever get married, have children, take risks, or start new careers. There is no right time. There's just . . . what you want to do and what you're going to do. And what you don't want to do. I just wish you'd be man enough to admit I'm not the one. You don't want to marry me. End of story. *Next!*"

He paced the kitchen, his pajama pants slung low

around his hips, his palms moving back and forth over his buzzed head. "It's not that simple, Sarah."

I hopped up on my kitchen island and kicked the drawers with my heels like a child. "What's not that simple? Getting married? I feel like a bully, Ethan. Do you know how awful that is? Even if you ever proposed, which, let's face it, is never going to happen, it would be ruined because I've talked about it so much and pushed so hard. And I don't even like weddings."

He smiled in an attempt to change the mood and shift the charged air. But I was at my breaking point. I couldn't sleep with him, wake up with him, give him my whole life, and just get *maybes* in return. Or the intention of "someday." I wanted now. I needed definites. I needed an investment. I looked at him and swallowed the crater in my throat. "I can't believe I'm going to say this, but—"

"Don't." He lifted his hand. "Don't you dare break up with me because we aren't engaged yet. Don't you fucking dare."

"What else am I supposed to do? Do you think I want to break up with you? I'm sitting here telling you that I want to marry you. That you are the only man I have ever wanted. I don't want to give you an ultimatum. That's what I'm saying. I've become this girl, and I hate her. I literally hate her."

"Aghhhh!" Ethan screamed, a loud pierce that filled my silent, white, clean kitchen. "Why can't you ever just do things at my pace, Sarah? Why?"

I dropped down from the island and moved to him, craning my head to meet his eyes. "I've done nothing but love you from basically the first day we met. I literally can't live without you. I don't *want* to live without you. But I can't just live with you . . . without something more."

Despite the situation, he laughed. "Is that like a word problem?"

I squeezed his arm. I watched the imprint of my fingers appear after a few seconds, long, tapered, and pink.

"I'm sorry. It's just the way I feel. I can't help it."

"Sarah, come on," he whispered. "Please don't do this." His voice was husky.

"I have to." Our lives together flashed in sequence: walking into his furniture shop all those years ago and asking him out; our first date hiking, where I'd twisted my ankle and he'd carried me down the mountain on his back; the time we'd both had food poisoning and he'd managed to drag himself to the store for broth and crackers; the night a piece of wood in his shop had crushed his shin and I'd had to take him to the emergency room to get stitches; the day his mother told me he'd never been this in love with a woman; the afternoon he'd helped my dad after he drank too much and couldn't drive home. All of the real moments—not just the happy times—gave me pause. There was so much substance here, so much time put in, so many memories. Was I willing to give all that up because I didn't have a ring?

He grabbed the back of my neck and leaned in. I let him kiss me, my love trapped by frustration, longing, disappointment, and fear. He yanked at my clothes, and they tumbled to the tile as we made love in the kitchen.

After, we laid together, his fingers stroking my cheeks and hair.

"I love you, Sarah."

"I love you too." But it wasn't enough. I knew loving him wouldn't fill the void. Not anymore.

Three hours later, Ethan left my condo for the last time.

during

The woods form a blooming, visible line behind the school and blocks of houses. It seems so easy that children would go missing here: one moment playing in their backyards, the next being swallowed by the trees.

I ride my bike around the block, another row of houses on the other side of the forest, the trees a dividing line down the center. This means the woods aren't thick; to come out of them, you have to cross over into someone's backyard. It isn't a good cover and makes it impossible for children not to be found.

I check my watch a thousand times as I ride, making loop after senseless loop. I know that Emma's house is the twelfth down on the left from the school. I know to get there, I have a decent trek through those woods, and even then, I don't know if I will be able to see her. I do not know where the woods begin at the edge of her backyard, or if she will even *be* in her backyard. I know I have to be on foot for this—a bike just won't do—but I have no idea what my intentions are or what I'm after yet.

At ten, I ride back to the hotel. I shower, check messages, eat, wait until afternoon, then load up my bike and head toward the school. I park several blocks away, half-way between the hotel and the school, sliding my Tahoe in among other similar cars on the street. My bags are still at the hotel—a glaring oversight—but I don't have time to go back. I lock my car and start walking, searching for an opening to the woods. My only way in is at either corner. The woods start where the school begins and end about half a mile down. Above, the clouds are thickening and changing shape, blocking out what little sun has been on display.

I've never much liked the woods. Perhaps it's the cautionary tales we're told as children, how bad things happen to good little girls and boys in those dark, unmarked trails. I like tree houses, camping, open fires, crispy bacon, and coffee in a hot tin cup, but there is always something sinister about rows of trees that muffle sounds, house creatures, and bury secrets.

I rework my scarf, suddenly aware that it could get caught on a tree branch and rip. I wrap it tightly around my throat and tuck the ends into my long-sleeved black shirt. I do not want to go in, but this is the only way.

At the end of the block, I stare directly at the forest. I start to wonder what the difference is between a forest and the woods. This stretch of trees doesn't seem long enough or dense enough to be classified as a forest. I shake my head—always the distractions—and study the side of the school on my left and the bank of houses on my right. The woods dissect both, cutting off what would have been bigger backyards in exchange for coniferous trees blasting in a dense line into the sky.

I casually step onto the grass, keeping my eyes peeled for passersby. I come to the opening of the woods, toeing the line, and then I slip inside, everything becoming black, cool, and damp. I blink, let my eyes adjust, and shuffle forward, feeling branches like tiny bones snap beneath my shoes. I move to the left, because that's where the school is—just a few feet ahead. I can already hear the children, outside for their afternoon play. I push branches out of my way and come to the edge of the tree line. I can make out the privacy fence, but I can't see the children running, climbing, and shouting on the other side, like tiny primates.

A shudder of disgust takes hold. I hope no one with sinister intentions has ever stood just where I'm standing. I retreat, suddenly breathing hard, as contempt rots my insides. *What the fuck am I doing?*

I sit on the ground, which is shockingly damp and soaks through the back of my jeans. I drop my head to my knees and breathe in an attempt to figure this out.

I should stand up, walk back through those trees, get in my car, check out of the hotel, and go home. Go back to my life and my business. Get on with everything. Get over the breakup. Put myself out there. Meet someone new. Move on, move up, move away. Just *move*.

I stand and brush off my jeans, checking the back to see just how wet they have become, when I hear a teacher's voice. My ears twitch, and my stomach churns. I move closer to the edge of the trees.

"Emma!"

At the sound of her name, my heart wrenches in my chest. I press my hand over it, as though that will calm my most erratic organ, and listen.

"Your sitter is here!"

I go slack with relief—*a sitter! she has a sitter!*—and move back, knowing I have ground to cover to get to her house. If I stay close to the tree line, I can make out the houses on the left.

I start to walk, far enough back that no one in their garden, fence-free, sees the crazy lady on the move. What will I see when I get there? The fact that she has a sitter makes me wonder if life is really so bad. She's at school during the day; she has a sitter in the afternoons. Maybe dinner and bedtime aren't awful. Maybe I have it all wrong.

But I just want to see her one last time. I want to see her playing, jovial and happy. I want to see her sitter engaged, to have verification that someone is on her side. I want to watch her mom come home, witness the exchange, see just one hug, an arm around her shoulder, something to assure me that this girl will grow up and prosper. I keep count of the houses, watching the different hues and styles pass by. *Four, five, six . . .*

I don't know if I will beat them there, if she will go outside today, or if she's even allowed outdoor play once she's home. Does she get a snack? Does she need to rest? Does she just sit in front of the television until Mommy or Daddy appear?

Suddenly, I am running, watching for knotted roots or branches. I want to get there before they do. My foot catches on something and twists, hard. I slow down, my ankle throbbing, and keep moving, calming myself. I check my watch—I've only been moving for a few minutes. I've got three houses to go.

I take deep breaths and trot past the last few houses, ignoring the dull pain near my Achilles tendon.

Almost there, I tell myself. *Almost.*

The backyard is messy. The grass is at least ankle height, and patchy. I believe you can tell a lot by someone's backyard, how they really live. The front yard is easy to keep pristine. It's visible to the world—you get judged if it's not manicured. But the backyard is like the inside of a home—a truthful afterthought, a catchall for the remains of your daily exhaustion.

The yard is small, shaped like a rectangle, and angles up toward the woods. They have no fence, which is surprising with two young children. The woods are only about twenty feet out, but I can see clearly. Old, plastic toys litter the yard, as if someone took a sack of forgotten parts and flung them into the grass. There's a Big Wheel—did they still make those?—a kid-sized plastic table and chairs, a red and yellow playhouse sheathed in mud, a soggy teddy bear, and a lawn mower. Their patio is bare and dusty, except for a pair of rain boots. The yard sweeps onto a gravel drive, a toolshed, and those few battered toys.

I've been moving for fifteen minutes. I crouch at the edge of the woods, my knees popping, and wait. I finger the skin over my ankle, checking for swelling. My other foot bumps into something under the dirt. I move it with my toe and realize it's a beaded necklace. I scan the ground and see a few more toys, half buried, suggesting time spent in these woods. Emma?

I'm careful not to touch anything, not to disrupt the story these woods tell. I glance again at my watch and strain to see with this much tree coverage. I'm assuming the sitter walks her home; they should be arriving shortly. I can imagine Emma chattering as she skips, showing her sitter the pictures she drew, telling her all about the friends she had fun with or what she learned today. It's my favorite thing about children—their wild, unbridled enthusiasm— but even as I imagine it, I can't quite picture Emma like that. She's not animated, this much I know, even from the short time I glimpsed her in the airport.

I wait five minutes, then ten. Finally, I hear something coming from the left, and I see Emma run up the drive, alone. She immediately darts into the backyard. I scramble backward, afraid to be seen, and crouch even lower, my breath fractured. An involuntary swell of protectiveness sweeps over me at the very sight of her. The red bow, the same dress, the scuffed ruby shoes. Is this her uniform? I try to remember if the other kids wore uniforms when I visited, but I can't.

Emma runs into the playhouse and slams the door behind her. It makes a dull thud. I peel my eyes for the sitter before I see a young woman walk up the drive with Emma's backpack in hand.

"Emma, I'm going inside now."

Emma says nothing. The sitter sighs and disappears around to the front of the house. I hear a door close. Then, Emma exits her playhouse and walks to a patch of grass. She sits and plunges her fingers into the soft dirt.

I change my position so I can better see her. I watch as tufts of grass rise above her head and then fall like confetti. I want to talk to her, to tell her to come to the trees. I want to have a conversation. I just want to—

The back door slams and out walks the sitter. Her arms are crossed and I can tell, even from this distance, that she looks mean.

"Emma Grace, stop tearing up the yard. You know your mother won't like that."

Emma looks up, and her hands freeze midair. She stands and wipes her fingers on her dress. She says something that I can't hear, and the sitter nods.

They both go inside, and I slink back. I don't know what to do. Why is everyone so *annoyed* with her? Is there something I don't see? Some hidden quality that changes her into a child monster?

I sit for an hour. I have to pee. It is the start of summer, and the sun sets later now, but in this region, the sun is more of a concept than a given. Before dark, a car rolls up, its headlights shooting into the trees. I pull back, careful not to be spotted, even though I'm in all black.

I'm getting colder; my black jeans are still wet. Night is imminent, and I have to get out of these trees before then. I'll have to use my cell phone light to pave the way back, which will give me away to nosy neighbors. I move back to the edge of the trees and wait to see who is in the car: shitty mom or shitty dad?

Shitty mom exits, goes to the back, unstraps baby brother, and walks around the front of the house. I hear a door shut, and then nothing. A few minutes later, a second car pulls in behind Amy's, and I hear the front door slam.

I listen as intently as possible, but it's strangely quiet, no neighborhood children yammering about. I'm still for ten minutes and then the back door opens and out charges Emma—not running, *sprinting*—and suddenly, she is in the trees, heading straight for me.

"Holy shit," I whisper as I watch her, just feet from me, crouch and fold into a tight little ball. A red orb against a black, early night. She doesn't see me. She is afraid of someone.

Her mother rockets out the back door, the baby missing from her hip, and she yells at the top of her lungs: "Emma Grace, come here right this instant!"

There's an annoyed mother's tone and then there's *this*—poison mixed with something dangerous. Emma stands and teeters back and forth. She steps out of the woods as I reach for her, my hands closing in on air.

Amy takes a few steps forward, and Emma takes one small step back toward the woods.

"How many times have I told you not to go into those woods? Get over here right now. It's time to go inside. I mean it."

She moves as deliberately as I've ever seen a child move, as if time has been stilled and she is a slow-motion mime.

"Emma, now!"

Emma walks with her head down until she is standing a foot away from her mother. I'm holding my breath, and then Amy's hand is around Emma's elbow, and she is shaking her until tears prick my eyes.

"What is wrong with you? Why can't you ever just listen? Just *listen* to me! Just once!"

Emma screams something and her mother lets go, her chapped cheeks trembling with fury. She is like a cartoon—so lively, inflated, and enraged. I'm witnessing something about their relationship here. In their backyard, in Washington, I am learning the truth of their daily interactions. I watch the struggle on Amy's face—*do I walk away or do I unleash?*—and I wait to see which side of this woman wins.

She comes within inches of Emma's face. She bends over her daughter, her stomach pressing against her tight pants. All of the complexities of motherhood fester: her anger, her contorted face, the timeline of her life. In front of her stands her beautiful, unblemished daughter, who doesn't listen and has her whole life ahead of her. Some relationships are that simple—Amy is large, mean, and aging, Emma is young, small, and beautiful—and therefore, Emma is a reminder of all that her mother no longer has.

Emma says something to her mother, and her mother whispers something back. I have no way of hearing, but Emma shakes her head, sits down, and starts wailing, which takes me by surprise. It's as much emotion as I've seen from the girl, and then Amy is turning away while Emma goes after her, arms outstretched.

I know all the digs, wounds, and stings that can compose a childhood, domino after affected domino tumbling down with so much heaviness. There are so many ways a mother can inflict pain: intentional, physical, subconscious, verbal. Which one is this?

Amy pivots, towering, and then hinges at the waist, her body making a loose right angle. Emma reaches for her—an apology? a hug?—and Amy lifts her right hand and strikes the girl across the face, knocking her slight body back into the dirt. I cover my mouth with both hands and bite back my protests.

In that lift of Amy's hand, I feel my own mother's fingertips across my cheek, a manicured rake of open palm to soft, young flesh. I learned subtraction from counting those imprints: $3-2=1$, $5-1=4$, $4-2=2$, $5-5=0$. Each hour, a finger would disappear, and I'd continue subtracting until there were no more left.

Emma holds her face and screams uncontrollably, and Amy gathers herself and walks back inside. It's then that I realize I know that cry. It hits me in a primal wave. The screams I heard are Emma's screams. The neighborhood shrieks are hers. Emma stumbles to the door and pounds on it, claws at it, hysterical now, and I am looking for neighbors—where are the neighbors?

I lose sight of her as she runs around to the front door and then again to the back. Finally, she sits down in the grass again. The sun begins to set as she wails. Oh, how she wails.

Emma tugs at the green strands, her cries finally tapering off. I can barely make out a five-fingered mark, red and raw, along her cheek. Every couple of breaths, she glances over her shoulder to see if someone is coming for her, if her mother will scoop her up in a tearful apology, but she does not.

I gather myself, my knees stiff, bladder bursting. The stickiness of her name pulls at the back of my throat. It isn't too late to turn back now. I can retreat, get in my car, and return to regular life. I can make an anonymous call to the authorities, or her school, and hope they get this family the help they need. But I know how hard it is for mothers to change, even when the stakes are the highest.

A shaky breath vibrates against my ribs. My ankle throbs. I blink and make my decision. I stand, every joint below my waist on fire. As though underwater, I whisper the two syllables from the trees.

She stands—I can hear her gasp, even from this distance—and then she is moving toward the tree line, as I whisper her name again.

"Who—who is that? Who's there?" It is only the second time I have heard her speak. Her voice pierces my chest with its sweetness. She hiccups as she asks who's there again, her chest shuddering in that absolute way after a hard cry. It's all I can do not to take her into my arms, hold her close, and tell her that it's all going to be okay.

But I don't. I don't say anything. I hold steady as she looks back at her house, where there is still no movement. Maybe a door will open, maybe her mother or father will come out and pretend this argument never happened and trill, "Sweetheart, it's dinnertime! Come eat!"

But no one comes. It is silent, so silent, and there's only this moment, the woods, and us.

She takes another step and another, and then she is swallowed by the trees. I stand just feet from her, shifting from foot to foot. She blinks until her eyes adjust and looks left then right. Her eyes land on me, and her little mouth shifts into an O of surprise at seeing an actual person in the woods.

"Please don't scream. And don't be scared. It's okay," I say, which I realize is what every bad person has probably ever said to a child.

She takes a step back out of the woods, and desperation weaves a second, tougher skin. "Wait, Emma. Please wait."

She turns to me, and that's when I see it. Even in this dim light, her exceptional eyes, which are large, gray, and piercing, register a level of sadness that I recognize from my own childhood.

I gather the words in my mouth, words that will forever change my life and hers. I reach out one hand and swallow. Night is closing in, and we have a little ways to walk, and fast. I take a breath. "Will you come with me?" I ask.

She bobbles on her feet, left and right, her red bow fluttering in the wind. I can smell the rain before it hits; I know it's coming. We have ten minutes, maybe fifteen, at best. She takes a fractional step forward, as uncertain as a fawn discovering her legs.

She closes the gap and looks up at me. My hand is still extended. She studies it, her arms at her sides. I manage a smile and secure my lips against my teeth. "I just want to help you," I say.

I am going to take you away from here.

She takes another breath. Her whole body balloons and then deflates. She bends the fingers of her left hand, then lifts her right toward mine.

It makes contact. I squeeze and press her hot palm to mine. Our bodies link. Our eyes lock. She nods, and my voice catches in my throat as I begin to pull her away from her mother, her house, and her life.

amy

during

The door rattles. The lock clicks.

Richard looks up from feeding Robbie, bits of rice already latching to the hardwoods.

"What the hell was that about? I could hear Emma screaming all the way in here. What happened?"

"I just . . . can't. I can't do this anymore. I quit. I quit parenting."

"Jesus, Amy. She's *five*. Stop being so dramatic."

Emma appears outside the dining room door, her palms slapping the glass so hard, Amy fears it will shatter into a thousand pieces. She turns and shrieks at the top of her lungs: "Go play! *Right* now!" Her eye twitches as she yells, a new and unfortunate habit that renders her virtually insane. Emma jiggles the doorknob again and again.

Richard covers Robbie's ears with his large hands. "Are you really locking our child out of the house right now?"

Amy huffs through the living room and locks the front door too. Emma can stay out there all night for all she cares.

"What are you doing, Amy? She's five years old, not sixteen! You can't lock a five-year-old out of the house." He stands and unlocks the back door, but Emma isn't standing there anymore.

"Really, Richard? Our daughter is five? I didn't know that! Thank you for reminding me." Amy stands between the dining room and kitchen, seething, with no one else to take it out on.

Richard knows what's coming and turns his attention back to Robbie. He lifts him from his high chair. "Come on, little guy. Let's get you cleaned up and ready for a bath." He glances at her. "Go handle this, Amy. You're supposed to be the adult here." A litany of veggies, rice, and chicken unroll from Robert's bib and scatter across the floor—another mess for her to clean in the list of unending messes.

Amy smacks her hand onto the kitchen counter, her palm stinging, just as it had moments before. "That is it! I have had it!"

Richard rolls his eyes and carries Robert to the bathroom. Amy looks at the back door, now unlocked. She should leave it alone and take a few minutes to calm down. Emma will come in, go to bed, and they will all start over tomorrow. But something in her won't let it end at that. In three steps, she crosses to the back door and twists the gold button on the lock. She watches Emma sitting in the grass, sniffling.

Amy stalks to the bedroom, wanting to slam the door, to splinter every inch of wood. Instead, she closes the door and kicks the bed. A searing pain shoots from her big toe to her knee to her crumbly inner thigh. "Fuuuuuck!" She throws herself on the mattress and swallows a mouthful of duvet on the way down. She screams and screams into the white cover, smelling her own acrid breath, mixed with sweat and tears.

She is losing control, losing her mind, losing her life.

———

What feels like days later, she peels herself from the mattress, her clothes sticky, a small puddle of drool next to her ear. She's fallen asleep, hard, which probably says more about her temper stemming from lack of sleep than anything else. She opens the door, calmer now, and vows to stay calm. She wills herself to just get through the nightly routine, have a fractured night's sleep, and start all over again. Tomorrow will be better. She will make it better.

She walks through the house, but it is silent. She checks the clock on the stove: nine o'clock. Has she been asleep for three *hours*? Where is Richard? She tiptoes down the hall and peeks into Robert's room. Her son is asleep in his twin bed, his limbs around Richard, who is snoring beside him. She closes the door and heads back down the hall to Emma's room, hoping she's not still awake. She's not in the mood for negotiations tonight.

Her room is empty, her bed untouched. A small button of panic presses against her abdomen. *Where is Emma?*

She searches under the covers anyway, sorts through her crammed closet, the bathroom, the living room, the hall closet, and even the damp, moldy garage. *Would she go in the attic?* No, never. Emma is afraid of the attic. She peers toward the backyard, most of it dim except for where the bulbous streetlight casts an eerie graveyard glow onto all the dirt-smattered toys.

She exits the back and checks both cars—in, around, under—before tearing the yard apart: the crappy playhouse no one uses, the wagon, the various tools and trash. She can feel her breath in her throat, the panic a real, actual, living thing now. *I fell asleep and now my daughter isn't here.*

Her sore body strains up the sharp incline, cutting left, right, then in pointless, random circles. She hopes her knees will stay intact and not decide, right at this moment, to explode like a can of dough. Her breath is labored; it is warm out, and a new drizzle makes everything slick.

Amy stands in the center of the yard, knowing the only place Emma could have gone, the only place she would go after an argument, is the woods. She swallows and stares, the line of brown trunks and ominous branches shooting up into the sky and then dissolving into the misty clouds.

This has happened before; Emma has gone into the woods on two separate occasions, but she only wandered a few houses down before a neighbor returned her. What time did she leave Emma out here? Six? Did Richard not come to check on her? Did he forget to unlock the door? Surely a neighbor has her . . . could she possibly be in the woods somewhere, alone or asleep?

Amy moves back inside and rummages through the junk drawer until she finds a gray, heavy flashlight. She charges back into the yard and up to the wood's edge. She dissects the trees with pale yellow light, trying not to think of all the bad things associated with children and woods.

The buttery light trembles as her hands shake. She steps over sticks and scours the ground for clues of any sort. She walks right, then left, and feels close to passing out. *Her daughter is gone*.

"No. This isn't . . . this isn't happening," she pants, as she heads back to the house to wake Richard. She does one more walk-through, ignoring the muddy footprints she will have to clean later, making sure Emma isn't hiding somewhere obvious. Kids are like that: disappearing under piles of laundry, curled up in unassuming corners, sometimes even under their own comforters, flattened, still, and so easy to miss. She turns on every light and calls Emma's name. The syllables crack in her throat as sharp, acidic bile rises after them.

It is all becoming sickeningly clear. Her daughter is missing, and it is her fault and her clueless husband's, who hadn't thought to go outside and check on her. She'd locked the door again, when she could have left it open. Because she locked the door, her daughter is out there somewhere, five years old and alone.

before

She was spent.

Rather, her day was spent, and never in the way she wanted. Emma was in preschool, while Robbie was in day care—only for four hours, only four days a week—and Amy was taking a personal day from work, though there was nothing personal about it.

She would spend her precious child-and-husband-free time scrubbing cooked oats from a cool pan, flicking dried cat food off their kitchen tile with her blunt, unpainted fingernails, doing endless loads of laundry, and then staring at the mounds of fluffy cotton and denim, still hot—especially those scalding silver jean buttons—not knowing where she was supposed to even begin with folding.

In the timeline of her life, it was always the same—kids, work, cleaning, cooking, errands, kids—unless she took a day off, which meant there was always *more* in her day, not less. She was perpetually behind, no matter how she organized her days.

On the rare mornings she let her husband take over due to her incessant complaining about never getting even one morning to herself, she'd wake early anyway, because he was doing everything just a bit too loudly. She'd stand in the center of the kitchen in her fraying, stained robe and judge her husband's every movement, commenting without even one bit of self-consciousness, because their marriage, by this point, was based entirely on hurting each other's feelings. She already knew how her comments translated, in his mind, as she watched him slice slightly moldy strawberries with a butter knife.

"Should you be doing that?" (*You're an idiot.*)

"What kind of oil did you cook that in?" (*You're incompetent.*)

"Robbie can't eat *nuts* yet, Richard. Jesus. He'll choke to death." (*You're a terrible father.*)

The coated insults stacked up like all the laundry, and some days, she said the thing she actually meant, and Richard would let it roll off his bony, mole-shrouded shoulders, because he was spineless, careless, muted. Sometimes, when he was standing there, head bent over his phone, she could tell he was just waiting for a heart attack (he was too skinny), an act of terror (he rarely flew), or some freak accident (he only went to work, home, and back to work again) to put him out of his misery. And hers. Lately, she fantasized about Richard having an affair. She'd catch him in the act of sweaty, spread limbs and divorce him. But she knew Richard would never have an affair. He wasn't that type of man.

Amy looked at herself in the mirror on the way to the kitchen. It was one of those cheap, full-length mirrors she'd bought on sale with one of the endless 20 percent off coupons from Bed Bath & Beyond. She stood in front of it, feeling like a fleshy, red whale. Was this who she'd always been or who she'd become? Childbirth had taken a few things from her, sure, but she wasn't like one of those women who went from a sizzling 10 to a 6 on a scale of 1 to 10. She, at best, had always been a 4 and was now hovering between a 2 and a 3, so that the differences, although there, weren't jarring. She didn't have to spend her time agonizing over stretch marks, how her skin had changed, or the clumps of hair that came loose in the shower like weird, ropy sea kelp.

She'd always thought she was lucky not to be beautiful, because when beauty faded, and you didn't have other things to offer, you were basically just a shell. You weren't real. Her mother taught her that because she wasn't attractive either, and that's what less-than-pretty people told themselves (and their daughters). All the pretty people she had ever known spent their entire lives dissecting imperfections or judging others: pinching flesh, gasping at wrinkles, doing everything to make themselves lighter, tighter, and younger, when they all would end up the same heavier, looser, older versions of themselves. It seemed such a waste of time to focus the majority of one's time on looks; she was just too lazy to tweeze, pluck, wax, and spackle.

So she settled for a red, pocked face—the tragic result of horrific childhood chicken pox, followed by a staph infection, resistance to antibiotics, shingles, and yet another staph infection—a gummy waist, and thighs that rubbed together so much, she had sores on the insides of her legs and labia. She got horrible gas, went to the bathroom just twice a week, and always had some ailment she was sure would require surgery or result in an immediate death sentence. She should exercise, get outside, get inspired, find something she loved, meet a group of people, live. But she didn't, and she wouldn't, and the whole thing—all the things—pushed her to a maddening form of being, or not being. She felt like a nonperson.

This wasn't always her life. Before Richard, before Emma and Robbie, she was a semi-okay woman with an affinity for romance novels and single-serving frozen satin pies she'd devour after her nightly baths. She had been alone then, and she'd loved it. Now, there was just noise.

She moved from the mirror to the kitchen, resolving something. *So what?* So she wasn't beautiful—should it come as such a shock by now?—but she wasn't funny, overly nice, kind, or insanely smart either. She was a ruddy person with a ruddy complexion in the middle of a ruddy life.

Except for her daughter. Except for Emma.

She'd been told that two regular people could produce one beautiful one, but she'd always rolled her eyes at such nonsense, until the doctor placed her newborn daughter in her arms. She'd looked down at this still warm, pink, pretty bundle—just an eight-pound slab of meat that had, moments before, been pulled from her hairy, swollen vagina—and lifted the newborn back up to the doctor, as though her baby, her *real* baby (probably with a smashed face, a cone head, and skinny little arms and legs, like Richard), had been swapped and was now munching on someone else's tits.

Emma was exceptionally beautiful, which was kind of a cruel joke, because Amy didn't know what to *do* with beautiful. She was afraid it would crumble in her hands, like meringue. It was just too big a responsibility. No one in her family had looks, but this child—oh, *this* child— she got stopped everywhere they went. Strangers commented on everything from her ruby lips (*She looks like she's wearing lipstick! Is she wearing lipstick?*) to her mammoth gray eyes (*They will change color, you know, but my, aren't they spectacular?*) to her flawless, ivory skin (*How is her skin so creamy? You could eat her with a spoon! You really could!*), which drew constant attention to Amy, which made her self-conscious because now people were looking. She couldn't hide.

Now, after having a second child, she was a full-time mother and was forced to strike up conversations about babies and childbirth, and *wasn't it all so wonderful?* The anger formed a helix inside her. Richard, on the occasions he could tell she was about to burst, would ask her why.

"I'm not angry," she would insist, spitting the words, as though he had insulted her even by insinuating she was anything other than a pleasant human being. (Because she was a whale; because she was married to a wimp, but she married him anyway; because who else would she marry?; because she hated being a mother; because she hated her job; because she hated Washington; because she was so fucking tired all the time; because she was too old, too fat, and too ugly to do anything about it.)

"You seem angry," he would reply.

"Well, you seem annoying. Why are you so annoying?"

"Because I'm married to you."

They'd go on this way for minutes until one of them just gave up and went into the den or for a drive, and then they'd join in the same bed hours later, each of them tucked in to the very edge of their lumpy sides. After so many years of marriage, she'd squirm in the beefy dark, trying to figure a way out of what she'd gotten herself into, but this wasn't some movie where she could change her life, divorce her husband, quit her job, lose the weight, toss the anger, and move to somewhere shiny and new. She had children now and that tethered her to this life, these dishes, the endless to-do list, and this filthy house for the next two decades, at least.

Whenever Emma and Robbie left their house, years later, with their entire childhoods, acne, backne, crazy hormonal shifts, boyfriends, girlfriends, and toxic teenage outbursts behind them, Amy would be too resigned to do anything but sit in a recliner (Would they still make those in the future? Did they even still make them now?), eating crappy food and watching mindless TV until she died from cardiac arrest, boredom, or from choking on a fat corn dog, which she loved so much and often ate too fast.

She rarely chewed, which was probably why all the gas, and she loved cheese even more than corn dogs, which, as every magazine, website, diet pill ad, and doctor told her, was unhealthy. Every day, she sliced clean rectangles from block after block of cow and goat cheese, which probably explained the lack of poop. Maybe she wasn't fat; maybe if you cut her open, you'd just see congealed mountains of cheese clogging everything up? That had to impede her colon somehow. Maybe she should get a colonic? Maybe that was the answer to all of her prayers! Maybe, after, with a sore asshole, she'd be thinner, happier, and feel better about her life?

Amy began the painstaking process of washing dishes, loading dishes, wiping countertops, sorting laundry, picking up random toys and various Emma and Robbie messes, vacuuming, making lunch, eating lunch, having her post-lunch cheese, cleaning up her own damn dishes, going to the grocery store, picking up Emma, then picking up Robbie, all while trying to placate her very loud children while she decided on dinner.

She heard Richard shuffle through the door right at six, dropping his heavy bag, removing his light shoes, and crashing his thirty-seven keys onto the tray by the door. Why couldn't she just cross the threshold from anger to acceptance, kiss her husband hello, and ask him about his day? Why, now, was this so hard, when it was pretty much the unspoken lifeline of marriage?

Because they weren't that type of couple, that's why. It was too late for them. She heard Robbie perk up, cooing at the sound of his father's footsteps. Robbie struggled in his purple Bumbo, an eager toddler desperate to break free. Emma dislodged his chunky, creamy thighs and allowed him to take off toward their father, before she threw her own small limbs into his long, lanky ones. Amy busied herself in the kitchen and tried not to feel the bullets of jealousy at her children's preference for him rather than her.

She heard Richard's blasé voice hitch up an octave as he greeted his daughter and scooped her into his arms. Then Robbie. He entered the kitchen with a sigh, his standard post-work, my-life-is-harder-than-yours-because-I-am-the-breadwinner-and-because-I-have-a-penis-therefore-I-get-paid-more-than-you-do-to-sit-behind-a-desk-all-day-so-I-am-granted-this-daily-sigh sigh.

When was the last time they'd made love? Kissed? Hugged? She'd brushed against him in the hall the night before last, and they'd both startled, almost embarrassed by each other, by the brief, unwanted contact, by their sham of a marriage.

Her work friends said they'd find their way back to each other eventually. She didn't tell them much because they were always talking; they chattered constantly, as though their jobs—and lives—depended on it. They talked about everything: groceries, the weather, the upcoming election, neighbor noise, child discipline, dairy, anal. Sometimes, they'd throw in a casual, "What do you think, Amy?" to which Amy, having checked out after the first two minutes, would murmur, "I totally agree with what *she* said." If their fleeting attention ever landed on her for more than a few seconds, she fed them small, insignificant morsels about her life over turkey sandwiches in their cubicles. They'd all been there, they said. She had children; therefore everything was allowed to be on pause. She would blink into their pretty faces and realize, even though they were all women, she couldn't be more of a foreign species if she tried.

"I don't know what to do for dinner."

Richard placed Robbie on the ground, and he was off, rocketing down the hall on his flat, wide, heavy feet. Emma chased after him.

"What do we have?"

Amy shrugged. There was a pinch in her neck—was she out of alignment again? She felt absently for a lump, hoping it wasn't a tumor or something like lymphoma, but the skin gave way under her fingers, warm and full, like the rest of her. "The usual. I picked up a rotisserie chicken. Want to do something with that?"

"Sure." Richard sorted the mail with one hand and adjusted his glasses with the other. Why didn't they both just get out of the house? Throw a babysitter at the problem once or twice per week? Have girls' nights, guys' nights, and date nights? Toss back some cocktails, get reckless, let their chests expand and contract with laughter, or at least the opposite of annoyance? Maybe even let their mouths meet in some sticky, wet semblance of a kiss?

It was so hard to recollect their beginning—both of them dripping with inexperience and insecurity. They'd connected because there was just nobody else. Theirs had been a sloppy and inefficient pairing, but they'd done it without all the passion, falling "madly in love," and drama of other couples. They'd taken trips, gone on dates, gotten engaged, and had a lovely two-person wedding with one witness. Had there been laughter? Had there been real love? She felt it was harder to regain something you might never have had in the first place; this left her unsure of what it was she was supposed to want, and for that, she was stuck.

Robbie screeched from somewhere down the hall, and

Emma started crying. It was the fake cry, though; the one that screamed for attention and nothing else. "Will you deal with that, please?"

Richard set off after his children. "How'd you get in here so fast?" he cooed to Robbie. She could hear him groan as he picked up their heavy toddler and then plopped him into the playpen in the family room, where China-made toys filled the silence with their aggravating, repetitive songs. They worked around each other in the kitchen, discussing bills to be paid and daily logistics as Amy sliced off pieces of clammy chicken and Richard fried up some red potatoes in canola oil.

As the kitchen heated and Emma rambled to Robbie in the next room, Amy felt her real self banging inside the prison of her own mind, jangling the bars and trying to find another way out—or in.

after

"Richard. Richard, wake up." She struggled to keep her voice calm, when all she wanted to do was shake him, scream, and place blame on her incompetent husband. She pulled his thin body up to a sitting position and motioned for him to come out of the room. Richard stuffed two pillows on either side of Robert and groggily followed.

"God, what time is it?"

"Emma's gone."

"What? What are you talking about? She was just outside." He swayed back and forth, never one to come out of sleep without a struggle.

"She was just outside three hours ago, Richard! I fell asleep! Why didn't you get me up? Did you just leave her out there all night by herself?"

His eyes were shiny, heavy, and confused. "No, I . . . I don't think so. Wait." They moved to the kitchen. He leaned against the counter and wedged his palms over his eyes. "Robert was super-fussy, so we did bath and story time. I laid down with him, and—"

"And you fucking fell asleep and forgot our five-year-old daughter was outside, alone!" She was hysterical. Her whole body itched.

"I wasn't the one who locked her out! I unlocked the

door! I thought *you* were with her. I thought you two were working it out. I wanted to give you space."

"You didn't want to give us space. You forgot." What she meant was: *We both forgot, we always forget, we are not cut out for this.*

"Jesus, Amy, does it matter who did what? We need to call the police right now." Richard reached for the phone, but she stopped him.

"Just wait. Wait. You know the last two times she showed up."

"She wasn't gone for three hours, Amy. And it wasn't at night."

"Still, you know they won't do anything until she's been missing twenty-four or forty-eight hours or whatever that ridiculous rule is. We need to see if we can find her first. Should we call the neighbors?"

"We don't have any of the neighbors' information."

"Well, then, we'll knock on their doors. I don't know."

He re-cradled the phone. "Don't you think if the neighbors had her they would tell us? Or bring her home?"

"Not if they don't know where she lives."

"Well, some of them know us. And Emma knows her own address."

They wouldn't bring her home if they saw her sore face or had heard their loud fight. The reality of the situation clamped hard. How would she explain their argument? The slap? How could she possibly tell authorities that they'd just left their child outside, *alone*? That she'd hit her and then locked her out? She reminded herself that people left their children in hot cars while doing simple things like going to the grocery store or to work. They were so tired, they just forgot, while their children suffocated to death. But what she'd done was worse than forget.

"I think we need to call the police," Richard said.

"Fine. Yes, you're right. Call the police. I'm going to start knocking on doors. Stay here."

"But I want to help, Amy."

She slapped one hand to her forehead. "You can't leave our *other* child alone, Richard! Why is this so hard? We have *two* children who need to be looked after. Two, not one."

He hated her. She could see it, could feel it. There had been a small window after Robert was born where they found their way back to each other, where he finally had his boy. She had given him that, and then, like so much else, it had all fallen away, and here they were again, enemies.

"Why don't you stay with Robert and I'll go knock on doors? If I'm not back in half an hour, call the police."

He zipped up a windbreaker and was out of the house in seconds. She exhaled and felt a sharp pain in her chest. Was she going to have a heart attack? Was this the event that would finally push her over the edge?

She massaged her chest, went through the house again, and then back into the woods with the flashlight. Richard would find Emma, they would all go to sleep, and Amy would be better in the morning. This was her wake-up call. She'd start going to anger management or back to hypnotherapy. She'd done so well when she was going. She'd been happier, calmer. She'd felt better about the world; she'd been a better mother because of it.

She charged through the trees, getting snagged and whipped by rebounding branches. She kept track of her steps and turns and heard her own voice, small and ineffective, call out a name that was instantly swallowed by the trees.

An hour later, she and Richard stood in the kitchen, just having reported Emma missing. The police force in Longview was small, and up until this point, irrelevant in their personal lives. She had no idea of their capabilities or what the protocol was for an event like this.

The officer on the phone, Barry, suggested they enter Emma into the National Crime Information Center Missing Person File. Amy had almost protested—her child wasn't really a missing person, was she?—but the gravity of it came pressing down; the reality of their chaotic mother-daughter relationship was about to be unraveled. They'd talk to the school. They'd search their home. They'd look at her—miserable, overweight, perpetually stressed—and make immediate judgments.

"They're going to put out a bulletin to the community, though there'll probably be little movement tonight," Amy said.

"Are we supposed to just go to sleep like everything's normal? Knowing she's . . . out there? Amy, what if someone took her? What if someone hurt her? *Is* hurting her right now, while we're just sitting here, waiting?"

She thought of the handprint that was probably on Emma's face, the bumps and bruises up and down her arms and legs. Would *she* become a suspect? "I have no idea. They're sending officers over right now. Let's just . . . I don't know. I don't know what." *This is your fault. I hate you. I never wanted children. I should have divorced you when I had the chance.*

Fifteen minutes of pacing and checking in on Robert later, two officers stood at the door: protruding bellies, puffy eyes, grayish teeth, wrinkled beige uniforms.

"Mr. and Mrs. Townsend? May we come in, please?"

Kidnappings didn't happen in their community. It was as vanilla as subdivisions came. Big news was about price increases at the local market, an overpriced hipster café, or the occasional automobile break-in. Not this. Not ever this. Not as long as they'd been here.

Richard found his voice and ushered them inside, flipping on lights as they went. Had they been standing in the dark this whole time? She couldn't remember. She kept her ears primed, as if Emma might pop out from behind a chair and say, *Surprise! I'm right here*. She wasn't that playful, and she wasn't behind a chair. She'd get in trouble if she pulled a stunt like this, and Emma knew it, so she rarely jumped, shouted, or hid.

"Would you two like something to drink? Water? Coffee?" *That's right. Nice host, nice mother, nice wife, nice life.*

Barry, the tall one, and Stan, at least five inches shorter, moved into the kitchen, their eyes casing everything. "Coffee would be wonderful, ma'am. Thank you."

Of course they wanted coffee at 10:30 P.M. Of course she'd have to busy her hands and not hear the entire conversation. They'd distract her, get her to slip. She already felt like a suspect.

They all stood in the kitchen. Barry scratched his head and extracted a small pad. Their lack of urgency annoyed her. They were here, so this was obviously something more significant than Emma just wandering off in the backyard. Her child was out there somewhere! Where were the detectives? The FBI? A search party?

"So, we just need to go over the details of what happened, so we can get all of the facts straight." Stan studied the kitchen floor as he said it. Her muddy footprints covered the tile.

"I was searching for her. In the woods. That's why there's mud everywhere."

"In the woods? Is that where you suspect she went?"

Amy looked to Richard, who'd grown conveniently mute. She was going to fall on a sword, all right. All by herself. "Yes, I suspect that's where she went." She poured the water into the carafe, sprinkled in some cheap coffee, and pressed *start*. "She's run off a few times before—in the woods, I mean—but she's always come back."

Barry shifted, his gun holster hitting their oven. "Is there a place we can sit to go over details?"

Amy led them to the dining room table and shut the door leading into the hall. "We have a little one sleeping in the back, so if we could keep this quiet."

"Oh, of course, ma'am. Though we will have to search the house."

"Search the house? Why?" Richard asked.

"For clues, evidence of foul play, to obtain the child's DNA. Completely standard. I'm sure everything is fine."

"Why don't we just start with what happened?" Stan folded his hands on the table while Barry was primed to take notes.

"Okay. Well, Emma was playing outside in the backyard, as she normally does after school and—"

"Approximately what time was this?"

She looked at Richard. "Well, she has a babysitter bring her home, so I assume she was outside before we arrived home from work."

"What's the babysitter's name? His or her full name, please?"

Amy gave it to them. "Why do you need her name?"

"At this point, ma'am, anyone who has a direct connection to the girl could be of help. Go on."

Amy heard the last gurgle of coffee hiss into the pot and wanted to get up and busy herself with pouring multiple cups. "So, when we both got home, I went outside to tell Emma it was time to come in."

"And did she?"

Amy looked at the table. "No, she didn't want to come in. We argued about it."

"Was this a verbal argument or a physical one?"

Amy opened her mouth, looked at Richard, and closed it. He didn't know she'd slapped her. Could she leave that detail out? If someone found Emma, would her cheek be bruised? Would she be able to place blame somewhere else? She'd watched enough shows to know that if they suspected physical abuse, this preliminary investigation would shift to her. The only important thing was to find her daughter, not muddy it up with irrelevant details. "No, it was verbal. I was very tired. She was being difficult. She's five, so . . ."

They nodded as though they understood. "That can be a difficult age, sure."

"So, I came back inside and Richard was feeding Robert, our son. I went to the bedroom, and I fell asleep. I didn't mean to, but I was tired and frustrated, and the next thing I knew, it was nine."

"And what time did you go back to your room?"

"I don't know. Six, maybe?"

"And did you get your daughter in from outside, sir?"

Richard turned the color of a beet and squeezed his hands together. "No, I didn't. I . . . I was on toddler duty and got him ready for bed and did the bath. I didn't know Amy had fallen asleep. I thought she was with her. I went to put Robert down, and I fell asleep with him too. Amy woke me up once she realized Emma was gone."

Barry and Stan looked at each other. "So, you're telling me *you* fell asleep while your husband took care of the baby, and then *he* fell asleep and forgot your daughter was outside? You don't know if she ever came back in?"

"That's correct."

"Was the door unlocked or locked?" Stan asked.

Amy had relocked the door. Richard hadn't seen her do it.

"Sir, did you lock up before bed?"

"I . . . no, I don't think so. The back door was unlocked. I just thought she would come in." He scratched his head and let his hands fall into his lap. "I thought they were working out their argument. That's what they normally do."

Amy looked at Richard, appalled. If she could have sliced him in half with one look, he would be in stringy, clumpy chunks at her feet.

Barry jumped all over that. "So, you two argue a lot? Is that accurate, ma'am?"

Amy stood and moved to pour them all coffee. "I wouldn't say a lot, but sometimes, yes. It's been a very stressful transition with the new baby, juggling work, bills, kids, you know. Would anyone like cream or sugar?"

"Black for me."

"I'll take sugar," Stan said.

She prepared their cups and brought them over, a little liquid sloshing over the top. "Sorry about that."

"You're fine, ma'am. Thank you."

"Can I have a cup too?" Richard asked.

Get up and get one yourself! Amy grimaced and went back to pour Richard a cup.

"Can we get your daughter's full name, weight, height, and what she was wearing tonight?"

Amy had no idea how much she weighed or her height. She was wearing what she always wore. She'd conceded to let Emma wear just one or two outfits, always some variation of red dress and red shoes, because the arguments about what to wear just weren't worth it. She gave the information as best as she could.

"Any distinguishing marks, such as a birthmark or scars?"

Richard looked at Amy and ducked his head to sip his coffee. "No, no real distinguishing marks. Other than a birthmark. On her hip." Why was *she* the one answering all the fucking questions?

"We'll need a written statement from both of you as to what she was wearing, any personal items she might have had at the time of the disappearance, as well as any specific mannerisms or identifying characteristics that could help us find her."

"Do we do that now, or . . . ?"

"At the station, ma'am. We will also need a list of friends, acquaintances, or anyone else who might know where she is. We'll start with the neighborhood. Does your daughter go to school?"

"Yes. It's just the Montessori on the corner, actually. We walk her there every day."

"Great, that's great." Barry's pen worked feverishly. "And we'll need a recent photo as well in case of distribution."

"Distribution?"

"Yes, in case the agency needs it, the media, or the NCMEC. Don't you worry about any of that now. Hopefully, we'll find her before it comes to that. Kids tend to run off and come home, especially in a safe neighborhood like this."

Richard looked back and forth between the two men. "Are you two related?"

Amy scoffed at Richard's inane, random question. What did it matter if they were conjoined twins? They just needed to find Emma.

"We are, sir. Brothers. Born and raised in Longview. We come from a long line of officers."

"What a small world."

"Richard, really?" She turned her attention back to the officers and drummed her fingers on her coffee mug. "What next?" She was a clichéd nervous wreck, but if she sat here one minute more, she'd combust.

The brothers stood and scraped their chairs against the hardwood. She winced.

"We are going to need to look at Emma's room and check the surrounding area. Can you show us to her room? We would also ask during this time that you not touch or rearrange anything."

Amy was shaking, her head fuzzy and full of details and questions. Her entire body felt cold, but she was sweating. She led them down the hall to Emma's room, which was bare and boring: a mattress on the floor, a few stuffed animals, a dresser—no happy, homemade art. Amy never let her keep toys in her room, because she inevitably destroyed it, tossing dolls and stuffed animals everywhere. It had been such a constant source of animosity between them—Amy always on cleanup duty, and Emma always destroying what she'd just cleaned up—that she'd made the official rule that bedrooms were for sleeping, and that was it.

Looking around now, she could see it through the officers' eyes, and she was embarrassed. In this day and age, kids' rooms often looked like shrines pieced together from Pinterest. Every time she opened a children's catalog and gazed into all those beautifully designed rooms, she felt wildly inadequate.

She stepped out of the room as they rifled through her daughter's personal things. They lowered their voices as they rummaged, sorted, and tagged. Amy poured herself a cup of coffee while Richard sat at the table with his head in his hands. Could anything in her daughter's room be a clue to where she'd gone? This hadn't been a deliberate act. There was no one in their lives who would ever take Emma, was there? The list of their friends and family was minuscule. It revealed their sparse, tiny life in this small town.

As Amy blew the steam off the top of her cup, she wondered if there was some secret part of her daughter's life that would give away the truth of her whereabouts. A journal with drawings of a faraway place. A stranger who'd offered her candy after school. Some crazy adventure where she'd stuffed a backpack full of toys and snacks and then set off through the woods—a child heroine in a beloved storybook tale. It didn't seem likely. None of this— the evening, the fight, the slap, the confession, the door, the sleep, the disappearance, the men in her daughter's room now, shuffling, tossing, and jotting—seemed real. Yet it was all real. And it was her fault.

As she sipped her coffee and watched Richard, who stared blankly at the wall with tears in his eyes, she knew she had to keep the slap and the deliberately relocked door to herself. Those acts looked intentional. Those acts appeared to show a woman at her breaking point. And a mother at her breaking point could do horrible, unspeakable things: drowning her child in a bathtub, driving them both off of a cliff, smothering an unsuspecting child while she slept. It was in the best interest for all of them if they actually found Emma instead of fixating on Amy as a possible suspect.

Nobody knew the entire truth, and she wanted to keep it that way.

It was well past midnight. Robert had stirred once. Amy's whole body throbbed with adrenaline. The three-hour nap coupled with the coffee made her feel she could trek through the entire length of woods faster than any detective could. Richard was still in with Robbie, probably passed out cold. He didn't handle emergencies well, and his emotions were all over the place. Amy had just two speeds: turned off or angry, neither of which would benefit her here, with this.

The officers called a detective, Frank Lewis. He'd obviously been woken from sleep when he arrived at their door. Dark scruff dotted his jaw, and his hair looked full of static. Barry and Stan led him into her home, as if they were now the hosts, and briefed him on what info they had collected.

Frank raked a hand over his face as he listened, a succession of rapid blinks as he nodded or murmured. He acknowledged her with a handshake and then combed their entire house before circling back to her.

"So, you said Emma was outside, but you don't know if this dining room door was locked for her to get back in?" His voice was filled with gravel and boomed across their quiet house. He opened the door, and there, all along the back of the grimy glass, were small, muddy handprints. They all stopped as the truth sunk in. Her daughter had been banging on the door, but she hadn't been able to get in because Amy intentionally locked it. The lie coiled in her throat, in battle with the awful truth.

"Like I said, I fell asleep accidentally, and Richard was taking care of Robert. She often bangs on the door when she wants to show me something."

"Is the door usually locked when she wants to show you something?"

"No, it's not usually locked."

"But it was locked tonight?"

She shook her head no, but didn't say the word. *If they*

knew she locked her out, they'd crucify her. If they knew she'd slapped her, they'd think she had something to do with this. She hoped the warmth in her skin wasn't giving her away.

Frank kneeled down to the glass and brought out a swab. "I'll need to see the girl's hairbrush and toothbrush."

"Why?"

"DNA. Hopefully we won't need it. It's standard procedure."

Amy showed him the bathroom and followed Barry and Stan back to the dining room for more questioning.

"Is anyone searching for Emma? Anyone at all? Why are we all just sitting here?"

"Ma'am, there's a very specific protocol. I know it's hard, but you have to trust that we're handling it. We just have to get all the facts first."

"What facts do you need besides my five-year-old daughter is missing? Every second we sit here, someone could be getting further away. At this point, it's been hours," Amy said. The panic tinged her voice.

"I promise, Mrs. Townsend, we will find her."

Amy nodded because she didn't know what else to do. She heard the drawers of the bathroom scrape open and closed, as Frank collected DNA from her missing child. Amy closed her eyes as Barry and Stan asked more questions. The room was spinning. She felt sick. Every emotion circulated through her system: worry, fear, anxiety, resignation, indignation, guilt. She gripped the table and willed all of this away. She just wanted to wake up, to start this day over, to do everything different.

Just bring her back, and I'll do better, I promise.

Just bring her back to me.

before

Amy pulled in to the shady lot and rechecked the address scribbled on the back of an envelope. The numbers were carved into a black sign hanging on a white door that was wedged between a few other businesses—a dry cleaner, a law office, and a bridal store servicing the lesbian community.

She hoisted herself from the car, already damp and craving cheese. She'd read so many books on past-life regression therapy that she felt electrified by the prospect; she'd be able to find out who she'd been and what she'd been doing in her last life. Possibly her last three lives, if she was lucky. Maybe she was a thin, wealthy socialite who sat around drinking wine all day? Maybe she was a dog, a janitor, one of the respected presidents? Even the thought of lying on a couch to be transported somewhere else felt like a vacation.

And she needed a vacation. She couldn't go to the spa (mortifying), on a real, relaxing vacation (kids), or find even a spare moment to herself (no proper lock on the bathroom door). So this was it. She smoothed the front of her pants and felt her underwear knotting up and into her cheeks. She scanned the lot and fingered out the fabric.

She stopped before opening the door. Maybe she

shouldn't even do this. What was the point? What if she got laughed out of the office, or offered help for her weight and not past-life regression? She thought about what was waiting at home—kids, chores, chaos, *him*—and decided to just go through with it.

"Hello." A set of bells chimed as she stepped inside. "Welcome to Back in Touch. How may I help you?"

Amy braced herself for judgment but saw only a friendly, professional smile and a cup of what looked like green tea steaming beside the woman at the front desk.

"I have a one o'clock with Barbara?"

The woman checked the computer. "Yes, Amy Townsend? Welcome. You can just wait right over there. Barb is finishing up with someone and will be out shortly. Would you like some tea, coffee, or cucumber water?"

Did she look like the type of person to drink cucumber water? "No, I'm fine. Thank you."

The office was small, white, and smelled like lavender. She scooped up a magazine from the coffee table and pretended to flip through. At two minutes before one, a scruffy man of about sixty exited the only door leading to the back, his eyes red, his cheeks blotchy. Several bunched Kleenex bulged against his chest. Behind him emerged a short, slightly overweight woman with an arm working his back in soothing circles.

"Take care, Brian. And drink lots of water, please." He pushed through the door to the outside, bells tinkling, head down, as Barb whispered something to the lady at the front desk before turning to focus on her.

"Amy? It is so nice to finally meet you after so much correspondence."

Twenty-three. They'd exchanged twenty-three emails about what to expect for today, what she would get out of it, how it worked, just how exactly each dollar would be spent. She had cashed part of her last three checks, so Richard wouldn't see this on the credit card statement.

"Do I pay now, or . . . ?"

Barb waved her off. "Oh, my. Heavens no. You can pay after we have a successful session. Please, right this way."

She opened the door to a slim hallway and led her to the office in the back. The lights were dim, the gray curtains drawn, and it took Amy a moment for her eyes to adjust. There was a diffuser in the corner spitting out essential oils.

Barb saw her eyeing the diffuser. "I find that the oils really help people relax. This work can be a bit overwhelming."

She showed Amy to the couch. She sized up the sofa and prepared, as she always did, by squatting three-quarters of the way down before sitting. She did this for wooden chairs, old couches, and God forbid, stools. The couch moaned as she made contact, and she coughed in a simultaneous apology for her weight. She clutched her purse tighter in her lap and darted her eyes from left to right like a giant, mushy cuckoo clock.

"Amy, dear, *relax*. You're safe here. This is going to be . . . educational." Barb reached for a timer and wound it to sixty minutes. "And fun."

"Fun?"

Barb patted her chest for her reading glasses and then absently pulled them from the front of her sweater. She sat in a chair a few feet opposite Amy, adjusting her slacks, her blouse, and her glasses. "Well, if you were a *murderer* in a past life, not so much, but you know . . . yes, it can be fun."

Christ. What if she'd been a murderer? She hadn't even thought of that. What if she was just as bad in a past life as in this life? What if that life was even worse and she was paying for all of the awful things she'd done then in the here and now? Out of everything she'd researched, that seemed to be likely.

Amy opened her mouth and then closed it. She set her purse by her left hip. "So, how do we do this, exactly?"

"Well, as we discussed, normally we'd do an introductory interview, but we seem to have done that already via email." Barb chuckled. "So today, I'm going to guide you through a gentle meditation. We might stop there if I sense any resistance, or we could go a bit further if you're open." She removed her glasses and leaned forward. "But if you're uncomfortable at any point, we'll stop, and the first session will be over. Okay?"

Amy nodded. "Do I lay down, or . . . ?"

"I find that usually helps. It allows the body to sufficiently relax."

Amy weighed her choices. Half her body would spill off the couch if she laid down; the couch just wasn't deep enough. And then she'd never get comfortable and would worry about toppling onto the floor like a bowl full of jelly.

Barb sensed her uncertainty. "But if you're more comfortable sitting, that's fine too. You can just relax back a bit. Let your head and shoulders rest. This is your time, not mine. So you decide what feels best."

Amy wished she'd stop saying that. Nothing was her time—it was never her time. Even here, she was faced with the obstacle of herself, the mountain of herself, the insecurities of her own body, and the constant, persistent scrutiny of the outside her, rather than the calmer, prettier, thinner inner her. God, she was so exhausted by constantly leading with her weight, her looks, and the unhappiness that made her yell, hide, and eat. She was cut from the same cloth as her own mother, who had been large and sturdy too, but while her mother had used that to her advantage, Amy retreated her way through life. She had disappointed her mother in that way, and herself. Why couldn't she be stronger and just deal with what God had given her?

Because she couldn't, that's why.

She cleared her throat, willing them to start. She'd never wanted more of a break from her own mind than right this second, on this skinny couch.

"I can sense you are ready." Barb leaned forward in her chair, hands on her knees, staring. "Are you ready, Amy?"

Amy nodded and leaned back, letting her eyes flutter closed. What was she supposed to do with her hands? She let them fall to her sides, palms open, and exhaled for a full five counts.

"That's good. Very good. I want you to take some good, long, deep breaths. Don't worry about the length of your inhales or exhales. Just let the rhythm of your own breath guide you. I want you to look up, as if you're trying to roll your eyes to the back of your head. With your eyes still up, imagine you are standing at the top of a staircase, and you're going to start taking steps down."

And so it began. She started to slip away, to retreat, her mind breaking apart like a dinosaur egg, layer by layer, in hopes of revealing something different, old, and sacred.

Amy woke as though she'd just taken a delicious nap via a sleeping pill. "Is it over?" Her tongue felt like a slug inside her mouth. She remembered nothing. Had it not worked? Had she not gone under?

Barb smiled. "It is over. For today, at least. You were *extremely* receptive to the therapy, Amy. That's very good." Barb leaned over and extracted a small tape from a recorder, popping it into another handheld recording device.

"This is for you. So you can listen to the session. See where we went."

"Where we went?" Amy felt foggy, her mouth thick with too many syllables.

"Yes, my dear. We went back. We weren't going to, but as you went under, it was immediately evident that you were open and receptive to the therapy." She flicked her watch around to see the time. "It's been almost three hours."

Amy sat all the way up. "Three hours?" She had to get home. She hadn't allotted for this much time away. "I thought we were just testing to see if I was responsive?"

"Oh, Amy, you were very responsive. Eager, in fact. We just went with it."

She could feel the everyday agitation coursing back already. This woman had *taken* her time, and she hadn't even been aware of it. Three hours were gone, and she had nothing to carry home with her besides a little tape?

"Why don't I remember what we just did?"

"Well, some people are in a very light trance state while others are aware the entire session. The subconscious mind can be different for everyone. Even when it doesn't feel like it, you're still aware of what's going on. Sometimes, it just takes a little while to reorient to the here and now and then"—Barb snapped her fingers—"it will just come to you. Often, when you listen to the tape, you become fully aware."

Amy wanted the tape. She extended her hand and Barb handed it over. "I'll just need the recorder back on your next session, okay? We have a lot of interesting work to do here."

Amy stood and the room swayed. She sat back down.

"Let me get you some water, and you can sit here as long as you need before you drive home, all right?"

Amy nodded and flipped the recorder over in her hands. She drank the small paper cup of water and then was ushered out the front, but not before paying and booking her next three sessions.

In the car, she fumbled with the recorder's tiny buttons and pressed *play.* Static blasted the silence, and she cranked the volume down. Then she heard Barbara's voice, soothing and sure, leading her under with a string of words. After a few moments, she heard herself, in a voice entirely deep and measured, being taken back to 1963. Her name was Greg. She, Amy Marie Townsend, was a meek, calm man named Greg! And then she talked. And talked. About life as a newspaper editor, about parents who had abandoned him when he revealed he was gay, about his crippling, debilitating depression, and then, about his final day, with a glass of scotch, snotty tears, and a Smith & Wesson balanced on his pressed gray slacks.

Amy talked about the cold steel entering her mouth, but it wasn't her mouth, it was Greg's. She could feel, as she talked, her own teeth, which were small and square, gripping down on the barrel like those X-rays at the dentist. A man's guttural anguish ripped through her throat. She closed her eyes, then opened them, and her fingers, Greg's fingers, pulled once on the trigger. There was a loud, fiery pop, a warm blast at the back of her throat, and then blackness.

She burst out of her memory, gasping and choking, and Barbara came to her rescue, talking to her in a succession of commands to bring Amy back to calm.

She pressed *stop,* one hot hand over her mouth. She remembered. She could feel it. She rewound the first part and listened again, and then again. Is this why she hated loud noises and guns? Is this why she cringed more than others when she heard about anyone who had committed suicide? Why those stories stuck with her for days, nights, sometimes even months afterward, haunting her with their gory details, while others brushed them off as cautionary tales? She had committed suicide in a former life. She had pressed the barrel of a gun into her throat and dared to pull the trigger . . . didn't that tell her everything?

Her fingers fumbled as she shoved the tape recorder into her glove compartment and checked her phone. She had four missed calls from Richard. He rarely texted and never left a voicemail, so she never knew if something was wrong or if he was just being impatient. She put the car in reverse and struggled to come up with an excuse for where she'd been and how shaken she felt. She wanted to know more about who she was, and if that person, Greg, was any better than who she was now and what she was returning home to.

after

"Are you sleeping?" Richard stirred beside her, removing and then replacing his legs under the blanket every minute or so. Amy wanted to scream.

She blinked into the dark, as she had so many times over the years, though tonight, the worry was far from trivial. *Her child was out there somewhere, and they were in here.* "Of course I'm not sleeping. I don't know if I'll ever sleep again."

Richard sat up, grappled for his glasses among the sea of books, nose spray, and magazines littered on his nightstand, and then slid them on. She heard something pop—knee? hip? shoulder?—and resettle as he got out of bed. "I just can't sit here all night. Where's the AMBER Alert? Why hasn't it hit yet?" He went to the bathroom, and she could hear his powerful stream of urine hitting the toilet bowl. Was he sitting or standing? Lately, he'd taken to sitting while peeing, which had given her an entire new wave of judgment to contend with.

Amy glanced at the alarm clock beside them. It was 4:00 A.M. Barry, Stan, and Frank had stayed with them most of the night and were taking next steps. They'd cased the neighborhood and had put out local alerts. A detailed woods search would follow, but not until daylight.

Amy sat up too, pulled her robe from her dresser, and walked to the kitchen. She'd been up so many times at this exact hour for different reasons: heating bottles, crying babies, pregnancy cravings, pregnancy indigestion, colic, racing heart, labor, stomach flu, food poisoning, hangovers, unexplained adrenaline. She put the kettle on and rummaged in the cabinet for tea.

Amy was good in a crisis. She memorized necessary information and detached herself from everything else—namely, emotion—a lucky trait picked up from her tough-as-nails mother, and her job as an executive assistant at a high-powered firm. Barry had left a sheet about AMBER Alert criteria—at Richard's insistence—because, as far as her husband was concerned, their child was the only one who'd ever gone missing in the history of the world, and it demanded everyone's attention.

"What are you doing in here?"

She startled. "Jesus, Richard. You gave me a heart attack. What do you think I'm doing? I'm making tea." She shuffled through the loose bags: Earl Grey, Darjeeling, passionflower, hibiscus, chamomile, black. She held up a few, fanned out like condoms in her fingers. "Want some?"

He nodded and picked up the stack of pamphlets Barry and Stan had left. They were titled "When Your Child Goes Missing: A Family Survival Guide." Amy had almost laughed when they gave them each a copy, as though it were a test they had to study for and then hopefully pass. There was a twenty-four-hour-period to-do list, and then the "long-term" search, which meant anything over forty-eight hours. But Richard was fixated on the AMBER Alert criteria, going over and over each numbered point.

"Number one: Law enforcement has to believe our child was abducted. I mean, what else can we do? She's *gone*! Number two: Law enforcement has to believe Emma is in serious danger of injury or death. Well, it seems any child who's disappeared is at risk of that. Let's see, let's see." He pulled his finger down the page. "Ah. Number three: They must have enough descriptors to issue the alert." He grew silent at this one, because they both knew they didn't have many recent photos. Simply saying a child was beautiful with brown hair and big gray eyes did little to help provide those minute, intimate details only a family would know. "Okay, so we're working on this one. So we don't take a lot of photos. So what? People take too many photos these days. Think about when we were kids. I think I have like three photos from childhood. Okay, here. Number four: The child is under seventeen. Well, of course. If a kid runs away over seventeen, I think they call it moving out. Am I right?" He gave his speech to a party of one, while Amy waited for the kettle to whistle. "And lastly: The child has been entered into the NCIC system. What is that? How are we supposed to know what that is?"

"It's the National Crime Information Center," Amy explained. She brought down two mugs. "And she hasn't been entered into that yet."

The papers fell to a defeated slump by his side. "How do you know what that stands for? How could you possibly know that?"

"Because I have the same handout as you. And because I read it." Secretly, she was just as frustrated as Richard. There was a ridiculous *process* to it all, just like getting your license or doing taxes. Paperwork, intake forms, waiting, and questioning—often, the same questions posed a million different ways. Couldn't they just record it once, so they could be left alone to do the important stuff? Barry, Stan, and Frank assured them they were doing everything they could. It had only been ten hours. There was still hope. She could still be out there.

"Why would she just disappear like this? Do you think she ran away?"

Amy recoiled. She couldn't think about their last exchange, couldn't share the ugly truth of it—those awful words she'd said, the actions taken—how that might prompt a child to get as far away from home as possible and never return. Whoever picked her up would have seen the ugly handprint across her face, and then what? Panic squeezed her throat. Would she then become a real suspect?

She was good with Robbie. She'd never hit him or even yelled at him. She could prove she was a good mom; that she was just tired, cranky, and had a shit-for-brains husband who literally—in less than twenty-four hours—was barely functioning.

She grabbed the kettle before the whistle came to a full whine. Richard was weeping over the survival guide, mouth open, snot running, his torso folding over onto itself.

"Richard. Richard. Here." She dunked a teabag in his mug and handed it to him. Why wasn't she crying too? Why hadn't she cried yet?

Because she knew Emma. If she'd run off on purpose, she was probably hiding in a place even the cops couldn't find her. She was a clever girl. Amy took a sip of chamomile and thought about her child's handful of years on earth. Emma never told Amy anything. She never answered questions about her days, her friends, or her teachers. She felt like a perpetual outsider to her daughter's life, which made her angrier, and made Emma more closed off.

"Richard, sit down. Let's just sit down."

They both sat and his tea sloshed onto the table—another mess. She sighed, wanting to just go back to bed and to sleep until this whole thing was over. But she couldn't. "Look, I—"

The landline pierced the silence and Richard lunged to get it, huffing as he stretched to grab it on the first ring. "Yes? Hello? Hello? Did you find her?"

He pinched his lips together with his thumb and index finger until his lips were bulging and purple. "Okay. Okay, yes. That's good. That's a start. Thank you. Yes, we'll be right there."

He hung up, his eyes rabid. "They've issued the AMBER Alert. Locally. If they need to coordinate with other states they will, but . . . it's issued at least." He exhaled like this was a huge relief, but all this meant was that the criteria were serious enough to warrant Emma as missing. This was no longer a game of hide-and-seek.

"What else did they say?"

He was already heading to the garage to put on his shoes. "They need us to come to the station to answer questions. Take a polygraph."

"What? A polygraph? Now? What are you talking about? It's four-thirty in the morning! Why would we have to take a lie detector test?"

"I'm sure it's standard procedure. Just to weed us out of the equation. It's not like we have anything to hide."

She would look like a liar. She knew it. They would ask her about the events of tonight and she would be telling the truth—but a selective one. She couldn't reveal that she'd hit her daughter, that she'd said those horrible words. She should have told them already, but she hadn't. And she couldn't tell them now, after the fact. It was a vital omission in Emma's disappearance. "Richard, we have a sleeping toddler in the other room. We can't both leave. What if Emma comes back?"

He shrugged on his windbreaker for the second time.

"I'm going to go. I'll ask if someone can come and man the house. I'm sure they're all over the neighborhood already. You stay here with Robbie. I'll call you. Keep your cell on."

He was out the door, a man on a mission, something she'd never seen from her husband in all their married years.

She took a sip of tea, but it was already cold. She startled as Robbie began to cry and she went to him, finding solace in a bit of normalcy.

She kissed his cheek and tucked him back in. He rolled to his side, a girthy thumb wedged between parted lips. He was the easy one. He'd been a total pregnancy surprise—the one time they'd had sex in at least a six-month window—but he'd shown her tolerance. She was kind to him.

Emma was the chaos, and now, in her absence, there was even more. She was like a tiny wrecking ball, knocking down everything in her path just to see how much damage she could get away with.

Amy decided to take a shower, get dressed, and do some research on polygraphs. Wait for Richard to call and then go down to the station, where she would have to carefully craft the story of mother, daughter, and their complicated life.

sarah

after

Bozeman, Montana wasn't the kind of place you picked for family vacations or sightseeing. Like all those states clustered together that were an afterthought—Idaho, the Dakotas, Iowa, Nebraska—you'd hear people praise Montana, but no one ever *really* visited, besides mountain men. Bozeman was a forgotten blip, situated close to the mouth of Wyoming, right above Jefferson. It was one of those cities you didn't realize you were missing until someone brought you there.

The first time Ethan told me he owned a lake house, I visualized long weekends, hot baths, and skinny-dipping in crystal blue water.

"It's a bit of a drive," he'd offered casually over tacos.

"So? I think we take good road trips together."

He sucked his juicy fingers, squirted a blob of Sriracha onto his third taco, and tipped back his beer. "Is eleven hours too long?"

I bristled. "Eleven hours? For a weekend trip? With *you*? Ugh. Torturous. No way. Not happening." I took a swig of my own beer and watched his face rearrange into a smile.

He draped his arms along the back of our booth. "Perfect. When do you want to go?"

"Next weekend?"

Next weekend turned into two weekends per month, then three. Weekends became three days, then four, and sometimes the entire week, when our schedules allowed. The lake house wasn't really even in Bozeman—it was about an hour out and sat close to Fairy Lake, one of the only bodies of water for miles.

I teased him about the name—that couldn't be the actual name of a lake, could it?—and he told me that it was the real name, that it was full of fairies, leprechauns, and pots of tiny gold you had to examine with a magnifying glass.

He'd been traipsing to the house most of his life; once he'd gone into woodworking, he'd gained new inspiration and old wood, carting it back to his shop in a loaded van. When I started tagging along, I'd sketched and created the early designs that had become TACK's first digital activity books while Ethan foraged for lodgepole pine.

We made endless pots of coffee, and I would harass him to try just one cup, which he would, before spitting it out, a hot brown stream dribbling down his chin. Instead, he'd fill his mug with water or whiskey and sit beside me in the mornings or early afternoons, so that I'd have someone to drink with.

The house was a throwback to the 1980s, a time when style was interpretable and interior decorating resulted in many unfortunate pairings. His grandfather had been a rancher and had built the lake house for his wife, Mae, before she'd passed away in 2000. Since then, he'd lived and worked in the cabin before dying from a broken heart. I'd seen the photos of his grandfather in his prime—standing next to sexy cars or on the back of his motorcycle, an arm possessively flung around his wife—and I couldn't get over the resemblance he and Ethan shared: that same charisma, the identical noses, crooked on the end, the broad shoulders, the tapered torso, the huge calves. They even had matching smiles.

Much to my surprise, Ethan wouldn't touch the cabin after his grandfather's death—wouldn't change one thing, even—because he wanted to keep his grandfather's memory intact. I was surprised at the sentimentality, as I could see all the great potential in the high beams and endless square footage—but he refused.

"It's not my place. It's his. He'd want to keep it this way." There'd been an edge to his voice when I first mentioned it, a protectiveness he'd never quite shown with me.

I'd met his grandfather a year into our relationship and had come to know him well. We took to each other instantly, often ganging up on Ethan when he was being difficult, staying up late with scotch and cigars, making huge omelets in the morning with buttered toast and coffee thick as fudge.

Ethan joked that I enjoyed his grandfather more than him; I would insist that Bill was more attractive and would he ever remarry?—to which Bill would clap a warm hand over mine and say, "Only for you, sweetheart. Only for you."

We'd gotten the call late in the night, as with most bad news, when his grandfather passed. He was fit as a fiddle, no heart issues, no medication. It seemed he'd just decided one night, after a heart-healthy dinner and a drink, that he'd had enough. He'd gone to sleep and just hadn't woken up. I'd never seen Ethan so distraught; no amount of insisting he was with Mae, that he chose this, that he was still with us, would help.

The cabin was left to Ethan in the will, which, in my book, meant he could do whatever he wanted—however *we* wanted. Instead, he treated it like a relic, not wanting to tarnish a single memory, move a single photograph, or improve a single light fixture.

After Bill's death, I felt like an intruder inside a museum. Ethan would snap if I dropped something on the carpet or left a dirty towel on top of the washing machine. Our easy work sessions became loaded, our conversations tinged with sarcasm.

The weekend visits became shorter; the happy times less frequent; the inspiration all but dried up. But I still loved Bozeman and what it represented. I still loved Fairy Lake, the strong coffee, and the memory of Bill, tucked into every room or Bozeman story. I kept the house close to my vest, hoping one day I'd return, with Ethan.

Almost twelve hours after we'd started, the familiar crunch of leaves flattened under the tires, the smash of gravel beneath dirty rubber. I loved that sound—a signal, really—that the day's drive was over. On the weekends Ethan's grandfather vacated for us to use the cabin, I used to throw Ethan a hazy smile under the canopy of trees, as we mashed lips and teeth and stripped off our clothes, often before we'd even unlocked the front door.

I'd turned off my phone four hours in. I couldn't be trusted not to call everyone I knew. The AMBER Alert had to be out by now. I was sure it was infiltrating the surrounding cities, social media, and news outlets with as much speed and importance as a charged political campaign. She was a child from a decent community. I understood how these things worked, how certain preferences went to certain children. As one-sided as those preferences were, I knew the authorities would do whatever it took to find her.

My hands danced on the wheel. Every time I'd ever

received an AMBER Alert on my phone or seen some tragic kidnapping story on the news, I would flip it off in disgust, thanking God I didn't have children just so I would never have to worry about them being snatched. I'd heard unbelievable cases of kids disappearing from shopping carts, from car seats, from bedrooms in the middle of the night. It was a strange and scary time to be a kid.

I sifted through the memories of my own childhood, thinking of all the opportunities someone would have had to take me. How I'd trusted the world, how my dad had trusted the world, how I'd let myself in our house after school and then hit the pavement post-homework, walking blocks and blocks to who knows where, ducking into ragged backyards with three-legged dogs and creepy men propped up in lawn chairs.

I peeked in the rearview and watched Emma's chest rise and fall beneath the buckles of the brand-new Graco Highback TurboBooster seat. I'd had to read the directions four times and checked and double-checked that it was installed correctly. Friends of Brad's had lost their four-year-old recently when their car was rear-ended by a Jeep. Everyone walked away but the boy, who was killed instantly due to an improper car seat installation. What would I do if something happened to Emma on my watch?

I killed the headlights and sat in the early morning light, the rows of trees hiding us. Emma's chortled snores filled the silence. A prick of worry knitted my spine. Were kids supposed to snore? What if she had an underlying condition that hadn't yet been detected? What if she needed medication? What if she had an accident and I had to take her to the hospital?

I exited the car, wincing as I gave it a firm push closed, but Emma didn't budge. We'd driven straight through the night after the trip to Walmart, with only one stop, in a seedy gas station bathroom. Emma had been asleep for most of the ride, leaving me with nothing but my anxious, riddled thoughts.

I jogged to the side garage door, sliding my fingers into the dirt until I found the key box. I popped it open, and there it was: safety. The must of the garage was a welcome memory. How many times had we come through this garage, laden with cheap groceries to make pizzas and Toll House cookies before binging by the fire?

I crossed the tidy garage and unlocked the interior door. The mudroom was the same, the linoleum a dingy yellow, worn by time and footsteps. I rounded the corner and stepped onto the carpet, which was designed to look like hardwood floors. When I thought of Ethan's grandfather, in the early eighties, laying this carpet, thinking what a good find it was because it looked like hardwood—but it was carpet!—it melted my heart. What a good man he'd been. I missed the way he'd set up board games and activities for our longer visits. How he'd sit and ask me about city life. How he'd always join me for coffee or let me pick his brain over my newest digital book.

I moved to the bathroom. The carpet was thick, beige, and moldy around the standup shower, an old running argument. I'd begged Ethan to consider changing this one feature because it was unsanitary. *Please, just change the carpet! Your grandfather won't mind!*

I'd get out of the shower, my feet damp on the soggy carpet, and I'd bitch and moan about never feeling clean. The pressure wasn't right. The water was soft, which left my hair feeling oily, no matter how many times I rinsed. At night, we'd get into the Sleep Number bed, which was studded with dog fur from Ethan's uncle, who let his big mutts sleep in the bed when they visited twice a year. We'd have blowout arguments about buying new sheets, because no matter how many times we washed them, the small, stiff dog hairs would latch on to our skin.

I moved into the main room, the kitchen on the left, the lofted living room on the right. I always marveled at the big beams suspended from the ceiling, dissecting the room at beautiful, woodsy angles. I used to joke with Ethan about climbing up there and swinging around like monkeys on vines.

Not a thing had changed. Not one piece of furniture. Not a single dish towel or utensil. There were the same few books lining the bookcases, the same board games dusty and worn on a spare shelf, the same rocking chair with the ancient pillows, the threadbare couch, the old-school TV and round table and chairs. There was a bedroom upstairs with two twin beds and a small bathroom, and a finished basement with a bar, a living room, and another, window-less bedroom.

After making sure we were indeed the only intruders here—Ethan never visited the cabin at the start of summer—I hurried back to the car. Emma was still asleep, her tender snore rattling the silence.

I unloaded our bags, unbuckled Emma, scooped her into my arms, and carried her inside. Her head dropped to the crook of my neck, her legs heavy around my hips. I laid her in the middle of the king bed in the master bed-room, removing her shoes and tucking her in. The black-out shades were drawn, which pitched the room in utter darkness, despite it being daylight. I unpacked the night-light I'd bought and plugged it in near the foot of the bed.

Once our bags were in the front hall, I checked on her again before pulling the door shut and moving to the living room. My stomach growled. We'd have to get food today. I looked in the cabinets for anything edible and saw a jar of peanut butter. I checked the expiration date, opened it, and plunged a spoon into the oily mix. I sucked the spoon dry, wiped my hands, pulled my computer from my bag, and sat down. I needed to know what the world was saying about Emma, but I was scared.

I used to think no one could ever get away with kidnapping a child in this technologically advanced age. How could they? But I was soon realizing, in some ways, it was easier. You knew where the authorities were looking, who their lead suspects were, if they had something or nothing, if the parents looked hopeful or resigned in their press conference videos. The investigation was available— evidence was searchable. Nothing was private anymore.

I took a breath and attempted to log online. Normally, I'd be able to connect instantly, the password having been the same for the last decade. I tried and retried with no luck. Who could I call? Ethan? The thought was preposterous. I stood, rummaged again in the cabinet in search of coffee, and found an old bag. I sniffed it, filled the coffeepot with water, and shook some grounds into a crinkled filter. I pulled my phone from my pocket and turned it back on, walking to the living room and pausing outside of the master bedroom. I fired off a few texts to Brad, Madison, and Lisa: *Feeling a bit better from the flu, but I'm going to stay with my dad awhile. He's not doing so well. Will connect tomorrow.* Once the coffee was brewed, I returned to the living room with my oversize mug, pulled up Safari, and typed in "Emma Townsend"—Emma finally told me her last name—and "AMBER Alert."

A new window appeared with a list of hyperlinks, only two of them about her. I clicked on the top article and scanned the report. I had *caused* this. This article and subsequent search were my fault. I tried to come to terms with the gravity of the situation as reality sunk in.

LONGVIEW—An AMBER Alert has been issued for a

5-year-old girl who has been missing from her Longview home since Thursday night.

Emma Townsend was last seen around 6 p.m. Thursday at 1232 Cranston Drive.

Police say Emma was playing in her backyard after school and disappeared sometime that evening.

Authorities activated a CodeRED notification in the surrounding neighborhoods and asked for Washington State Patrol's help in searching the area.

Read more on KLTV.com.

I read the article again, trying to decipher the next official move. It was early—less than twenty-four hours since she'd been gone—and there was no more information on the case: no leads, no suspects. How careful had I been? How easy would it be to find us?

I pondered as I swallowed the last of my coffee. I had no connection to Emma; no reason to take her—

"Sarah?"

I jumped and dropped my phone, the heavy coffee mug almost slipping from my grip. I set it down and walked around the couch to kneel in front of a very sleepy Emma.

"Hi, sweetie. Do you need anything? Do you need to pee?"

She nodded and shoved her knuckles into her eyes, attempting to rub the sleep out like an infant.

I re-pocketed my phone, my heart thudding in my ears. "Would you like to get into pajamas?"

Emma looked at the sunlight streaming in through the windows. "But it's day."

"That's okay. Pajamas are fun for day sometimes."

She yawned and moved to the bathroom, her hair in one fuzzy knot at the back of her head. She wiped at herself clumsily before flushing the toilet and then stood on her tiptoes to wash her hands.

"Let's brush your teeth too."

I went to one of the plastic bags and removed her new purple toothbrush and toothpaste.

"I can do it." She took them from me and expertly squeezed out a small amount of paste and worked it over her teeth in a gentle but effective manner.

"You're a great teeth brusher," I said. She looked at me and smiled, her teeth frosty. The skin of her cheek bulged below her eye. "Does your cheek still hurt? Do you want some more ice?"

She shook her head no and then we took off her new outfit, the collar getting hung around her neck. I took those few seconds to check her skin for bruises, as though looking for ticks or shifty moles. I hadn't had time in Walmart's dressing room, but now we weren't rushed. It was hard to see in the dim bathroom light, but the bruises were there, scattered up and down her legs like rocks, a few shaped like fingers on her torso and upper arms.

"How'd you get all of these bruises?"

She looked down at her legs, as though just seeing them for the first time. "I don't know. Maybe school?"

"And these?" I pointed to her torso and arms.

She shrugged again and looked down.

"Emma, honey, did your mom give you these?" I lightly touched the bruises.

"I don't know."

"Emma, look. This is just for me to know, so I can make sure you don't get any more bruises. Okay?"

"Okay." Her voice was small, but I could sense it: she trusted me. "I think Mommy gave me those. She squeezes hard sometimes. Too hard."

"Yeah? I bet that doesn't feel good, does it?"

"No."

Here was the patchwork of bruises, bared for the world

to see. Here was this innocent little girl, real, warm, safe, and confessing. She touched her cheek and dropped her fingers.

"Emma, you don't have to worry about that anymore. I promise. Do you believe me?"

"Yes." She yawned again, and I helped her into a set of PAW Patrol pajamas. Her pant leg got tangled, and she had to jump up and down to set the fabric loose, her hands balanced on my shoulders. She laughed and gripped my neck, her cool, minty breath moving across my cheek. I took the opportunity to give her a hug, and she squeezed me back.

I released her and we walked into the living room. Emma stared at the unfamiliar surroundings. She sat on the edge of the worn couch, with its scratchy fabric, and crossed her legs. "My grandmother had a house like this."

"Oh, really?" I collapsed in the rocking chair across from her, pushing my feet to begin the sway. She looked so much older than five—those eyes telling me something I couldn't quite comprehend.

"Did you like going there?"

"It was so fun! She had a farm with chickens and pigs too."

"How cool is that?"

"So cool." She scratched her hand. "But she died."

"Oh no. I'm sorry."

She looked at the television. "Why is that TV like that?"

I laughed. "Do you mean these?" I pointed to the antennae. "Because it's about one hundred years old."

"It is?"

I shook my head. "Not really. But it's pretty old."

"Can we go outside now?"

"Sure."

"And I can still wear my pajamas?"

"Of course. Do you want to go see the lake?"

"A lake? Yes! Can we play in it?"

I told her the same tale Ethan had told me: about the small fairies and pots of gold. Emma's eyes widened at the possibility of actual magic in the water.

She hopped off the couch and grabbed my hand before I offered it. I opened the back patio door and together we tumbled down the steep incline to the mouth of the lake, where we remained for the rest of the day.

After a day spent on the water, we loaded up on groceries and sunscreen at the market just outside of town and ate outside, under the stars. We'd had an exceptional first day—no tears, no questions about her parents, no worries at all. She ate a huge dinner, asking for a snack later, and then I let her watch one cartoon on my phone. After, she handed it to me.

"Is it time to go to bed now?"

I glanced at the large clock on the mantel. "What time do you normally go to sleep?"

"Whenever I fall asleep."

I wondered if anyone read her bedtime stories, if she got tucked in, or if her dad or mom sang songs. Did her mother brush her hair after bath time? *Was* there a bath time? Did anyone tell her she was special? That she could grow up and do anything? Tears burned my eyes, but I blinked them away and cleared my throat before they fell. It was pointless to wonder about such things.

"Are you sleepy?"

"Kind of."

"Want a bath?"

"Can I? Like a real bath?"

"Do you not take baths at home?"

"No, Mama says we never have time, and it wastes all the hot water. Can I? Can I do it right now?"

There was a small bathtub upstairs. "Let's go fill it up."

I sat beside her as the bath filled, while she splashed and played with two Barbies we'd gotten her at Walmart. I caught up on work emails on my phone, fired off more texts, and waited until she was done playing to wash her. I folded her in a fluffy towel and carefully carried her downstairs to the bedroom. I helped her put on the same pajamas and she crawled into the tall bed.

"Does anyone ever sing to you?"

She shook her head no.

"Would you like me to sing to you, or do you just want to go to sleep?"

"Could you?" Her voice was small and curious.

"Of course I can." I racked the recesses of my brain for a nursery song I might still remember: "Hush Little Baby"? "Twinkle Twinkle"? "Itsy Bitsy Spider"?

She waited and pulled the covers up to her chin. I smoothed the hair from her face and started with "Twinkle Twinkle Little Star," my voice cracking in the still night.

She let out a sigh and found my hand in the dark, winding her warm fingers through mine before pulling my entire hand to her chest.

My voice shook with emotion as I stroked her face with my other hand. The words turned to humming as her breath deepened and she slipped under after only a few minutes.

I finally removed my fingers from hers and watched her rib cage expand and contract in the darkness. The gravity of this little girl in a stranger's bed took hold. I didn't even know her and already I was falling in love. I hadn't gone through the daily grind with this child the way mothers all over the world did every single day. But I knew that she was special; that I was supposed to meet her; that I would do anything—*anything*—to keep her safe and unharmed, here, with me.

Outside, we could hear crickets and frogs. Emma jerked wide eyes at me—a question. "What are those?"

"What? Those sounds?"

"Yes." She edged closer on the log.

"Oh sweetie, those are just crickets and frogs. They like to sing at night. Singing, singing, singing. That's how they talk. Kind of like what we're doing now." I leaned forward and threw a few more sticks onto the fire.

"I don't like frogs."

"Well," I draped a protective arm around her shoulders, "did you know that some mama frogs lay up to one hundred eggs and she carries them around on her back?"

She burrowed beneath my arm. Her skin was hot. The baby-fine hairs of her arm pricked against mine. "Like eggs that you eat?"

"No, like eggs that turn into babies. Can you imagine having that many brothers and sisters running around?"

She giggled. "Tell me more about the froggies."

I rambled on about any random facts I could remember about frogs, digging into the bag by my feet to find a marshmallow. I stabbed one of the fluffy white cylinders with the skewer and handed it to Emma.

"Have you ever roasted a marshmallow before?"

"No."

"Well, this was one of my favorite things to do when I was little. Can I teach you how?"

Emma scooted to the edge of the log. I showed her how to stick the tip of the marshmallow and skewer into the fire, constantly rotating it so as not to blacken and char just one spot. As soon as hers was ready, I pulled out the graham crackers and thick squares of chocolate and let Emma squish the hot, sticky mess into a sweet sandwich. "Now press down."

Emma pressed hard, her top cracker splintering from the pressure. "Oh no! It broke!"

"It's fine. They always crack. See the way it's melting now?"

She inspected her waxy marshmallow. "Can I bite it?"

"It might be a little hot. Let me try first." I bit into mine, the flavors transporting me back to roaring fires and camping trips with my father. "I think if you blow on it, it shouldn't be too hot."

Emma blew on her s'more and then took a bite. She squealed and pulled the sandwich away from her mouth, a long, fluffy string falling into her lap. "Look! It looks like glue!"

"It does look like glue, doesn't it? The marshmallows get all long and stringy." I took another bite. "Do you like it?"

She bit into hers again and nodded, smearing chocolate and white goo all over her chin. We chewed, the crackle of the fire disappearing into the sky, an alert that there was life out here, in the woods, if anyone was looking. That Emma, the little girl the whole world was worrying about, was safe, happy, and eating s'mores with someone who just wanted her to have a better, happier life.

An hour later, we climbed the steps to head back inside. I made the familiar rounds to lock all the doors. I lifted a section of my hair and inhaled the pungent smell of smoke as I walked upstairs from the basement. I wondered if Emma's smelled the same, if we'd have to scrub her hair twice at her next bath just to erase the stench. On the main floor, Emma was already curled on the couch, asleep.

I covered her with a blanket and kissed her forehead, dropping into the rocking chair across from her. My heart started palpitating as I watched her sleep—a persistent occurrence these last few days—suddenly aware of everything ahead of me, of us.

Those first tenuous days had turned into a week, and then two. And here we were, hidden from a world obsessed with the hunt. I'd kept up with the reports on my phone, but they were all the same. Nothing new, no specific information, no real leads yet.

I closed my eyes, the slight squeak of the rocking chair lulling me somewhere else entirely. I'd read endless stories about unspeakable childhood tragedies, and most of those kids went on to lead happy, productive lives. It was the parents who fucked them up more than anyone; the parents who unloaded their own insecurities and hurt onto their children; the parents who taught them that the world, their world, was limiting instead of limitless; that most of their intuition was wrong, that they had to watch out for strangers, cars, and sugar; that they weren't capable of doing what they wanted when they wanted, because the world was just one big, dangerous place. And parents knew best. Even when they laid hands on you, yelled at you, and made you feel like nothing.

I stopped rocking and opened my eyes. Emma hadn't even mentioned her family in the last week . . . hadn't said anything about her mom, dad, or brother even once. Didn't that mean something? Wouldn't a child from a good home beg to go back? Was there a way to get a message out that Emma was okay, that she was safe, and to call off the search dogs? I had no way to prove I wasn't some single, child-starved crazy person distraught from a tough breakup. No way to prove that I would never lay a finger on this girl, that those bruises—now gone—hadn't come from me, that we just seemed to understand each other, often without saying much of anything.

I got up, too antsy to sleep, and went into the bedroom. I fished my phone from my purse and glanced at the time: ten-thirty. I knew he'd be awake. He'd moved on with his life, and here I was, in *his* cabin, with a child who wasn't my own, ready to bring him in as . . . what? An accomplice? A voice of reason?

I placed the phone on the nightstand, changed into pajamas, and got ready for bed. I was beginning to miss the city sounds. Would I ever return to a normal life? Would I ever be able to get up, traipse across my home with a cup of hot coffee in hand, and gaze outside without thinking of Emma?

Even if I got out of this without going to prison, I knew the consequences of what I'd done would mean a different life. Work would be different. My personal relationships would be different. In essence, I'd be sacrificing the life I'd built—and the people in it—for a girl I barely knew.

The next day, I stepped outside and listened to all ten of my voicemails. I skipped through several from Lisa and my dad, vowing to carve out time to call them back. I'd been doing as much work from my phone as I could, but I needed laptop access. Brad and Madison had each called twice. I paused on the last message.

"Sarah, where are you? Do you know what's happening here?" Madison's voice hissed through my voicemail, charged with insinuation. "I was watching the news and heard about that little girl who was taken."

My pulse drummed in my ears.

"There's a little girl who got taken from that school we went to—Emma something or other? From the Montessori!

So I was going through the photos from Longview, you know, to see if I could help or anything, and we have a photo of her, Sarah." Her voice dropped to a whisper. "*Three* photos of her, actually. On our camera. And now you're gone, and I'm freaking out, and I need you to tell me what to do. Right now. I mean it, Sarah. Call me back. Please."

I'd never heard Madison so frantic. I knew, left to their own devices, my team would probably hand the camera over to the police and volunteer to set up search parties for Emma, because they always wanted to help. If Madison hadn't charged over to my dad's house already, I was sure she would be on her way soon if I didn't call her back. Except I wasn't at my dad's. I was at Ethan's.

I'd brought the team here once, several years ago. Ethan loved grilling burgers and bantering with Brad, who made continuous (but innocent) sexual innuendos aimed at Travis, who only had eyes for Madison. Madison, however, couldn't take her eyes off of Ethan, and as a result, I'd felt I had to watch her a little more closely than the others. She was young, beautiful, and impressionable. Why wouldn't she have a crush on Ethan?

I listened to Madison's message two more times as I moved back into the house. Did she know something? Did she *suspect* something? I'd never told Brad, Travis, or Madison about seeing Emma in the airport all those months ago. I hadn't even told Lisa, even though I'd wanted to. If I had, would that have made it better or worse? I didn't want to drag them into this, but those photos . . . why hadn't I remembered to delete those photos?

I cracked the door to the master bedroom. Emma was sprawled in bed, on her back, in a deep afternoon nap. We'd spent the morning hiking and canoeing and then we'd splashed in the shallow end of the lake, picking rocks and digging for worms.

She had some good color on her arms—not exactly brown, but not pink either. Her hair had already lightened to a buttery gold, and she'd plumped a bit in her arms and cheeks. It made me wonder what she ate in Longview.

I stepped back outside and walked around to the rocks, the water glittering and warm. I played with my phone, spinning it around in my hands before punching in Madison's cell.

"Sarah. Christ! Where are you? Where have you been?"

"Hi, Madison." I tried to keep my voice calm, though my feet were tapping madly against the dirt. "I got your message. Sorry. I don't have great reception where I am."

"At your dad's, are you?"

I could hear the sarcasm in her voice, and I imagined her manicured nails squeezing her Gucci belt as she paced her office.

"Why do you say it like that?"

"Because I called your father. We know you're not there."

"Oh." I shifted on the rocks and squinted into the sun. "You're right. I'm not there."

"Then where are you? What's going on? I mean, we go to this school in Longview and then there are these photos, right?—photos that *I* took—and then this girl goes missing a week later? What do I do? I've never seen that girl in my life, I swear, and what if they think . . . what if they think I had something to do with it? The parents— these parents seem like they are the worst, by the way, you should see them—they don't even have a current photo of their daughter. Who, in this day and age, doesn't take photos of their children? They don't have Facebook. They don't even seem to be real! But I have these photos, and if someone has her, I can help, right?"

Madison was spinning, her thoughts vomiting directly into my ear. I knew her well enough to know she needed to get them all out, to let them loop around each other like a rubber band bracelet.

"Madison, take a breath."

I could hear shuffling in the background, the closing of a door. "Okay. I'm breathing."

"I want you to sit down. Are you sitting?"

"I am now."

"Listen to me. Do not contact the police or her parents. Do not get involved with this at all, do you understand me? It's too complicated. You could end up becoming a suspect." I cringed as I said it, but it had to be threatened. All Madison had to do was imagine herself in an orange jumpsuit, stripped of her wardrobe and her lattes, and that would be enough.

"Sarah, are you there?"

I pulled the phone away from my ear. I had a measly two bars of reception. I stood and walked back to the house, the connection becoming clearer. "Did you hear what I just said?"

"Yes. You just kind of cut out for a second. Where are you?"

"I'm . . . I'm at the lake house."

"*Ethan's* lake house? As in Ethan, your ex we all hope contracts an infectious disease and loses half his face—that Ethan?"

"That's the one."

"You're there? With him? Oh my God, now this all makes sense! You're back together! You've gone off the grid because you reconciled. I'm sorry for going on and on about all of this. You'll have to tell us everything when you get back. At least we know you're okay. God, wait until I tell Brad and Travis. They will be so ha—"

"Stop. I'm not here with Ethan. We're not back together. I just . . . I just needed space. And I knew he wouldn't be here. So I came."

"But why? You could get space anywhere. Why there? Isn't that . . . I don't know, painful or something?"

"It's the right place to be. For me. For now. Look, I need you to promise me you're not going to do anything with those photos."

"I promise. I'll tell Brad."

"You told Brad?"

"Well, yeah. When I couldn't get you, I had to tell someone."

"And what did he say?"

"He said what you said. He doesn't want to get involved in this, either."

"Look. Just delete the photos. I need you to take care of the business—to focus *solely* on the business—and I will be back soon, I promise. My schedule has been grueling, and I just needed to unwind and take the vacation that I never take. Okay? I've got some new ideas brewing."

"Ooh, awesome!" I could hear Madison perking up, the thought of new creativity almost an excuse for my absence or poor behavior. "Take all the time you need, boss lady. We've got it covered. Though you might want to give Brad a call. He's freaking the eff out."

I laughed at her inability to curse. "Just tell him not to get his panties in a wad and enjoy the run at being the boss. I'll keep in better touch, I promise. I just need a bit more time to myself, okay?"

"Okay. So everything's okay." It wasn't a question, more of a Madison pep talk. I could see the assurance falling into place, like her hair—smoothed, spritzed, and shiny.

We hung up, and I stepped back inside, checking on Emma again, who was in the exact position she was before. I couldn't believe how tired she became on a daily basis. She would play for two hours and then not be able to keep her eyes open for three. I reminded myself to get some vitamin B12 and maybe even vitamin D at the market, in case she was deficient.

I moved to the couch, plucking an old novel off the shelf. Not getting on the internet was driving me mad. I had my phone, but I hated waiting forever for pages to load and reading the tiny print. Every article said some version of the same—

"Hello? Who's here?"

I bolted upright. Footsteps shuffled hesitantly from the garage to the laundry room and back again. I ran as fast as I could without making too much noise. There, with a knapsack and a vibrant blonde at his side, stood Ethan, hand outstretched as if ready to fend off an intruder, a look of deep concern carved into the lines of his face. I'd parked my car by the lake and found an old tarp to drape over it. He couldn't see it from the drive.

Our eyes locked. His look of concern morphed to surprise and then outrage. "Sarah? What the fuck are you doing here?"

I looked over my shoulder and ushered him out into the garage. "Shh! Keep your voice down."

He recoiled as if I'd bitten him. "Excuse me? Keep my *voice* down? This is my cabin, Sarah! Why are you here? Are you with someone?"

The blonde looked uncomfortable but bit her lip in an attempt to hide an embarrassed smile.

"I'm not here with someone. I had to get out of town for a while, and I knew you wouldn't be here. I know it was wrong—"

"You bet it was wrong. Do you know I could have you arrested for trespassing?"

Dread corseted my middle. If he called the cops, they would find so much more than trespassing.

"Sarah?"

We all turned as if a gunshot had gone off, the garage door creaking on its ancient hinges. There, in her one-piece watermelon bathing suit, stood Emma, her face still full of sleep, her hair resting in a tangled heap at the nape of her neck. She looked from me to Ethan to the blonde and back to me again.

"Sweetheart, can you go inside for a second? I'm just talking to my friends."

She nodded and retreated into the house. My guts twisted. All the blood rushed to my face. I turned, and I could see it in Ethan's eyes. The registered shock followed by the grave realization of . . . her.

He knew who she was. He knew what I'd done.

He knew.

amy

during

Amy lugs Robbie and her bag inside. Carla is on the couch, reading a magazine. She jumps like she always does when Amy barges through the door, as if she's been caught. "Emma's outside. I tried to get her to come in, but she won't."

Amy sets Robbie down, then her bag, and arches her back as pain shoots down her legs to her feet. She feels as though she might have a partially torn Achilles tendon, sciatica, and an umbilical hernia, because there is something round and hard protruding from her belly button that juts out when she strains.

She can't think about any of this now, of course; she has to pay the babysitter, wait for Richard, and make sure Robbie doesn't swallow bleach or pull the TV over on himself. She has to heat up the leftovers for dinner and deal with her daughter, who, at the moment, is nowhere to be found.

She barely remembers the days of coming home to an empty house, pre-children, and how indulgent that now seems. There was literally no agenda, which at the time seemed boring, but now seems like the only thing worth living for. She hears Robbie start to cry from somewhere inside the house. She fishes some wrinkled bills from her wallet and hands them to Carla, who bursts out of their house as fast as she can.

She is an odd girl, but she's the only one they've got. Amy could quit her job, be home more, pick up both kids from school, but she doesn't want that stay-at-home life.

Robbie is in his closet. She grabs him under his chubby arms and braces herself as she lifts, carrying him to the living room to place him in front of a cartoon. Richard should be home in five minutes. He can feed Robbie tonight.

She goes to the kitchen and sees Emma outside the window, pulling up the grass again after they have explicitly asked her not to. She uncorks the wine from two days ago, takes a whiff, and then drinks straight from the bottle. It is sour, sweet, and a bit vegetal, but she drinks it anyway and then lets out a long, juicy burp. Robbie laughs from the living room, and she smiles, because he is such an easy, quiet toddler, if not a tad dumb.

She steels herself and glances out the window again, but Emma isn't there. She leans forward over the sink, looks left, then right. Why had they never bought a fence? She feels the anger swirling, as it always does, and then she is out the dining room door, screaming. "Emma Grace, come here right this instant!"

She waits—she's in the woods, it has to be the woods—and then her child emerges from the trees, dirt-smeared and lovely, and it takes everything in her not to cry. "How many times have I told you not to go into those woods?"

Emma stands there. She always just *stands* there, and just like Richard, the absence of words is the catalyst. It's always the catalyst to her complete undoing. "Get over here right now. It's time to go inside. I mean it."

Emma slows everything down—the way she has so many times—because she knows that nothing annoys Amy more than the silent treatment and moving at a glacial pace.

"Emma, *now*!" A thousand curses push to her lips, and she wants to say them all. She wants to take out her shitty day and her shitty life on her unblemished daughter right here in their shitty backyard.

Emma stops a foot from Amy, rather than just bounding inside like a normal, happy child, eager for dinner, so thankful to be alive. *Yes, Mama! What's for dinner?* How hard could that be? How fucking hard could it be to just do what you are told?

She hears Richard in the kitchen, banging pots and pans, taking out the leftovers. He won't come out here to help her—it's always her against Emma—never a united front as parents, never a team.

Amy's fingers close around Emma's bony elbow, and she thinks about squeezing it until she hears the crack and pop of bone. "What is *wrong* with you? Why can't you ever just listen? Just listen to me! Just once!"

She is shaking her, but Emma does not break, because Emma never breaks. She smiles at her mother—she actually smiles!—and then her daughter decides to rip apart her stoic silence with this: "Because I don't love you, that's why!"

Emma screams it, and now the neighbors know that her own daughter doesn't love her, and she is so embarrassed to be spoken to this way. After all this time, after five years of feeding, providing, and keeping her alive and safe—after all this *silence*—this is what she says?

Amy releases her elbow and turns. *Go inside. Eat dinner. Leave her alone.* But it's not that simple—it's never just that simple—and she turns back and leans over Emma, spitting words right back into her perfect little face.

"I don't love you either. I *never* have. Did you know that?"

There is a beat, a challenge, and then her daughter comes unglued, shakes her head, and is screaming for Amy in a way that Amy has never heard. But she has said *those awful words*. She can't take them back, and she doesn't know if she wants to. Something has to change, and maybe this is it. She's said the worst thing a mother can ever say to a child. The damage is done.

Amy stomps back to the house and Emma runs after her with outstretched arms. She should feel bad, she should give her a hug, she should let both of them start over. They both deserve a break.

She turns back—just for a moment—and sees that her daughter's tears are fake, because she *knows* that forced cry (the cry when she wants a toy and doesn't get it; the cry for constant attention; the cry when she blames Robbie for doing something he did not do), and she is so insulted that she rears back and strikes Emma as hard as she's ever been struck. Richard is not standing at the window. If he were, he would not stand for this.

Her hand makes contact with Emma's soft cheek, and she's afraid she's split her daughter's face into two distinct parts. She removes her hand and looks at it—half-expecting to see baby teeth and jaw adhered to the skin of her red, red palm.

She feels the wine bubbling up her esophagus, but she swallows it and walks back toward the house. She prays there are no neighbors; that her child will stop screaming; that she will wake up from this Groundhog Day of her life to find something different in the morning.

She steps through the door and locks it, her husband

and other child looking at her with similar, worried expressions. She cannot face them now. She cannot face her daughter. She takes a shaky breath, ignoring the ferocious sting in her hand and the anger strangling her heart.

after

People wore T-shirts with Emma's face, a photo taken by the school six months ago. They held banners, wore stickers and buttons, and handed out fliers. Had someone paid for those? Amy adjusted her blouse, sweating and clammy, her makeup, applied with a sponge the size of a pancake, already slick and melting off her jaw.

She blinked into the cameras and lights. Why were they doing this? Why did families ever do this? A kidnapper would never watch this and just hand the kid back. So who was this for? Not them. Not Emma.

She heard the hot pop and click of the cameras, the testing of microphones, the heated lamps that were blinding. It was for them—the media—the piranhas of all tragedies of mankind.

Frank was at the helm of the investigation and promised it would be fast and painless. But it hadn't been painless. They had ransacked their home, bagging and tagging personal items: combs, toothbrushes, clothing, shoes, paperwork, printed emails, files. They'd searched under furniture, at the backs of drawers, and in their cars. They had dusted their entire home for fingerprints. They'd tracked more muddy footprints into her kitchen, across the backyard, and into the cloak of woods that was their best and only lead.

Amy had frozen in the hallway on the second day when they located her stack of tapes from her past-life regression therapy sessions. Those had been hidden in her glove compartment. She watched as they sprinkled the tiny tapes into a bag, sealed it, and hauled them away. She'd panicked at what was on those tapes—the stories, the insecurities, the confessions—and how they might twist the contents to use against her.

She'd almost told Frank as much but hadn't. She was embarrassed to admit she'd developed a crush on him. He was in his late forties, maybe early fifties. She imagined he'd had a hard, productive life full of cases, bad news, and miracles. She wondered if he spent his summers riding motorcycles in the unforgiving sun, crashing at his lake house, all while chopping firewood and killing his dinner bare-chested with a rifle. She swallowed as she imagined his toned, furry chest. He was a widower. She knew that much about him, at least. She figured this job was all he had, and he definitely had his hands full with their case.

This was the official press conference—the only one she had agreed to do. Richard's emotion—which would help in a situation like this—had suddenly been wiped away as he stood beside her, stone-faced, swaying, and as uncomfortable as she felt.

"Thank you for coming today," Frank began. "We are here to discuss the disappearance of five-year-old Longview native Emma Grace Townsend. If you or anyone you know has information, please . . ."

Amy tuned him out, pretending he was talking about someone else, somewhere else. This couldn't be *her* Emma Grace Townsend. The whole world couldn't be looking for her daughter. She hadn't even gotten as far as thinking about Emma's return and what that would mean too: the trauma, the aftermath, the effects, the therapy. How would they afford it? What if she was even more closed off, emotionally damaged, or physically wounded?

Amy's entire life would be devoted to the rehabilitation of their daughter. They would quit their jobs, go into debt, let Robbie chew on wooden spoons, and fend for himself. No, this could not take over their entire lives.

Richard nudged her with his elbow, and suddenly, it was her turn to speak. What was she supposed to say? She looked at camera one but was directed to turn to camera two. She cleared her throat and heard herself speak, though the things she was saying were laughable. "Mama loves you. If you're out there, come home. We need you at home. If someone out there has Emma, please bring her back. She needs her family."

How preposterous. No one had coached her on what to say, and as the generic pleas left her mouth, she heard a snicker from somewhere in the back of the brightly lit room. Frank squeezed her shoulder. She turned into his grip. Her eyes searched his for approval, and he nodded that she'd done just fine.

For the next twenty minutes, they fielded questions from the media. Amy was asked about her and Emma's relationship at least twenty times. Someone had been digging. A neighbor could have heard one of their million fights and given her up, because they didn't like her. Someone at the school could confess that Emma was covered in bruises and wore the same dirty clothes. Carla could tell them what she was *really* like as a mother, how hard she was on Emma. She could be crucified.

Finally, Frank ushered them away from the podium to the back. She collapsed in a chair and fanned herself.

"God, that was awful. I'm sorry. I didn't know what to say."

Richard slumped against a wall and began wailing. She swallowed the urge to slap him, to tell him to pull it together.

Frank fired off a text on his phone. "Look, we're getting calls from the tip line we set up. Which is a positive step. We'll have to work our way through them, of course, to establish any validity, but there is movement."

"And the search party?"

"The woods came up clean. There was activity near your yard, but that was to be expected. There were also footprints throughout the woods, but teenagers often use it to—well, they use the woods for things. And it rained, so . . ." Frank reddened, which Amy found adorable. Did he date? Did he have children? Were they grown?

Richard lifted his head and wiped his eyes. "If she was in the woods, then where did she go? Was she taken from our yard? Did she just disappear into thin air? Was she abducted by aliens? What?"

"The dogs picked up her scent very strongly near your home, but they faded off near the school."

"Oh my God. Do you think someone from school took her?"

Why hadn't she thought of that? All those smug Montessori parents judging them because their child didn't pack an organic lunch or wear clothing woven from recycled plastic. Maybe some selfless, do-gooder mom had decided that Amy wasn't a fit mother and taken Emma in? "Have you checked with all the families from the school? I think Richard might be right."

Richard stood and stuffed his shirt back into his khakis. "You know, I've seen some of those mothers looking at Emma and me when I drop her at school. Judging looks, you know? What if she's with one of them? She has to be. That would explain everything."

Frank pocketed his phone and held out his hands, one toward each of them. "Let's all just calm down here. We are looking into every family at the school as well as the neighborhood and the surrounding areas. We are prepared to look at all leads accordingly." He glanced behind him, at Barry motioning for him. "I've got to take care of something, but I'll see you both at the station?"

Robbie was with Carla. It seemed that most of their free time would be spent at the station. Richard grabbed her elbow and she let him steer her toward the exit, as they both pushed through the sea of press to their car.

She heard questions, shouts, and accusations and was perplexed at how odd the world was and yet how predictable. She should get a lawyer. Ronnie was a longtime friend and had helped with her mother's estate after she died. He would know what to do, how to handle all this backlash. Richard locked the doors and started the car, not even bothering to buckle his seatbelt before he took off.

"Put on your belt, Richard."

He did as he was told as he navigated the back roads to the station. The radio was off, and Amy could hear her pounding heart working overtime in an erratic symphony of angst and stress, beating against her ribs.

"I just can't believe this is our life now," he said. "How did this even happen?"

Amy stayed silent, not wanting to admit her role in all of this.

"Seriously, I want to know. How did this happen?"

"How do any tragedies happen? You're just going along with life, la, la, la, worrying about things that don't even matter, when boom. Tragedy strikes. And life is never the same."

He looked at her as he blasted over a speed bump, and they both bounced and pitched forward in their seats. "You say the most awful things sometimes."

"At least I'm honest," she murmured, looking out the window as the station came into view. Just the sight of the squat brick building filled her with dread. At some point, they would get their answers in there. The police would either bring Emma home, or give them the most tragic news a parent could ever hear.

Amy could not deal with all this waiting. She had to do something—*they* had to do something—she just didn't know what.

sarah

after

Ethan turned to the girl. "We have to go now."

"But we just got here. What's . . . going on?" She looked at both of us, obvious questions unanswered. "Ethan?"

The way she said his name—dripping with intimacy—wrapped its jealous fist around my heart and squeezed. I tightened my ponytail and glanced down at my ripped jeans and dirty tank top. Not exactly the best reunion outfit, even in these tenuous circumstances.

"Nothing. Sarah and her . . . daughter have showed up here, and I think it's best we go." He ushered the girl out. There was the quick engine rev, the rolling of aggressive tires on gravel. I watched the taillights snake through the long, wooded drive before I exhaled. I wanted to burst into tears, pack everything, and hide.

He knew.

I walked back inside with this information, the truth swirling like an internal tornado. Emma was sitting on the floor, playing with a puzzle we'd bought on the way in. "Who was that?"

"That was an old friend. This is his cabin. I forgot to tell him we'd be coming here, so he was mad."

"Who was that pretty girl?"

I bristled at the word *pretty*. "I think she was a friend."

Of course she was pretty. Though Ethan and I had never shared anything about our past relationships—because we wanted a fresh slate—I'd never wondered if he'd brought other women here. Had Bill welcomed other women? Had they simply laughed at the carpeted bathroom and the hairy sheets and gushed about how perfect everything was? *Oh, Ethan. It's so charming and so perfect* just as it is. *I could live here* forever.

The thought made me sick.

Ethan never came here in early summer. There was always too much going on with the shop and too much to do in and around Portland; he'd always said that the cabin was best suited for cold nights and warm fires. And now he'd made the conscious choice to come here with someone else.

"Are you hungry?"

Emma nodded, and I moved to the kitchen, pulling out a loaf of bread and some peanut butter. She liked the sandwiches best when I fried them in coconut oil and mashed a banana in with the peanut butter. Over two weeks, and I knew her palate—how limited it was but how easy to fix her things she would eat. I tried to sneak in the veggies when I could, which was tough with the old Oster blender that could barely blend water, let alone hide chunks of broccoli or kale. Luckily, she loved sweet potatoes and carrots and had recently discovered she liked the crunch of red peppers dipped in hummus.

As I heated the pan and scooped out a tablespoon of oil, watching the white blob melt into clear liquid, I tried to stay calm. What should I do? Call him? Beg him not to turn us in? Hope there was the slightest chance he didn't know who she was?

Ethan was many things, but he wasn't stupid. He watched the news every morning. Unless he was screwing old Blondie every waking second, then he'd seen it. He knew who Emma was. He knew what I'd done.

Should we pack up and leave? Where would we even go? I told myself to stay calm—if I wasn't calm, then I wouldn't be able to think—and just wait. I grabbed my phone from the bedroom, making sure the ringer was turned all the way up. If he called, I would answer. I would tell him everything. I just hoped he would give me a chance to explain.

Despite the turn of events, we spent a calm afternoon by the water. I'd discovered that Emma didn't know how to read yet, though she loved looking at all the pictures. We were studying sight words like *and, the, for,* and *are,* and she was starting to understand. I'd even ransacked my car, looking for a spare TACK kit.

We were working on remembering the days of the week, the weeks in a month, the minutes in an hour, and important holidays and dates. She'd just turned five in April, though she couldn't remember the exact day.

"What did you do for your birthday party?"

She scratched her nose. "What's a birthday party?"

"You've never had a birthday party?"

"I don't think so."

"Well, maybe you can have one next year."

"But what is it?"

"It's a celebration where all your friends get together and bring you presents and celebrate you turning another year older."

"That sounds fun."

"It is fun. I think you'd love it." I hugged her—I couldn't help it—and held her there. She was young, so maybe birthday parties weren't in the cards yet, but I was angry with her parents anyway. Birthday parties were some of the best parts of childhood. I hadn't had many of my own, because my mother was always too tired or would just promise me we'd do it next year. Often, I'd eaten a store-bought cupcake with no candle, only a match that had been lit and stuck in the top to take its place. Just another way we were alike, Emma and I.

We came back up to the cabin before dinner, shaking the water from our hair, careful not to step on sharp rocks or sticks. I checked the front, just to make sure Ethan hadn't come back, and ushered Emma inside.

"Do you want to help me make dinner?"

She nodded—an eager nod—and we changed into dry clothes and then got to work. Emma dragged a dining room chair to the countertop and climbed on top of it, helping me peel and safely chop carrots, sweet potatoes, and chicken to drop into the pan.

"Do you cook a lot at home?"

"No. Mama never lets me help."

"Why not?"

"Because she says I'm too little and I just mess things up."

"But how else are you supposed to learn?"

"I don't know."

"Well, cooking is messy, but that's part of the fun. I promise you're not going to mess anything up here. Okay?"

"Okay."

I handed her the lettuce to throw into a bowl for our salad—would she eat salad?—and kept chopping tomatoes. "Do you miss your family?"

She was silent, sifting through the greens before placing them in the white plastic bowl one leaf at a time. "Sometimes."

"Like when?"

"In my dreams. I dream about them."

"Are they good dreams?"

She nodded, a small smile. "My brother is laughing and so silly in my dreams."

"Your brother sounds funny."

"He is. He barely ever cries. Mama is so nice to him."

"Does that hurt your feelings because she's not nice to you?"

She shrugged.

"Do you ever do anything fun with your mom?"

"No. But I do with Daddy. He takes me to the playground."

"I love playgrounds."

She dropped the lettuce and looked at her damp fingers, before spreading them out on the cutting board. "But you're a grown-up."

"So? Grown-ups can still play. I wish we had playgrounds for adults."

She scrunched up her face. "That would be crazy!" She popped a leaf into her mouth and crunched through it. "I love the slide and the monkey bars."

"Me too."

"Did you know what? I can go all the way across by myself."

"You can? Are you part monkey?"

She laughed. "No, I'm a person!"

"You are? I thought you were a monkey for sure. Let me see." I inspected her arms and made her open her mouth wide. She laughed so hard she began hiccupping.

"Well, monkeys don't hiccup, so I guess you're not a monkey."

"I told you!"

"So, your dad takes you to the playground. And you're not a monkey. When else are they nice to you?"

"I don't know. They leave me alone a lot."

I bristled. "But do they take you anywhere? Like out for ice cream? Or shopping for new toys? Or do they give you kisses and tell you what a smart little girl you are?"

I handed her the tomatoes to sprinkle into the salad. She dropped a handful in and wiped her hands on her shorts. "No, not really."

"But you do know what a special little girl you are, right?"

"I don't know."

"Well, you are. I happen to know you are the most special little girl I have ever, *ever* met. And I've met a lot of little girls."

"Are you going to take me back?"

The question stopped me cold. I set down my serrated knife and tried to breathe. "Do you want me to take you back?"

"No, I love it here."

"You do?"

"It makes my love light shine."

"What's a love light?"

"It's this thing my teacher taught us, and when you do good things, it makes your love light shine, but when you do bad things, your love light dims. Mama makes my love light so dim."

"Emma, I want you to look at me and listen, okay? This is very important. Here." I set her back on the ground and wiped my hands on a dish towel. I motioned to the couch in the living room, where we both sat.

"Am I in trouble?"

"Oh honey, no. Of course not. I just . . . I want to explain something. And it's complicated. Do you know what *complicated* means?"

"Like when something is hard?"

"Yes, exactly like that. Um . . ." I didn't know where to start. "When I saw your mom being very mean to you, I felt protective over you, like you were my responsibility. Almost like I felt like you were my daughter. Does that make sense?"

"Like you were my mommy?"

"Yes, just like that."

"But you would never be mean like Mommy."

"No, I wouldn't."

"Is my mommy going to get in trouble?"

It was my turn to shrug. "I don't know. *I* could get in big trouble, because I'm not your mommy."

"But I like it here better. I don't want to ever go back."

There. That's what I'd been waiting for, after asking myself so many questions: Did she prefer it here? Was she happy? Did she feel safe? I placed a hand on her hair and twirled a few strands before trailing my fingers across her cheek. "I like it here too, Emma. I just want to keep you safe. But we have to figure out what we're going to do. Because if people find us here, then we could both get in trouble."

"Like that man?"

"What man?"

"Your friend. Could he get us in trouble?"

"I don't know. I sure hope not."

"Can we eat now? I'm hungry."

I laughed, a small one, and stood up from the couch. "Let's finish our meal, master chef."

"I'm not a chef!"

"Tonight, you're a chef. The best chef."

She giggled, and we walked back to the kitchen, finishing our prep and enjoying a quiet meal in the country under the stars.

The next morning, we woke late, both of us now comfortably sleeping in the king bed—a mountain of room between us—and I began making coffee and breakfast.

We rotated between oats, toast with peanut butter, pancakes, eggs, and smoothies. Emma never seemed to prefer one thing to the next, which made it easy to surprise her.

I glanced at the clock—it was already ten!—and had just settled in to drink my second cup of coffee when I heard someone bang through the side garage door.

"Oh fuck."

Emma turned her head sharply from her spot on the floor, shocked at my choice of words. "You said a bad—"

"I know. I know, honey. I did. I'm sorry. Look. Stay here, okay? I'll be right back."

I gripped my mug of coffee, trying not to slosh any onto the floor, and met Ethan in the hallway by the washer and dryer.

His breath was labored, his face drawn, his hair disheveled. He looked like he hadn't slept, which, if he'd driven all the way to Portland and back without stopping, I assumed he hadn't.

"I—"

He took the mug from my hands and set it down on the washing machine. He grabbed my elbow—too firmly—and steered me into the garage. He loosened his grip, stared at my elbow where the imprint of his fingers was already fading, and mumbled an apology. After a dramatic sigh, he paced the garage in his work boots. I noticed the sweat rings under the arms of his gray T-shirt, the low-slung jeans, the slip of belly as he raked a hand through his hair.

"I don't even know what to say or where to begin," he

started, so softly I had to lean in. "Number one: You have no right to be here without my knowledge. We broke up. This is not your place."

"I know, I'm sorry."

"Do not talk. Do not say anything, Sarah—not one word—or I swear to God, I will lose it."

I closed my mouth and folded my arms across my chest.

"Number two: If that little girl is who I think she is, you are either going to the police right now, or I will. Do you understand that by me even *seeing* her here, I could go to jail? That you could go to jail for the rest of your life? Unless you just stumbled upon her here in these woods and are on your way to the local authorities, you better start explaining yourself. Now."

I refrained from making a joke about being able to talk and instead rubbed both hands across my face. I needed to get my story straight. I needed to not have my heart thumping at seeing Ethan again over half a year later.

"Let's go inside. I don't want to leave Emma by herself."

"Oh, Christ. So it is her?"

I turned around and let the screen door shut. "What do you mean? You already knew that."

He slapped his open palm against a worktable. "I didn't really *want* to believe that, Sarah! I was hoping—I don't know—that you'd adopted a kid or something! Not that you kidnapped a child the whole country is looking for!"

"Well, so sorry to disappoint you that I haven't adopted a child. Just calm down. It's not what it seems. I can promise you that much."

He lifted his hands in the air, his go-to exasperation move. I remembered that gesture well. "Oh, well thank God it's not what it seems. I feel so much better having a kidnapper and her victim on my private property. My grandfather must be rolling over in his fucking grave."

"Oh, don't use Bill in any of this. I'm not some creepy kidnapper, and she's not some helpless victim heading to her demise. I'm not trying to *harm* her in any way. I'd think you, of all people, would know me better than that."

"Oh pl—"

"And your grandfather would completely understand why I did this, for the record. If you'd give me two minutes to explain, you would too."

I let the screen door slam behind me and scooped up my coffee, taking a giant sip. I winced as the scalding liquid burned my throat and tongue.

Emma was playing in the living room.

"Hey, sweetie, remember my friend Ethan? He wants to talk to me for a few minutes. Do you think you could go downstairs and play for a bit?"

She put down her toys. "By myself?" She swallowed, her eyes revealing the typical childhood fear of basements.

"Or, you know what? Ethan and I are going to go right here—" I slid the patio door open and set my coffee cup on the folding table outside. "You just stay right there and play and just knock on the glass if you need something, okay?"

"Okay."

"And eat those oaties."

She giggled and sat back down, taking a big spoonful and disappearing back into her play world. Ethan stood at the edge of the fireplace, his face registering what?— shock? acceptance? disbelief?—before stepping outside to the metal table and finally lowering himself into a chair.

I slid the door shut and sighed.

"I just can't believe this is happening. Start talking."

And so I told him. I started with my work trip, my first sighting of her in the airport, how it stuck with me, but how I didn't think much of it until we went on our job to

Longview. I told him about the photographs Madison had taken, about going back just to check things out, about what I'd seen in her driveway, and later, after school in the woods.

I told him I'd made a rash decision—even though I had plotted to come back—and that I'd just run with it. If Ethan knew anything, he knew I wasn't overly spontaneous. If I did something like this, it was for good reason.

"But why not just tell the authorities? Or take her somewhere official? Why not have the parents investigated?"

I took another sip of coffee, now lukewarm. "Because the world doesn't work like that, and you know it. They wouldn't believe me, and even if they did, she'd be carted off to social services or put in foster care, or I'd be asked why I was even involved. Proving child abuse, neglect, or that the parents aren't fit—I'm not the Department of Child and Family Services or a social worker, obviously—but even I know it's almost impossible once you get the law involved. I mean, even drug addicts get to keep their babies, because they are their babies. It's hard to go against biology."

He knew what I was saying; I could see it in his eyes. Even if he would never dream of doing the same thing, even if he didn't agree with my choices, he had to understand why I did it.

I glanced at Emma, who was still on the carpet, playing, her oats abandoned in exchange for conversation with a doll. "I mean, through all of this—she's been so happy, Ethan. She's eating. She's sleeping. There are no more bruises. She doesn't even want to go home. We've talked about it. That family, the way they are—I just can't give her back knowing what kind of life she's going to lead. What could happen to her."

"But you have to, Sarah. It's not your choice. Do you

even know how lucky you are that you haven't been caught already? What a miracle that is? You still have a chance to do the right thing."

"And the right thing is . . ."

"Giving her back to her family. Even if they're awful, they are still her family. You are not her family. You will never be her family."

I felt more like her family than he could possibly know. "So even if they're harmful, that's okay? Do you even hear yourself? As though biology excuses that type of behavior? This is an actual child we are talking about, Ethan. A human being. Not a piece of wood."

"Thanks for that clarification, Sarah. Christ." He chewed on his bottom lip. "You don't . . . you don't really know how they are every day, though, not really. You might think you do, but you can't really know. They could have been having a bad day or going through a stressful time. You're just not . . . you're not a parent, so you can't possibly know what it's like."

"But I do know what it's like. I had a mother just like hers. A mother who left."

"Exactly. Emma didn't choose to leave. You took her. There's a difference."

"I know." A mosquito landed on my arm, and I swatted it away. "Who was that girl, by the way?"

He opened his mouth to speak and shut it. "Nobody. Just a friend."

"Uh-huh. She looked like a real buddy type of girl."

"Stop it, Sarah. It's none of your business."

I cleared my throat. "Do I have to worry about her? Piecing this together, I mean?"

"No. I don't think so. She doesn't watch the news."

"Not old enough to stay up?" I joked, bringing the cool coffee to my lips.

"Funny." He stood and stretched, his arms arcing wide over his head and then back down, heavy and relaxed, at his sides. "I need to sleep. I've been up for two days straight. Once I rest, we'll figure this out. But not right now. I'm just . . . I just need a clear head. I can't think. I'll sleep downstairs."

"We?"

"Well, *we* don't have a choice, now do we, Sarah? Because you've magically pulled me into your sinister little web."

I shook my head and walked to the patio door, then paused. "You know, Ethan, you have no idea what these past six months have been like. No idea. So don't you dare, for even one second, judge me. I did what I thought was right, and though I regret how I did it, I don't regret what I did."

He turned away again and scanned the lake. "Are you talking about her or about us?"

"Does it really matter?" I pried the door open and stepped through to the living room, sliding it shut behind me. I smiled at Emma. "You doing okay?" I poured myself another cup of coffee, leaning against the kitchen counter. In another life, this was what I'd always wanted: a little girl on the rug, Ethan outside, our beautiful family tucked away in these woods on a spontaneous summer getaway. How cruel and unusual life could be. Yet here we were, together at last. Finally.

before

I hid near the bathroom, on all fours. I tried not to giggle, though it was hard because this was a fun game and my mother didn't allow much fun unless her friends were around. I loved when they had their Friday-night card games and I could stay up late, spending time eavesdropping near their ankles. It was the only time I could be free, when I could get away with reading books late into the night or watching movies until my eyes felt glassy and raw.

The six of them were talking over each other, their voices sloshed with alcohol. White plumes formed and then spread, heavy with the scent of tobacco. My father kept waving his hands through the smoke, as though he were picking through cobwebs. He had an allergy to cigarettes, but he would never make my mother go outside to smoke. Instead, he'd be up half the night coughing and wheezing, and she never even bothered to ask him why. I listened to them talk for a while, mostly about adult things I had no knowledge of.

I scooted forward a bit more, feeling like a baby, crawling toward the dining room. My knees pressed into the hardwood. It grew quiet as the game got serious, the slap of the cards and poker chips filling time. Billie Holiday crooned on my father's record player. My mother loved jazz, vinyl, 1920s costumes, long cigarette holders, and especially Billie Holiday, with her warped, delicious voice and tragic life.

My dad liked anything she liked. He told me she'd gone nuts when she'd first seen his record player. She'd immediately bought armfuls of records, and they'd stayed up drinking whiskey and listening to old-school country, classic rock, and authentic blues the whole night. He told me that's when he fell for her, when he glimpsed how excited he could make her from such simple things. That excitement could easily power a room, or in his eyes, the world.

I edged closer so I could hear our neighbor, Marilyn, who tended to whisper instead of talk, as though she were always letting you in on a secret.

"It's just . . . children like yours. You know."

"Children like mine? What's that supposed to mean, Marilyn?" My mother's voice was clipped as she counted her chips for a tentative bet.

"Oh please, Elaine, you know what I mean. You have it so *easy*. That child follows you around like a morose little puppy dog, so eager for your affection. All she wants is for you to notice her, which you never do. You treat her like a nuisance. Like she's not even yours! You have no idea how rough it could be. My boys are just so difficult . . ."

I sat back, trying to understand what she'd just said. Children like me? What did that mean? I didn't follow her around like a puppy, did I? I didn't even particularly like my mother, and I figured everyone could tell. I pricked my ears to see if my father would defend me, but he stayed silent. They were already on to another topic of conversation. I had just been preparing to crawl into the room and scare them, hoping their chips would come filtering down like rain, but now I didn't want to.

I stood, shook out my left foot, which had fallen asleep,

tiptoed back to my room, and roughly palmed my bunny rabbit, Roxie, from my bed. I plucked at her soft fur, yanking out small tufts and balling them in my fingers like dough. I wanted to go back out, to spy, but I felt defeated. Did my mother talk about me behind my back? Did she let strangers and friends say bad things about me too?

I slipped under the sheets, my curtains parted so I could see the bright moon hanging like a hook in the sky. It was barely more than a sliver, but I could see the man in the moon, smiling down at me with only half his face. It seemed the whole world was smiling, but not me. Not tonight. I didn't have anything to smile about. My mother thought I was a nuisance, apparently. Everyone did. I would look up the word *nuisance* in the dictionary tomorrow and ask my dad what that really meant and if he would describe me that way too.

I pulled my rabbit closer and made a decision that I wouldn't ask my mother for anything ever again. I'd make sure I wasn't following her around, that I wasn't asking for affection or attention.

I closed my eyes, but their laughter shook my walls and kept me up late into the night. Well after midnight, I got up and stuffed a towel at the base of my door to block the cigarette smoke. It always clung to my hair and clothes and made me want to take a shower. Finally, when it was beginning to lighten outside, I drifted off, after their friends had left, the rev of their engines alive in our driveway, and my mother and father went off to bed.

Over the next few months, I tried my best not to bother my mother. She was gone more and more, so it was just me and my father, which I didn't mind. We played catch, went for ice cream, and made dinner together on the nights my mother went out. She wanted to be an actress and was always auditioning, meeting casting directors, agents, or other actors for drinks. All she'd ever wanted was to be on TV. She insisted that would never happen in the Midwest and told my father over and over she wanted to move to Los Angeles.

He had a small but important job at the local steel mill, and he couldn't just leave without someone bringing in income. Los Angeles had more glamorous work than what my father was used to, and they constantly fought about him not being able to find work if we moved to California.

Once, my mother had landed a commercial for Dawn dish soap. She made a copy of the check and framed it in our kitchen. Whenever my father talked about budget, poring over our finances with a huge calculator and his specs, my mother would tap her fake nails against the frame and insist that she contributed.

Though all my clothes came from Goodwill—because she rationalized I'd just get brand-new clothes dirty at school—my mother came home with purses, jewelry, and vintage clothes that were heavy, colorful, and looked very expensive. I never asked her where they came from or why she didn't think to get me some new clothes, or even a toy. Sometimes, when she was gone, and I was bored of playing dress-up with all of her clothes, I'd start in on her makeup and bras, pretending to be an actress too. I painted my face and spritzed her perfume on my collarbone, the way I'd seen her do a thousand times.

If she ever asked where something went, my dad would make up some lame excuse that he'd moved it, washed it, or that her makeup had rolled under the bed. He knew what I was doing, could hear me in their room, singing and dancing in my mother's clothes and favorite cosmetics, but he never told me not to.

On the weekends, I played with other kids in the neighborhood, though I never had a real best friend. Indiana felt temporary—maybe because my mother wanted to live anywhere else but here—so I never invested too much in the other kids. I went to school, did my studies, and played.

But my heart wasn't in it, and my friends could tell. I was never on the invitation list for parties or sleepovers. They'd all come into school after so-and-so's birthday party, excited with the retelling, and I would just sit and eat my lunch out of my brown paper sack and pretend it didn't bother me. I wasn't unpopular, but I was forgettable. A nobody. A nuisance.

My mother was the personality in the family, and there was no room for anybody else. There were so many days when I wanted a sibling, just someone I could play with or take care of. I would never utter a word of this to my mother, who carried a disdain for children the way most people did for spiders. I was secondary to whatever she was feeling, doing, or thinking. I learned to live small and tread lightly. I didn't ask for much, and I expected even less.

Every time I got excited about something, disappointment would edge its way in, so much so that it became a way of life for me. So I would pray. I wasn't sure if I believed in God, or who He was, or if maybe He could be a She, but if there was one, I'd wish for something to happen. Something to change.

I needed something solid—a sign, a best friend, an awesome vacation, a new mom. I was too young to be so disappointed, but that's what my mother—in all her self-absorption and Hollywood dreams—had done to me.

after

Ethan woke late. I'd already put Emma to bed and decided to drown my sorrows in a pot of decaf and a peanut butter and banana sandwich. I heard Ethan before I saw him, his heavy footsteps coming out of the basement like a warning. I was just licking the last crumbs of bread and peanut butter from the knife when he emerged from the shadows at the top of the stairs.

I cleared my throat and busied myself with sifting the pre-ground Peet's into the cone filter. I filled the carafe from the tap, poured it all the way to the top, and pressed *start* before turning around.

"No more Chemex?" he asked. It was the closest thing to a peace offering, so I took it.

"Oh, you know. Didn't really plan this all out very well."

We both laughed, a sad, long giggle that sputtered and died in the living room. "I'm sorry for ruining your plans . . . with your friend."

He waved me off and walked to the kitchen, crossing his arms and leaning against the island. I could smell the earthiness of his skin. My whole body began to tingle, and I cleared my throat again. He was only a foot away. How easily I could close that gap and fall into him.

"So what now?"

"I'm not sure."

"I mean . . . where does work think you are? How is the whole world not looking for you? Did no one see you take her?"

I bristled at the word *take,* but I knew he was right and that I was more than lucky. I shrugged and stood on tiptoes to pull down a mug from the cabinet.

"Can I have some too?"

I looked at him, startled. "Coffee? You drink coffee now?" The rage coiled inside me. I could see him drinking coffee with his new girlfriend, and it made me want to scream.

"Sometimes." He shrugged. "It's grown on me."

"Well, it's decaf, so it's not like you're going to get a caffeine boost or anything."

"That's fine."

I begrudgingly pulled down another mug and waited until the pot was done to pour us both a cup. Almost six years of begging him to have a single cup of coffee, and he wanted one now? When we were dealing with this?

We blew on our cups and sipped with hesitation, both of us careful not to burn our tongues. How else had he changed? What other secrets did he have?

"So, this family. Give me details," he said.

"I'm sure the media is telling the world more about them than I can."

"Well, I haven't watched much, but you know . . . a missing white girl gets a lot of media attention." He cracked his knuckles and exhaled.

"Yes, she does. However unfair that is."

"I think I saw there was a petition to clear the woods."

"The woods . . ." The woods had given me cover. The woods had allowed me to get here.

"The woods what?" He took a long swallow.

"Nothing. I've been reading everything, but from my phone. Which gets spotty service at best. The password changed." It came out accusatory. "I mean, it just takes forever for things to load."

I moved to the dining room table and pulled my sweater tighter around my chest with my free hand. No matter how hot it was outside, the temperature always dropped inside the cabin after sundown. It was inevitable. "I mean, I know this is crazy. But if you'd seen these parents . . . her mother, the way she shook her and yelled at her. And how hard she slapped her. It was awful."

"I'm sure it was, but . . ."

"I know, I know. But I did something terrible too."

"You have to remember that one slap is not abuse. Think about how you were raised. How I was raised! I got spanked all the time. It doesn't necessarily mean—"

"Stop. I know what I saw. I know what I heard. The way she screamed, it was . . . primal almost. And I know parents have bad days. I'm not saying they don't. But she was the same when I saw her in the airport, months ago. Emma wasn't even doing anything, and her mother was just terrible to her."

"Wait, so you've seen this girl more than once?"

"I told you that."

"I was practically sleepwalking a few hours ago." His body deflated into the chair across from me. "Besides all of that, you just don't—I mean, she could be sick or, I don't know, problematic, or have issues. You just don't know, Sarah."

"And again, we've been over that too. I know all of this. But she had bruises all over her body and that awful handprint from the slap and—"

"But those could be from anything. Not the slap, obviously. But the bruises."

I slammed my hand on the table. "Look, this girl hasn't had a single issue the entire time I've had her. The entire time! She's literally the easiest damn kid I've ever been around. She sleeps as though she hasn't slept in years. And eats everything I put in front of her. I *know* children. Children are my life, my business. And I know—I know that she's better with me. She's safe."

"Okay, great. She's safe. So just turn her parents into CPS and call it a day."

"Are you kidding me, Ethan? Do you seriously not remember anything we discussed when you got here? That system is broken. There are good people who work for these children and do the best they can, but the system is just too big for them to make a difference. It's a horrible process for the child, and it's almost impossible to prove neglect from parents by a total stranger. At best, she'd get placed in social services. That's not happening. I won't let it happen."

Ethan spun his mug around. "It's just not your place to say what can or can't happen. You took an actual child from an actual family. This isn't hypothetical or whatever. It's a crime. An actual criminal offense. That you could go to jail for. That *I* could go to jail for, even. Do you understand that?"

"Yes, I understand that."

He leaned forward. "No, but do you really? Do you understand that this is real? I mean, this isn't like a reaction to our break—"

"Oh, give me a break. This is not some desperate plea for attention."

Ethan drummed his fingers on the table. "I can't believe you took a child. How does that even happen?"

I rolled my eyes. "I know. Trust me. It's insane. I realize that. But, I don't know. When I saw her again, it's like

I was supposed to do something. Like I was *obligated* to. Haven't you ever known something to be, I don't know, just . . . true?"

He locked eyes with mine—a torturous moment—and then looked away. "There's a difference between saying something and doing what you did. You have to know that."

"Of course I do."

An awkward silence fell between us. "Anyway."

"Wait, no." I put a hand on his, and the warmth startled us both. I pulled back. He stood. "Ethan, please don't shut me out. Just talk to me."

He walked back and forth, clasping his fingers behind his head. Finally, after a few tense moments, he sat. "About what?"

"Let's just put this situation aside for one second."

"Fine."

"I just want to know why."

"Why what?"

"Why it wasn't me." God, I sounded pathetic, like some bad *Sex and the City* episode. *Why wasn't I The One, Mr. Big?*

Ethan folded his hands in front of him and looked at me with more intensity than he ever had. He was silent for a full minute. I wanted to shake him, demand he tell me everything already, to just explain it to me so I could finally move on with my life. But I had waited this long. I didn't want to push.

"Look . . ."

"Sarah?" Emma stood in the doorway, her eyes closed from the bright kitchen lights.

I jumped up. "What is it, sweetie? Are you okay?"

"I'm thirsty."

I grabbed a small glass from the kitchen, filled it halfway, and handed it to her. She drank with her eyes closed and wiped her mouth with the back of her hand.

"Do you need to pee?"

"No."

Ethan's eyes were on us, sizing us up, judging. I walked her back to the room and helped her climb into bed.

"You just get some good sleep, and in the morning, you can help me make pancakes, okay?"

I could feel her smile in the darkness. "With blueberries and chocolate chips?"

"And real maple syrup."

"Yay." She pulled the covers up high to her chin and was back to sleep in minutes. I crept out of her room and pulled the door shut as quietly as possible.

"You're good with her."

"You sound surprised." I grabbed the coffeepot and refilled our cups.

"Well, given the situation, I am. It's just surprising how—"

"Normal it all seems?"

"Well, not normal, no. But something like that, I guess."

I sat across from him again, eager to pick up our conversation. "So you were saying?"

He shook his head. "It doesn't matter. Another time. We have to figure out what you're doing with her. You can't stay here. You know that, right?"

"I know. And I'm sorry for bringing her here. I am. It was just . . . remote enough and far enough. And I didn't think you'd be here now. I thought—well, I don't know what I thought. Sorry."

"You put me in a horrible position. Horrible."

"I know." We both drank our coffee and listened to the sounds of life outside. "We never came here too much during the summer, you know."

"Sarah, I have to tell you something."

The sickness flopped in my belly, a fat, wild salmon just caught in a gill net. *Please don't*, I wanted to scream. If he was getting married or having a baby, I would literally kill him with my bare hands and add murder to my kidnapping charge. I wouldn't be able to take it.

"Wait. I need more coffee." I got up, hands shaking, and poured myself the last of the pot. I stayed in the kitchen, at a safe distance, reading him. "Do I even want to hear this?"

"Probably not."

"Great. Just get it over with, I guess."

"I'm moving. From Portland."

I opened my mouth, closed it, and took a few steps toward the table. "Wait, what? Moving? As in *moving* moving? But your whole life is in Portland. You love Portland more than I love Portland."

"I know."

"And your shop. What about—everything?" I sat across from him. "How can you be moving? Did something happen to someone in your family?"

"No, no, nothing like that. It's just . . . I don't know. Time for a change."

"But why? Your whole life is all about—"

"I know."

"So, why then?"

"Like I just said, it's time for a new start."

Nothing in what he said rang true. Yes, we had gone through a hard breakup, but Ethan wasn't the type of guy to just pick up and start over. He'd put down roots. We'd talked explicitly about Portland being our forever place. No matter where we traveled or how far we went, it was home.

"I'm shocked."

He shrugged.

"When?"

"Soon, I think." He took another sip and sat back in his chair.

"Does it have something to do with us?"

"What? No, of course not."

The breath collected in my chest, circulating. "Then does it have something to do with . . . *her*?"

He opened his mouth, the hesitation apparent. I stood so quickly, my chair clattered behind me. I moved to the back patio and unlocked it, slamming the door against its frame and throwing myself outside. I didn't have shoes on, but I ran down the sloped backyard anyway, my heels ramming into jagged rocks and branches as gravity and speed carried me to the edge of Fairy Lake. There'd been so many promises made here, and now he was abandoning all of that and moving who knows where with some girl he'd known for a few months.

I started laughing then, which turned into a hysterical cry, then a guttural scream. Why did men always do this? I'd heard so many stories about the next person in line being the one who got everything. It was such a sad, overdone story, and yet I was the pathetic star this time. It was happening. I had a child I would do anything for, a thriving career, a town he'd made me love, and he was leaving all of it.

He was leaving me.

I fell to the ground and let my head rest on my knees. Nausea pushed bile to the base of my throat, and I swallowed it back with long, deep breaths. In minutes, Ethan was outside, crushing branches under his boots as he moved toward the lake.

I lifted my head in the dark. "How could you do this?"

"Do what? Move?"

"No, us. This. Everything! You ruined all of this."

He let out a bitter laugh. "*I* ruined it? You better recheck your history books, Sarah, because you're the one who broke up with me. What was I supposed to do?"

"I broke up with you because you didn't want what I wanted! You didn't want to be with me."

He came to me then, so much anger in his voice, it scared me. "You have no clue what you're talking about. No clue." He turned and took a few steps toward the shore.

"Ethan, I have to ask you something."

"What?" His voice was flat and sharp, his back a beautiful silhouette against the shiny black water.

"Did you have a ring?"

He said nothing, his hands still stationed on his hips. A full minute passed, then two.

"Ethan, answer me. Did you have a—"

"Yes, I had a ring."

My entire body felt like it had been dunked in ice. I grabbed his elbow in an attempt to turn him. "When? When did you get a ring?"

"Early."

"Like Cannon Beach early?"

He looked down and sighed. "Yes. I had the ring at Cannon Beach. And I'm assuming you found it."

"I did." My entire world was spinning and flipping. I glanced back to the house, wondering if we should go back up. "I don't understand. We were together six years, and you never once . . ."

"I know." He sat, then laid back on the rocky shore, covering his eyes with his arms. "I don't know what to say, Sarah. I talked myself into and out of it so many times. I wanted to. I wanted to right away. I wanted to ask you, but then . . ."

"Then *what*? What happened?" All the air had left my body. I felt like I was melting. "You just decided not to?"

He sat up, a few rocks clinging to his shirt. "Yes. I just decided not to."

"I don't even know what to say to that." The pain in my voice echoed in the night.

"I'm sorry, Sarah."

"Whatever. It's over, right? It doesn't matter now."

"I wanted it to be you. I did."

"Please don't say something ridiculously cliché like that."

He looked at me, a sad smile in the dark, a cheap offering in the interminable silence. "I really did want it to be you."

"So why wasn't it?"

"Because I suck."

I snorted. This was it, and we both knew it. The true finality of us, disintegrating like graham crackers in milk. I couldn't breathe. *He had wanted to marry me and then he changed his mind.*

We sat there for a few minutes more, then I finally stood, shaking out my stiff joints. "We'll leave in the next few days. You don't have to worry about anyone finding us here." My voice sounded hollow, dead. "I need to go check on her." I started to walk back, searching for roots or branches in the dark.

"Sarah?"

I turned, still focused on getting one foot to move, then the other, back up the hill and into the house.

"You have to take her back home. Straight from here. Do you understand?"

"Yes, I understand that you want me to take her home."

"No, I'm not telling you I want you to take her home. I'm telling you that you *have* to."

"Or what, Ethan?"

"Or I will turn you into the authorities. Do you hear me? It's not a request."

"Are you serious?" I faced him in the dark, his face an inky blob beneath the moon.

"I've never been more serious in my entire life. I will turn you into the police if that girl is not back home in two days. I mean it."

The dread spread through my body, a numbing agent. I nodded, an imperceptible movement at best, and walked the rest of the way to the cabin.

He would turn me in? He wouldn't. I ducked into the bedroom and laid there, waiting for movement, the click of the patio door or his footsteps on the basement stairs. How could you suddenly hate someone you had so easily loved?

I stayed awake the entire night, Emma breathing hard beside me, occasionally throwing a limb in the air, mumbling, or grinding her small teeth.

Sometime after the sun came up, I finally drifted off and was jerked awake by Emma babbling to a stuffed animal beside me.

"Well, good morning," I croaked, feeling hungover, the taste of decaf like fur on my teeth. I got up and scrubbed my mouth, rinsed my face, and threw my hair into a messy ponytail. I left the bathroom and searched the kitchen for signs of life. I went to the basement door, took a deep breath, and descended the stairs.

The room was dark and bare, the bed made as if he'd never slept. I ran back up the stairs and outside to the driveway. His truck was gone.

Ethan was out of the city, soon to be out of our city, and banished from my life forever. I was all alone in this. Only, the threat of being turned in hung over my head like a noose.

My phone buzzed, and I looked at the text.

I meant what I said. You have 48 hours.

I had a choice to make, a bluff to call, and a girl to protect. I had no idea what to do next.

after

We got to the market just before closing.

It's when we always went, the workers too tired to care who was there. It's when the mothers were at home with their children, which was both good and bad. No parents would be in the aisles to pay attention to us, but the employees might. Emma wore a hat and had a LeapFrog in hand, so she was utterly and completely occupied.

I shopped in bulk—I didn't want to make too many trips—and we had a regularly rotating menu. We wound our way through, the cart heavy, one wheel not rolling just right. My cash was dwindling, but we would make it. I weighed the reality of being turned in against the reality of Emma's family. What would she be returning to? And how would I get her back without the whole world watching? Ethan's moral compass led him to think he knew what I should do, but he hadn't seen Amy and Emma together.

He didn't know her the way I did. The thought of dropping her at a police station crossed my mind again, but I wouldn't trust anyone—even officials—to get the story straight. How would I ever explain myself? How would I ever say goodbye? I was now faced with an impossible, even more urgent decision, and I hated Ethan for putting this expiration date on it.

I made pleasant conversation with the woman at the checkout as she scanned the groceries and tossed them into brown plastic bags.

"Sweetie, would you like a sticker?"

My heart fluttered as the woman talked to Emma, who was still engrossed in her game.

"Oh, she's fine. Thank you, though."

"Are you sure? Sweetheart—what's her name?—are you sure you don't want a sticker?"

As if in slow motion, Emma lifted her head, coming out of her electronic haze. She nodded and smiled, and the woman pulled out a long roll of stickers and offered her a choice of a dog, a butterfly, or a frog. Emma pointed to the butterfly.

"That's a beauty. Good choice."

"Can you say thank you?" My voice was high and tight. I needed to pull this woman's eyes back to me and off Emma's face.

"Thank you," she said, a small, shy smile at her lips.

The cashier handed me my change and looked from me to her, her eyes lingering on Emma just a little too long for comfort. "She's adorable. What beautiful gray eyes. I've never seen eyes like those before."

"Thank you."

"Such a great age too. How old? Five? Six?"

I nodded, afraid to speak, my entire body pulsing with nerves.

"I'm five," Emma said, wagging each finger on her right hand. "And then next year I will be six!"

"When's your birthday, sweetheart?"

Emma looked to me, and I thanked the woman, and began to roll the cart outside, casually glancing over my shoulder. The woman was looking at us, and her face had changed.

"Oh God." I turned back around and struggled to keep the pace neutral as we rolled to the Tahoe. I looked behind me again—had she seen my car? my license plate?—before lifting Emma out of the cart and into the backseat.

"Why are your hands shaking?"

"Hmm?"

"Your hands are shaking."

"Oh, I'm—I'm cold."

"But it's not cold."

"I know. But sometimes I get cold when it's hot."

"That's silly." She laughed at the absurdity of my explanation and tucked back into her game. I hurriedly unloaded the rest of the groceries and parked the cart right by the car. I got in and closed my eyes, willing my breath to slow. I waited a beat before putting the key in the ignition. With steadied hands, I reversed into the parking lot and made a sharp U-turn at the end of the row. I kept my eyes peeled for the cashier, for the sound of sirens, for someone to follow us back to the cabin.

There was no one—yet—but that had been my final clue. Threat or no threat, it was time to leave Montana.

We unpacked the groceries, grilled bison burgers, and baked sweet potato fries. I told myself I was being paranoid, that we were safe, that the cashier couldn't possibly know who she was.

After dinner, I pulled out a map I kept stashed in my glove box and smoothed it on the table. The thick, waxy paper crinkled beneath my fingers. I rummaged for two markers from Emma's craft stash and handed her one. "Okay, so here's what we're going to do. We are here," I marked Montana in pink, "and we are driving all the way over here." I circled Connecticut.

"But that's so far."

"It is, but you know what? I've always wanted to explore this great big old country, and who better to do it with than you?"

She smiled and pulled at the skin of her lips with her teeth. "Where's your house?"

"It's right here." I circled Portland.

"What's exploring mean?" Emma scratched her head with her finger, her purple marker raised in the air like a cigar.

"It means we are going on an adventure. We're going to look at this map and pick four or five places we want to see."

"But I don't know any of these places."

"That's okay. I can explain what's in each city, and we can decide if we want to go there or not, okay?"

"But where will we stay?"

"We'll need to rent places, like hotels or houses. Or maybe we can go camping? Have you ever been camping?"

She shook her head.

"I can promise you one thing."

"What?"

"We are going to have *f-u-n*. Do you know what that spells?"

She sounded out the letters. "*Fun*! It spells *fun*!"

"That's right. Are you ready to help me?"

She nodded, her eyes focused on the task at hand. I had to be strategic about where we went. Bustling communities were good, unless people watched national news. Rural communities were generally safe, except finding an Airbnb would be more of a challenge. As we got into the exercise, Emma warmed, eager to scribble giant, looping circles around our destinations.

I let her mark the map with her own art as I scraped the rest of our food into the garbage, loaded the dishwasher, and wiped down the countertops. "Ready for your bath, sweet pea?"

"I'm not a pea!"

"Sweet broccoli?"

She popped the cap on her marker. "I don't even like broccoli!"

"You don't?"

I jogged to the back of her chair and tickled her. "Do you like the Tickle Monster?"

She giggled uncontrollably as I found the ticklish spot behind her neck. "Hold me upside down! Upside down!"

"Okay, on the floor."

She flattened herself on the ground as I counted down from five, hoisted her by her ankles, and carefully lugged her to the bedroom to get ready for her bath.

After an hour of splashing, bubbles, playing, and washing, I drained the sudsy tub and toweled off her hair.

"Hey, Em. What do you think about a haircut?"

"Why?"

Because they're onto us. Because Ethan threatened us. Because that lady might know who you are. "Well, sometimes it's fun to get a different haircut. I was thinking maybe some bangs and kind of like here—under your ears?"

"But that's short. I'll look like a boy."

"You could never look like a boy. Plenty of girls have short hair. Did you know my hair used to be this short?" I moved my hands an inch from my forehead.

"But it's so long now."

"Well, it's been all different lengths. That's the great thing about hair."

"What is?"

I leaned in close and whispered. "If you don't like it, it grows right back. You know how?"

She shook her head, her breath warm on my face.

"Magic."

She grinned, but I could sense her uncertainty. She fingered the slippery strands of her hair.

"How about this? How about we cut some bangs, and if you like those, then we'll do the rest?"

"Okay."

I searched the house for scissors while she put on her pajamas, finding a dull pair in the kitchen junk drawer. I'd cut my own bangs a million times, but I feared that she was going to end up bald if I wasn't careful.

"Do you want to see how I do mine first?"

I grabbed a section of hair and snipped the ends, my own dark hair fluttering into the sink. I'd have to clean every last bit, just in case anyone traced us here. Should I cut my hair too? I snipped away at my bangs, cutting them into a blunt, even line above my eyebrows. Emma smiled as the strands spread across the porcelain.

"It's like streamers!" she said.

"It is like streamers."

I hoisted her onto the sink and sectioned her hair into three parts. I'd watched enough YouTube videos to have this down, though I'd never cut a child's hair. "Okay, now I need you to be a big girl for me and sit super-still, okay?"

She smiled and wiggled her toes. "Okay."

"You can even hold your breath, if you want. I'll count to five. Ready?"

She inhaled, her small lungs filling, and let me snip as I counted. I managed to cut them right above her eyebrows, which completely changed her face. I made sure they were even before letting her look. She gasped and leaned forward. "I look different!"

"You do. I love it. Do you?"

She nodded and fingered the bangs. "Let's do the rest!"

I told her to hold still again, more nervous about trying to cut a bob. I'd only done this to Barbie dolls as a child, most of which had ended up with lopsided cuts and some with completely short, uneven pixie 'dos. I started an inch above her shoulders, which ended up being closer to her ears after the first few cuts. I tried to tell her a story while I worked, keeping my hand steady as the dull blades sawed at her fine dirty-blond hair.

Twenty minutes later, I was looking at a Parisian princess. The haircut so drastically altered her face, no one would ever recognize her as the same girl. This little girl was tan and about five pounds heavier. Her hair had lightened and now, she looked sophisticated and around seven, not five. I brushed the stray hairs from her shoulders and clapped my hands. "Emma, oh my gosh, are you ready to see?"

She kicked her heels against the counter and squealed. I turned her around and she screamed, smoothing her small fingers over the bob. I could see a few uneven parts, but I could fix those with better scissors.

"Oh. My. Goodness. I look so beautiful!"

I squeezed her to my chest. "You do look beautiful. You're the most beautiful girl I've ever seen. Do you know that?"

She looked up at me and smiled, squeezing me harder. "I love it! I love it so much. Thank you."

I patted her on the back and finished getting her ready for bed. As I tucked the covers around her chin, she pulled me close to her face.

"I have a secret," she whispered.

"Oh yeah? What's that?"

She cupped her warm fingers around my ear and pulled

me close. "You're my favorite person in the whole wide world."

The tears came before I could stop them, and I crushed her against my chest and held her, not ever wanting to let go. What had I gotten myself into? What had I gotten this child into? I pulled back and gingerly held both of her cheeks in my hands. "You're my favorite person too, Em."

I sang her to sleep and crept from the room, leaving the door cracked. I poured myself a giant glass of wine and then extracted my computer from my bag, connected with the password Ethan had left—*woodisgood#1*6*—and keyed in the search. It was time to absorb any minute detail I'd missed; to see if the woman today recognized us, if Ethan had made good on his threat yet.

The rainbow wheel appeared, making me work for it—why wouldn't I have to work for it?—and then a list of articles appeared, stacked on top of each other like headlines of war. I'd read every single one. I moved the cursor all the way down to the first piece of information I could find, several days after I had taken her from the woods, and reread the article.

Missing Girl Rocks Longview Community— Search in Woods Continues

June 5, 2016 (Longview, WA) Late Thursday afternoon, five-year-old Emma Grace Townsend wandered off into the woods and has not yet been recovered. Police say she was playing in

the woods after school. The search is
on for the missing girl, and the community is coming together to scour
the neighborhood for clues. This is not
the first time tragedy has rocked this
small community, though this is the
first time a child has gone missing . . .

I continued to pore over every headline, though I had already memorized all the facts, looking for clues to actual leads. The titles went from generic to more specific, listing not only Emma's name and age, but weight. Where were the mentions of the bruises, the under-eye circles, the smacked face, the sadness, or the lack of proper nutrition? Had her teachers not seen the marks? Had they not asked her about the same clothes she wore day in and day out, the lack of happiness, or her appetite?

There were comments and facts from her teachers—Emma had been attending the school for a year and was a quiet student. Her parents were hard workers, blah, blah, blah. My fingers stiffened. It was insane how a living being could be reduced to stark facts—height, weight, hair color, birthmarks, shoe size—instead of the real details that composed them.

I knew Emma was a loving, patient child, despite everything. I knew that she didn't like cereal—that she preferred oats loaded with blueberries, peanut butter, and honey instead. I knew that she had to have the same rotation of songs sung every night to fall asleep, and that she loved when I changed the words to something silly. I knew that she didn't need a night-light, but liked a sliver of light coming from somewhere—the moon, the window, the bathroom, or the crack of a door. I knew that she did a special dance post-shower or bath to shake the water off, sometimes running through the cabin at full speed (anything to avoid a towel). I knew that she loved bugs but was afraid of snakes and frogs; that she sometimes took what you said literally, so joking was something of a concept. I knew she had a small birthmark on her right hip, and that it was shaped like a raisin. I knew her toenails grew faster than her fingernails, and that the fingernails of her left hand grew longer than her right. She was right-handed, but preferred to throw with her left. She had mismatched ears, a small gap in her two front teeth, and eyelashes that were so long, they brushed the tops of her cheeks when she slept. I knew she preferred pants to skirts, dresses to shorts, and *always* wanted to wear flip-flops. She had terrible balance but was very strong, and though she loved the water, she was afraid to be let go in it, panicking and screeching if the water dipped above her waist. I knew that she could sit for hours and study books, though she could only read a few words, and that she sometimes inverted her letters and numbers. She scanned the page right to left, skipped words in sentences, and had a choppy, slow cadence that made me worry about dyslexia. I knew that she drew her twos like the letter *S* and scribbled her *N*'s backward. I knew that she had memorized almost all of the fifty states, but she didn't know about other countries, or the people in them. She could recite the first five presidents and was extremely good with her hands, though she hated washing them. She had a small cavity in her lower right molar—one we brushed repeatedly—and I hoped it wouldn't get worse. She didn't love candy, though I suspected she ate it often, and strawberries were her favorite fruit. She slept without covers, no matter how cold it was, and still wet the bed on occasion, so that we had to buy the largest size pull-ups I could find—and I think it embarrassed her.

Her teachers knew her. Her babysitter knew her. I knew her. I realized her parents didn't know how she thought—they told her how to think, how to behave, and what not to do. But they didn't know the real Emma—the Emma beneath all the ridicule, rule following, and excess punishment.

I delved deeper, discovering Amy was an executive assistant at a large firm and Richard worked at a factory in Longview that made deli meat. Beyond the basic details, they had no digital footprint. No Facebook account. No Twitter. No Instagram. No Pinterest.

I got up and poured myself another glass of wine and settled onto the couch, slipping my headphones on. I switched from Web to video. There were only three videos, one four days after I took her, one a week after, and one from just three days ago. Why had I not thought to search for video broadcasts? My fingers hovered over the *play* button. Did I want to see these?

I played the first one—waiting for the video to load. It was a local news broadcast. The reporter was wearing a red tailored jacket and red lipstick, her blond hair an unmoving shield across her shoulders. The irony of the red—it was almost too much. She just needed a red bow flapping in the wind to make it a complete tribute to Emma.

She cleared her throat, her manicured nails flexing around the slim black microphone. "It's every parent's worst nightmare," she began. "Last Thursday, five-year-old Emma Grace Townsend was reported missing from her Longview home. A small community, Longview has banded together in its search efforts to find the missing girl, who is suspected to have run off into the woods late Thursday afternoon after routine play gone terribly wrong."

The reporter stood outside Emma's home, a glimpse of the woods behind her, menacing, deep, and dark. The camera cut to her babysitter, who looked like an animal primed for slaughter.

"She, um, she likes to play in the woods sometimes. This isn't the first time, um . . ." The babysitter trailed off. "We always talked about it. I told her not to play in the woods, that it was dangerous—that it *could* be dangerous."

The camera cut back to the reporter. "Her teachers confirmed nothing unusual happened on Thursday or the week of her disappearance. The babysitter, Carla Shirley, picked her up from school and took her home. Her mother came home after work and spent quality time with her daughter that very afternoon, though Emma was allowed to play outside until dinner. Nothing reported would give reason for the little girl to run away."

I snorted. If only they knew.

"This is a very safe community," an elderly neighbor said. "Kids play outside, even until dark. It hasn't been a problem before now. Everyone helps everyone around here. It's just . . . it's just so awful what happened."

Another neighbor had a different opinion: "It's too dangerous. Anyone could get lost in those woods. There's no dividing line. It's too hard to keep an eye out. I think the woods should be cut down, especially after this tragedy."

The reporter straightened and motioned one arm toward the trees behind her. "The woods you see here have been an ongoing concern for parents of this Longview community. There have been many failed petitions from concerned citizens to get them cleared. While many children know not to go into the woods, some still do. It seems that Emma was one of them."

The camera panned the woods again, showing search crews combing through with flashlights and dogs. "Police are doing everything they can to retrace the steps of Emma and bring her safely back to her family. If there's a clue here, they will find it. From KLTV, I'm Stacy Tucker. Gina, back to you."

I removed my headphones and twisted my necklace around and around my throat. I thought about our trek through the woods. Yes, this was well over two weeks ago, which meant they probably hadn't found much, but what about our footprints? Our scent? Could they trace that? Or had the rain taken care of it? Even so, could those results show intent? That she didn't just wander off—that she was encouraged to come with someone? A size-eight-shoed female, perhaps? Would that change their search tactics, lead them my way? A neighbor spotting my Tahoe, maybe? Someone at the hotel?

I'd watched enough crime television to know they targeted family and close friends first, but still. It had been sudden and careless on my part. I'd taken her in public. I'd taken her into my hotel. What if people remembered seeing her red dress and red bow? Anyone could remember anything when pressed.

I looked at the next two videos, one another update, and the last an actual press conference with Emma's parents. I scanned the comments first, the usual internet trolls making horrible comments about the family, about who took her, about how she was probably dead. I wondered if by taking her, I had somehow cracked the fake-parenting armor and given people insight to how her mother really treated her.

I scrolled back to the top, took a deep breath, and hit *play*. There they were, Amy and the dad, Richard Townsend, blinking into the bright lights. He stood beside her, a string bean to her short, round frame, both of them positioned behind the podium. They weren't crying. Their faces were bland, revealing nothing. Richard spoke first.

"Please, if you know anything about our little girl, about, um, Emma, please tell the authorities. We just want her back at home with us, where she belongs."

I watched Amy as he talked, scanning her every feature, her dead eyes. I wondered if, deep down, she thought she deserved this; if her cruel, abhorrent behavior warranted some tragedy like this. She had to know it could happen. She had to believe karma like that existed in some capacity.

Richard shifted his glasses, the flash of camera lights and murmurs from reporters filling the awkward gaps in his statement. He urged Amy to speak with his right elbow, nudging his sharp points into her side.

Amy cleared her throat and swayed from foot to foot. Her face was soaked in heavy foundation that ran off her jaw. It divided her red—now brown—complexion from her creamy neck, and I could see the ruddy cheeks emerging through, the large, open pores, and the sores she was hiding. She was sweating, and as she swatted her upper lip, her fingers came away to reveal a patch of red. "Mama loves you. If you're out there, come home. We need you at home. If someone out there has Emma, please bring her back. She needs her family."

I shut the computer then, so disgusted by her fake pleas, I felt sick. How would Emma react if she saw this? Would she scream for her mother, demanding to go back, or would something inside her click? The bad memories, the shouts, the pushing and pulling, the bruises, the abandonment?

Not that these videos confirmed anything or changed the facts, but it was time for us to move on. The haircut would help, as would the slightly plump and tanned appearance. It had been nearly three weeks. What would happen after months of her being gone? Years? Some parents searched for decades, never giving up until they had absolute proof. I'd be like that, if I had a child. I'd never believe my child was really gone, unless I laid eyes on the corpse myself. Would Amy? Would they fight forever to find her?

What if I decided to just . . . keep her? Would the trail ever run cold? I thought of a book I'd read about a girl's faked death by an insane grandmother. How relatively easy it would be to prove that she was gone. Then the search would stop. We could disappear into a normal life. The sordid thoughts gave me chills.

I tossed the laptop on the couch and stared into my empty wineglass. What did I really know about being a mother? I'd waited for my mother to change before she'd left us, willing it, even. Instead, I'd grown up thinking: *How will I ever learn to love without conditions?*

"You already love without conditions," my father would assure me. "You love yourself, right?"

"Yes."

"And you love me?"

"Yes."

"And you love your mother, even though she's hard to love?"

I'd swallowed and said yes, though my stomach felt like those sea otters I'd seen turning wet, slimy somersaults at the zoo. Could you love someone who didn't love you back? I wanted to reserve that love—even as a girl—for someone who would appreciate it. Someone who would appreciate me.

"You know, Sarah, your mother does love you," he'd said, as if my thoughts were real. "It's just in her own way."

"What way?"

He shrugged. "It just doesn't come easy, but she still loves you. All mothers love their children."

"How do you know? You're not a mom."

"But I'm a parent. And I just know."

"But not all parents are the same. Elaine is different than every other mom."

"She is."

That was the end of the debate. What more could he say that I didn't already know? It wasn't the last time we'd visit the subject, turning it over like a ship in a bottle, unable to figure out how to get it out, or how it got in.

Those weren't normal questions to ask myself as a child, but the anxiety had wormed its way into my heart, keeping me up at night. It destroyed my father that I was thinking about love and conditions, instead of dolls and friends.

But I grew up with that chip about love, so I looked for the signs with everyone I met: lazy eye contact, lying, detachment, annoyance, judgment, or irritation. I wanted to tell Emma this: that love was difficult and sometimes ugly, but that didn't make it okay.

I closed my eyes and reveled in the safety of the cabin. What would it be like to enter into the real world with her? Beyond the quick run to the market or a gas station? If that clerk had spotted us—and there'd been no alerts to indicate she had—how risky would it be driving, stopping, and filtering in and out of random cities, restaurants, and stores? Could I really do this? Could I keep this child protected?

I stood and stretched, rinsing my wineglass in the sink. I would find a way. I had no choice.

after

We spent the following morning packing—Ethan's threat pinging at the back of my skull like a constant iPhone reminder, as the forty-eight-hour ultimatum loomed—and then ventured down to the lake. I did another search while drinking coffee, but found nothing. I'd set up a Google alert to keep me updated on anything to do with Emma's case when we first arrived, but now the stakes were higher. I couldn't afford to miss a step.

I looked at the slice of backyard, how it sloped and bumped toward Fairy Lake, how grass grew in some spots and then refused in others—like alopecia—leaving bald patches of dirt everywhere. It was hard upkeep, and I knew Ethan had someone tend to the yard monthly, just to keep everything neat and tidy. I hadn't thought of that, how some unsuspecting yard boy might descend upon us, startled and apologetic, and I'd have to ramble idiotically to make up a story about who we were.

Thankfully, we were on our way out. We'd eaten lunch under the haze of trees—hummus and tofu sandwiches, which Emma surprisingly liked—and laid on our beach towels to watch the leaves sway. We lapped up the cool breeze while Emma told me things: how she loved the color blue, even though she wasn't a boy; how she was not only afraid of snakes and frogs, but now bats; how she loved airplanes even though she'd only ridden two; how she'd sing to herself at night to calm down. She took to the woods often, wandering around her neighborhood, looking for something to do. She'd never just come right out and say it—*I hate my mother*—but I was pretty sure she hated her life with her mother, even if she was still loyal to her mother. There was a difference . . . that much I knew.

Now, Emma was squatting over her yellow bucket, gathering rocks by the shoreline. I could hear her happy chatter, that kid imagination taking hold, devising plotlines and characters. Her belongings were scattered about as though they'd been emptied from a bag in a windstorm. Her size-eleven sandals, her beach towel, her books, her latest plastic toys from the dollar store, her beach dress, balled like a white cotton egg under a tree.

This was summer: her pink cheeks and tanned knees, her dirty feet and constantly damp hair, her bathing suits and pasty white bottom. I was witnessing something here, in a place that I loved, with a girl I adored.

I scooped up each item, gathering the details of her life into my arms, all of our secrets and memories. I thought of her own backyard, the messiness of it, the bareness of it, how the layers of grime told its own lonely story, and how those screams, pounding fists, and running into a blanket of dark trees told another.

These were happier items from a different Emma. No matter what happened, the summer of her fifth year went like this: She was safe. She was fed. She had fun. She learned things. She was loved.

"Emma, let's start packing it up, okay? Time to hit the road first thing tomorrow."

"Hit the road?" She said it with wonder, her inflection shifting as it often did with funny questions.

"Well, we're not really hitting the road. It's just something that people say when they go somewhere new."

She stood and tipped her bucket over, the heavy gray pebbles spraying near her bare feet. "Like, we're hitting the banana peels."

I laughed, a genuine one, as she told each and every one of her rocks goodbye.

She pinched one between two fingers and raised it high, wagging it back and forth. "Can I keep this one? I want to name it Chalky."

"Sure you can. Why Chalky?"

"Because when you press it to the ground, it writes like chalk!"

"That's a good reason, then."

I linked my arm around her sun-kissed shoulders, that ginger smattering of freckles reminding me of my own summers as a kid.

"Ugh, I'm so tired," she said as she trudged up the hill toward the house, her empty bucket swinging from one arm, Chalky gripped tight in her other.

I rubbed her head, her roots wet, and reminded her to get changed before we loaded everything in the car. We'd pack everything today, make dinner, and start driving before the sun came up.

It felt like mourning something, leaving all this. How easy it would be to set up a life here—to carve ourselves into this small community, with groceries, an eventual garden, homeschool, and endless travel.

I could still do that, I thought, though not here. It would never work anywhere near here, even though we were far from Portland. Though I'd managed to keep up with work, fielding calls, pushing orders through, and answering emails, my team was growing antsy. I couldn't just stay gone forever. They deserved more than that.

I wasn't sure what came after this: after Ethan, after his threats, after abandoning work, after seeing what I was capable of, even in the face of sane reasoning.

"Sarah? Come on!"

Emma struggled to keep the sliding door open, and I smiled and jogged to her, one sandal coming dangerously close to toppling back down the hill. I followed her inside and let the belongings tumble to the floor. I turned, closed the sliding glass door, and locked it. This would be the last time for this. No more afternoon naps. No more adventures had by the lake after dark. A knot of something rose and twisted. I blinked, breathed, and shut it down. *Not here. Not now.*

In the afternoon, we made a stop at Sally's Beauty Supply for blond hair dye, scissors, and rubber gloves. I left Emma in the car, air running, doors locked, windows tinted, and made it in and out in two minutes. I lightened my hair in the basement bathroom sink, and Emma was fascinated and a little frightened at how completely it changed my face. She yelled something over the hair dryer. I clicked it off.

"What did you say?"

"Do you just love it?"

I looked in the mirror. I'd never been a blonde, and I couldn't help but think of Ethan's new girlfriend. "It's . . . different." I fingered my freshly chopped bangs. "Do you like it?"

"I love it."

I grabbed the scissors. "Want to look like twins?"

She nodded and bounced up and down as I snipped the ends of my hair just above my shoulders, working my way around my head. I collected the hair in a garbage bag. "Want to look exactly alike?"

"Yes!"

I opened the second box of hair color. "We are going to lighten your hair even more to look like mine. I want you to tell me if this burns at all, okay?"

"Burns?"

"Well, sometimes it can just tickle your skin a little, but it shouldn't." I painted her hair with the ammonia-free blond dye.

She sat on the edge of the sink. "Why is it purple? Ow, ow, it's burning my ear!" I swiped her ear with a towel and blew around her hairline.

"Just a few more minutes, okay?"

I washed it out before time was up, and put her in the shower, making sure it was completely rinsed. She was now a true blonde. We looked at ourselves in the mirror. We could have passed for mother and daughter.

"I like it. I look like you," she said.

"And I look like you."

We spent the rest of the day cleaning the cabin. I had our breakfast, lunch, and snacks loaded in the refrigerator in a small cooler.

"Are you sad to leave?" I asked.

"Uh-huh."

"What will you miss the most?"

She thought about this, her lips scrunched, finger tapping her chin. "I'll miss the stars and Fairy Lake."

"Really? That's what I'll miss the most too."

After an early dinner, Emma convinced me to take one last canoe ride. We floated in the water, her feet dangling over the edge of the boat, as I guided us against the current. Emma helped me drag the canoe back toward the shed once we were on shore, our final duty before we left in the morning. The big silver boat bumped over sticks and rocks. Emma struggled to push her slight weight against it, letting out a toot with the force.

"Was that what I think it was?"

She collapsed in a fit of giggles against the canoe, her fingers gripping her belly. Her blond hair swished across her cheeks.

"Don't make me laugh! I can't pull it . . ." I trailed off as she let out another fart and then another, a small butt trumpet propelling us toward the shed. After I caught my breath from laughter, I used my legs to drag the canoe all the way into the open wooden doors, my forearms burning with effort.

"There. Now watch out, okay?" I flipped the boat over, banging a pointed edge against my shin. Intense pain cracked across the front of my leg. I squatted down to inspect my shin. A hard knot bloomed under the thin skin.

Emma crouched beside me and blew on the wound. "Does that hurt? Do you need a Band-Aid?"

"It does hurt," I said. My eyes watered. I ran my fingers over the lump. "It's not bleeding though, so that's good." I shook my leg and finished propping up the canoe so the water could drain. "Hitting your shin is the absolute worst."

"Mama hit me with a stick one time on my shin, and I cried."

I was startled by the admission and stopped rubbing my shin. "Oh, Em, I'm very sorry that happened to you. How did that make you feel?"

"Sad. And mad. I threw the stick back at her, though." She looked around the dusty shed, packed with two more canoes, life jackets, paddles, and various tools. "Once we leave, are we never coming back again?" Her voice trembled.

"Probably not."

"Aw, but maybe we can someday?"

"We'll see." I placed the oars in their hooks. I guided Emma back outside, shut the shed, and wiped the dust from my hands. I hooked an arm around her as the last bit of light drained from the sky. There was a final burst of color—Emma called it her afternoon rainbow—and then day slipped into dusk. I guided her to the base of the stairs, my shin throbbing, when I saw blue lights ricocheting off the cabin.

"What's that light up there?"

Instinctively, I pulled Emma back to the edge of the shed. My heart ratcheted in my chest.

They've found us.

A thousand scenarios danced in front of my eyes, but I only had one decision to make. I dropped down to Emma's level and clutched her shoulders.

"Em, I need you to listen to me, okay?"

"Why are you whispering?"

I reopened the shed as soundlessly as I could. We shuffled against the sandy floor and fumbled in the dark. "I'm going to ask you to do something. It's your bravery test for the day, okay? Kind of like hide-and-seek, except you do *not* come out until I find you."

"I don't want to. It's dark in here."

"I know, but . . ." I peeked outside and saw a flashlight bounce through the front of the cabin windows straight through to the back. "Listen, there are some people at the cabin I need to talk to. But I have to do it alone, okay? It won't take long. And I really, really need you to stay here." I moved her deeper into the shed so she was hidden under the canoe. "And think about all the fun places we're going to go after we leave. I want you to think about those places and count as high as you can. Can you do that for me?"

"I can't count that high!"

"Okay, how about you count to one hundred, but really, really slowly?" I whispered. "And if you get to one hundred, start over."

"But it's too dark in here! I'm scared."

I fished my phone from my back pocket and flipped the flashlight on. "Here, but don't shine this around too much, okay? Just keep it close so you can see. Now, Emma," I gazed into her trusting, gray eyes and kissed the top of her head. "Promise me you will stay here. You have to promise me."

She nodded. "I promise."

"Good girl. You're safe in here, okay? I'll be right back. Start counting."

I shut the shed and slipped the large bolt through the lock. I prayed with every fiber of my being that she would not get scared and pound on the door to be let out.

I tiptoed to the back of the cabin, hugging the rear of the house, and let myself in. I crawled to the front and fingered the curtains apart to peek out the dining room window. There was a lone officer, radioing in something as he rattled my car doors. Locked, thank God. He moved around to the front of the house and knocked.

I had only one shot at this, and I couldn't screw it up. I stood, took the shakiest breath of my life, counted to three, and opened the door.

before

I kept up with the seasons from the car.

Summer was spent with my feet on the dash, the hot glass of the windshield warming my callouses. My father and I would stop to pick flowers or purchase overripe melons at fruit stands. My heels became tough during those unforgiving months, as I waded through waist-high weeds, crossed sizzling pavement, ran over pebbly shores, and plucked splinters from the tough, dirty flesh, while my father negotiated over heirloom tomatoes or farm-fresh corn.

Fall was coffee collars littering the backseat, muffin wrappers caught around seatbelts, thick scarves my father bought at secondhand shops, a litany of pumpkin patches and raked leaves, and boots marred by mud that I'd scrape off with dirty fingernails.

Winter, we would sludge through slushy highways, gray snow spitting onto worn tires. We'd often get caught behind massive semis that skittered left and right on the road, on the verge of toppling. Once, I'd watched a batch of sweaty pigs push against each other, squealing, shitting, and trampling pink heads and thick spines, all of them, as my father explained, trying to save themselves before slaughter.

Spring was bouquets of flowers pressed into back windows, petals crisped, browned, and forgotten by the sun. I begged my father to buy flowers everywhere we went, even though we didn't have a vase. I loved fresh flowers because they were the only good reminder of my mother. She'd had a small flower garden that she'd tended to, and when she was feeling generous, she'd let me water them from her bright pink watering can. She always filled our house with the fruits of her labor, arranging batches of colorful breeds in antique vases.

In the car, once the flowers died, I pressed the dried petals inside my favorite books, sometimes forgetting and opening a novel to have dehydrated petals disintegrate across my thighs.

I learned to sleep better in a car than on a mattress. I concocted stories as families traveled beside us on highways in their cars, vans, and Winnebagos. I wanted to argue with a brother in the backseat, sing songs with a sister, or even comb my fingers through my mother's hair from the back, playing beauty shop and smelling the distinct sweetness of her shampoo on my palms.

These were the staples of childhood. I had lived in a car with my father, listening to old jazz, reading books, and eating out of rumpled fast food bags. I'd spent months wondering if we'd ever find a place that felt like home, brushing my teeth in gas station stalls or at the nicer rest stops. I washed my underwear in bathroom sinks and let them dry on the roof of our car when we parked in the hot sun. I collected workbooks to keep up with schoolwork as we transferred from school to school, with no real attachment to anyone or anything.

Sometimes, I would expect to see my mother—at a gas pump, local market, or random store. Would she still recognize me and realize what she'd done? I wondered if she'd want us back . . . because how could a mother not want her family?

I'd figured out that familial love—something I thought to be unbreakable—was still conditional. Mothers still left. Fathers shut down. Marriages broke apart. Kids suffered. My own mother had walked away. What was more conditional than that?

I'd spent a lot of time on the question of forgiveness. I heard someone say that when it was the right person, forgiveness came easy. But why should I forgive my mother for what she'd done?

These were questions I could never ask my father, as he dripped his sadness all over the road, our car, our crappy rentals, and finally, into the city in Washington he would call home. As we set up our small, modest house with flea market finds and bulky items on lease, I would bring up my mother in conversation, because I was beginning to forget her.

I'd been a bit brash when she left, celebrating like that, making grass angels on our lawn, but she made me so self-conscious and angry. Everything was always about her, when I wanted, needed, it to be all about me. I was the child! It was my only shot at attention.

Now that she was gone, I was free, but my dad wasn't, so I still couldn't express myself. I was in a box, chained to my mother's memory. Because of that, I was learning things about love: its conditions, its fragility. No one ever taught me that there could be a different kind of love, but that's what I was looking for. I wanted to love someone, and I wanted that person to love me back. Not based on how I behaved, what I looked like, or what I had to offer, but because they saw the real me: the girl in the car, the girl who didn't have a mother, the girl who took care of her father when he couldn't take care of himself.

"Hey, Dad! Dad? You home?"

I pushed the door back on its hinges. Every Friday, I drove down from Seattle for the weekend. I brought pepperoni pizza, a six-pack of beer, and an obscure science-fiction movie. When I banged through the screen door, still with a patch of mesh missing in the lower left corner, I was eight again, then ten, then twelve. My teenage years had been a flurry of hormones and disappointment, and I couldn't wait to get away from this small, brown box and out into a world I'd never seen.

"Is that you, sweetheart?"

"No, it's your other daughter."

He emerged from the back in a pressed shirt and slacks. He'd dressed up for me, which tugged at my heart. "Is it Friday already?"

"Can you believe it?" I knew he lived for Fridays. He planned his week around these visits, hiring a housekeeper who lived in the neighborhood, Mrs. Fletcher, to destroy all the evidence of his bachelorhood. I'd seen the trash can full of empty bottles, and the mold she hadn't been able to completely scrub away along the rim of the bathroom sink. She had a crush on my father and cut him a massive discount—she cleaned his entire house every week for only thirty dollars—but he was too aloof to notice. He just thought that's how much it cost to clean houses.

We ate our pizza and drank beer in front of the television. We rarely said much beyond what was happening at school, what friends I'd made, if I'd met a nice boy, what I wanted to do with my life. He took no interest in his own, and when I asked questions about work or his personal life, he always answered with some variation of the same thing.

I was majoring in business, and I couldn't wait to make enough money to support both of us. Being around all that failure, giving up, and giving in as a kid had instilled in me the kind of drive you just couldn't teach.

After our pizza, I peeled the label on my beer. "So, I had a dream last night."

"Oh?" He ripped through another beer, set the bottle with the glass collection at his feet, and burped. "Excuse me. About what?"

"About Elaine."

He turned to me on the sofa, his eyes slightly unfocused. He pressed *pause* on the remote. "What was it about?"

"It was weird. I was watching her sleep. I kept petting her hair and rearranging her covers, like I was the mother. She was young, as young as when she left, and I felt . . . I don't know. I felt calm or something. Maternal. It was like closure."

My father's fingers twitched on the remote. I knew, just when I said it, that I shouldn't have. He'd take the next two weeks to work this dream over in his mind, partly jealous that I'd had it, the rest of him wondering if it meant she was dead because she was now showing up in my dreams.

"Do you ever dream about her?"

He hesitated. "No. I don't."

I knew he wanted to. I knew he slept for almost twelve hours a night so that he could hopefully see his beloved in his dreams.

"Yeah, me either. It was surprising. I just thought I should tell you." I wanted to say more. I wanted to tell him how it felt like I'd watched her sleep for hours, the curve of her body telling its own story with its tiny jerks and rapid-eye movement. I had stared at her and wondered: Did her mother ever do this? Had she ever done this with me? And when had I started to grate on her nerves, like a puppy, enough for her to leave?

"Want to watch the rest of the movie?"

He nodded, but neither of us was paying close attention. The lone thought that tumbled over and over in my head that I could never say out loud and never extinguish, even as a senior in college, was this: *Why wasn't I enough to make her stay?*

after

"Good evening, ma'am. I'm sorry to disturb you, but is this your property?"

"No, sir. It's my ex-boyfriend's property. Is everything okay?"

The officer shifted in his boots and leaned around me. His neck, doused in freckles, angled into the living room. "Are you here alone, ma'am?"

"Yes, I am." The words shook as they left my mouth, and I worked overtime to steady my voice.

He straightened and hooked his thumbs into his belt. "Well, we've gotten two separate calls about a missing child: one spotted at a grocery store in the area, and the other from a man saying he owns this cabin and there was a woman here with a little girl."

He'd done it. The bastard had actually called it in.

It hadn't even been forty-eight hours, and he'd called it in. "I'm sorry, what? Are you serious? A missing *child*?" I channeled every bit of high school drama I could and started laughing. "Oh my God, what a little shit."

"Excuse me, ma'am?"

I placed my hands on my hips. "This is all one giant misunderstanding. We used to share this cabin. My ex and I. I come up here all the time. I still have the keys. See?"

I scooped the set of keys from the kitchen counter and dangled them in front of his face. I dropped them back on the counter and fake pouted. "I needed to get away. I knew he wouldn't be here, so I came. But he showed up anyway. With another *girl*." I widened my eyes. "Naturally, I was irate. He called me crazy, told me to get out of here, which I was just about to do. We both calmed down and started talking. He told me about that missing girl report because of my job—I work with children—so you can imagine all the things I see. He also told me in the same breath to leave or else. He didn't specify what the 'what else' could be, but now I know." I tapped my foot on the carpet and crossed my arms. "I just can't believe he would say such a ridiculous thing to get me out of here. To lie like that. I guess he was desperate." I was talking too much, but I couldn't stop.

"Do you mind if I look around?"

"By all means." I pulled the door all the way open, and the hinges yelped in protest. "I was literally just about to get on the road."

He went from room to room. I prayed there were no lingering stuffed animals or a tiny lost sock crumpled in a corner somewhere. What if he checked the trash cans? The car?

"You keep a pretty tidy place here."

"I didn't want to give him a reason to get angrier than he was."

He looked at me, at my blond hair, short and wavy, with bangs. "Well, the clerk's description of the woman was a brunette."

I fingered my hair. "What does the little girl look like? I'll definitely keep an eye out."

"Brown hair. Five years old. Gray eyes." He looked at the stairs leading upstairs and down. "You don't mind if I just finish going through the home and take a look around the premises?"

I swallowed. "No, of course not."

He went upstairs, then down, and I counted the seconds in my head. I was dying to get to Emma, to let her out of that shed, to get the hell out of here. I could just make out the edge of the shed from the back window. What if she started screaming when she heard voices out there?

He circled back to the living room and jiggled the patio lock.

"Here, let me get that for you."

His radio squawked, and he hit the button. "Immediate backup requested at 4426 McCreary Lane. Possible domestic. Are you in range, over?"

"Copy that. On my way."

He turned back to me and pointed the end of his flashlight, unlit, toward me. "You stay out of places that aren't yours, you hear?"

"Yes, sir. Won't ever happen again."

He meandered back to the front of the house and out the front door, studying my car again, his eyes lingering on the license plate. I'd have to change it. Where would I change it? He said something into his radio, and I watched as he pulled out of the gravel drive and rolled safely toward the main road.

When he was gone, I sprinted out the back door and down to the shed, slipping the bolt off the lock with shaking fingers. I blasted into the darkness. "Emma, are you okay?"

She was crouched in a tiny ball in the corner, still counting, the phone flashlight in a tight stream beside her. "Can I come out now?" She uncurled. "Is it safe?"

I pulled her into a hug. "I am so, so sorry about that.

There was someone here I didn't know, and I just wanted you to be safe. Are you okay?"

"I'm okay."

"Let's get you out of here." I picked her up and folded her trusting body against my chest.

"Your heart is beating so fast."

"Is it?" I steadied my voice and carried her up the backyard to the top of the stairs. I smothered her hair with kisses and murmured my apologies. I relocked every door, wiped down every surface, took her to the bathroom, and cautiously walked her to the car.

"I thought we were going to leave in the morning?"

"Well, you know what? I thought it would be fun to do a little night drive instead. So we can see the stars and the moon. How about that?" The adrenaline drenched my body like the strongest caffeine. I fastened her in her car seat and reversed down the drive. We were on the main road in minutes.

"Can you put the radio on?"

I found a suitable station and watched her mouth the words to a pop song from the back, shaking her little fingers and clapping off beat. Despite my nerves, I smiled and sang with her, but all I could think about was the officer.

He'd seen me. He'd seen my car. He'd seen my license plate.

Now, it was a hunt for us both.

I gripped the wheel, the radio on something low and classical. Emma hummed in the background, lost in play. I'd driven straight through the night, one thought plaguing me with every mile: *Ethan turned me in.* He hadn't waited the forty-eight hours like he'd promised. He hadn't kept his word.

The ramifications slashed my conscience and tethered every breath. This wasn't make-believe; it was a child, and there was more at stake than a breakup, a business, or defaulting on a mortgage. I cleared my throat and reached for my water. I struggled with the bottle top, not wanting to remove my other hand from the steering wheel. I watched the speedometer, unwilling to get caught for any reason, especially speeding.

I'd been checking the Montana news updates obsessively since we'd left. Had the cashier's threat led to another lead? Had the officer reported my car?

"Which place are we going to again?"

"Valentine, Nebraska." Emma had chosen Valentine for its name, and I'd chosen it for its obscurity. With a population of 2,700, I hoped we were relatively safe from almost three-week-old Washington news.

"I'm excited." She flipped her floppy puppy over in her hands. "I know Pinky is excited."

"Pinky? Is that what you decided to name him? I like that." I watched my speed, my foot smashed hard on the pedal. I was seven miles per hour above the speed limit and eased up almost too much, looking for unmarked police cars or cruisers parked between highway bushes. "Do you have a real puppy at home? I forgot to ask."

"My dad is 'llergic."

"Allergic?"

"To the spit."

She started barking at her puppy, and the two of them were off on an imaginary tangent.

I turned the music higher and focused on the road. According to the map, we had three hours to go before our first destination. My back hurt. I was exhausted. We'd stopped three times, and she was wiggling again in the back. "Do you need to pee?"

She nodded. We pulled over at the next rest area and my body struggled to unfold from the driver's seat. I waited outside of the stall while she peed, looking at my wrecked complexion. I fixed my bangs and stared at my lopsided bob. My phone dinged. I hoped it wasn't a work emergency, or my father. I pulled up the new email, a Google alert: *Possible Sighting of Missing Washington Girl Rocks Four Corners*

"Oh my God."

"What?" Emma flushed and came out to wash her hands.

I read the short update hurriedly, soaking in every detail. The cashier's news was official. They did not have the make or model of my car (yet), but authorities were still scoping out the area in hopes of validating the claim.

Would the cop be able to track me from Four Corners to Bozeman to Valentine? We both had different hair now—authorities were looking for two brunettes—and that would help. But I had to think of something to buy us more time.

"Nothing, honey. Ready?"

"Don't you need to pee too?"

I shook my head and hurried her back to the car. Only a few hours and we'd be in Nebraska. We'd be safe.

The keys to the cottage were left for us in the mailbox, a lucky arrangement I was thankful for in these small parts. I'd found an Airbnb that required no human contact, just keys in a box. We stayed in for an entire week, resting, eating, and keeping a low profile. I kept tabs on what was happening, if any of the leads had turned into anything substantial. They hadn't.

After the dust had settled, we ventured out and drove

to Main Street, which was nothing more than a block of shops and a diner. I was confident with Emma's new haircut, floppy hat, and summer tan that no one would recognize us. Together, we looked like a family. The bell tinkled above the door as we stepped inside. Dirty linoleum and the smell of bacon and eggs drenched the booths.

"Just anywhere, hon," a plump waitress said. She had a pencil tucked in the waist of her apron. She worked a dirty white rag across the surface of a table by the window. I chose a booth near the back, and she was over in moments, offering us menus and flipping over a mug on the table. "Coffee?"

"Yes, please." The light brown water sloshed around in my cup. I shifted in the ripped booth, the leather sticking to the backs of my thighs.

"Doesn't that smell good?"

"Mmmhmm," Emma said, busy coloring the children's menu with the three peeling, stubby crayons left in a cup on the table.

"Em, do you know what today is?"

"No. What?"

"Today is the Fourth of July. Independence Day. Do you know what that means?"

She tapped her crayon against her head. "Hmm. I'm not sure. What?"

"It means that a really, really long time ago on this day in 1776, we adopted the Declaration of Independence. It's when we officially became the United States of America and weren't part of the British Empire anymore."

"That sounds like fun. Are we a part of that too?"

"Yes, we are." I laughed. "And it is fun, because there are usually parades, barbecues, and fireworks."

She looked up. "Is there going to be fireworks? Can we go?"

"Sure, why not?" I'd already checked to see if there was a fireworks celebration and figured we could blend in with the sea of people to enjoy one homegrown holiday in a small town. She deserved that.

"And I'll get to see real live fireworks?"

"You will."

"Yippee!" She finished her first picture. "This is for you. Do you like it?"

"It's beautiful." She'd drawn two stick figures with yellow hair, holding hands.

"It's me and you."

"Oh, Em, I'll keep it forever. Thank you." I cleared the emotion from my voice, folded the picture, and tucked it into my purse. "What do you think you want? Pancakes? Eggs? Bacon? Waffles?"

"Waffles! And bacon!" Emma exclaimed, while scribbling outside the lines of her next picture. "What's bacon made from?"

"What do you think bacon is made from?"

"Is it from a cow?"

"No."

"A chicken?"

"It's actually from a pig."

"Like a *real* pig?"

"Yep."

"Like a real pig that goes oink oink?"

"Yes, ma'am. Just like that."

She thought about it, her crayon raised. "Well, I love bacon so much, I just want to eat a pig's whole face."

"Well, that might be kind of hard on your tummy."

She giggled. "Are you going to get bacon too?"

"I'm not sure yet." I was suddenly starving.

"Are you ready?" The waitress walked over and looked back and forth between us. "You two from around here?"

"No, just passing through."

"You should come to the square tonight. Going to be plenty of fun for the little ones."

"We were planning on it. Thank you."

She scribbled our orders and refilled my coffee.

"Are we still going to the waterfall after this?" Emma asked.

"Yep. That's why we need to eat up, okay?"

I'd gotten Emma one pair of tennis shoes, which were purple and a size 11. I hoped they'd hold up if there were slippery rocks to climb. It was unseasonably hot for the beginning of July, and I already had our water, sunscreen, and snacks packed in a cooler in the car.

We ate in comfortable silence, the diner filling with regulars, happy, familiar conversation passing from booth to booth. I ate all of my eggs, toast with honey and butter, fried potatoes, and two pieces of crispy bacon. Emma ate half of her waffle and offered me the rest. I took a bite, diving into the sickly sweet batter. I left the waitress a big tip and slugged back my fourth cup of coffee before we headed out to Snake River Falls.

"Are there going to be real snakes there?" Emma asked, as I buckled her in.

"No, I don't think so. That's just what it's called."

"But there could be snakes?"

"Well, we're going to be outside, so I guess there could be. Because that's where snakes live. But you don't need to worry about them."

"But they scare me."

"I know they do, but most people are afraid of snakes. And you know what?"

"What?"

"Snakes are actually scared of you because you're so much bigger than they are."

"But they're so fast. And they have those tiny, mean teeth, like dolphins."

"Do dolphins have tiny teeth?"

"Yes, they're like this little"—she smushed her index and thumb together—"but they're like super-sharp and can tear through human flesh and things."

"Well, I don't think we have to worry about any dolphins."

"But the snakes, we do."

"How about this: I'll keep my eye out for snakes, and you just focus on the waterfall. Deal?"

"Deal."

A short ride later, we were at the mouth of the falls, parking the car and making sure we had everything we needed before heading up. Minivans lined the lot, some with patriotic stickers. I left the cooler, uncertain how far we'd have to climb. I grabbed Emma's hand and off we went, exploring nature in the heartland of Nebraska.

That night, we were sleepy from sun and exercise. The waterfall was exceptional. I'd convinced Emma to wade near it with me, both of us splashing in the cold water and drying ourselves on a nearby rock. We ate our sandwiches by the lake, and then went back to the Airbnb, rummaging for something patriotic to wear so we'd blend in.

We walked to the town square and stood on a street corner as a small parade marched by. A high school band, decked out in red, white, and blue uniforms, blasted off-key tunes. There were a few baton twirlers, which captivated Emma. I hoisted her onto my shoulders, and she screamed and clapped with the commotion.

"Where are the fireworks?"

"Not until dark. I thought we might get ice cream

first?" I lowered her to the ground and we walked to a small cart by the square. I got us each a scoop of strawberry on a sugar cone. We had to eat fast from the heat, as we moved with the throngs of townspeople toward the open lawn.

I'd brought an extra blanket from the house, and I spread it out, while Emma stood and stared directly into the sky.

After the sun set, bursts of color sprayed into the night, and Emma reached her hands up as though she could catch them, like rain. She clapped as every new firework went off.

A little girl sitting next to us offered her a sparkler. Emma turned to me, a question in her eyes, and I let her take it, as the small stick sizzled and lit her entire face. She danced around with the girl, as her parents watched and laughed, and I relaxed back in the lush grass of the small town square.

Out of the corner of my eye, I felt someone watching us. I turned to see the waitress from the diner staring and whispering something to a man beside her. I lifted my hand in a wave and she waved back, but she wasn't smiling. I told myself I was being paranoid; that her whispers had nothing to do with us. They couldn't.

"Watch, Sarah. It's like a sparkly monster!" Emma wagged her stick in the air in giant, cursive loops until all the sparklers were gone and she was begging for more. She climbed into my lap as the fireworks continued. The sky exploded in vivid colors, each one louder and more elaborate than the last. The sparks showered over us, filtering through wispy clouds and disappearing in shapeless plumes of smoke. Emma cheered, and I pulled her closer, her sweaty limbs stuck to mine.

I glanced to the left again, but the couple was gone. I scanned the grounds but didn't see them. I ignored the prick of worry, pulled Emma closer, and enjoyed the rest of the night.

We were on the road before sunrise. Emma was still asleep, her lips chapped from too much sun. I glanced at my phone and noticed several new texts. I needed to call Brad.

It had been thirty days since I'd taken Emma from the woods. Only thirty days and yet . . . *thirty whole days*. I thought of my own path to get here. Would I be able to find me if I were a detective? Would I be able to connect the dots from her to me?

I checked the time. It was early, but I knew Brad would be up, drinking his espresso and trying not to freak the fuck out that the boss was still out of the office. I slipped in my earbuds and cleared my throat as I dialed.

"Could it be?" Brad gasped as his greeting. "You're actually calling instead of emailing?"

"Very funny. Hi." I concentrated on using a soothing voice, flicking my eyes from the road to the mirror, not wanting to wake her.

"I'm sure you are calling to tell me you're two seconds away from the office, right? Because it's been a *month* since we've seen your pretty face. Which means something has to be going on beyond spending fake time with your dad. Are we folding? Did you sell? Did something happen? Talk! Where are you?"

I'd forgotten how rapid-fire Brad could be, how intense. Spending the last month with a child had left me drastically out of practice for his sharp edges and snarky tone.

"I've been handling business. As you know. From my computer. Which happens to be one of the perks of living in today's world."

"Working from your computer is not work. That's not the nature of how we do business."

"Email is how everyone does business."

"No, travel is how you do business. You're the face of this business, and we need you."

"Look, not everything is about the company. I've been dealing with . . . some personal issues. I needed time away."

"You mean the flu you faked or the family trip to see your dad you lied to your whole team about? It's not like you to lie."

It is now, I thought. I prayed they had not been following Emma's case; that they wouldn't put two and two together to realize the "spotted" brunette was me. "I thought you guys might not be able to understand. I went to Ethan's—which I'm sure Madison told you about by now—and then he showed up. With a girl."

Brad went silent.

"Hello? You still there?"

"Yes, I'm here." His tone had softened. I knew if the love of his life showed up with his new lover at his ex-lover's place, he'd have a heart attack.

"So, as you can imagine, it was mortifying. I can't even go into it. Long story short, he left, and then he came back, and we hashed it out."

"Well, that's good though, right? Closure and all that?"

"Kind of. He told me he'd . . . that he'd actually bought a ring. That he was going to propose."

"What? When?"

Getting engaged had been a topic of debate with my team. I'd never told them I'd found the box—it was too embarrassing. "He got it about seven months into our relationship. And then he just never gave it to me."

Brad exhaled. "I mean . . . wow. Did he say why?"

"He said he just changed his mind." My voice broke when I said it, which angered me. I was stronger than this. I had to get over it. *He'd turned me in.* As far as I was concerned, he no longer existed. I cleared my throat, checked Emma and my speed.

"Holy balls," Brad whispered. "I'm really sorry, Sarah. That's a lot to absorb. I don't even know what to say."

"I left after he did, and I've just been driving cross-country ever since. I'm . . ." I tried to think of something that would satisfy my team, that would allow me to just abandon everything we'd worked so hard on and be gone for as long as I needed to.

"Got any kits with you? You could make some pit stops along the—"

"Really?"

"Okay, okay. It's fine. Everything's fine. Are you on your way back?"

"Not yet. I've decided something." I felt a plan hatching.

"Please tell me you're not selling." Brad had sent me five emails over the last week about being bought out and one a few days ago that had given me pause. There was a huge toy company in California who wanted to absorb us. It was an ungodly amount of money—enough to sail through life without ever thinking about making ends meet again.

"Are you talking about the offer from Hal?" Even as I said it, I had to admit the appeal was there. I'd been working so hard for so long. I loved my job. But how did I ever go back to it after this?

"Yes. That one. It's tempting, right?"

"It is. And I'm considering it."

"That was a test, dammit. I didn't think you'd say you were actually considering it."

"I didn't say I'm doing it. But I am considering it. For all of us. It would be complete financial freedom. For you, Madison, and Travis. I'd make sure of it. I'll talk to Hal and find out the bottom line."

"So what are you doing now, then? Why aren't you back?"

"I'm going to find my mother." The lie slipped from my lips in an easy rush.

"You're what now? Your mother? Seriously? Do you even know where she is?"

"Not exactly. But I have an idea."

Brad slurped at his espresso and coughed. "So, this has been an all-around total life-changing month for you, then."

"Something like that."

"Does your dad know?"

"Not yet."

"Look." He exhaled hard into the phone. "You do what you've gotta do. I've got it all under control. Take some time. Not too much time, because we still need you."

"Thanks."

"And let me know when you talk to Hal. In fact," he whistled, "I am not kidding when I say I just got his final offer. Right this second." He was quiet as he read through the details. "We have forty-eight hours to respond."

It was my second forty-eight-hour ultimatum, though this one could provide freedom, not steal it. "What does it say?"

"You know what? I'm going to send this over. Read it when you're not driving. Because you might crash."

"That much?"

"More." His fingers pecked on the keys. "There. Sent. Okay, where were we?"

"You were giving me a guilt trip about not being in the office, though I've never been out of the office, except for work."

"I know. But things just aren't the same without you."

"They're probably better."

"Nice try." He cleared his throat. "So . . . how much time do you need, do you think?"

"Brad."

"What? I need a time frame. You know that. I work better with structure in place. Are you thinking a few weeks? Another month? Until you find your mom? Indefinitely?"

The word *indefinitely* hung in the air, thick with insinuation. Could I just walk away from my business indefinitely? The perfect life I'd worked so hard to build? The life I thought I'd always wanted? A month without my city and my business, in the situation I was in, and that version seemed like another, less important life.

"Let's not get dramatic. No one is going anywhere indefinitely. I'll continue to take care of our accounts. And I promise to check in more on the phone. And of course, if there are any emergencies—"

"I've got it covered. Everything's good here."

"I really do appreciate it."

"Please be safe. And I'm sorry about Ethan, Sarah. I'm just surprised. We all loved him."

"I know you did. Thanks. But it's okay. The door is finally closed." I put on my blinker and changed lanes. "I should go. I don't need to talk and drive when I have no idea where the fuck I am. Love you."

"Love you more. And don't get kidnapped or chopped up and buried in someone's backyard or anything. You know how those isolated areas are."

I bristled at the word *kidnapped* but laughed. "How do you know I'm somewhere rural?"

"If you're driving cross-country, you're rural, sweetie."

"Yeah, yeah. I'll try not to get killed. You know there's nothing scarier than a hillbilly."

"Girl, don't I know it. Try dating one."

"Oh, that's right." I laughed. "What was that guy's name? Paul? Patrick?"

"Try Pervis. His name was actually *Pervis*. He lived with his mother in their basement. I'm pretty sure he made skin jackets in his free time."

"Gross."

"Okay, girl. Call me tomorrow."

"I will. I promise."

We hung up. The weight of work lifted from my shoulders. Business was safe. Relationships were restored. Bills were still getting paid. My team was still on board.

It was my turn to figure out what I was doing, where I was taking Emma, and just how long I could keep up this charade.

after

At a gas stop, I took Emma in the stall to pee. I laid the paper on the seat and shut the door for her, asking every few seconds if she was okay.

"It's stuck in traffic."

This was her running joke when it took her twenty minutes to go to the bathroom. I laughed and told her to take her time, as I washed my hands and splashed my face, startled once again by the blond version of myself in the mirror. Did I look better or worse? I thought about the quiz I'd taken on Facebook that said I looked like Anne Hathaway. Who would be my look-alike now? I checked my phone, typing in Emma's name, and waited for any updates to register. And there it was: the same update with a different title. I swallowed as I read the headline.

Missing Girl Spotted in Montana

Emma flushed and exited, pulling her skirt out of her tights. "That bathroom's stinky. Shoo-wee."

I smiled absently as she moved to wash her hands. I scoured the article as fast as I could, absorbing any new key words: anonymous caller. Spotted in Bozeman. Emma with a slim brunette in an SUV. We were far from Bozeman, but it didn't matter now. They had to know I was heading east. I'd had every intention of making it to Connecticut, but I needed some place larger, some place I was familiar with, some place where we'd blend in with millions of people who were too absorbed in their own lives to pay any attention to two blondes in a Tahoe.

I checked my directions on my phone and mapped how long it would take.

"How would you like to go somewhere super-exciting? Somewhere we didn't mark on the map?"

She jumped up and down. "Are there toys there?"

"Toys? There are so many toys you won't even know what to do."

"Are there parks?"

"Hundreds."

"Playgrounds?"

"A million."

She squealed and bounced out to the car. "I want to go now! Can we go now?"

I nodded as we situated ourselves back into the car, and I deviated from our original plan.

That afternoon, I kept my eye out for healthy lunch options. We'd been existing on diner food and processed snacks. We both needed something substantial. We'd played the alphabet game four times, and I'd finally given in to her using the iPad.

My cell rang. It was a number I recognized, a number I'd been avoiding until now.

"This is Sarah." I made my voice as professional as possible, all of my fears and questions abandoned as curiosity took over.

"Sarah? Hey, finally. It's Hal. Hal Pierce."

"Hey, Hal. I'm so sorry I haven't gotten back to you."

"No, no. It's fine, really. I'm just glad I got you. So, I'll get right to it."

"Shoot."

"I'm assuming you received our latest proposal?"

After we hung up, I'd looked at Hal's final offer at a rest stop, and triple-checked the number of zeros. I'd read over the terms of the deal—all favorable—and sent it straight to my lawyer. It was the best offer I'd ever get, and we both knew it. In a way, it was now or never. Sell my life's work, or continue to play the game and hope not to become irrelevant in the sea of new businesses.

"I have."

He chuckled. "Hard to get. I like it. I have to say, Sarah, we've never made an offer this substantial, but that's how much we believe in your business. We want to get these kits into every school and home in America."

"Just America?"

"No, of course not just in America, but it's the best place to start. I know your international work is very important to you, and we understand that. We want to continue all the good work you've done and maximize our global reach after our domestic one is optimized."

I glanced in the rearview. A police car was hovering two cars back. A ripple of fear clawed at my spine. I cleared my throat. "You know, Hal, I am beyond flattered. And I appreciate it so much, but I'm just not sure it's the best time to sell. I thought I made that pretty clear."

"I know. And I understand. I do. But what we're offering doesn't mean you have to just hand everything over and walk. We can have a partnership. You can even drive the ship if you want. But, if I've learned anything in business, it's that your first baby isn't your last. TACK is amazing, revolutionary even. But don't you want to know what's next?"

"Next?"

"Yes, next. Your next venture. With a mind like yours, this won't be your only business."

My first business coach told me the same thing. *Don't settle for your first business idea because it's never your last.* "Honestly, I hadn't thought about it."

"Well, you should. You're young. This is only the beginning of your career. And what we're offering can literally fund your next venture. Entirely. You can even take the same team with you, if that's what you choose. Nothing has to change."

Except everything. It seemed Hal had all the answers. But the betrayal my team would feel . . . the responsibility I had to all of those children. How did I just give that all up for a check with seven zeros? I glanced at Emma in the backseat and thought: for her. Money was the only way I could disappear with Emma. Not some money. *Enough* money, where we could lay low for years if we had to, only reemerging when we were certain we would never be found. When going on worldly travels would result in me having spontaneously "adopted" an older child, and then I could introduce Emma to the people in my life as my daughter. Would anyone believe me?

The police car I'd been tracking suddenly darted into the left lane and flicked on its siren, a blue wash of lights blinding this late in the afternoon. Hal breathed into my ear, a patient predator. Choices bounced around my brain. At once, the police car shot back into the right lane and pulled within inches of my trunk, its aggressive signal to pull over. I checked my speed and glanced to see that Emma's headphones were still on.

"Hal? Hal, I'm so sorry, but I'm going to have to call you right back." I ripped off the earbuds and dropped my cell on the passenger seat. Every fear I'd ever had bumped up against some version of the truth I would need to concoct. All of the options ran in one large liar's list, a dump of information I couldn't quite sift through. The steering wheel jerked to the right, startling Emma, as the tires skidded onto a thin expanse of grass. The metal of the car shook with the close proximity to the highway.

Emma looked up. "Why are we stopping?" she yelled over the sound of her iPad. She removed one of her headphones.

"Hey, honey. You just keep listening to your show, okay? We're just stopping to talk to this man for a second."

She nodded and let her large headphones snap back over her small ears. After an interminable wait, a large officer loped to my window. Brown slacks tucked into muddy black boots kicked dust into tiny clouds. A round belly strained against a police uniform top. A gun rested at his bulging hip. I closed my eyes and took a deep, steadying breath.

A set of knuckles landed on my window before I could open my eyes, tapping hard enough to shatter glass. I lowered my window, urging the automatic system to work faster. The officer looked directly past me and found Emma in the back. He scanned the scene: child in a car seat, watching a show, the various contents of our road trip strewn across the seats like a shaken-out trash bag. Emma, as oblivious as could be, didn't feel the intense gaze of a stranger pressing into her.

Two blue eyes pushed far back into a doughy face came even with the open window and finally locked somewhere above my forehead. One of his hands rested on the roof. The whir of cars sped by dangerously close to his back, and I feared someone who might be texting and driving could crash into his mammoth frame and spit him out, chewed and torn, a hundred feet from here. The officer's breath smelled like tobacco and coffee. A violent red wart perched on the side of his nose.

"Know why I pulled you over?"

He chewed over his syllables, and I tried to slow my thoughts to match his casual pace and Midwest accent. "No, sir. I wasn't speeding, was I?"

He stood and sniffed. "License and registration, please." I fished in my glove compartment for the proper papers, glad I hadn't swapped out my license plate with something that wouldn't register in the system. I wormed my license out of my wallet and handed it to him.

He stared down at the license and back at me. "Different."

"Excuse me?"

"Your hair. Different."

I smoothed a piece behind my ear. "Yep."

"Be right back."

I watched him take his time as he sauntered to his car, pushing through wayward sticks and bunches of gravel. The weight of his lower half groaned as he sat in the driver's seat and entered my information into his special computer. Luckily, I'd never had so much as a speeding ticket or traffic violation in my entire life. But what if that officer in Montana had made my license plate? What if word of the two blondes had traveled to these parts? What if everything I'd done was about to come to a startling conclusion and Emma was ripped away? I literally couldn't bear the thought of her being taken from me.

In minutes, he was back at the window and handed me my papers. "Where you headed?"

"Chicago. Visiting my folks."

He sucked his teeth. "Quite a drive from Portland with a little one."

"She's used to it. Loves road trips. So, may I ask why I was pulled over?"

"Taillight is out. Right rear. Gonna need to get that fixed before you do any night driving."

The relief filled my entire body until it felt like I might float away. "What?"

"Taillight. Right rear."

"But I just had a tune-up."

"Nah. They gyp you. Especially women."

I ignored the slightly chauvinistic comment and feigned humility. "Well, thanks so much for letting me know. I'll get it fixed right away. So sorry about that."

He nodded and glanced to the back again. "Those things sure do keep 'em quiet, huh?"

"I'm sorry?"

"The iPads. Screens. Keeps 'em entertained."

"Oh, yes. They do. It's the only way to make it through a road trip in one piece." My attempt at humor fell flat, and he stood to his full height and arched his back in the same way I'd seen very pregnant women do a hundred times in my life.

"You two have a good day now. Be safe."

"Thanks, Officer. You too." I watched him walk back to his car and let out a shaky, guarded breath. My fingers ached on the gearshift. The dash swam in front of me. I waited until he peeled back into traffic and then followed, gunning the engine to navigate back onto the highway.

All of the mistakes I'd made gathered in a sloppy bundle: the red dress, the red bow, the hotel, all of the store runs, the public outings in small towns, Ethan, the cashier, the cop at the cabin, the license plate, the car, the stops, the fireworks, the waitress, the paper trail of receipts, and the two of us, heading across the country, east.

Emma had become too important to me to be so careless. We were too far in to climb our way out. I only cared about what happened to us now; the us that had formed in the last month and transformed everything I knew about myself into someone else.

It was too late to pretend we were ever going back. Something had been decided on that phone call with Brad, with Hal, and here, with this officer, who had taken a singular look at my life and tried to make sense of a two-minute scene in his day. To him, I was a mother driving her daughter to see her grandparents in Illinois. If he looked a little closer, he could have seen the truth. How our features didn't quite add up; how our car supplies suggested too much time on the road. How the descriptions of the vehicle, the woman, and the missing girl matched us here, on this trajectory from west to east.

The miles fell away as the thoughts plagued me. That officer could still wake in the dead of night, in an attempt to scratch an itch, when he realized the real reason that child's face looked so damn familiar. Because she was someone else too.

But by then we'd be too far. If I had to ditch my car and get another, I'd do it. If I had to disappear to the other side of the country with lies in my heart, fine. Whatever it took to get us out of the public eye in these small, nondescript, but highly observant towns. I wanted a new, more anonymous reality. No more clumsy attempts to hide out. No more sneaking in and out of hotels and rentals. We had to shrug on our new identities like familiar overcoats and *believe* in who we were becoming. Emma was no longer the girl in the red dress with the red bow. She was the blonde in a jumper with a round belly and stories from the road. I was the woman who'd changed her and given her another choice.

I knew, from my own past, that if I'd been offered a

hand in the woods—to stay put or to take a new, uncertain path—I would have run. Because girls like us didn't have much to lose. Emma had a whole world to gain, and I wanted to be the one to give it to her. I wanted to give her a second chance at a life I wanted to live.

after

We bumped along I-90 East. Traffic was thick as we crossed into the city, slowing almost to a crawl as the "L" rocketed past us—the blue line, if I remembered correctly. We'd stopped on the outskirts of town to get a bulb for my taillight, and I'd looked up a video on how to install it myself. As long as I didn't speed, there should be no reason to be pulled over, especially not here.

"See that Emma? That's called the L train."

"Why is it called the L? Is it like the letter *L*?"

"Yes, it is like the letter *L*."

"Maybe because it's really l-l-loud?"

I laughed. "That would make sense, wouldn't it?" I switched lanes. "It's actually short for the word *elevated*, which sounds like the letter *L*. Do you know what *elevated* means?"

Emma stabbed the air with her index finger. "Like up?"

"That's right. It's aboveground. Most of the trains run on top of the ground here instead of underneath the ground. Isn't that cool?"

I pointed out the skyline. The buildings rose up and down in a straight line like uneven Legos, black and reflective. I missed the dissected view of Portland mountains, how they outlined the buildings but never detracted from them, how they were an enhancement to all the shops and people happily meandering about. Here, it was just rows and rows of buildings clustered in a neat little grid.

I'd checked the temperature on the way into Chicago. They were in the middle of a cool week—a mere sixty-five degrees—which was a welcome reprieve from the recent summer humidity. I realized I had no appropriate clothes for cooler weather, other than a few pairs of leggings and cardigans.

We eased forward, closer to downtown. We were going to stay at the Sofitel, which was right in the thick of it, just off the edge of the famed Magnificent Mile. I'd stayed there once with Lisa and had almost died from happiness. It was quiet and walkable to much of the city. The valet service would be an expensive nightmare, but I didn't care. It was time to relax in a bit of luxury.

We'd have to go shopping—maybe on Michigan Avenue—or perhaps even to that horrible American Girl place Lisa had dragged me to on our last girls' weekend so she could buy overpriced dolls for her daughter.

My gut clenched thinking of Lisa. I'd communicated with her via text only, telling her I was busy with work. She was used to my insane travel schedule. We often went weeks without speaking. I could have concocted the same story about finding my mother, but I knew if she heard my voice, she'd figure something out, and I wasn't ready to blatantly lie to my best friend.

I pointed out the Willis Tower—I still thought of it as the Sears—and the John Hancock Building. I told Emma about Millennium Park, the new Maggie Daley Park, and the outdoor ice rink. Chicago was one of my favorite target markets for TACK. I'd spent the last few years here on business trips, and I never tired of the city.

"Can we go to that park? Can we go there now? Please?"

The thought of finding parking and not losing her in the sea of children and props made me nervous. Here, I'd have to make sure she held my hand and looked both ways before crossing the street.

This child had been in the car more the last month than she'd probably ever been in her entire life. I felt guilty. She needed to run, jump, stretch her limbs, study the skyline, and think of nothing but being a child and playing with other children.

"You know what? Sure. Why not?"

I knew how to get downtown, but I had no clue where to park. As we inched along with the late afternoon traffic, I let myself relax into the anonymity of all of these faceless people.

We found parking five blocks away for an exorbitant hourly rate, and I pulled a sweater from her bag and helped her shrug it on. I was kicking myself for not having one with a hood, but she insisted she was fine.

"Why is it chilly here when it's summer?"

I took her hand as we began walking toward the lake, the wind biting into our cheeks and ruffling our hair. "Chicago sometimes gets really cool weather out of nowhere."

"It's so windy," she said, and I had to lean down to hear her soft voice over all the noise. Her breath smelled like apples—she'd been obsessed with saying, "Smell my breath!" lately after she ate anything—and I nodded at her observation.

"Chicago gets very windy. Do you know why it's called the Windy City?"

"Because it's windy?"

"That's what I thought too! But it's actually because Chicago was famous for some of the bad people who used to live here. They blew a lot of hot air from their mouths, which means—"

"How do you blow hot air?" She exhaled. "My breath isn't hot."

"It's just an expression, like 'it's raining cats and dogs.'"

"But it doesn't rain cats and dogs."

"I know! And that's like these bad people. They told a lot of lies, and the city's nickname just kind of stuck."

"Do they get tornadoes here?"

"Not in the city. There are too many buildings."

"What about earthquakes?"

"Not that I know of." I ruffled the top of her hair, hoping to ease her mind.

We came to Michigan Avenue, and I smiled. It felt good to be in a city again and out of the sticks. I reveled in the chatter of passersby, in the hiss of buses and cabs weaving in and out of traffic.

We waited to cross and then fell into step with all the locals and tourists. I could see the giant silver bean gleaming a hundred feet away, and I pointed it out to her.

"Is that a real bean? Can you eat it?"

"We could try!" I said, and we jogged toward it, my hand glued to hers. *I will not lose her.*

Emma pushed through the small gaggle of children to stand in front of the sculpture, her fingers instantly abandoning mine. I tried to stay calm, to keep sight of her as she stared up at her own reflection in the enormous metal exterior. She pressed her palms to it, as though she were going to give it a hug.

"You try, Sarah!"

I joined her and extended my arms against the shiny surface. Our magnified reflections bounced and curved in the afternoon light.

"We're giants!" she screamed.

We traipsed toward Maggie Daley Park, stepping onto a curvy bridge that twisted over the street.

"This looks like a snake, Sarah. Look!" She ran ahead and hoisted herself up the side of the walkway. Cars zipped below. I placed my hands on her hips and soaked in the scaly metal beast dissecting the park from downtown.

"Do you see the lake over there? That's Lake Michigan." Straight ahead, off the bridge and across Lakeshore Drive, the twinkling teal water jerked with hundreds of boats and passengers all fighting for summer space.

"The park! There it is!" Emma took off running. I trotted behind her as we arced around the last few feet of the walkway and spilled onto the perimeter of the park.

Fake boats, cargo nets, ladders, oversized swings, bridges, winding gardens, and massive steel slides huddled in their own contained cocoon against the city skyline. An ice ribbon snaked around a segment of the park; children squealed, shouted, and climbed on wooden towers joined by a rope bridge. Colorful rubber matting gave beneath our shoes like a sponge. Everywhere I looked, I could see the tinkling glass and various mid- and high-level skyscrapers erected around us.

"Holy moly," Emma exclaimed. Her body tensed, preparing to run, but I caught her by the shoulders.

"Emma, you have to stay where I can see you, okay? It would be very easy for you to get lost here."

She nodded, her mind already on the man-made paradise that awaited her.

"Can I do the slides?"

I'd never seen Emma so excited. I nodded and followed her up a tiny hill, elbowing my way past a small child to hop on the slide next to hers. We raced each other down, and I kept pace with her, jogging, climbing, and playing until beads of sweat erupted at my hairline. She begged to take her sweater off, but I said no.

Kids were running everywhere, frantic parents trying

to keep step, to not lose sight, to just *hold on*. In my bag, my phone vibrated. I made sure to keep my eyes on Emma and grabbed it, noticing my dad's number. My father never called during the day—what if something had happened? "Hello?"

"Sarah. Sarah, is that you?"

I moved forward to keep up with Emma. "Of course it's me, Dad. Is everything okay?"

"It's loud. Where are you?"

This was just like my father to call me for something and then get caught up in the minutiae. He had the attention span of a fly. "I'm . . . I'm at a school playground. Research for my next kit. What's going on?"

"Well, I have some news I need to share with you. It's about your mother."

I felt as though I'd been punched. He had not said "your mother" in years. Had I somehow willed my mother into existence by making up a story of looking for her? I turned my back—it was only for a moment—to register what he was saying. It was three seconds, tops, but when I turned back around, realizing my mistake, I'd lost sight of her. I dropped the phone, my heart seizing. Should I call her name? Did that expose me? I panned my eyes—left to right, right to left—but I couldn't see her. *No. No, no, no.* I picked up the phone. "Dad, let me call you back."

I hung up and began racing toward the drawbridge, doubling back to where we'd last been. The hysteria bubbled and swirled. I wanted to laugh at the irony and cry from fear. This couldn't be happening. Would she run away? The thought was as devastating as being forced to give her up. After all this time, did she want to get *away* from me?

I made continuous circles, looking for her cropped hair, her pink sweater, her tight red pants, her ankle boots that were just a little too big. Her name was in my throat, fighting a desperate bid to keep my mouth shut—but I couldn't. This was too much; it would be too much if I lost her.

I gathered all the air in my belly and swallowed the fear clogging my throat. I opened my mouth and screamed her name as loud as I could. I refrained from using her middle name—how stupid could I be?—but a couple of parents looked my way and then started looking with me, for me, searching for her.

"Emma? Emma!" The mania seized my voice. What if I couldn't find her? What if I had to report her *missing*? It was so large here. Anyone could snatch her and disappear into the mass of bodies without a trace. There was too much ground to cover. What did I do? Where did I go? I summoned every spiritual part of my being and prayed to anyone or anything that was listening.

Just bring her back. I will take her home. I will do the right thing. But please, please God. Just bring her back to me.

amy

after

This means something. This has to mean something." Richard paced the living room, the furniture cleared weeks ago to tack up possible leads on a corkboard. He'd morphed into a crazy person, becoming more manic as Amy became more resigned to the fact that she wasn't coming back.

"It doesn't mean anything." She sighed. What it meant was the reins on them would loosen; the authorities, grasping at accusatory straws, would actually start looking into someone else besides them. They'd questioned her at length about her hypnotherapy tapes. *Why had she gone? What did it mean? Was she having murderous feelings toward her child?* Her privacy to her own thoughts, feelings, and past lives had been incinerated, along with the truth. She'd tried to point them toward possible suspects in their own lives—the teachers at the school, the parents, even Aunt Sally, because she thought Amy was a terrible mother—but they had all led to dead ends.

She worked out different scenarios—kidnapping, torture, murder—but she couldn't shake one lone thought from her head: what if Emma chose to run away and never wanted to be found? She was only five, but it was still possible.

"Of course it means something. Why would you even say that? She was spotted with a woman in Montana! That could only mean they are heading east, because where else would they go? It also means she's not with some lunatic rapist, thank God. Maybe this woman is trying to help! Maybe she's trying to get her home but has no way of knowing the news in Washington. Emma knows your cell, doesn't she? Didn't you quiz her on that? And she knows our address. Or at least the street number. She's probably just so scared and confused. Would she know how to get home? Oh God, oh God, my poor baby. She must feel so lost."

He'd become so addicted to feeling. He'd grown a beard and stopped eating. The more he refused to eat, the more she ate for the both of them. She'd put on twenty pounds in the last month. She didn't even know weight gain like that was possible. "Richard, even if she is with a woman, that doesn't mean a woman can't hurt her too." *Exhibit A.*

"Well, it's a hell of a lot more likely that a man would . . . oh Jesus, oh no, I can't even think about it. This is good. This is *so good*. She's going to make her way back to us. Montana authorities have been warned. She's coming back, Amy. I can feel it."

She looked at the time line tacked to the wall. He'd bought two cheap maps from Dollar General and had markers and notes pinned on multiple states. Emma had been gone for thirty-two days. Thirty-two days, and still no results.

Over the past month, she'd made every sort of bargain with the universe. She'd stop eating so much. She'd get back to hypnotherapy (but stash the tapes). She'd go on medication if that helped with her mood swings or depression. She'd find a better job. She'd be at home more. She'd join a moms' group. But nothing had worked. The police had given countless press conferences, contacted the media, and organized search parties. They'd turned their neighborhood upside down, night and day, for weeks.

There had been false sightings—so many girls looked like Emma—and Amy had to believe this was a false sighting too. She'd had to detach from all emotion, which caused everyone to think she was a horrible mother. (She was.) Some websites said she'd buried her daughter in the woods, that this was all planned, that she was a murderer. She'd read all of this with a sick fascination that *this* is what people would forever think about her. Didn't they know she already thought so little about herself?

Richard walked back and forth, dragging his finger across the time line from the night of her disappearance to now. "We've missed something, Amy. We have, I know it."

This ordeal had forced them together, had thrown the daily grievances out the window and helped them focus on keeping Robbie alive, safe, and shielded from all this nonsense. Amy let Richard take over, mostly. She was afraid to get too close to Robert, as if that meant something, as if that would determine the outcome of Emma's return.

"Richard, we've done everything we can." She looked at the time line to confirm—they had done everything. They'd gone over personal calendars, community events, and even searched newspapers to see who might have been in the vicinity on the night of her disappearance. They'd each taken a polygraph (inconclusive), requested the NCMEC to issue a broadcast fax to law enforcement agencies around the country (pointless), scheduled press releases and media events, hired a media spokesperson, issued a reward ($50,000—more than they could afford), reported extortion attempts (three), had a second line installed with a trap-and-trace feature in case the suspect called (they wouldn't; they didn't), worked with volunteers, made exhaustive lists, called Emma's doctor and dentist for medical records and X-rays . . . just in case.

She'd forked over the entire history of Emma's life and gotten nothing in return. They'd even issued a land, sea, and air search, and Amy and Richard had prayed for the very first time together, right here, on their hardwood floors, that they would not pull Emma's clammy, blue body from a river or lake (they hadn't). There were tracking dogs and investigators, and the further they got into it, the more removed she felt.

She wasn't cut out for this. It was like labor: she was so exhausted—mentally, physically, and emotionally—that she just wanted it to be over. Whether that meant a happy, healthy child or a horrific, unimaginable outcome, she just needed it to end.

"But look. Look at this. From day three until day twenty-three—day twenty-fucking-three!—they focused solely on *us* as the suspects. They had no other leads. None. With the UCLA campus shooting, the Orlando nightclub shooting, the political endorsements, the health care bust, the news turned to other things. And our girl . . . she was just out there somewhere."

"Her story didn't get buried because of worldwide events, Richard. It got buried because people have zero attention span. Do you know how many children have gone missing this year alone?"

He blinked at her, a scrawny deer caught seconds before its death by hunter.

"Eight hundred thousand. *Eight hundred thousand!* And that doesn't even begin to count the sex trafficking or the—"

He pressed his hands over his ears like a child and stomped his feet. "Stop! Stop it! I will not think about my little girl in a sex trafficking ring at five years old!" He ripped his hands from his ears and glared at her, his chest heaving. "Why would you even *say* that to me right now? Do Stan and Barry—does Frank know about things like this? Where did you even find this out? What's the age group?" He disappeared from the living room to his laptop, which was scattered among loose printouts on the dining room table. Their entire house had been hijacked for the sole purpose of gathering information, when the only thing that mattered was the act of finding Emma.

She looked for somewhere to sit and settled for the floor, her legs in front of her, her back rounded in a soft, cervical C. She laid all the way back and took deep breaths. When would this all be over? How would it end?

Richard mumbled, cursed, stood, sat, and then walked around the dining room table.

"Richard. Richard, come here."

He ignored her, so lost in doing sex trafficking research that she had to scream his name at the top of her lungs. She didn't care if she woke Robert. This had to be said. He came to her after a full two minutes, rocking in the doorway. "What? Why are you laying like that? Did you fall?"

She sighed, closed her eyes, and reopened them. "I want a divorce. After all of this is said and done, whatever the outcome, I want a divorce." She rolled her head to look at Richard, at his bloodshot eyes, leaky nose, and beard that looked like it had been pieced together from pubic hair.

He placed his hands on his hips, opened his mouth as wide as it would go, and bent forward until he was inches from her. After a moment of awkward, gaping silence, he screamed directly into her ear.

She scooted away, protecting her right eardrum. "Jesus Christ, Richard! My *ear*!"

"I fucking hate you, woman! I *hate* you! Don't you know that?" He stood back up and raised his hands, like his favorite sports team had just won a championship. "I would love to get a divorce! Please! God, please, yes, let's get a divorce! That's the best news I've heard all year!" He started laughing then, high, like a hyena. He hitched his knees up as if dribbling a soccer ball and ran around and around her in celebration. She thought he had officially lost it, that he'd taken all her craziness and anger and transformed it to absolute hysteria. And here she was, left on the floor as the calm one, while her husband became officially unhinged.

And then she realized: she was calm because Emma was gone. Emma was to her what she was to Richard. They were a toxic combination as a family. She knew that now. She would never admit it to anyone, but even with the chaos of this investigation and everything crumbling around them, not having the daily battles with her daughter had been an immense relief.

She let him laugh, kick, and twirl and then turned her head back to stare at the ceiling. Who would get Robbie in the divorce? Especially after the type of mother she'd become known as in the press? She closed her eyes, blocked out the world, and reminded herself that this wasn't her *entire* life, just a segment. It was too late for all of them as a family. She could see that now. Everything would be different, was different. But it wasn't too late for her.

The telephone rang, and Richard jumped all over it. "What? *What?* You're kidding! Oh my God, oh my God, Amy! So . . . what does this mean? The other leads are? Okay, okay, we'll come right down. Thank you so much, Frank. Thank you, thank you." Richard screamed and bounded to where she still laid, their previous conversation having dropped from his blasted memory.

"They have an *actual* lead. An actual lead! They have authorities working on it and didn't want to tell us unless they thought it was real. But this time it's real."

"How do they know it's real?"

"Because they saw Emma with the same woman. Different hair, but the same one! A cop in Montana got the woman's license plate. And now they're in Nebraska . . . a waitress spotted them at some diner or something."

Amy sat straight up. "Nebraska?"

"Yes, with the same woman. It has to be her. It has to."

"Wait, wait. Please start at the beginning." She was tempted to just call Frank himself, because Richard was behaving as though he'd had a mini-stroke and was trying hard to get on with it but couldn't quite make sense of how things worked. He would scramble details, facts, and timelines. Sometimes, he hung up the phone on the oven or put the notepad in the freezer.

"There was a waitress. Thought she looked familiar. It was her eyes. Those beautiful eyes of hers. I don't know. But it's her. I know it has to be!"

"*Where*, Richard? What the hell are you talking about?" She pinched her forehead between her fingers and tried to remember how to talk to an imbecile. "Who is this woman? And how do we know it's actually Emma?"

He shook his head and sat down, cross-legged, on the floor. "Just let me think, let me think. Frank said . . . he said that this woman worked in a café or a restaurant or something and that Emma came in."

"Is she hurt?"

"I don't know. But the people—"

"What people? Is she with someone other than a woman?" She wanted to strangle the answers from his scrawny body, but she knew the more she pushed, the less he'd reveal.

"That same woman. Different hair. Officials are all over it. They've issued an AMBER Alert in Nebraska, I think. This woman better not have hurt her, Amy, or I swear to God—"

"So what? Do we go to Nebraska? What do we do now? Are we supposed to just sit here?"

"Frank said not to get our hopes up, but based on the description and the pattern of driving, it sounds solid. But . . . anyway. They're talking to the waitress, so officials can talk to her, and then . . . well, I don't know, but this just happened a few days ago, so they're on top of it."

"This happened a few *days* ago? What do you mean? And they haven't found her yet?"

The constant running goose chase was making her crazy. All the ups, downs, twists, turns, accusations, and judgments. They were starting to define her.

"I don't know. One of us should go talk to Frank."

"I'll go." She had to get out of this house. Knowing Richard, he'd get into a head-on collision on the way and burn to a crisp before he got any definitive answers. "Are you okay to stay with Robbie?"

He blinked, as though he'd forgotten who Robbie was. "Of course I will. Go. Record what he says. Use your phone."

"I'm not going to record what he says. That's illegal." She grabbed her purse and stepped outside, hoping there wouldn't be people clustered in her front yard, waiting to bomb her with insults. What a horrible time this had been, the way the world knew the intimate lining of her life.

She got in her car and drove the short distance to the station, parking and asking for Frank once inside. Ronda was working the front and motioned for her to go on back.

Frank was sitting on the corner of his desk, on the

phone. "Let me call you right back," he said. He hung up and turned to her.

"Mrs. Townsend. Nice to see you." He was being nicer now that there was an actual lead. Perhaps he was beginning to think she wasn't responsible.

"Richard just told me about Nebraska. I just wanted to get all the details."

He clenched his hands in his lap. "It's the best lead we have. There was a house call in Montana about a report of a woman and a child. There was no child found, but the cop thought something was off and called in the license plate. It took awhile to make its way here, but the same car was spotted at a Nebraska diner a few days ago, where a waitress matched the description of the same woman in Montana, but she was with a little girl."

"And the little girl looks like Emma?"

"Yes, let me see here." He looked at a piece of paper. "It seems to be about the same description, but you know, Amy, sometimes these things are pretty vague." He lowered the page. "Especially when there's a cash reward involved."

"But it could be Emma." She could feel the first signs of hope and dread flickering simultaneously. "What about her eyes? Everyone who meets Emma goes on and on about her eyes. Did this waitress get a good look at her? Richard said something about her eyes." She swallowed. "Was she . . . injured?"

"She was not visibly injured, no. That wasn't reported."

"Did you get the diner's exact location?"

"Yes, we are working on that now."

"But this could be false, or . . . ?"

"It could be something, or it could be another false lead, yes. We don't know yet."

"Does that happen? Is that what you think this is?"

"False leads happen all the time. Look, Amy, we're doing all that we can do. We'll get to the bottom of it. I promise."

"But you've been saying that for over a month, Frank. And she's out there somewhere, without us."

"I know that. I know. Just let us do our job. You and Richard should really try and get some rest. Get back on some sort of normal schedule."

She laughed, a dusty, hollow bark erupting from the back of her throat.

"I know it's tough. But I really feel we're headed in the right direction."

"Is there . . . is there anything positive I can bring back to Richard? I'm not sure how much longer he can cope with all of this."

"I know it's hard. But the moment I know any new details, you two will be the first to know. Now go home and take care of that son of yours. And get some rest."

She gave a stiff nod and walked out of the station, the familiar sounds of ringing phones, handcuffs, and bookings an odd comfort. She climbed into her car, both hands flexed around the wheel. Should she drive to Nebraska? Find this woman who called in the lead? Reorganize her house? Talk to a divorce lawyer?

The ridiculous options of her stalled life flashed before her. She'd told her daughter she didn't love her, and now her daughter had been gone for thirty-two days. Was this the world's way of telling her she wasn't fit to be a mother? Was she supposed to come out of this with the meaning of life under her expanding belt?

She stopped at the local cheese shop on the way home. Virginia, the only woman who hadn't completely turned on her, greeted her as she entered.

"Amy, *dear*. How are you? The usual today?"

Amy nodded, plucking a French baguette from the warm basket and paying for her cheese with cash. She ate it by the window, ripping off pieces of crusty bread and spreading the white, creamy cheese across each generous slice.

She chewed and swallowed, the tears coming on so suddenly that at first, she thought there was a leak in the ceiling. The bite turned to white, lumpy slime in her mouth, and soon she was sobbing like Richard. Customers were looking, and then Virginia's plump arms were around Amy's even plumper body, and it all came tumbling out, here, in the middle of town, in her favorite cheese shop.

She struggled between crying and swallowing and hung tightly to Virginia's yeasty shoulder as she let everything out—her grief, her remorse, her ineptitude, her guilt, her love, her uncertainty—all of it real, hard, and imperfect, like her.

before

The airport had been a disaster. Richard, as always, was zero help. She rarely traveled with the kids, or ever, for that matter, but this was necessary, and they were finally here.

Richard complained as he pulled the luggage from the rental car, leaving Amy to get the kids out of their car seats. It had been two years since she'd been back to Iowa. Her mother had guilt-tripped her about it often in her cursive, handwritten letters she sent once a month. She never told Richard about the letters—because they were hers—and he was scared of her mother anyway.

Betty was a gruff, stout, matter-of-fact farmer's daughter who'd worked her entire life without so much as a single complaint. She wore overalls to dinner and often had hay stuck in her gray, cropped hair. Her skin looked like it was made of leather, and her calves were the size of baby watermelons.

Amy had been raised on farm-fresh bacon, grits, and fried eggs, but Amy wasn't a worker like her mother. Betty was sturdy where Amy was soft, and she had always envied her mother because of it. Despite their differences—and there were many—when the two of them got together, drinking pots of coffee and reminiscing about their other, current lives, Amy felt understood, seen.

Amy was an only child, a fatherless child, and now, tragically, a motherless daughter. The only time she'd asked Betty about her real father, she'd gotten a sharp crack across the cheek. But Amy, stubborn as a young girl, had gone snooping through her mother's things and fished one photo from her wallet. It was a crumpled black-and-white that had been folded three times. She'd taken the photograph into her room to study it. Upon closer inspection, the sight of the man standing beside her mother had disappointed Amy. She'd expected some farmer with lanky limbs, mischief in his eyes, or a craggy face marked by the sun.

Instead, the man staring back at her was shaped like a smear. He had no definitive edges; the weight of him simply poured outside the sharpness of his joints, so that it was hard to figure out where he ended or began. But she recognized herself in this man. This man was her biological father all right. She took the photo to her aunt to confirm it. He had died when she was only a baby, and her mother never spoke of him again.

"This is going to be weird."

Amy snapped out of her thoughts and turned toward Richard. "What's going to be weird?"

"You know. Staying in your mother's house. Without your mother."

"It's not like she died *in* the house, Richard. She was in the barn." The farmhouse was beautiful. It was cavernous, warm, and everything she'd imagined she'd want when she'd first started a family. If it had been somewhere besides Malcolm, with all of its nosy neighbors, tough memories, and rundown businesses, she'd just uproot everyone and move straight in.

She almost said as much, the thought on her lips, as she turned on all the lights and rubbed her hands over her arms. The kids took off, and she didn't even tell them not to. A stack of fresh firewood rested by the fireplace, as though her mother, even after death, had been expecting her. She tended to the fire, a full blaze roaring in less than a minute. Richard whistled.

"What?"

"That's impressive." He smiled and gestured toward the blaze. "The way you just did that."

She clapped the soot from her hands. "If we had a real fireplace, I'd be doing this all the time."

She walked through all the rooms. Her mother was a tidy woman, thank God. She emptied out the fridge, sorted through the bills, and watched Emma chase Robbie outside. A huge white picket fence marked the perimeter. Maybe she'd take them to see the horses and pigs in a bit. Feed the chickens. They could have fresh omelets for dinner.

"What time is the funeral tomorrow?"

"It's at ten." She sighed. "I'll need to go to the funeral home to check on arrangements in a bit. Do you think you can watch them?"

"Of course I can. Sure."

She hesitated then locked eyes with him. "Thank you."

"You're welcome." He took one step closer to her. "You seem—and I don't want you to take this the wrong way—but you seem different here. More relaxed. Not that these are happy circumstances or anything—"

She cut him off, gave him a lifeline. "No, you're right. I am. It's the only place in the whole world where I can just be myself. It's always been like that here. I'm not sure why."

"Because you grew up here, I'm sure." Richard looked at the ceiling, composed entirely of wood. "This is a truly stunning home. Are you sure you want to sell?"

She nodded. "It's just too much to take care of. There's no way we could handle the upkeep." She checked her watch and tied up the garbage bag full of old food. "I'm going to dump this and head to the funeral home. I should be back in time for dinner. Can you handle things here?"

"Yes. Call me if you need anything."

Richard slipped out the back. Emma squealed and ran from him while Robbie chuckled. She smiled, feeling, if only for a moment, like a real family that was temporarily unbreakable.

The service was long, painful, and impersonal, as they usually were. Her mother would have hated it. Amy shifted on the pew, adjusted her tight black dress, and blotted her face with a tissue. Aunt Sally sat next to her and clutched her knee with a death grip. Veins ran an obstacle course under her aged skin, and Amy began to count the veins in an effort to keep from crying. Uncle Ted was on the other side of Sally, Richard and the kids to her left. Emma was playing with the hem of her dress, the thread beginning to unravel. She shot her a look, but Emma didn't even acknowledge her.

"Emma," she hissed. "Stop pulling on your dress."

Emma nodded, let her hands go, and then, just one minute later, started again. Amy could feel the anger tugging her away from the sermon, the coffin, the dark blue veins of Aunt Sally's left hand, and the digital slideshow that showed her mother as a younger, more handsome version of her older self. She shielded the side of her face with a program just to block out Emma and keep her rage in check.

Emma knew what she was doing. She knew just how to push her buttons, and now, Amy was on the verge of losing it and snapping at her daughter here in the house of the Lord. She took deep, cleansing breaths as Aunt Sally leaned over and whispered, "Oh Amy, what are we going to do without her?"

The burial was sparsely attended and swift, with a cheap coffin and a handful of tulips tossed on top. Amy watched as they lowered her mother's corpse six feet under and sprinkled the box with dirt. At the house, she took Saran wrap off casseroles and porcelain dishes, opening the home to her mother's community of friends, relatives, and acquaintances.

She felt strangely envious—her mother had had such a full, wonderful life in the middle of nowhere, while Amy had a small, lonely life in the bustling Pacific Northwest. Her mother had always seemed woefully content with her life, never wanting anything other than what God had given her. And Amy had done nothing but squander every single cell of her loose, unfortunate body, wanting anything but what she'd been given. She had it all wrong.

A few other kids were running wild with Emma and Robbie on the wide plank floors, shoes on, but her mother would have loved the noise. This was her mother's house, not hers, and Amy didn't have it in her to scream, scold, or chase after them. It had been such a nice distraction being away from their daily routine: the house, work, and the endless chores. She didn't have to be a dictator here—not until they got back home and it would all start to trickle back into place: the impatience, the schedules, the sleeplessness, and the many annoyances.

"Amy, how are you doing with all of this?" Aunt Sally stood beside her, crooked and brittle, a shawl wrapped over the pointy bones of her shoulders. If Amy pressed a finger into her clavicle, she was afraid it would go all the way through and pop out the back of her spine.

"Oh, you know. It's hard."

"Well, you just *never* got to see her. She always talked about you. She just wished she could have done more for you and the kids, you know . . ."

Something in Amy began to fester and twitch. She cleared her throat and looked for another casserole to de-foil. "Did you get something to eat?"

Sally waved a bony paw in her face. "You know, I rarely eat. Always found the fountain of youth is to eat *less*. And I never snack. You know they don't snack in other countries, but the way we snack here is just disgusting, isn't it? And all these *fat* children . . ." She squeezed her arm. "Besides, you can get away with exercising less. When you don't eat." She laughed, a throaty rattle that sounded like emphysema or pneumonia.

She watched the debate on Sally's face as she gauged her next words. "Not that you take after me in that regard, or your mother, really. She worked so hard, laboring day after day for all those years. By herself."

Amy slammed a casserole dish onto the butcher-block island, and Sally smacked a hand to her chest. A few others looked their way, and Amy wiped her hands on the apron she'd found at the very back of her mother's pantry. "Is there something I can do for you, Sally? Or do you just want to guilt-trip me about how fat and sedentary I am, and what a shitty daughter I was?"

Sally stumbled over her next words, and Richard came to the rescue, steering her aunt into the living room. He glared at Amy, his mustache fidgeting over his top lip, and mouthed, *Really?* She shrugged.

"Amy?"

She blinked into the face of an older man she didn't recognize. "Yes?"

"I'm Gary, a good friend of your mom's. I'm so sorry for your loss."

"Thank you."

"Is that one yours?" He pointed out the kitchen window at Emma, who was halfway up a giant swamp white oak. "I know most of the other kids, but I've never met her."

"*Christ* . . . Yes, it is. Thank you." She looked around for Richard.

"I was going to get her down, but I didn't know how you'd take to a stranger grabbing your girl, so I just thought I'd alert you."

Gary's words faded as the fury took over. *Just once.* She couldn't even mourn at her own mother's funeral without Emma hoarding all the attention for herself.

She stormed out the door, slipping into rain boots, and screamed Emma's name into the sprawling acreage. Robbie toddled below her at the tree's base, next to the other kids, all of them covered in mud and pig shit. Had they let out the pigs from their pens?

Emma ignored her and climbed higher—so high that by the time Amy got to the tree, Emma kicked off a shoe and it tumbled down to hit Amy's shoulder. She snatched it from the damp earth and threw it back as hard as she could, narrowly missing her daughter's head. Emma's eyes widened and Robbie began to cry.

The other children went inside, sensing danger, and there they were again, facing off, a battle of the genetic wills.

"Amy! Amy, go inside. I've got it. Pumpkin, come down from there, please!" Richard sprinted toward the tree and waved his arms in his attempt at interference. She let Richard switch places with her as she searched the yard for

Robbie and spotted him close to the back door. After a moment of encouragement, Emma slithered back down the trunk and dropped into Richard's arms, her tangle of pale limbs clutched around his middle in a spray of bark and leaves.

Amy just wanted Emma to respect her, and she just wanted to respect Emma. She could imagine her own mother laughing, telling her to calm down, that it all goes by so fast, that it's not a big deal. Her daughter was safe, feet on the ground again, her will unbroken. And wasn't that enough?

But it felt like a big deal. It *always* felt like a big deal, and no matter how hard Amy tried, she couldn't let her anger go. Emma fried the mechanics of her nerves and pushed her to an anger that felt raw. Amy always promised herself that tomorrow would be different, but it wasn't. Every day played out the same way, with her daughter dictating the sequence—politeness, acceptance, annoyance, rage, screaming, hitting, defiance, forgiveness—until the cadence of her days ran just like that, hot and cold, and she had no one to blame but Emma (and herself). The explosiveness of their relationship was becoming too much, and she felt there was nothing and no one to help.

sarah

after

My voice was hoarse from screaming. By now, the entire park knew a girl named Emma was missing. Would anyone make the connection to the news? I didn't even care—I just wanted her back, and I would do whatever it took to get her.

Time was stretching in waves. Had it been a minute? Two minutes? Fifteen? *Think, Sarah. Where would she go?*

A hand brushed my elbow and I turned, even though I knew the hand was too high and large to be hers. I came face-to-face with a man wearing black-rimmed glasses. He was only a few inches taller than me.

"Ma'am? Have you lost your daughter?"

"Yes, I . . . she's not my daughter, she's my niece."

"Okay. What does she look like?"

I rattled off a description—pink sweater, red pants, gray boots, blond hair, large, gray eyes—and he told me he'd take the left side of the park. He had a small person attached to his left hand, who looked as worried as I felt.

"Thank you," I managed to get out. "I . . . I can't believe this is happening."

"Don't panic. Let's meet right back at this bench in," he glanced at his watch, "five minutes or so. Okay?"

I nodded and stumbled forward, trying to steel myself

against the possibility that she was gone and this time—
this time—something bad could actually happen. The
world of difference between my actions—a reverse kidnapping to help a child, not harm—and an actual kidnapping made me almost capsize with grief. This was only
happening because I'd taken her from the woods. There
was no one else to blame.

I made the rounds again, fitting my body up the wooden
tower, my ankles wobbling on the bridge as I scanned all
the moving bodies below. Where was she? How far could
she have gone? Maybe she'd run back to the bean. A frayed
loop of her actions played in my brain. Sometimes she
ran off. Sometimes she got excited and forgot to ask for
permission.

But sometimes, kids also just disappeared.

It wasn't like her to run off from me, but then again,
she had a history of wandering off in general; it's what had
given us the cushion of escape in the first place. Maybe
this was just what she did in crowds.

I climbed down and looked at my watch. I'd never felt
more on the verge of coming undone. I retraced my steps
back to the bench, but the man wasn't there. I sat on it and
dropped my head into my hands. If I hadn't taken that call.
If I hadn't been so stupid to turn my back for just a few
seconds. But I knew, more than anyone, that a few seconds
was all it took.

I made a million deals with myself as the squeals of
excited children cut across my conscience. If one was
Emma, I'd do anything. If one was her, I'd make it all okay.
I took off from the bench again, staking out the same path
I'd just been through, the two syllables of her name rolling off the back of my throat. I saw girls in similar outfits;
girls with similar hair. I lunged at each of them, startled
parents gripping their children in worried fists. Wild, cau-

tious eyes stared back at me as I extended hand after hand in apology.

"I'm sorry, it's my niece. She's run off. I'm sorry, have you seen a little girl? I'm sorry, can you help?"

I ran until my calves seized, and I'd circled the park three times. I huddled back at the bench as my lungs burned and my heart closed in on itself.

"Miss?" I heard the man's voice somewhere around my shoulders and looked up. His son was on his right, fiddling with his baseball cap. To his left, a hand cupped loosely around her shoulders, stood Emma. She held a pile of flowers, roots dangling, in her fingers by her right hip. "Is this her?"

I dropped to my knees and seized her to my chest. The crunch of petals smashed against my shirt, and she screamed in protest.

"My flowers! You crushed them!"

"Emma, my God, are you okay? Where did you go?" I kissed her forehead, her cheeks, and her eyelids. "Why did you run off? We've talked about this. You have to stay where I can see you at all times. Do you understand?"

"I *didn't*," she said, squirming out of my embrace. "I went to pick flowers right over there. I wanted to get you some. And you broke them."

Blood coursed through my entire body, my bones limp with relief. I looked up at the man—my savior. "How did you find her? I swear I looked everywhere."

"Well, Charlie here has run off a few times, and it's always near the perimeter. They have all those flowers and bushes. Sometimes, when they crouch down, you can't even see them. So I took a wild guess, and there she was, picking flowers." His voice was light, relieved.

I stood, one hand still firmly on Emma, my knees cracking from all the miles in the car and sudden sprinting through the park. "I can't possibly thank you enough . . ."

"Ryan. Ryan Bailey. And you're very welcome."

I dragged my eyes from his face and looked down at his son. "And this is Charlie, I'm assuming?"

"Yes, this is my son, Charlie. He's seven."

I pulled Emma closer. "I really, really don't know how to thank you. I've never been so scared in all my life."

"Well, especially if it's not your child," he said. Emma glanced at him, her eyebrows cocked in question, and I searched for something to say before she could. "Well, you guys have a good day. Thanks again. Truly."

"Oh, okay. You too." He squatted down to Emma. "So glad you're okay." He stood and lifted his hand in a wave as Charlie ran off. Ryan followed a few feet behind him.

"I want to go play with that boy."

I crouched into a deep squat, my nerves still firing with adrenaline. "What's that, sweetie?"

She pointed to Charlie, who was running farther and farther into the park. "I want to play with him."

"Well . . ." I turned to look at Charlie and Ryan. That had been as close a call as any, but she was back, and it was fine. Everything was fine. I knew the chances of some-one being familiar with the missing persons reports from Longview, Washington—or now, Montana—were im-probable. And Emma didn't talk about her family. I knew she wouldn't just start gabbing about who I was or where we'd been.

"Look, you can play for just a few more minutes, but only where I can see you."

She took off where Charlie was, and I lingered close to Ryan.

"Hello, again."

"Hi." My hand felt limp as I raised and lowered it.

"Are you guys from around here?" Ryan was standing a few feet away, his gaze split between Charlie and me. I stood, eyes glued to Emma.

"What's that?"

"I was just asking if you were from around here? Or just visiting?"

I shook my head. "No. Just visiting." I felt an urgency to get away from the prying questions. Charlie held up something to show Ryan from a distance, and Emma laughed.

"Hey, Em! We need to go, sweetheart."

She turned. "But we just got here! And you said I could play!" Her voice was high, shrill, and testing. She was tired and hungry, and I could see a tantrum brewing in her balled fists and lifted chin.

"Ten minutes, okay? Then we need to go."

She nodded, already climbing a rope behind Charlie. "You'll have to excuse me if I don't look at you."

Ryan laughed. "Understood."

We moved closer to where the kids were, and I reminded Emma to stay where I could see her. We broke into separate groups as Emma insisted on climbing the tower again, and Charlie wanted to go look at the ice ribbon. We climbed, ran, and chased, our cheeks growing pink, our bodies warm. I slid down one of the tallest slides, Emma perched on my thighs, and we rocketed out of the bottom, flying forward and landing on our hands and knees.

"Again!"

She went back up alone and then flew down the slide into my open, waiting arms.

"Whew, kid, I'm beat. Are you getting hungry?"

"Yes! Can we go eat?"

"Yep. And I think I know just where to take you."

"And then can we come back here?"

"Maybe."

She pulled on my hand as we started back to the car. At the edge of the park, I heard Emma's name, and there were Ryan and Charlie, trotting up to us.

"Hey. You guys taking off, Emma and . . . ?"

"Oh, sorry. Sarah. I'm Sarah. And yes. We are." I smoothed Emma's bangs. "I can't thank you enough for your help. Seriously. You basically saved my life. Our lives."

"Any time."

"He didn't save my life," Emma stated.

"It's just an expression, sweetie. I know he didn't actually save your life."

"Then why did you say it?"

"Because that's just what people say."

"Where are you guys headed?" Ryan asked.

"To eat." I swung our hands back and forth. "This one is super-hungry, and we all know how that goes, don't we?"

"We do, don't we, Charlie? Do you know where you're going to eat, or . . . ?"

"Oh, I'm not sure really. I was maybe going to take her to Tempo? She loves breakfast for dinner, and their omelets are exceptional."

"You don't have to tell me. They're the best." He adjusted Charlie's hat. "Would it be totally rude to crash your party and join? We haven't been there in a long time either."

I looked down at Emma. "Oh, um . . ."

She yanked my arm, a plea. "Say yes, Sarah. Say yes! Please, please, please?"

Ryan gestured to Emma. "How can you argue with that? It's not like this is fate at work or anything, right? I mean, helping a complete stranger locate a child is *totally* a normal way to meet someone. It's not like you should buy me dinner or anything for 'saving your life,' as you just stated yourself."

"Laying it on pretty thick."

"So that's a yes?"

I couldn't just throw caution to the wind, but we needed a distraction. Emma needed a friend. And I needed a break. "Sure. Why not?"

"Great." Ryan squatted down to shake Emma's hand. Her fingers dangled in his firm grip. "It was super-nice to meet you, Emma. You're a great flower picker. We'll see you soon?"

She pushed into me, shy, and nodded.

He stood. "We'll meet you over there?"

"Sounds good." I gripped Emma's hot fingers and walked back to the car.

Emma gushed about her new friend Charlie as we drove down Michigan Avenue. I pointed out the buildings, the art museum, and the droves of people clustered on either side of the street. We found parking on State Street, a fragrant blast of air drifting up from the grates as I paid the meter.

I pulled open the double doors of the restaurant and let her walk through. "This is Tempo. They stay open all day and night, and you can get any type of breakfast dish you want. Waffles, pancakes, or huge omelets they serve in a skillet over crispy potatoes."

"Do I like omelets?"

"Well, you love eggs. And omelets are made from eggs, so I would guess yes?" I scanned the restaurant for Ryan and Charlie. They were already in a booth by one of the windows. Emma yelped and ran over to Charlie. I followed.

We slid in across from them, shedding our coats. Our booth faced State Street. We watched people pass by as they left work or ducked onto the L. We helped the kids with their sticky, oversize menus and ordered our food. Ryan folded his hands on the table as the kids colored on smaller, paper menus. "So."

"So."

I expected Ryan to ask me why I had my niece, what the story was, but he didn't. He rearranged the jams in the basket. "So, you're from . . . ?"

"Indiana. But I live out west."

"Like California out west?"

"Portland. How long have you and Charlie lived in Chicago?"

"I've been here fifteen years. Love it here."

"Me too. I've been here a ton for work. Great city. One of the best." I kept him talking about the city and his life as a dad, deflecting as many questions as I could. He wore no ring and didn't talk about Charlie's mom, so I didn't ask.

Our orders arrived, and Emma's eyes grew to cartoonish proportions. "This is all for me?" The kids compared their giant omelets and waved their Greek toast around like flags.

"And you? What about you? I've been talking nonstop. Are you married? Serious with anyone?"

I laughed and pointed to Emma. "Yes, she and I are *very* serious." I took a bite of eggs.

"Where are you guys staying?"

"Probably at the Sofitel. I have points. Where do you guys live?"

"Wicker Park. I was lucky and bought before it turned into 'the coolest neighborhood ever.'" He glanced at Charlie. "I mean, I know we just officially met and everything, and this probably sounds super-sketchy, but you guys are totally welcome to stay if you don't want to spend the points. Or if you need a kitchen. I know how inconvenient it can be with kids and hotels."

"Oh, wow. That's incredibly nice of you." I searched my arsenal of excuses, trying to find one that wouldn't offend him.

"And definitely, probably a bit creepy, right?"

"Maybe a little."

"I promise I'm not a serial *k-i-l-l-e-r*."

"I can spell, Dad." Charlie rolled his eyes.

"I know, I know."

"Are we going to do a sleepover, Dad? Can we? Can we watch movies and stay up late and eat popcorn?"

Emma pulled on my arm. "A *sleepover*? A real sleepover? Can we? Can we, Sarah? Oh, please? Can we?" Emma bounced so much in the seat, my body started to sway. I pressed my hands into her shoulders to calm her.

"I know that sounds like fun, Emma, but we really can't. We don't want to impose. Plus, we're not staying long."

"Well, if you need a place just to crash for the night or something, you're welcome to. Charlie's summer vacation lasts forever, because they don't go back until September, so you'd actually be doing us a favor. Only-child syndrome and all."

Emma looked like she was about to burst. Which would be riskier? Staying in a public hotel with a paper trail, hotel staff, and elevators, or a private house? Wasn't this the kind of anonymity we'd been looking for?

Ryan waved at the waitress for the check and sat back. There was so much at stake here. I closed my eyes, took a breath, and rolled the dice. "Okay, for one night only. And then we get a hotel. I mean it, Emma." Emma and Charlie began to shift in their seats and talk about what movies they wanted to watch.

"I promise I'll behave," Ryan said with a wink.

"That's not what I'm worried about. I just don't want to impose."

"It's no sweat," he said, chatting with the waitress as she brought our bill. He paid before I could protest and scribbled his address on the back of the receipt. "Do you think you can find that? Or do you just want to follow us?"

"We'll just follow you guys if that works."

"That works."

We all stood and walked toward the exit. Emma and Charlie were laughing about something. We pushed through the double doors and into the crisp, loud night.

"We're over there," Ryan said, pointing to the left.

"And we're over there." I pointed right.

"Cool. Do you want to circle around the block and pull behind us?"

"Sure."

"So we'll see you shortly if you don't decide to *d-i-t-c-h* us?"

"Dad! Again, with the spelling!"

"Yes." I laughed and tucked Emma's hand, now gummy from ketchup, into mine. "We'll see you shortly."

"Promise?" Charlie looked up at me, adjusting his hat.

"Yes, I promise."

"I promise too!" Emma added.

"See you soon," Ryan said.

Charlie and Emma splashed in the baby pool. They'd made fast friends over the last twenty-four hours. It was amazing to watch her with another kid, the way they talked, played, and joked, their own private language. She never talked about friends at home, or people that she missed. I was glad to give her this, even if it was temporary.

I hated lying to Ryan, but I didn't have a choice. Every nerve ending sizzled on high alert. I had to watch everything I said or did—keeping myself primed to make a quick exit or to cover up something Emma said.

"Amazing weather, isn't it?"

Ryan was stretched on one of his lawn chairs in the backyard.

"It is. It's also amazing you have a backyard in Chicago."

"It was a prerequisite with this one," he said. "He gets tired of parks. And frankly, so do I."

"Yeah, I guess you can't lose him here, huh?" It was supposed to be a joke, but it came out flat and hard.

"Seriously, don't beat yourself up about that. It's fine. It happens all the time. You're definitely not the first person to lose sight of a child in a massive park. I once lost Charlie in a parking garage. And a pet store. And at the Water Tower."

"Well, I'd never forgive myself if something happened."

He waved his hand, a dismissal. "I just think it's amazing that you're taking her on such a big trip. Your sister must really trust you."

I swallowed and wished I had something to do with my hands. "I really love Emma."

"I can tell." He sighed and crossed his arms over his chest. "How crazy is this?"

"What?"

"You? Me? This? Here? This kind of stuff doesn't happen, except in cheesy movies and romance novels."

"You read romance novels?"

He pressed a hand to his heart. "Fabio is my all-time-favorite book-cover model."

"I see. Well, on that note, we should really be going," I joked.

We laughed and then settled into comfortable silence. "It is definitely an odd way to meet someone, though." It came out more flirtatiously than I meant it to. "I mean, not *romantically* meet someone . . . maybe you were just supposed to help find Emma. And buy us dinner. And then let us stay here for free."

He leaned over and squeezed my knee. "Calm down. I know what you mean."

My phone began to ring, and I dug it from my bag at my feet. It was my father. "Oh crap. This is my dad. Do you mind if I take this?"

"By all means. I'll keep an eye on these two trouble-makers."

Emma looked at Ryan, her ears primed. "I'm not a trouble-maker!"

"You're *not*?"

"Hello?" I turned my back and stuck a finger in my ear to hear better. "Dad?"

"Sarah, why haven't you called me back?"

"I've . . . I had a bit of an emergency. It's fine now. Sorry. I was going to call you. Is everything okay?" The fact that my mother could be dead and I hadn't bothered to call my dad told me more than I wanted to know about myself.

"Yes, everything is better than okay. Are you ready for this? You should sit down. Are you sitting down?"

"Jesus, Dad. Out with it, please."

"Okay, okay. I'm just so—anyway. Gosh, listen to me! I'm like a babbling schoolboy! Ah, wow. It feels good. It does."

"What does, Dad? What are you talking about?"

"She *called*, Sarah." He was breathless. It sounded like the phone was smashed against his lips, the way I used to do when talking to my boyfriends after bedtime. "She made actual contact."

I took a few steps toward the three-flat patio door. "What do you mean she made contact? What does that mean? Is she in a spaceship?"

"She . . . she just called, Sarah. Out of the blue. Can you believe it?" He was whispering like he'd won the lottery and didn't want a single person to know. "I mean, just . . . after all this time . . . and . . . and everything. I don't even know how she got my—"

"Dad, Dad, slow down. Take a breath." What *I* really needed was a breath. I needed to process the words he was saying as much as he did. I did the quick mental calculation—it had been twenty-five years since she'd walked out. *Twenty-five years!* I'd never received a single birthday card, phone call, or surprise visit, not even a lame Facebook request as an adult. Even though I was relieved when she left, that small part of me still hoped she'd at least recognize the important days of my life: birthdays, holidays, graduations, a potential engagement, a possible wedding, maybe grandchildren someday.

The protective hold on my father blossomed. Already, he sounded like a different person. I hadn't heard him with this much energy since before she'd left. He wouldn't survive a second heartbreak. He just wouldn't. "Just start from the beginning, please."

"She—where are you, Sarah? It sounds like you're in the middle of a vacuum."

I moved farther away from the pool, motioning to Ryan that I was going inside. He gave me a thumb's up—he would watch both children with hawk eyes—and then I was in his bedroom, which happened to be the first room off the kitchen. I was startled by the intimacy of it, the dark blue duvet (why did single men always choose dark blue linens?), the books on the nightstand, the clothes laid in a lazy little pile by the door. "Sorry. I'm with a friend. Is this better?" I sat on the edge of the mattress. It was one of those memory foam mattresses, and my legs sunk in until my whole body relaxed into a warm puddle, and all I wanted to do was sleep for a year.

"Yes, better. So, I was doing my usual Sunday routine: get up, make coffee, read the paper, what have you, when the telephone rang. Didn't I tell you there was a reason all these years that I didn't get rid of the landline? Didn't I insist that one day she could call—"

"Yes, Dad. Continue, please."

"Okay. So I get up to answer the phone, and I say, 'Hello?' and I hear this raspy breath, and that's when I know—I *know*, Sarah—that it's her, that she's come back to me."

"Dad, slow down. No one is coming back—"

"And then she says, 'Roger?' And that voice sounded like an angel, and I almost started crying right then and there. But I didn't. I *didn't*, Sarah. I just kept my voice steady, and I said, 'Elaine? Is that you?' And she started laughing—remember that laugh? God, it was one for the books—and then she asked if I was expecting someone else. She still has her sense of humor, I'll give her that."

My stomach churned at his gullible enthusiasm. This was the woman who'd left us, the woman who'd made us walk on eggshells twenty-four hours a day, seven days a week. But all of that was forgotten with a laugh and a hello? It made me nauseous. "So, then what?"

"Well, we talked for an hour."

"And?"

"And what?"

I peeked my head back out to the baby pool. Emma was

splashing with Charlie, while Ryan talked animatedly to them. "And did you find out where the hell she's been for the better part of our lives?"

"I . . . well, no. I didn't ask."

"Wait, you're kidding, right? You didn't even ask where she's been? You just let her off the hook like that, like she didn't do the worst thing a mother could ever do?"

He fumbled with something in the background. The more nervous my dad got, the clumsier he became. I used to think it was an endearing trait; right now, much like the rest of him, I found it pathetic.

"Well, I know she lives in Boulder."

"Of course she does. Not Hollywood, right? She's not some famous actress now?"

"That's not nice, Sarah. You know how cutthroat Hollywood is."

"No, I don't, actually. I know how cutthroat my own childhood was, though," I hissed. "Do you remember that at all, or has all of that been erased because she finally decided to pick up a damn phone after twenty-five years?"

"You were always so hard on her, Sarah. Just try to understand. And she . . . she asked about you. She wants to see you."

I pulled the phone away from my ear as though he'd screamed at the top of his lungs. I tried to settle down, to remember this wasn't my father's fault; it was hers. I could hear him calling my name. "I'm here."

"Did you hear what I just said? She wants to see you."

"Why? Why now? What does she want?"

"Why would you think she automatically wants something, Sarah? She wants to see her own daughter. I think that's reason enough."

"Gee, Dad, I don't know. Maybe because I run a very successful business and she wants money? Why else would a woman who abandoned us suddenly come back into our lives? Did she say she wanted to see you?"

His breath was heavy and slow. "Well, no. Not exactly. She—"

"Don't you dare defend that woman to me. Just don't. I have to go now."

I hung up, my fingers shaking as I struggled to calm down. This was ludicrous. Twenty-five years, and now she wanted to see me? That was an entire adult life. That was an irreparable amount of time. That was a first-degree-murder prison sentence! The irony that I'd lied about going to find her and now she wanted to find me was just too rich.

I stepped back outside and tipped my face to the sun.

"Everything okay?" Ryan asked.

I studied him. He was the exact opposite of Ethan, but suddenly, I just wanted to fold myself in someone's arms and have them tell me it was all going to be okay. I wanted to stop running.

"That was my father. My mother called him out of the blue."

"Are they divorced?"

Emma and Charlie were playing with Transformers. Every time Charlie would splash one into the water, Emma would bring hers up.

"What?" I looked at him and shook my head. "Oh no. She walked out when I was eight years old. Haven't heard a peep from her in twenty-five years."

I waited for the obligatory *I'm so sorry, that must have been rough* to come. "So you're thirty-three. Practically ancient."

I looked at him and laughed. "Really? That's what you just got from what I said?"

"Hey, at least I can do quick addition, right? And P.S.

Your mom sounds like a certified narcissist. Or a bitch. Want a drink?"

Emma jerked her head to Charlie at the word *bitch,* and then she darted her eyes my way. "He said—"

"It's fine, Emma. He didn't mean to."

I smiled at Ryan—the first genuine smile I'd given another male since Ethan. "Yes, she is. And yes, I would love a drink. Thank you."

I relaxed into the lawn chair, gazing at his small patch of earth in this urban metropolis. I closed my eyes and soaked in the children's sweet voices. They were talking about whose Transformer could do more tricks.

My mother wanted to see me.

Those words should have no impact, except they did. Ethan had always tried to get me to hunt her down, but I never had any interest. I'd never googled her or tried to look her up, not even once. She wasn't in my life, and it had been better because of it.

I watched Emma. Was *this* why I had taken her? To save her from a horrible relationship with her own mother because I couldn't save myself? Surely I wasn't that messed up from childhood, yet any therapist would identify the parallels. The similarities were there: absent mothers, verbal, physical, and emotional abuse. . . .

Ryan returned with a whiskey on the rocks, and I thanked him. He sat in the lawn chair and reached his glass out to clink mine.

"To complicated relationships," he said. I looked at his twinkling blue eyes, his straight, white teeth, and the small tuft of black hair sprouting from his open T-shirt in a single, wavy line. He was sturdy and dark, and there was something so neat, handsome, and dependable about him. He seemed like the kind of person who would understand anything, but I still couldn't tell him the truth.

Instead, I raised my glass and touched his with mine. "To complicated relationships." We both drank, our ice cubes clattering against our teeth, as we watched the kids. Is this what normal life could feel like? How easy it could all be?

Emma turned to me. "Can we stay here again, Sarah? Please? Just one more night?"

"What did I say yesterday? Just one day, remember?" I looked at Ryan, ready to apologize, but he shrugged.

"Why don't you guys stay another night? Charlie and I can show you the sights, isn't that right, buddy?"

Charlie nodded, and Emma nodded with him.

"We don't want to impose any more than we already have. We have to get back on the road soon."

"So get on the road soon. But stay for tonight. We'd really love the company." He looked at Charlie. "Right, buddy? Wouldn't we?"

"Yeah, yeah, yeah!" Charlie splashed.

Ryan turned back to me, regarding me lightly, but there was something else. A small prick of desire began to stir, but I pushed it away. I wanted to say yes. I was so tired of driving—if I never set foot in a car again, I would be happy—and so was Emma. She wanted to play and run free. I was exhausted from driving to senseless locations, worried about getting caught, worried about what Ethan had done, worried about the Montana lead, worried about exposing ourselves to more and more people, worried about getting sick or needing something out of my reach. We were so far from Washington. What if my Tahoe broke down? What if we got into a wreck? What if someone recognized us again?

I looked at Emma's eager, innocent face, her legs jumpy and slick in the pool, poised to celebrate if I said yes. "Okay, but only if you are absolutely sure. And thank you.

Really." I bit into an ice cube, feeling the shocking cold crunch against my teeth.

The kids let out happy shrieks and kept splashing and playing. Ryan and I laughed at their cuteness, finishing our drinks and sitting in happy silence, watching the sky turn from blue to pink to orange to black.

The next morning, over cereal and juice, it was as if Ryan knew what I was thinking.

"So I have a proposition for you."

He poured each of the kids more cereal.

"Oh, yeah? What's that?" I wrapped my hands around my mug of coffee, which was deliciously strong.

"Why don't you guys stay a little longer?"

"We stayed last night."

"I know, but I mean like a proper stay."

Emma dropped her spoon and looked at me. "Yes. Let's stay! Yay!"

I sighed. "Emma, we talked about this. We have more terrain—more places to see."

"I know, but we can show you some adventures, can't we, Charlie? We can go to Wisconsin or Indiana. There's extremely flat terrain there."

"I'm from Indiana, remember?"

"See? There you go. It's a homecoming."

"I am definitely not going back there." My voice was light, but my thoughts were heavy. It would be so easy to hole up here for a while, playing house, letting her just be a kid. But every day we stayed was one day closer to Ryan—or the world—finding out the truth.

"When does Emma have to be home?"

I shot up straighter in my chair. "No specific time, really. But soon."

Ryan knew there was a story there, but he didn't ask. I waited for Emma to say something, to allude to the fact that her home was somewhere else.

Instead, Emma watched Charlie's every movement, mimicking the way he held his adult utensil, some of the milk not making it into her mouth as she brought her own large spoon to her lips.

"So we can stay?" Emma finally asked, wiping her chin with the back of her hand.

"For a little while."

Charlie pushed away from the table and brought his bowl to Ryan. Emma did the same. "Can we go play in my room now?"

"Sure, buddy. Watch out for her, okay? Make sure she's okay on the steps."

Emma looked at him. "I'm not a baby."

He ruffled her hair. "I know that. You're a big girl."

She nodded, and they were off, parading through the three-flat as though they were elephants.

"Will they be okay up there?" I asked, rising to get more coffee.

He took my mug and refilled it. "You mean, besides all the drugs and guns? Sure, they should be."

"Ha ha. Very funny." I suddenly felt naked in my T-shirt and pajama pants. "This is good coffee. I haven't had good coffee in forever."

"Coffee snob?"

I took a sip. "Excuse me?"

"Are you a coffee snob? You do live on the West Coast, after all."

"Yes, I am, proudly. I am a huge coffee snob." I moved to the living room and sat on his couch. The backyard was sprayed with toys from their playtime yesterday. "Looks like another beautiful day. I love the weather here."

"Come visit in winter. You'll hate it."

"Nah. I don't mind the cold. Makes me think of the holidays." I folded my legs underneath me. Once summer was over, holidays would be rolling in: Halloween, where buckets of candy would get stuck in tiny teeth and cobwebs would hang from doorways, then changing leaves, buttered, basted turkeys, twinkling multicolored lights, snow, Santa. The fantasies tore at me: carving pumpkins with Emma, cooking a Thanksgiving dinner, decorating a Christmas tree with hand-me-down ornaments, sitting in front of the fire, reading stories. It seemed so easy, so *right*.

"Do you have time to sit for a second?"

"Sure." He wore sweatpants and a T-shirt, his hair messy, a slight line of stubble darkening his cheeks and jaw.

"You'd tell me if you wanted us to go, right?" I wanted to stay. My body wanted us to stay. I was pretty sure he wanted us to stay. But I wanted to be sure.

He hung his head and let out a dramatic, playful sigh. "Sarah, for the love of God. How many ways can we ask? We. Want. You. To. Stay."

"Okay, okay. Just making sure." I looked around. "We need to go shopping today for a few things."

"What's the story there? Why do you have your niece? You two could pass for twins, you know."

In that moment, I wanted to tell him. Something told me he might understand, but then I remembered he was a real parent, and nothing could make him sympathize with me. "Her mother is . . . tough. Verbally. Physically. I'm taking care of her for a while." I said nothing more. It wasn't exactly a lie.

"Whoa. That's complicated, Sarah. I'm sorry."

"We don't talk about home, or her parents. It just upsets her. And frankly, it upsets me."

"Got it. Say no more. It's *f-u-n* from here on out."

"Are you going to be spelling everything from here on out?"

"You *k-n-o-w* it." He winked.

"Great." I stretched my legs in front of me and yawned. "So, what do you normally do during a typical summer day?"

"Well, we usually do brunch and some outdoor activity, like the zoo. I know they just ate, so what do you think about going to the zoo?"

I knew Emma would love the zoo. I wondered if she'd ever been before. "We'd love to go."

Ryan leaned forward then, so much that I could smell his laundry detergent and remnants of last night's cologne. The front of his T-shirt brushed against mine as he brought his lips against my ear. "I hear the monkeys have gigantic balls," he whispered, and I slapped his arm and pushed him away, laughing so hard I almost spilled my coffee.

"Let's go tell the rug rats," he said. My legs felt wobbly. I needed to exercise, to burn off some of this energy.

He was right behind me as we went up the stairs. I could feel the heat from his body, and I wanted to turn, to lean my chest against his and just be held. We stopped outside of Charlie's room. He stood beside me and pressed his fingers to his lips as we both peeked around the doorframe.

"It goes like this," Charlie was saying, showing Emma how to make the top of a castle from Legos. She watched and then fit a few pieces together and stuck them at the top.

"Now, let's make a moat," he said, all business.

"What's a note?"

"Not a note, a *moat*. It goes around the castle, like this."

We slipped past them and giggled, my back against the hallway wall. *They are so cute,* I mouthed, placing a hand over my heart.

And then Ryan was in front of me, his lips inches from mine.

"You are so cute."

In that moment, everything flashed before me: meeting Ethan, breaking up with Ethan, drowning myself in business, taking Emma, seeing him again. I let all of that evaporate as I moaned and pulled this new man against me, gripping the back of his neck. His skin was smooth and hot under my fingers and his lips—once pressed against mine—were sure, full, and warm. I let my hands explore the muscles of his back as his fingers tugged at the fabric of my T-shirt. There was a hunger there—for both of us—as our tongues entwined and our breath caught, and he erased everything from my mind but a single, repetitive thought: *This means trouble.*

I pulled away, gasping, and placed a hand on his chest. "I'm . . . I'm so sorry, I—"

"No, no, I'm sorry. Shit." He adjusted his glasses and raked a hand through his hair. "I'll let the kids know we want to go soon."

I nodded and moved back downstairs to the guest room, everything unraveling. How stupid could I be? How safe did I think I was? I closed my eyes, wanting the choices to be easy. I liked Ryan, but I couldn't get in any deeper.

As I changed my clothes, my body pulsed from the kiss. It had been so long since I'd kissed another man. And it felt . . . amazing. But it had to stop before it started. I couldn't do that to him, to me, to Charlie, to Emma. I threw a few items into my purse, and my phone vibrated. I rummaged around and extracted it. It was an alert. My fingers hovered over the email. I didn't want to open it. I didn't want to know. But I had to. It was my sole responsibility to know what was happening with her case, a case that I had caused. I took a deep breath, still smelling Ryan on my fingers and in my hair. I shook away the thoughts and clicked the email. I read the first headline: *Emma Grace Townsend Spotted in Nebraska Diner*

"Oh God. Please no. Not again. Not now." Nausea ripped through my body as I began to read the short article. We'd been made again in Nebraska. The waitress from the diner? So my instincts had been right in the town square. She had recognized us. I scanned the last few lines. They had the make and model of my car. The cop in Montana must have called it in.

Ryan knocked on my door.

"Come in."

He opened it and leaned against the doorframe. "You're not going to suddenly leave, are you?"

I tossed my phone back in my bag and kept my hands from shaking. "How'd you know? I was planning my great escape."

"Look, Sarah." He sat next to me on the bed, the mattress groaning under his weight. His knee brushed mine. "I know you're going through a lot, but I promise, I have good intentions. I'm not here to complicate your life."

"I know." I turned to him. "Actually, do you think you could do me a favor?"

He wiggled his eyebrows. "What kind of favor?"

I shoved him playfully. "Do you think you could watch Emma for a little bit? There's just an errand I need to run before we go to the zoo."

"Wow, I feel flattered that you trust me that much."

I stared into his warm eyes. "I do, actually. I do trust you. I'll be fast." I swiped my keys and wallet and hesitated by the door. I walked back to him, cupped his face in my hands, and leaned down to kiss him again. "I'll be right back."

"Take your time. We'll be here."

It took everything in me to leave Emma with him, but I had no choice. Outside, I unbuckled Emma's car seat and cleaned out all the junk, leaving it piled in a neat corner in Ryan's detached garage. I plugged in the address to a nearby CarMax. The alert had just hit. Surely, my car wasn't in some sort of nationwide system yet.

The thought of parting ways with my Tahoe—however trivial—made me sad. It was my first purchase when I'd sold the premiere kits in bulk from TACK, and I'd paid for the car in cash. It was in good condition, though it had seen some wear and tear in the last few months.

The trade was quick. The car more than covered what I chose, a white Ford Focus. I signed the papers and ran a sentimental hand over the hood, realizing all I'd done in this car, both good and bad. A heavy weight slipped from my shoulders. If anyone was looking for my SUV, they wouldn't find it now.

I raced back to Ryan's and parked a few blocks away. I'd have to explain the car to Emma, but I wasn't ready yet.

Emma squealed when I came back in, and she wrapped her arms around my middle. "Charlie said we can go to the zoo? Can we?"

"Of course. Did you have fun while I was gone?"

"Yes! Can we go to the zoo now?"

"Let me just go wash my hands."

Ryan wrangled the kids as I went to the guest room and folded the paperwork into my bag. Her excitement was contagious. I brushed my teeth and reapplied my lipstick in the mirror. It was settled: I would give Emma today and tonight—one more day of playing house. And then we'd be back on the road, in a car no one was looking for, headed somewhere else, alone.

———

The zoo was thick with Chicagoans. They weaved along the trails and squished noses to smudged display windows to look at all the wildlife pacing in dirty, tired circles. I'd never much liked zoos—one look at the depressed animals' faces did me in—but they seemed to exhilarate children, and Emma was no exception. She hopped from monkey to tiger to giraffe to elephant. She and Charlie had made fast friends, and he checked that she was constantly beside him.

I struggled to smile, clap, and *ooh* and *aah* with them, but I couldn't think of anything other than what was ahead of us, of what leaving here would mean. The truth was getting closer—I could feel it, something was going to slip—and I couldn't get caught in the crossfire. Even here, at this zoo, with Ryan and Charlie, I was exposing her on an entirely new level. Maybe Charlie would talk about "his new friend Emma" at school, which could get back to a concerned parent who kept their eyes out for nationwide AMBER Alerts. It could happen just like that—I knew it could. It was time to end this once and for all.

I didn't know how to get out of this current situation, how to explain our sudden departure to Ryan and Charlie, and especially to Emma. Finally, she was warming up to a real life with a new friend in a city that held so many fond memories.

Ryan adjusted his glasses and bumped shoulders with mine. "Who died?"

I was too close to Ryan already; he could read me—though my mood must have been somewhat transparent—and I found myself wanting to kiss him again. It was preposterous. I'd spent so many years of my life hyperfocused on the wrong man. And now, the first honest, nice guy I'd met in ages came with a built-in family, and I wasn't—couldn't—be available.

"Ryan, I—I have to tell you something."

"Uh-oh."

"No, it's not about you, or what happened earlier." I linked my arm through his and cast a quick look toward the children. They were face-to-face with a majestic tiger, only a thin sheet of glass protecting them from getting mauled. "I just got word that my sister is going to press charges if I don't bring Emma home. She wants her at home, but I'm scared to take her back. I have no real grounds for obtaining custody. It would be a legal battle. One I wouldn't win."

He scratched his neck in that same thoughtful way Ethan used to do. "Can you get a lawyer?"

I shook my head. "Again, it would be a legal nightmare. I need to do the right thing here."

"Isn't this the right thing?" He used his free arm to motion to the kids. "Anyone can see how happy and loved she is, Sarah. I can't see her having a better upbringing than with you."

His words, though based on only partial truths, validated something in me. "Thank you."

We stepped closer to the children. "So you have to go?"

I nodded. "We do."

"And there's nothing I can do to help you stay? Or help you with your situation?"

I unhooked my arm from his and readjusted Emma's ball cap. "We'd love to stay, we would. You have no idea how much."

He shoved his hands in his pockets and looked down. "Well, we have really great timing, I think. Don't you?"

I laughed. "Thank you for taking us in and being so understanding. I hope—well, I don't know what I hope."

He turned to me. "No, just hope. Hope's a good thing. There's not enough of it these days, right?"

I wanted to kiss him goodbye, but I didn't, so instead I squeezed his hand and let it go, squatting beside Emma and saying hi to the tiger.

"Look, look at this tiger, Sarah! He's *so* close! Charlie and I are pretending to pet him!"

The exuberance was infectious—both of them were adorable—and I felt like I was doing such a shitty thing taking her away from here.

My phone buzzed in my pocket, once, twice. I moved back, motioning to Ryan to watch the kids while I checked my phone. It was another alert about the Montana spotting. I thought of the man I'd made the trade with at CarMax, how busy they'd been, how quick the exchange. Even if a report had been filed, it obviously hadn't made it to Chicago yet. The cop who pulled us over flashed through my mind again. He had to know about my car by now. And I'd told him exactly where we were headed. Yet another mistake. Though I knew the car was now safely out of the picture, we weren't. If my car was investigated, the new car would soon follow. They'd know exactly where to find me.

But that wasn't what stopped me. I scrolled down a little further and saw a second article: *New Prime Suspect in Longview Missing Girl Case.*

I read it in shock, a million emotions without names crashing against my chest. I glanced at the kids, at Ryan, and back at my phone, rereading the words and trying to make sense of them.

No matter what I felt or what I wanted, this article changed everything. We had to get out of here. Now.

We had to go.

amy

after

The leads died. All the sightings vanished into nothing—the woman in Montana, the sighting in Nebraska, the SUV—and they were left just as they started: searching.

"But this woman has to have her, Amy. The one she's been spotted with? It's the only logical explanation. Where else would she be?"

"I have no idea."

"I know, but don't you think it's all just . . . suspicious? That the only leads we had just died? That everything just vanished?"

"Why are you whispering?" She handed Richard a glass from the dishwasher. "I'm sure they are doing what they can. They can't be everywhere at once."

"I know, but this woman. It seems like she's nice, right?"

"What does being nice have to do with anything?"

"I don't know. Maybe she's trying to help her."

"Help her what?"

"Live? Bring her back?"

"*Live*? Like keep her? What is wrong with you?"

He shrugged. "I mean, it's better than some scary, aw-ful, mean person with our daughter, isn't it? No one has reported an abusive, horrible person with our daughter. That has to count for something."

"It's not our daughter."

"What are you talking about?"

Amy stopped unloading and squeezed her hips with her hands. "Richard, don't you think if Emma was out there, really out there, that they could actually bring her back again? What would she be doing in Montana? Or Nebraska, for that matter? There are a million little girls with gray eyes and mothers. It's not her. I know it's not."

"What do you mean?" Richard gripped a glass to his chest. "You can't possibly know it's not her."

Amy snatched a plate and shoved it in the cabinet. "I know. Mothers *always* know."

"What is that supposed to mean?"

"It means that I don't think she's out there, Richard."

"What? But Frank is on it. They can even project where she will go next."

"And *have* they? Have they brought us anything but dead leads?"

Her cell buzzed and then Richard's. She wiped her hands and took it from her pocket, while Richard grabbed his from the counter. It was a text from Frank.

Can you both come to the station, please? Thx.

Richard held up his phone and all the color drained from his face. "This isn't good. Oh my God, this isn't good. I feel sick. I feel sick!"

"Richard, it's fine. Calm down. Just give me a minute." Amy called Carla, and she was there in minutes. She kissed Robbie, made sure he had his snack, and tapped Richard on the shoulder; he was busy drilling his head against the refrigerator.

"We don't even know what this is. It could be—I don't know—more paperwork or something."

He looked at her, a purple splotch blooming on his forehead. "Paperwork? But you just said you didn't think she's out there and then Frank just asked us to come in!"

"I know what I said, but I think it's just paperwork. Or something equally banal."

"Banal? Since when do you use words like *banal*?"

She rolled her eyes. "Give me the keys. I'm driving."

They piled into the van, and she switched on the radio because she couldn't stand to listen to any more of Richard's moans, gasps, cries, or crazy conversations. She drove on autopilot, taking two lefts and a right before pulling in to the almost empty lot.

Inside, they were ushered straight to Frank's office, Barry and Stan joking about something around the coffeemaker. Amy nodded in their direction, but they avoided eye contact and stared intently into their coffee cups.

"Did you see that?" Richard hissed. "Something has happened. I know it has. I can feel it. Hold my hand."

She looked down at his hand. It had been so long since they'd held hands . . . years, maybe. But if she refused, which she wanted to do, he would throw a tantrum in the police station, and she wanted to get out of here with as little fuss as possible. His wormy fingers barely fit into the tight spaces of her fluffy knuckles. Frank was sitting behind his desk, arms behind his head, reclined. She wondered, for a brief moment, what would happen if he tipped over. He motioned for them both to sit and then closed the door behind them.

"Thanks for getting here so fast, folks."

"Just tell us. Tell us, or I'm going to explode right here all over your desk."

Frank had grown accustomed to Richard's strange outbursts and odd requests. He didn't blink. "Well, it appears

we have a new lead. Someone has come forward to produce a motive for murder."

Richard grabbed the sides of his face and started pulling his skin so hard it looked like it was going to tear off
and drain into his lap. "She's *dead*? I knew it! I knew she
was dead! My baby!"

"No, no, Richard. She is not dead. Emma has not been
found. I want to make that perfectly clear. She has not been
found."

Amy readjusted in the chair, not quite understanding.
"Wait, I'm sorry. What are you saying? Murder? Why
would you say that, then? Who has a motive? Is there a new
lead?"

Frank wouldn't look directly at her. "Do you know an
Evelyn Lee Ross?"

Richard looked at her to confirm or deny. He was
terrible with names. "Of course," Amy said. "She's our
next-door neighbor. To the left. Well, to the right if you're
in our house, but yes. Why? Is she a . . . suspect?" The
thought of Evelyn Lee Ross with her homemade pies, lu-
lulemon pants, and *namaste* everything hurting so much
as a gnat seemed impossible.

"No, but she's come forward about the night Emma
went missing."

"Did she see who took her?" Richard leaned toward
Frank, his hands white on the arms of the chair.

"She saw Emma." Frank flipped a pencil over and over
in his hands. "With you, Amy. She saw you both outside."

Amy flinched. "So what? We *were* outside. I've told you
all that about a million times. What does that have to do
with anything?" *She knew exactly what it had to do with.*

"She gave her statement a few days after Emma went
missing, and told us she saw you both outside, but she left
it at that. But then she came down here yesterday, since

all of these leads have turned up cold, and she asked again about the night in question. Wanted to amend her statement. Said she saw it all through her fence."

"Saw *what* all through her fence?"

Richard looked at her, confused. "What's he talking about, Amy?"

"The fight with your daughter. The fight you only partially told us about." Frank pushed back in his chair again, arms crossed, smug. She hated him now, hated that she'd ever fantasized about him and her after all of this.

"No, I didn't partially tell you anything. I told you we had a fight and then I went back inside. And fell asleep." It sounded so ridiculous that even she would question herself if she were the police. "The polygraph proved that."

"No, the polygraph was inconclusive at best, because it seems you left out some important details."

"What details?" Richard's head volleyed back and forth between them.

"Amy, this is your chance to tell me exactly what happened that night."

She lifted her hands and dropped them. "What else can I tell you? We argued. We *always* argued. She was in the woods. I told her to come out. She did. I told her to come inside and she wouldn't. And then she told me—" She looked at Richard, embarrassed. "She told me she didn't love me."

"Oh, Amy, you know she didn't mean that. She—"

"And then I told her I didn't love her either."

"Did you hit your child, Amy?"

"I'm sorry . . . you said *what*?" Richard was shaking his head as if he hadn't heard correctly. "You told her you didn't *love* her?"

"Yes, I did. I know it was a terrible thing to say. But

we're terrible together. Everyone knows it. But that doesn't mean I would ever hurt her."

"So you didn't hit her?" Frank asked.

"Of course she didn't," Richard said. "You didn't, right? That's ridiculous."

Richard was so clueless. "I slapped her. I did. I lost my temper." She sniffed. "I don't think I'm the first parent in history to ever slap a child."

"And then you went inside and locked your child out of the house and your husband fell asleep with Robbie, correct?"

"But the door wasn't locked," Richard said. "I unlocked it."

She darted her eyes at Frank. He knew. "Yes, I relocked the door. I was angry. But I did fall asleep. I have no idea what happened during those three hours."

"You locked the door?" Richard asked. "Are you serious?"

"Why aren't you asking him what he was doing during those three hours?" Amy offered.

"You were asleep, weren't you, Amy?" Richard was clinging to the truth she'd created; it was his only lifeline.

"Of course I was asleep! I locked the bedroom door. How would I have gotten out? Did I climb through a window?"

"Can you support that, Richard? Was the bedroom door locked?"

"I didn't—I never . . ." He looked at Amy. "I never checked. I was too . . . I'm sorry. I never checked. I thought you were with Emma. I never thought to—"

"And why did you think Emma was with Amy? Did you see your wife with her after she went back inside? After the fight?"

"I . . . no. No, I don't think so. Wait." He dropped his

head in his hands, her forgetful, stressed husband who could literally sentence her right now if he wasn't accurate with his memory.

"This is ludicrous! I did not hurt my daughter! What, was I supposed to murder her while Richard sang Robbie to sleep? And do what with her body, exactly? I don't know if you've noticed, but I'm not the most physically fit person in the world. There are no bodies buried anywhere in our backyard. Dig it up. Dig it all up."

The hypnotherapy sessions came barreling in, and for a brief, transient moment, she wavered. They'd listened to the tapes; they knew. In those sessions, she could transport back to a former self. She was in another place, in another time, living another life. It all felt so real, but she was still conscious, straddling the line between this life and that. A few words, the tick of a clock, and she was under an indescribable trance. Had she somehow reverted to one of those states and then dropped Emma off a cliff? Drowned her in the bathtub and then buried her where no one could ever find her? Could she have done that without being aware of it? "This is all so preposterous, I don't even know what to say. I mean," she fiddled with the strap of her purse, "where would I have even supposedly taken her?"

"That's what we're asking you, Amy. Look." Frank leaned forward and folded his hands on the desk, a bargaining play. "This has all been stressful. On everyone. Parenthood is hard. Marriage is hard. We know there have been difficulties, and that's okay. That's perfectly okay. No one is here to judge you. But this is your one and only chance to come clean before things get messy."

"To come clean about what?"

"Did you kill your daughter?"

Amy shook with rage. Her fists opened and closed as

fast as her heart could pump blood. She made her voice as small, still, and certain as possible. "No, Frank. I did not kill my daughter."

He looked at Richard and stood. "Richard, I'm afraid we're going to have to keep Amy here for a little more questioning. Just to get this all straightened out. Okay, buddy?" He clapped him on the shoulder and Richard pitched forward in his chair.

"What? What's he talking about?" Richard looked at her again, but this time, uncertainty stared back. And then it all made sense: *This* was what Frank was after. Not for her to confess—there would be time for that. What he wanted was to plant the seed of doubt into her husband's fragile, fraying mind, so that Richard would spill all her dirty little parenting secrets.

"It's fine, Richard." Amy sat up straighter and glared at Frank. "I have nothing to hide. Ask me anything."

Frank ushered Richard into the lobby, his hand glued to Richard's back. Two could play at this game. Let the real kidnapper get away while they spun their wheels and tried to nab the horrible mother. Because a monstrosity like this had to have someone to blame, right? That's what the public wanted, so the police would give it to them. With or without the truth, Amy was now, once again, the prime suspect.

An hour later, Amy sat in another smaller, hotter office. There were no windows. A large recording device rested in front of her. She'd seen shows like this, how they asked you the same questions a million different ways to coerce you into a false confession. They'd hounded her in the beginning—her and Richard—and now, because of Evelyn Lee Ross, she was sitting here again, a liar, an awful mother, and, in their eyes, a child killer.

They made her wait with her little Styrofoam cup of water and pack of chips she'd snagged from the vending machine. She opened them and stabbed the roof of her mouth with the first triangle of baked corn. She winced, dug out the sharp edge, and checked for blood.

Frank entered after a thousand years, a woman behind him. "Sorry about the wait, Amy. It's been an unusually busy night. This is Detective Richards. She's going to be sitting in on this, if you don't mind."

"And if I do?"

"Well, I'm afraid you don't have a choice."

Amy nodded as though this were the answer she was waiting for—what was allowed and what wasn't—before folding her hands on the table, just as Frank had done in his office.

"Where would you like to start? When Emma was born? Before? I can tell you as much as you want to know. About how I didn't want kids. About my shitty marriage. About how good I am with my son, but for some reason, Emma and I are like oil and water. I can tell you about all the times I've spanked her in a fit of rage and then regretted it. How I made deals with myself that I would never do it again, and then she'd piss me off, and I'd pop her on the leg or hand, or yes, even her face. I can also—"

"Amy, Amy, slow down. We haven't even started yet. We're just going to have a casual conversation."

"Oh, really? Then why is that here?" She pointed to the recording device—ancient, dusty, too big for the room. "Is that for casual conversations only?"

Frank and Detective Richards looked at each other. She sat across from Amy, her shoulder pressing into Frank's.

Amy wondered if they were sleeping together due to all the tragic cases and late nights.

"Look, Amy. We know this is hard. No parent-child relationship is easy. And yes, we know you're not the first person to ever hit a child. But you did hit your child. Moments before she went missing. She was left outside, alone, and then there are three hours that are unaccounted for that neither your husband nor you have alibis for. Now, what would you surmise from that?"

"That we were guilty of being pretty shitty parents but not murderers. God. I've been far too busy fucking her up mentally to even worry about really hurting her physically yet." The joke fell flat, and Frank looked away, his head shaking back and forth.

"Why aren't Barry and Stan on the case anymore? Why have all the searches stopped? Why isn't anyone *doing* anything?" She could hear the tick of the clock, an old, wide orb with giant red hands.

"Because those leads are false. They've led us back here. This new testimony from Evelyn gives us good reason to believe your daughter is dead, Amy."

"And why is that?"

"We think you know why."

Amy reddened. "I want a lawyer. Right now." She scraped back her chair, leaving her chip crumbs and Styrofoam cup on the table.

"Amy, we're not finished."

"Am I under arrest? Do you have any evidence to support these ridiculous claims? No, you don't. I know my rights." She took a few steps toward the door and turned. "How about instead of wasting your time with this absolute nonsense *again*, you go out and actually find my daughter? I'll be at home if you need anything else."

She slammed the door. She had to call Ronnie. He was the only lawyer who would touch this. And she had to get to Richard, had to get him back on her side. Now, along with everything else, it was about damage control.

before

On her last trip to Barb's office, she came with questions. Questions about who she'd been in former lives and how that affected who she was today. She felt doomed. Every life she'd led had ended in turmoil. They'd all had their pocks and bumps, as if life were nothing but a suffering hole. She told Barb as much, all but demanding a refund.

"Well, I'm sorry you think of it like that, Amy. But everyone has a silver lining."

Amy rolled her eyes—they were past all pretenses of manners at this point—and squeezed her handbag beside her. "I want you to hypnotize me. I want you to hypnotize me to stop being so angry. I don't want to be angry anymore. I can't be."

Barb leaned back in her chair and assessed Amy. "While that's a noble thing to want, as you know, until you deal with the past, you can't get rid of your anger today."

Her blood began to rumble and warm. She could feel herself getting hotter, madder, and more frustrated. "You're not hearing me right. I have to get rid of this anger, or I'm going to be the worst mother on earth. The worst person on earth."

"Oh, tsk, tsk. No one is the worst mother on earth, I

can assure you. You're probably Supermom compared to most."

Amy stared at this portly woman who'd probably given birth a million years ago and couldn't remember what it was like to handle even one day with a young child. "Do you have children?"

Barb extended a hand and batted away an invisible truth. "Me? No, no. Wasn't in the cards for me."

Amy laughed. "So you're telling me that I'm a good parent, but you're not a parent? How can you . . . I don't even understand that. How can you give me advice if you have no idea what it's like to be me?"

"Oh, dear. Well, it's not about having a child or not having a child. It's just about relationships. People. Like me and you."

Amy's jaw stiffened. Her fists fastened. She worked to steady her breath, to not feel betrayed by this woman who knew who she was, what she'd done, and where she'd been. "And tell me. What do you think of me?"

"What do you mean?"

"As a person? What's your professional assessment of who I am as a human being?"

"Well, that's not really in my job description to assess who you are. It doesn't matter who I think you are."

"Indulge me." Amy folded her arms on her belly and waited.

Barb straightened, and the fake smile drained from her lips. "Okay, if you really want to know, Amy, I think you suffer from never having had a father. Your mother was very capable, so you grew up around capable females, but you resented her because she wasn't a victim, like you. She got on with her life, but you didn't. You ate your feelings and placed blame on everyone and everything around you. You let your life become circumstantial. You are a person who is *built* on circumstances. At any minute, you could look at your life and see all that you have to be thankful for—a loving husband, two healthy kids, a steady income—but instead you throw it all away because you're harboring some warped vision of the way your life was supposed to be instead of the way it is."

Amy inhaled. She opened her mouth then snapped it shut. How could Barb have gotten all of that from these visits? How could she look at her and just know who she was to the very core? Amy felt insulted and yet truly seen for the first time in her life. This woman saw her for who she was, not who she wanted to be. She could spout off some nasty remark and leave her office for good, or she could stay and face the truth of herself, of who she was no longer willing to be.

"Amy? I asked how that makes you feel? Hearing all of that?"

Amy stared at the clock on the wall, at the desk that was always messy, at the silver filing cabinets that housed hundreds of secret lives and tapes. She finally found Barb's eyes behind her glasses: milky gray irises that reminded her of how Emma's would shrink and droop someday. She wanted to stand and run, but instead, she stayed and sat.

"Tell me more," she said. "Tell me more about me."

after

Amy dropped her bags on her desk and took the Tupperware to the office kitchenette. Her coworkers, Mary and Christina, were already huddled around the coffeemaker, deep in gossip.

They barely batted an eye as Amy squeezed behind them to put her labeled, preportioned lunch in the refrigerator. She was starting a diet—today. She'd had it with straining, sweating, and so much heaviness with every step and breath.

The first time she'd tried to diet after Emma was born, she'd called her mother in an absolute panic about all the foods she had to give up. She always called her mother if there was a problem, because her mother wasn't emotional and could highlight the ease of a task without all the feelings surrounding it. Her sturdy, blunt mother, true to form, had told her to close her damn mouth and start moving her legs. "Come out to the farm for a while. You'll move so much you can eat anything you want."

Amy was trying Weight Watchers. It was the only plan where she could still have cheese and dessert and come in under her point tally. She turned to pour some coffee, but Mary blocked the way.

"Can I?" She reached an arm toward the cabinet for a mug.

Mary did not move. Amy looked at her, startled. Mary was many things, but she wasn't rude. "Is there a problem?"

Mary and Christina crossed their arms like a pair of preteen mean girls and studied Amy. "You know . . . I've spent the last two months feeling *horrible* for you, organizing search parties, trying to think of anything I could do to help," Mary said. "And now this."

"I can't believe you're even here today," Christina added.

Amy looked back and forth between the two of them. "And now *what*? What are you talking about?"

Christina shook her head. "We know what they are saying about you. Everyone knows. It's all over the internet."

Amy's fingers began to shake, and she shoved them into her pockets. "What's all over the internet? That I'm a suspect? I would never, ever hurt my daughter. People who know me know that."

The women looked at each other, and Mary took a step closer. "We saw that video, Amy. The one from the market."

"What video?"

Mary rolled her eyes. "The video. Of you and Emma with the grocery cart!"

What were they talking about? There was a video of her and Emma? And a grocery cart? "I have no idea about any type of video."

"Just save it, Amy. You shouldn't be here."

The two women left Amy facing the cabinets. She poured herself a cup of coffee and went to find Patrick, her boss. His door was closed, which meant he didn't want interruptions, but she knocked anyway. After a few beats, he barked for her to come in.

Amy shouldered the door open—it always stuck—and tried to keep her coffee from spilling. His face fell when he saw her. He sighed and motioned for her to sit.

"What is it?"

"I just had a few questions about the Delaney file," Amy said. "I'm a little behind."

"Amy, look. I've been meaning to find you and talk." He clipped the cap on his Montblanc and smoothed his tie. "I . . . we can't have this publicity here right now. I know work is probably the only thing keeping you afloat, and I get that, I do, but this is just . . . it's too serious an accusation. Until you get cleared, of course."

"Are you serious? You want me to go home?"

"I think that would be best."

Amy spun the mug in her hands, a slow, hot circle. "But why now? They accused me in the beginning too. That's what they do in these cases when they have no leads. They got some false traction and now they don't have anything, so the investigation turns back to me. That's all this is. They have nothing. They're just pointing fingers."

"I get that, Amy. I do. But I have a company to protect."

"But how am I supposed to pay for things? Richard has totally lost it. He hasn't been to work in over two months. I'm the only one supporting us right now."

He rolled the pen around in his fingers, a pen that cost more than she made in a month. "We'll give you six weeks' pay until this gets sorted. Okay? You've been here a long time. People are just . . . well, they're reeling about these latest accusations. You know how the media is."

She nodded, thanked Patrick, walked back to the kitchen, and dumped the rest of her coffee in the sink.

She scooped her Tupperware into her tote, collected a few things—her brand-new stapler, her laptop, her notebooks—and left with her head held high, the snickers and whispers of an office who barely used to know her name now filled with judgment.

Once in her car, she tapped the steering wheel and felt the absolute exhaustion of these past few months sift through her body like poison. Where could she go? She put the car in drive and headed straight to Ronnie's office. He'd know exactly how to help.

She'd set aside a chunk of her mother's house fund to cover potential lawyer fees in case she had to prove her innocence. Even though Ronnie was a friend, he was still expensive. She wanted to be prepared.

His office was small and unpretentious, with a reception desk and a single corner office flanked by windows, filing cabinets, and countless legal boxes. Ruth was answering a call and waved her back as she entered. She tapped on Ronnie's door.

He looked up, removed his small spectacles, and motioned for her to sit. "I wondered when you'd be coming in."

"Why do you say that?"

"Because you're the prime suspect."

Amy listened to the words leaving his mouth, the way they twisted the truth into something completely different. *Because you're the prime suspect.* Amy had done so many things wrong as a mother, but the fact that this investigation had actually turned back to her boggled her mind.

"Amy. Did you hear what I just said?"

"What? Sorry."

"You look exhausted. Are you getting any rest?"

"No, it's not that. I basically just got fired from my job."

"Oh. I'm sorry."

People kept saying that—that they were sorry, that she should just go home, lie down, and get some rest. She'd never thought there could be something worse than being overweight, in a crappy marriage, or raising a difficult child, but this was it. People thought she was a murderer. She wasn't sure how you bounced back from that. "And these girls . . . these girls at my work just now. They were talking about some video?"

"What video?" Ronnie feared negative media attention the way other people feared the flu. He'd do anything not to catch it.

"I don't know. Some video of Emma and me in the grocery store? I mean, I don't know why there would be a video. I never took a video."

"What's on the video, Amy?"

"I don't know, Ronnie. That's what I'm saying. I haven't seen it."

He pecked away on his computer, squinting his eyes, his bushy white eyebrows like caterpillars on a slow mission to find each other. "Oh, Amy. Oh my God." He hung his head and shook it, and she practically yanked his desktop screen her way.

"What? What is it? What could someone possibly have . . . ?"

Ronnie stopped the video, restarted it, and twisted the screen further toward her. It had recently been uploaded to some mainstream media site, and now the local news was all over it. Amy was looking at a version of herself probably six or seven months ago. Robbie was in the cart, chewing on a toy. And Emma was beside the cart, a wad of her hair having somehow gotten caught between the handle and the body of the cart. Amy was pushing the cart, oblivious, yelling at Emma to stop screaming. Emma could barely keep up as she cried and attempted to pry her hair free. The person taking the video was muttering obscenities, and people in the aisle were clutching their canned soups and bagged chips, appalled.

The video shut off. "Amy, I don't even know what to say."

"Ronnie, I didn't *know* her hair was stuck, I swear! I thought she was just, you know, being Emma and crying about something. Someone came over and let me know her hair was caught in the cart. I had no idea."

"But she was walking right beside you."

Amy rolled her eyes. "Ronnie, until you've worked a full day, then picked your kids up from day care, then had to go to the store to figure out what to get for dinner, all while being sleep-deprived, you can't possibly tell me what I would and wouldn't pay attention to. I was a professional at tuning her out when I needed to."

"But Amy . . ." He motioned to the screen.

"Look, when we got there, she kept swinging her hair near the cart. I kept telling her to stop, and she didn't. Her hair somehow got wound all the way around it. I thought she was just throwing a massive tantrum, like usual. As soon as someone pointed it out, I stopped and untangled it for her. Where's the video of that? That I helped her?" She fanned herself. "I basically had to rip a handful of her hair out, and then I rubbed her head and trimmed her hair for her when we got home. I swear."

"Amy, it doesn't matter what you did after. It matters what this makes you *look* like." He shook his head again, the disappointed grandfather, and turned back to his computer.

"This doesn't make any sense. Where did this video come from? Why didn't someone submit this months ago when I was first accused?"

"I have no idea. Probably because other leads surfaced. When there was movement in Montana and Nebraska, I think people probably thought it was an actual kidnapping. But now that it's turned back to you, well . . . you know how people are with their phones these days. People take videos of everything."

"But it is an actual kidnapping. I didn't *do* anything."

"We've got to go on the defensive immediately. We might need you to issue a statement."

"What?" Amy recoiled. "I'm not issuing a statement about something that happened months ago and wasn't even anything! I literally stopped seconds after that asshole stopped taking that video! I didn't even know we were being filmed. I mean, isn't that illegal?" She clutched her purse in her lap and squeezed. "I swear, I hate our world today. You can make anyone look like they are doing anything, and then sit back and just judge, write comments, and crucify parents who are, by the way, doing the hardest job imaginable—"

"People think you killed your daughter, Amy. This just corroborates their story, establishes a pattern! Don't you get that?" He rubbed a hand over his wrinkled forehead. "They're after Richard to give up even more instances like this. It's not good. Don't you see that? Don't you see what trouble you're in? How they are turning everyone against you?"

Amy took the cold, hard truth like icy water splashed in her face. "I'm sorry, Ronnie. Yes, you're right." She uncrossed and recrossed her legs, struggling to grab hold of an ankle. "What have you gotten from Richard in all this?"

Ronnie shuffled through some papers and coughed. "Well, he's . . . he's struggling right now, Amy. He really is."

"Ronnie, please, I beg of you. Cut the shit. Just tell me." She knew Richard didn't trust her. In the past week, she'd caught him at night, duvet pulled up to his chin, staring at her. He'd started sleeping with a baseball bat. He cried all the time: in the shower, over coffee, putting on his thin socks. Frank had turned him. He believed them, not her.

"He wants full custody of Robbie."

Amy sucked in her breath and rummaged in her purse for a cough drop. The menthol soothed her throat and opened her sinuses. "Can he do that?"

Ronnie chewed his lip into embarrassed, tactful angles and shrugged. "Well, technically, with everything that's happening right now? Yes. Yes, he can."

Amy bowed her head and sighed, accidentally sucking the lozenge into the back of her throat. She grabbed her neck and coughed, once, but it was lodged. She stood up and coughed as hard as she could. The blue mint rocketed out of her mouth and landed on the back of Ronnie's wrist.

"Oh my God, I'm so sorry, Ronnie. I was choking. I was . . ." She exploded into laughter, looking at that blue mint balanced on her lawyer's aging, sun-spotted wrist. He smiled, pinched it with a tissue, and deposited it in the trash.

"Amy, it's fine. Are you okay? Do you need me to get you some water?"

Tears streamed down her cheeks, and she collapsed in the chair, laughing and rocking back and forth until she thought she might pee.

"I'll be right back. Just take a minute. I'll get you some water, okay?"

She couldn't catch her breath. The whole world thought she was a *killer*. Her, a killer! Her husband now wanted to divorce her, and he wanted full custody of their other child. In a matter of a few months, everything about her life had changed. And isn't that exactly what she'd wanted?

Ronnie entered a few minutes later with a cup of water,

and Amy thanked him and took it. "I'm so sorry about that. I think everything just caught up to me. I haven't laughed in . . . God, I don't know how long."

"Perfectly normal, Amy. Everyone handles situations like these in different ways."

Ronnie pulled up something on his computer.

She set the glass on his mahogany desk, unable to locate a coaster. She slid a piece of paper under it as a courtesy. "Can I ask you something?"

"What's that?" He pressed *enter* and looked at her, that sloped smile—the result of a stroke a few years back—pulling his face down and to the left.

"Do you think I killed Emma?"

Now it was his turn to laugh. "Amy, dear. No, of course not. I've known you for years. You have a temper, sure, and you don't always paint yourself in the best light, but I know you would never *kill* a child."

She sat back, relieved. "Now, how do I prove that to the world?"

"Listen." He sat forward. "That's my job, okay? And so far, they have nothing. They've dug up your backyard. They've taken DNA. They've searched in rivers, lakes, the woods, and anywhere else you could have gone in *any* direction within a three-hour radius. They have nothing. They have a neighbor who saw a fight you've already confessed to. You've been open about everything else. Well, except this video. This damn, dreadful video. But we'll deal with that. We will." He turned back to his computer, read something, then focused on her. "If you were guilty—and I know you're not—you wouldn't have painted such an unattractive picture of your mother-daughter relationship. You wouldn't be so forthcoming about . . ."

"About what?"

He dismissed the thought with a wave of his hand and

went back to typing. "You know what I mean. The slap. What happened that night. Everything."

"So what now? I feel like I'm on trial. What am I supposed to do? I mean, is there going to be a trial?" The thought of courts and a jury made her feel instantly sick.

"No, there won't be a trial unless they can find some shred of concrete evidence to convict you. And I won't let that happen. I promise."

She nodded. Someone was on her side. Someone was giving her assurance. Someone believed in her, and that's all she needed to make it out of this alive.

On the way home, she stopped at the market to get eggs, cheese, and a loaf of bread. She wanted cheesy French toast—Virginia's cheese shop was closed, so she'd have to settle for the cheap stuff—and a bad movie. Fuck the diet. Robbie was with Richard on a dad-son date, and this would be one of the first nights she'd ever been in their house alone since she'd had children. As she popped a loaf of bread into her cart and turned down the dairy aisle, she could hear someone snicker beside her. She turned to see one of the school moms glaring at her, jaw clenched.

"May I help you?"

"You oughta be *ashamed* of yourself."

Amy looked at the cheese and butter in her hands. "For this? It could be worse. I'm already fat." She scooped even more butter and gooey cheese off the shelves and let them topple into the cart.

The woman pulled her sweater tighter and walked away, leaving her cart in Amy's way. Amy bumped it and grabbed a few more items before heading to the checkout.

The cashier was gabbing away with the man in front of her, but when Amy unloaded her groceries on the belt, the woman didn't say a single word. She took her groceries to her car herself—the checkout boy didn't offer to help—and found three eggs splattered across the side of her van. She turned around in the parking lot, shame and anger working over her entire body. She got in, locked the doors, and sat there, her breath coming in gasps.

She'd gone into labor with Robbie in this very parking lot. Emma had rubbed her belly, told her to breathe, and to do her "moz." Emma had been so little, and in that moment, Amy thought that she could be a good mom, that she *would* be a good mom. It was a sweet moment, a rare moment, and the memory of her daughter's small hands on her huge belly rocked through every bone in her body.

She cleared her throat and put the car into reverse, making sure the doors were locked, almost afraid to go home, to see what was awaiting her. Should she buy a gun?

As she pulled in to the driveway and the headlights flicked over the playhouse in the back, she had the same glimmer of hope she did every time she came home: *Maybe tonight will be the night Emma returns.*

She crept out of the car and tiptoed toward the barren playhouse, opening the door. Dirt covered the interior. The entire plastic house reeked of mildew and loneliness. Tears pricked her eyes. All she needed was a chance. One chance to do it again, to start over, to be better.

One more chance to make it right and show the world—and herself—that she was better than she'd been.

sarah

after

I climbed out of the car and let Emma explode onto the community playground. Droves of children shrieked, climbed, and chased each other. We were somewhere in Kansas. Emma charged straight to the swings, clenched the metal chains, and hoisted herself up on the hot, rubber seat. She leaned forward and began to extend and bend her legs to gain momentum. I shook the pins and needles from my legs and took a large gulp of coffee. We'd driven so many miles, I'd lost count.

Leaving Chicago had been excruciating. I marveled at how I could feel so connected to someone I'd just met. When I hugged Ryan goodbye, I wanted to tell him everything. I wanted to tell him about my mother. I wanted to tell him what I'd done. I wanted him to help. I wanted to go everywhere as a foursome, gorging ourselves on Coal Fire Pizza, winding through the Art Institute of Chicago, the Shedd Aquarium, and the Adler Planetarium. I wanted to pack a picnic lunch and eat in Grant Park. I wanted to live a normal life.

As Emma glided up and down, gaining height and speed, I smiled. I had so many decisions to make, but watching her here, like this, wasn't one of them. When I looked at her, all I could feel was joy. Our time together had been full of uncertainty, yes, but our connection had been pure. My phone buzzed in my pocket. My father.

Have you made a decision yet? Your mother would really love to see you.

My father had been calling obsessively as we charted our next destination. The irony wasn't lost on me that we were in Kansas and could easily drive to Colorado. I considered what it would mean to see my mother. All of the old hurts that would rear their ugly heads, all of the memories that no longer served me. I thought of Emma's mother. Did she deserve a second chance? Did my mother? Did all mothers deserve a second chance to right past wrongs?

Emma ejected herself from the swing. She overshot, tumbling forward before brushing off her knees.

"You okay?"

She thrust her thumb in the air and kept moving toward the ladder. My mind was numb with information. Information about Amy, about her being the main suspect. About my license plate, the car swap, Ryan, the waitress, my mother, all of it.

Emma flew down the slide, her feet spraying wood chips as her bright pink Converse made contact with the earth. She darted right, and I let my eyes sweep over the trees, the bike path, and the skate park that sat on a small hill ahead of us. The slap of colorful boards dropped in, squeaky wheels against concrete. Emma stood and watched the young boys and girls in their helmets and baggy shorts, descending off ramps and sliding across skinny metal beams to attempt new tricks.

I took another sip of coffee. We couldn't keep running. I couldn't keep evading my business. I couldn't keep avoiding my dad. I couldn't pretend that the reality of Amy getting sent to jail might happen if I didn't intervene.

I stretched my back and neck, my chin almost touching my chest as I looked down and then up at the cloudy sky. I turned my attention back to the playground, all of the children circling around each other like sharks in a feeding frenzy. Emma was climbing the ladder again and patiently waiting her turn as kids trampled on top of each other to fight for space on the way down. We'd washed her hair obsessively until the blond had been toned. She was wearing a ball cap, the ends of her short hair tucked up tight in a small bun.

I winced as a boy flew down after her, cracking her in the skull with his elbow. She rubbed her head, adjusted her hat, and kept jogging toward the small snake sculpture she could crawl through. A mother bounced her baby on her chest and yelled at her little boy to be more careful. She cast an apologetic look my way and I waved her off.

"It happens," I said.

My phone buzzed again with the unanswered text, and I sighed and pulled it from my pocket.

Fine. Give me the details. I'll see what I can do.

I pressed send before I could think about it. One decision made. Next. Cyclists moved across the windy path, a few joggers stretching in the grass. Emma sprinted toward the giant bush behind my bench and rustled a few of the prickly leaves with her palms.

"Hey, Em. Stay where I can see you, okay?"

She reemerged and came to take a sip of water. "I'm hungry."

I extracted her baggie of snacks and opened it, shaking out a few slices of orange and a handful of pretzels into her waiting palms. She popped the oranges and pretzels into her mouth at once, crunching and sucking loudly.

"Are you having fun?"

"Uh-huh." She slurped the juice rushing down her wrist

and shook one more pretzel into her mouth. "Can we stay awhile?"

"Sure."

She was off again, and I relaxed as I watched her, trying to clear my mind. I'd asked myself so many times what the "right" thing to do was, as though a clear, defined answer existed. It didn't. I wanted to keep her, of course I did. But would I be denying Amy her second chance? A second chance I would want if I was in her shoes?

Fear began to strangle me again, but I willed myself to stay calm. The thought of handing her over. The thought of never knowing what might happen to her. The thought of saying goodbye. No. I shook my head and drained the last of my coffee, tossing the paper cup in the trash.

A Toyota Corolla idled in the spot next to ours in the parking lot. I peered a little closer. A man with a beard sat behind the wheel, staring at the children. Engorged circles strangled the flesh beneath his eyes. There was no child in his car. Did he have a kid on the playground? I stepped back to the bench, a few leaves shaking loose from the tree beside me. I moved to the trunk and stared up into the web of tangled branches. Another child, a boy, was gripping the trunk and shimmying higher in his untied tennis shoes and red shorts. He whimpered.

"Are you okay?"

"I don't know how to get down!"

I scanned the playground for Emma, making sure she was okay, and looked around for the boy's parents. "Just step down on that branch right there, okay? You're not going to fall. I promise."

The boy's legs trembled as he found the lower branch and clung to the trunk. Finally, he was within reach, and I helped him slide down the bark and plop softly on the grass. He took off running, and I sat back down.

The mother with the baby approached. "Thank you for that. I have three boys here, and I can't ever keep up."

"No problem."

No one questioned if I was a parent. It had all been so natural and easy, despite the circumstances. But a child belonged to her mother. That was the law of nature. No matter how much I loved her, no matter how much I wanted her, no matter how much I cared.

The man in the car revved his engine, and I shuddered. Would Amy be able to protect Emma from strangers? Would Amy pay enough attention?

Chills pocked my skin. Clarity was coming, sweet and painful, but I wasn't ready to accept it just yet. I thought of what it would mean to return home without her. What was waiting for me there. I knew how easy it was to slip back into routines, to drive myself into an early grave with obsessive work. All the travel, the deals, the late nights and early mornings. In such a short period of time, I'd been awakened to other ways of life that had nothing to do with my business.

I opened up my email and fired off a final response to Hal, checking and rechecking it before I sent it. This was the right thing to do. It made sense.

My phone buzzed again. The address to my mother's house. I mapped it, calculating how long it would take. Not long. I motioned to Emma and she came running, her hands smeared with dirt. "I'm making mud pies!" she exclaimed. Tiny hot circles lit up her cheeks, and I kissed her forehead.

"Can I help?"

"Come on! This way! I'll show you the kitchen."

I followed her to the base of a tree, where dirt was saturated from leftover rain. I sat down beside her, thinking of the baby wipes wedged between the passenger door and the seat. We would clean up later. "Okay, tell me what to do."

"Well, we have to start with the main ingredients."

"Which are?"

"Mud, mud, and more mud. In that order."

I laughed as I collected compacted dirt in my palms, shaping, patting, and rounding out a perfect circle on the earth. I'd made so many bargains with myself. I'd promised to do with the right thing when she was found in Chicago. I'd made promises after the close run-ins with the cops, with Ryan, and the Google alerts. But I hadn't held up my end of the bargain.

I packed more dry dirt into the wet and attempted to pick up my pie. It disintegrated into brown bits that trickled against the tops of my thighs.

"Uh-oh. You have to start again. Let me show you how I do mine so it won't break."

I let her hands guide mine, her dirty fingers pressing into the tops of my hands. It reminded me of the dirt we'd scrubbed away back in June. The swollen cheek we'd iced. Those first timid conversations we'd had. That felt like another lifetime. A lump began to rise in my throat, but I swallowed it.

I willed myself to stay in the moment with her just a little bit longer, for as long as I possibly could.

now

We pull up to the address. I double-check that I have the right place.

"Who lives here again?" Emma asks.

"My mother."

"And you don't live with her anymore?"

Her innocence tugs at my heart. "No, sweetie. Actually, my mom left when I was young. I haven't seen her in a very long time."

"Why? Did she go on a trip somewhere?"

"Something like that." The engine idles, and I tap my fingers on the steering wheel. I don't want to do this. I don't want to be here. But I am here for my father, not her, because there is nothing on this earth she could ever say to make me hate her less for what she's done.

I told my coworkers I was going to find my mother, and here was the opportunity to actually do it. Finding my mother wouldn't erase what I'd done and all the repercussions to follow, but it would make one part of my story true . . . even if it was a small fragment. Now was my one shot to get it over with, to appease my dad, to give him something when so much had been taken away.

While I was able to move on because I was a child and that's what children do, my father wasted the best parts of his life sitting in that sad house, becoming a full-blown alcoholic, waiting for her to come back. Never mind she didn't know where we lived all those years. Never mind that he never went looking for her. He didn't think about those details. He just gave up. He was the victim and hoped she'd somehow find him. And yet, all that pain had simply sloughed off from the euphoria of one recent call, like it was nothing but a twenty-five-year nightmare. He seemed to be forgetting one critical detail: it's me she'd asked to see, not him.

I ask Emma to wait in the car. We've been in and out of the car enough for me to know she won't touch anything or do something unsafe. I unlock the doors, making the decision that I am not going into my mother's house. I will stand on the porch and hear what she has to say, then I am getting back in the car and driving far away from here. I twist around to flip on Emma's LeapFrog, and she is instantly immersed, the world becoming a backdrop as she homes in on the game at hand. I leave the car running, air-conditioning on high, music turned low, because it is hot out, and because I don't want her to hear.

I smooth my tank top, and look at the modest house, a ranch, just like the one we'd grown up in. I wonder if she has a husband, boyfriend, or even more kids? The thought slaps me in the face—could I have a half-sibling?—but I make my legs move toward the front door because I just want to get it over with.

In all the years she's been gone, I never imagined me coming to her. I figured I'd see her somewhere—in a movie, if she'd made it as an actress, or in a coffee shop, if it were random—but never at her new home with a life she'd built without me.

I walk up the porch steps and crane my neck to make sure Emma is still in her car seat, buckled and playing her game. I slide on my sunglasses and knock. Suddenly, I am a child again. I am foolish, and I am imposing on a woman who couldn't care less about me. All I have ever done in her world is fill time.

She pulls open the door before I can make contact with the knocker, and she stands there, shifting forward and backward, wanting to hug me—I can read it all over her face—but knowing that our relationship was never built on physical affection, she refrains. She is still strikingly beautiful, which both irritates and pleases me. She has a classic face, like she was born in the wrong era, which is probably why she was so obsessed with old-school movie stars. Her hair is still brown and slicked back into a ponytail, and her face is bare except for her bright red lipstick. She wears small black readers and stands in a gray V-neck T-shirt, fitted jeans, and expensive sandals. She looks refined and casual—not at all like the uptight, rigid woman I grew up with—and I'm literally at a loss for words as she drinks me in.

"Oh my God, Sarah. Is that really you?"

I want to make a joke about blondes having more fun, to lighten the mood, but I can't, so I simply nod. Then her arms are around me after all. She smells like freesias. I close my eyes and remember a million things that weren't entirely awful, all folded somewhere neatly inside me, like origami.

"You look beautiful," she breathes as she pulls back and holds me at arm's length, assessing and deciding with a curt nod that I am acceptable, that I am okay. "Please, please come in. It's so hot out."

I shake my head and glance at the car. "I can't."

She peers around me and squints at the Ford, which is about twenty feet away, where she can just make out the top of Emma's head through the windshield. "Oh my." She presses one delicate hand to her mouth, and I can see the blue veins roped beneath her thin, white skin. "Is that . . . is that your daughter? Oh Sarah. Am I a grandmother? Roger didn't mention it."

Hearing his name on her lips snaps me back to who it is I am dealing with. I straighten and resettle. "Look. I'm only here because he asked me to come see you. I have no interest in rekindling a relationship or connecting or whatever. I just . . . I'm sorry to say, I don't want you in my life. I'm here for him."

A million questions hurtle to my lips: *Where did you go? Where have you been? Did you ever think about coming back? About calling? About finding us?* But I don't, because I don't want even more drama stacked onto my back like bricks. I stand, stare, breathe, and step back to block her view of Emma, who seems to hold all the attention.

"She's so beautiful, Sarah. She looks just like you."

I want to laugh at her naiveté and fake compliments for a granddaughter that doesn't exist. If only she knew what she'd made me. "Enough, Elaine. Seriously. Stop. Just tell me what you want. Why did you contact Dad? And why now?"

"I—?" She startles, adjusts her glasses, and crosses her arms over her chest. "Are you sure you can't come in for a second?"

I shake my head but say nothing.

"I wanted to see how he was doing, I guess. I've thought about both of you through the years. *All* these years. I read about your business, and I just wanted to tell you how proud of you I am."

So there it was. I was right. This was about money. "Not that it's any of your business, but yes. My business is doing well. I'm doing well. Is that all?"

I turn to go. I just want out of this place, away from her, but she reaches for my elbow. "Sarah, please. Don't make this so hard."

I spin around. "Me don't make this hard? What exactly do you mean by *hard*, Elaine? The fact that you made my childhood a living hell, or the fact that you abandoned your eight-year-old daughter and a husband who worshiped you?"

She looks as though I've slapped her, and I think about actually slapping her, how good it would feel after all the times she's slapped me, that bright hot sting spreading across my open palm. But I've never hit anyone, and I'm not about to start now.

"You don't understand everything," she says.

"What's *everything* supposed to mean?" I angrily stab the air with quotes. "Where did you go? Why'd you really leave? Was it a man? Drugs?"

"It wasn't like that. It wasn't for somebody else. Or for something else." She readjusts in the doorway. "I went to Hollywood. I never planned to be gone for more than a month, maybe two. But once I got there, I just . . ." She shrugs. "You don't understand, Sarah. I wasn't cut out for motherhood. Your dad knew it. I knew it. I think you knew it too."

"So what? That qualifies you to just walk away? Do you know how many mothers feel like that every single day? That it's all just too much? That's called being a *mom*. It's hard. But you don't just—Jesus, you don't just walk away from your family. It doesn't work like that."

"I know it doesn't work like that. I was so selfish. I know that. I do."

I close my eyes and reopen them. "So you've been in Hollywood this whole time, then? Acting? Until you decided to move out here?"

"No. That didn't really pan out. I traveled for a while. I wrote to you, Sarah. I wanted you to know I was thinking of you."

I look at her, stunned. "No, you didn't."

"Yes, I did. I wrote to you. But you never wrote me back, so I figured Roger either didn't give you the letters or you just didn't want to write."

My heart burns with this new information. She actually wrote me? I rack my brain for any memory of mail with my name on it. My father was always the first to the mailbox, sorting, stacking, and tossing with the obsessiveness of a postman. Was this the reason why? Would my father keep those letters for himself? "I have to go," I say, almost tripping down the porch steps as I move to the car.

"Sarah. Sarah, wait." She runs after me, and she is surprisingly fast for her age. I try to calculate how old she is—only sixty?—and she closes the gap before I can open the driver's side door. "Look, I know you can't forgive me. Jesus." She scratches her head and sighs at the sky, which is clear and blue. "I don't know how to do this. I mean, listen to me. I sound like a bad movie script."

I nod because she does, and we are almost laughing, and I forgot about how sometimes, in the rarest of moments, we'd come together over something silly and just get each other in a way my father and I never could.

She reaches up to touch my hair, and I let her. "You are so, so beautiful," she whispers. "I'm sorry I messed it all up. I'm sorry I was so horrible. But we still have time. We can start from here, right? People do it all the time, don't they?" She is desperate and we both know it.

I shake my head, get into my car, and reverse down her driveway before I start bawling. I don't even check to see if Emma is still buckled—I'll stop the next block over—but I have to keep driving before I lose it.

My mother is back in my life after twenty-five years, with no real explanation for where she went or who she was with, and for some unexplainable reason, I *miss* her—I miss her to my very core—but I hate her too, which seems to be the problem with mothers. Mothers like Emma's. Mothers like mine.

now

"New to the area?"

I look to my left and a man of about thirty-five or forty is talking to me, his eyes trained on the playground. "No." The conversation flatlines, because I am cautious. I reveal nothing.

"Which one's yours?"

He is asking all the right questions, the nice-stranger-at-the-playground-so-maybe-our-kids-can-be-fast-friends questions, but I have nothing to offer. I will not give myself away, will not tell this stranger who I am and what exactly I've been up to for the past several months. Not that we've been halfway across the country and back, not that I've almost lost her, not that we have been in Utah, stalled, as I grapple with my final decision.

Instead, I extract my phone and pretend to answer a nonexistent call, giving him an apologetic look before moving away. I keep my eyes on Emma, watching her beautiful face as it transitions from stark concentration as she navigates the monkey bars to absolute glee as she coasts down the slide.

This is a different child than she was at the beginning of summer. Fear doesn't follow her like a shadow. There is no yelling or cowering here. We have a rhythm I've never had in any relationship, familial or romantic. I trust her. She trusts me.

I tell Emma we have five more minutes before we go. She climbs up a pole, squeezing her thighs around the cold steel.

"Sarah, watch this! Watch this, Sarah!" She pushes herself off the pole and lands in a gymnast's stance, arms thrust back, head up, knees bent, a perfect landing.

"Nice job, Em!"

I am still reeling over the case updates from several weeks back. Not the spotting from the Nebraska waitress, which is a problem in and of itself, but the one about Amy. The one for *murder*. I think how easy it would be to let the cops dismantle her life; to keep looking and pushing for a confession that doesn't exist. As much as I hate this woman, I do not want her to go to jail for a crime she did not commit. She is a bad mother, but she is not a killer. Her child is gone, but she is not dead.

I keep my eyes on Emma and know what I must do. I step away from the other parents and dig around in my bag until I find the burner phone I bought at Walmart. I fish the toll-free number from my wallet and recall the story I concocted—a good one—and dial. The phone connects and rings. I clear my throat.

"Emma Grace Townsend tip line. How may I help you?"

"Um, yes, hello? Is this the help line?" I shock myself at my own country accent and struggle to keep my breathing steady, my voice light, praying Emma does not come running over and interrupt.

"Yes, it is, ma'am. May I help you?"

"Well, yes, I sure hope so. I'm a nurse in the walk-in clinic here in Destin, Florida, and I just had a little girl come in here I'm pretty sure is that missing girl that I saw on TV?"

"Ma'am? Can you give us the details, please?"

"Why, I sure can! Well, she was just the cutest little thing you ever did see, but I noticed she had dye all along her temples, like her hair had been colored or something? Because it was jet black and you could see her brown roots, and my sister is a hairdresser, so I know when something's not real."

"Yes, ma'am. Please continue."

"Oh, okay. I'm using this funky phone of my brother's because I dropped mine in the toilet, can you believe it? Well, anyway, she had just the most startling gray eyes, and I thought, where have I seen those eyes before, and then I asked, 'Honey, what's your name?' And she looked at the woman and the man who brought her in there, and they immediately jumped in and said, 'Violet. Her name's Violet.' And I said, 'Well, that's a pretty name. Where did that come from?' And the man and woman just asked me to treat her and to stop asking questions, which I thought was rather rude. They were dirty, you know, like they hadn't bathed in a while, so I just did what they asked. So, I began examining her—she came in because she was having a hard time breathing and was complaining of severe stomach pain—and then I noticed the cutest little birthmark when I was pressing on her tummy, like a little raisin or something by her right hip? And I thought, 'Now, why does this little girl look so familiar?'—and that's when it hit me! I'd seen that broadcast, and I read all the details of that little girl's case, and I knew it was her. Of course, no one said she had a birthmark shaped like a *raisin*, but I remember reading about a birthmark, and there it was." I say the magic word—*birthmark*—and I can hear commotion in the background. Someone else comes onto the line, a man.

"Ma'am? Can you tell me where you are, please?"

"Well, don't you sound official? Hi there! This is Jenny Grayson, and I'm a nurse at the walk-in clinic here in Destin, Florida. Anyway, like I said, I didn't trust these people. They had two other kids with them who looked just like them, I mean they were the spitting image of them, but this little girl just looked—well, I hate to say it—but she was just so pretty, and she seemed scared. Like she was afraid to say anything. She had a real bad bug and a bladder infection, so I fixed her up and sent her on her way, but I got the make of the car. The license plate was covered up. But it was this sketchy red van. It was an old Chevy Express cargo van, I believe. My daddy was into vans and cars, so I know these things. It looked a bit older too. But this couple, they paid cash and hightailed it out of there, and something just didn't sit right with me. Which is why I called you. I know it's the girl. Emma Grace Townsend, right? What a pretty name that is, isn't it? But I do. I just know it was her."

"Ma'am, can you give me your exact location, please? And when this happened?"

"Hello? C-can-ou-ear-e?" I pretend to break up, giving bits and pieces of an address.

"Ms. Grayson? Hello? Can you hear me?"

"Hello? Hello? Yes, I'm at—" I hit the *mute* button on and off while I keep talking, giving the zip code in its entirety so they can hear. "I think I have a bad connection. Did you get that?"

The line goes dead. I take a massive breath. I walk farther into the grass, drop the phone, and stomp on it, feeling it explode and crunch into fat, black pieces beneath my boots.

I have done something for Emma's mother. The police now have a new lead from Jenny Grayson of Destin, Florida. They will be looking for a couple with two kids, a red van, and a little girl with jet-black hair named Violet. They will not be looking at Amy. At least for a little while. And they will not be looking for two blondes. They will not be looking for me.

I tap my watch. Emma comes running. She smiles and wipes sweat from her eyes. Her teeth are lovely and small and will one day be large, goofy, and square. Will I miss when her first tooth comes loose and she places it under her pillow and wishes for the Tooth Fairy to bring her treats? I catalog all of her: her tiny shoulders, the fine, blond hairs on her lower back, her crazy long toenails, her uneven earlobes, her freckles that sprinkle along her nose and deepen in the sun. I clear my throat and stand straighter, draping an arm around her shoulders. "Are you ready, spaghetti?"

She leans into me. "I'm not spaghetti!"

"Oh, sorry. Are you ready, meatball?"

She giggles in a loose way, pushing in closer and closer to my hips. She is an affectionate child—now, anyway. I buckle her in, hand her a bottle of water, and start the car. Fall is not so far away, and soon, the first dappled leaves will begin to change. Emma points out the science of it when we are driving, how the green leaves will turn gold, red, and orange; how they will catch the light, flutter toward the earth, and scatter in the wind.

I put the car into reverse, and we start driving.

"Where are we going now?" she asks.

I want to tell her where we're going, but I can't just yet. "It's time for a new adventure."

She nods and hugs her stuffed rabbit—chosen over her dog, Pinky—to her chest. She is used to the sudden changes and shifts; she has become a gypsy, just like I was a gypsy. On to the next place. A childhood spent on wheels. I choke back tears, and Emma asks me if I'm okay. I take a sip of water and assure her I'm fine, that I just swallowed wrong.

"Swallowed wrong?"

I make a funny face and noise to demonstrate, and she breaks into a real giggle, and my heart scrapes inside my chest, a heavy, red lump. We pull onto the highway. We are just two females, charging across the open road toward our final destination.

I cling to every moment as though it is my last. I memorize her every feature. I listen to her sweet voice as she asks me random questions and tells long, ambling jokes to her rabbit. I want to cry. I want to pull over. I want to buy a house and live in our happy, two-person life. But I don't. I can't. I keep driving.

I must stick to the plan.

Emma presses her hands to her cheeks and splashes in the water, head angled, jaw slack, letting the rays absorb into her skin.

I will remember her like this, unburdened and damp from the steady rain. She is shoeless, pantless, shirtless, just dancing in her underwear, a smile stretched across the delicate skin of her face. In a matter of months, she has grown, changed, lengthened. Her hair is shorter and lighter, but her body is longer, except for the round belly that juts forward like a pogo ball. It's the haircut; it's the fresh air; it's the freedom from verbal abuse, I'm sure. It's childhood.

She wades deeper into the water, the raindrops coming faster and harder now. I clench my fists and watch. She is up to her hips—*be careful, now!*—and she swivels and attempts to run in place. The water is calm. There are no alligators or big fish, but still, my heart clamps as I sit on the shore, away from her.

Her body has the awkward coordination of most five-year-olds, each appendage acting independently from the rest. Her elbows flare and her knees hike and angle inward, giving her the appearance of pigeon-toes and knock-knees.

She wants to swim, I can tell, but I don't trust myself to guide her under the water, though I want to. I cannot have her choke, sputter, and look at me with wild, fearful eyes. I can't put her in a position like that, where her rubbery limbs could slip from my arms and then she is under, and I am thrashing about, trying to bring her back to me.

"Sarah, watch this!"

Emma jumps out of the water, a starfish of limbs, and then she is down on her butt, and I am lunging for her, because I am scared of her going under and being swept out to sea. This is not the sea, it's a river, I remind myself, but still.

I take a swig of coffee, cold now, and tell her ten more minutes, and then we have to leave.

"No, I don't want to go!"

She's become more assertive lately, standing up for herself, knowing if she states what she wants, there's not going to be a tornado of words and fury to challenge her.

I am the patient one, and I want her to stick up for herself. This is training for her other life, for when fear comes rushing in, and she is scared. That's when I want her to remember me.

I stand, dusting off my legs, rough rocks and gritty sand sticking to the backs of my thighs. The rain is coming harder now. Both of us don't mind the wet; we are so used to it, we hardly even notice. It brings her to life, here and now, as she twists and twirls, and the only sounds I hear are her splashing and the rare fish flopping out of the river, silvery streak, before plunging back down into the deep, cold water.

Without asking, Emma trudges toward me. I grab her towel and hold it open. She lunges in and shivers, keeping close to my legs.

"It's really coming down," I say as I gather our things.

"Will you carry me?"

I hoist her up, my wet burrito, and start walking to the car. I slip on a rock and steady myself, and then her. "Well, that wouldn't have been good, would it?"

She giggles and waves her tongue to catch stray raindrops that splash our cheeks and hair. We make it to the car, and I lower her, a damp snake slithering from torso to shins. I play-dump her into the Ford and help her change into dry clothes. We pull onto the highway, and it all comes into focus: these past few months, my intentions, my realizations, my enormous risks. I glance at Emma in the rearview, her cheeks still pink from her exertion in the water.

I keep driving, thinking of the last bags to pack, the trash bags to fill and toss in a Dumpster. I readjust the mirror. She smiles at me, the damp tangles of her hair flattened against her skull.

The uncertainty of what lies ahead rips into me like a saw. What will happen to her? What will happen to me? But then a singular thought thumps through my head as the miles fade: *I have gotten away with it.* In this media-frenzied, multiheadlined world, Emma Grace Townsend is a story in an unending list. She has to contend with bombings, school shootings, and contentious elections. Her story just wasn't enough.

Later, in her bath, I run the conditioner through her ends and watch as she splashes with her toys. I squirt fluoride-free toothpaste onto her toothbrush and we brush her teeth in the bath while her conditioner sits. She spits into the water, a milky, foamy mess, and then smiles for me to inspect. I nod and rinse the conditioner. She hits the button to drain the water and stands, her arms open for her towel.

I fold the cotton around her, pick her up, and dry her damp hair. I smother her with kisses, read her four stories—and one chapter book—give her a banana, and rebrush her teeth. I sing her songs until she is sprawled on her back and breathing heavy, and then I slip from her room and head to my side of the rental.

I clutch my chest because it hurts, because it is all closing in. I pour myself a glass of wine, and I drink and stare out onto the street.

I think about calling Ryan—he knows we are heading back—because I just need someone to tell me it's okay, that I'm doing the right thing. Does he know the truth yet? Instead, I brace myself and call Lisa.

"Well, holy mother of God, where have you been, you asshat?"

She is hissing at me like Brad did, and I deserve it. But still, the profanity takes me off guard and makes me smile as the alcohol works its way through my system.

"Well, hello to you too."

"You better be in the hospital, secretly engaged, or hiding out because you won the lottery. I mean it. Those are the absolute only excuses I'm granting you for going so long without talking on the phone or seeing you. My kids think you've died. Or moved. But mostly died."

I laugh, a real laugh, in spite of the situation. "I feel like I've died. I'm really sorry, but you're not alone, I promise. I haven't talked to anyone. I haven't really worked. I'm . . . I've just been going through some *s-h-i-t*."

"Why are you spelling *shit*? Are kids around? You know I say *shit* twenty-five times per day. It's one of my favorite words."

"I thought *fuck* was your favorite word."

"*Fuck is* my favorite word. That's why I said *shit* was one of my favorite words." In the background, one of her kids shrieks, "Mama, you said *fuck*!"

Lisa rustles through her house, the kids barking out mommy demands, and then a door shuts—probably the laundry room—and I have her full attention. "Okay. Spill."

"Oh, Lees, I'm . . . I'm afraid I can't, exactly. It's complicated. At least I can't over the phone."

"Are you okay? Did something happen?" Lisa's mother died two years ago from colon cancer. She was one of those eternally fit women—a yoga teacher, a daily walker, a vegetarian, the owner of a nonprofit—and ever since then, even though Lisa is sarcastic, I know, in the back of her mind, she sometimes expects the worst.

"Well, yes and no. I really can't go into it on the phone."

"Are you, like, in legal trouble or something?" Her voice is high-pitched and nervous. I'm not sure how much to say.

"I promise I'll tell you when I get back. But I do have some Ethan news. And some other drama." I fill her in on the whole Ethan debacle—Lisa is the only one who never quite liked Ethan; she tolerated him but didn't think he was the one for me—and then I tell her about Ryan and Charlie.

"Why were you at a giant playground? In fucking Chicago, of all places?"

"I just wanted to check it out. Research. We're thinking of adding a line of physical education products. Just wanted to see what the kids gravitated to in other cities."

The lie slips easily from my lips, and while it could most definitely be true—because I have done just this very thing on numerous occasions—something rings false in my tone, and she can tell.

"So you drove all the way to Chicago to check out

a playground? For research? Instead of flying like you always do? Okeydoke."

"Well, that's not, you know—not the whole story, no. But guess what else? You'll love this. My mother called."

"Shut the fuck up! She did not. She *didn't*! Does she need money?"

"That's exactly what I said!"

"So did you talk to her?"

"Yeah, I actually drove to Colorado to see her."

"I'm sorry, but you did what, now?"

She's as outraged as I feel about it all, and this validates me somehow. I curl up on the stiff sofa and tell her about that too—how different my mother seemed, how calm, how honest, how devastatingly beautiful. I tell her about my dad, and how I have no idea how to handle his heart-break for the second time, and how angry I am that he kept her letters from me—unless that was a lie.

I talk and talk while she listens. I can hear the little fists of her children banging on the door to be let in.

"You need to come home. Come home, and we'll sort all of this out."

There's no way I can explain why I wouldn't be able to come home—not yet. "I have some bigger news, actually. Just confirmed today."

"I was in labor with all of you for days! Give me one minute! Sixty seconds! I have earned that."

"Hey, I'll let you go. I know you've got your brood."

"No, no, continue. What's your big news?"

"I'm selling."

"Selling what?"

"The company."

"What? But that's your whole life!"

I sigh. "You know I've been getting offers, right? And this latest one . . . well, it's a game changer. It could give me time to travel and relax. Take a break. Figure out my next venture."

"But you don't like breaks."

"Well, I think I might be ready to take a break. Just for a little bit. I mean, Lees, it's a lot of money."

"Like how much money?"

"Like ten million dollars much."

"Jesus, Mary, and Joseph. Are you shitting me right now? You're rich! What does the team think of—for the love of God, please stop banging on this door! I *mean* it!" Lisa fumbles with the lock, and then her kids are inside the laundry room, and one of them hijacks the phone—Jack—and barks, "Who is this?"

"Who is *this*?" I play-shout back.

"Sarah? Sarah! It's Sarah! When are you coming back? Where have you been?" The kids all fight to get on the phone with me, and I take turns talking to them and tell them I've been on a huge research trip for work. I give them all loud kisses through the phone, tell Lisa goodbye, and then down my wine in a single swallow. I feel better and worse for having talked to her.

"Sarah? Can you sing to me? I can't sleep." Emma is standing in the doorway, squinting through the low living room lights. I set down my glass and go to her, murmuring sweet words as I lead her back to her room. She loves my voice, this much I know. I cannot sing, have never been able to sing, but I can put Emma to sleep in three minutes, tops.

I stroke her hair and feel the tears falling onto the sheets as I sing her favorite lullaby. I rub her back and kiss her sweet cheeks. Can I go through with this?

I slip from her room—*good night, my sweet girl*—and wince as the door creaks and threatens to wake her. Our bags are packed. Her summer clothes are gone, left to a

Goodwill a few hours outside of Chicago. I have wiped down the countertops and loaded the car. This is it. This is the last night in a rental.

I'm antsy, restless to call someone else, to talk myself down. I want to call my father, to get to the bottom of the letters. Did he keep them from me on purpose? Did my mother really write? But I know how fragile my father is, how utterly selfish when it comes to Elaine, how any letter from her must have felt like a treasure written specifically to him, not me. I do not have the energy to ask him, and at this point, what does it really matter if she wrote to me or not? Seeing her has opened something in me much more than any letter ever could.

I think about Ryan again, how easy it would be to just pick up the phone and hear his voice. Instead, I dial another number. My skin electrifies as the phone rings twice, then three times. I'm on the verge of hanging up when I hear an uncertain hello.

I don't say anything for a full beat, and then I clear my throat.

"Sarah? Sarah, is that you?"

I wait, I breathe, I swallow. "Hi, Mom."

amy

now

She stands in the center of Emma's room and surveys the damage. She hasn't set foot in here since the detectives tore it apart, months ago. She passes by daily, but has been too afraid to touch anything.

Now, she dives in, a garbage bag in hand. There are pictures in scribbled crayon; hair clips and soft pink and purple rubber bands; diaper rash cream; skid-mark panties; hand-me-down leg warmers; children's books; work from school, half finished, her letters bunched and mixed between capitals and lowercase; an old bottle of balled, hard earwax from an extraction when Emma turned four; crumpled construction paper; coins; pipe cleaners; stuffed animals; a snot sucker; Band-Aids.

The contents of a five-year-old's life sift through her fingers, and for an excruciating moment, she is wrecked with grief. She tosses the pictures, places the toiletries back into their proper drawers, and shoves the clothes in the hamper in her closet. She disposes of the rest, knots the bag, and takes it out to the trash, feeling the rain and cool wind against her cheeks.

Everything is so confusing, but it also feels better. The police are off her back, the media on a new witch hunt now. It's as if suddenly she is free. She can breathe. She has room to think, digest, and sleep. Richard is speaking to her again, though he has moved into an extended-stay hotel, and she is fine with that.

She can't explain it, but her life is changing, and this awful event has been the catalyst to push things into motion. It is tragic and unthinkable, but this is her new normal.

She's always heard that sometimes tragedies happen to wake people up. Her daughter's disappearance has woken her up, and she isn't going back to sleep anytime soon. As she hustles back inside, wiping the wet from her face and arms, the same consistent thought rattles her entire core: *Emma isn't coming back.*

She knows it—call it mother's intuition, call it a hunch—but Emma is gone from their lives, hopefully very much alive, hopefully with someone better than these latest suspects. Emma has always been the odd one out—too pretty, too prideful, too full of life for what they have to offer. She deserves a different life.

Frank has gone radio silent, and she has not forgiven him. The only person she can trust is Ronnie, who promises if this lead comes up empty, she still won't be convicted because there is no body, no proof. They have nothing. She is stuck in this until something concrete surfaces, but she will do whatever it takes in order to prove she's not a murderer. She will have to wait a little longer for the divorce, the house, and the custody arrangement, but she is happier than she's ever been and wants to shout from the rooftops just how much clarity she has.

She can never admit it to anyone, or she will be condemned. But it's better; it's all so much better, because now, they all have a chance to live. She wants to sell the house, receive her buyout, and move as far away from Washington as possible. She's been to so few places in her life, she doesn't even know where she wants to start.

After much soul-searching, she has decided to grant Richard full custody of Robbie because Robbie is the only thing Richard has left to hold on to. He will fight her for him, and she doesn't have any fight left in her.

It is her ultimate sacrifice. She will still see her son, but she wants to be free from anything else tying her to this past life. Robbie makes her think of Emma. Emma makes her think of accusations, arguments, disappointments, and a version of herself she wants to shed like a second skin.

She thinks of all the past lives she now knows about, where she's been and what: the gay man who committed suicide in 1963 by shooting himself (her fear of loud noises); a French pastry chef in 1895 who died from a fever (her insatiable love of cheese); a prisoner in 1992 who was sentenced to death for murdering a ten-year-old boy (her disdain for children?).

None of these were pleasant lives except for the French pastry chef, but they give her purpose. They give her insight into her current life and the issues she faces. She is ready to get on with it.

No one understands her here. And that is finally okay. She is days away from receiving her final severance, cashing out the rest of her savings, getting gastric bypass surgery, and living out her life as someone else. She is tired of paying for past sins. She is tired of getting it wrong all the time. She is tired of monotony, disappointment, and so much grief.

Her child has gone missing, and the entire police force—in numerous states—cannot bring her home again. Her husband hates her. Her son prefers his father, which is okay after all. The police might still think she hurt her daughter, but she did not kill her. Though they are chasing the new lead, she knows the investigation will inevitably circle back to her, as it has before, as it will again.

However, she is ready this time. She has Ronnie. She has a defense.

The sun keeps shining, the days keep going, and her body keeps moving, despite all her efforts to destroy it. Her daughter is gone, and it is sad, but Amy shares this same story with millions of other parents, whose daughters are raped, tortured, chopped, buried, sold, bought, and snatched. They are tragic, twisted, unthinkable truths, and now she is forever tied to this community of mourners by her own sordid tale.

She is giving up her daughter—her red dress, her red shoes, her red bow, her silence, her defiance, her beauty, her memory, her grit—in order to embrace the second half of a damaged, unpredictable, very shaky life. She is giving up in order to move on.

She is giving up to live.

sarah

now

I shove the car into park and take a shuddering breath. This can't be it, but it has to be. It is now or never, and we both know it.

I hear the buckles of her car seat unsnap. The air is thick from the stalled night, the calmness of suburbia humming around us. I told Emma I will watch her until she rounds the corner. She promises she will run the rest of the way home. She's done it a million times before and knows just where to go. I've seen her run. I know how fast she is.

"Sarah?"

Her voice makes my chin crumple and my body convulse with sobs. I drop my head into my hands, shaking it as salty tears drench my palms.

Her small arms are around me—an awkward maneuver with the front seat bisecting us—but she squeezes me, and I let her. After too many minutes, we break apart and I shift in my seat to look at her.

"This is the right thing to do, okay? You belong with your family, even though I would love to have you stay." Whose voice is this? I don't recognize the tremors in it; have never felt this emotional about anything, or anyone.

How I love her.

I dab my thumbs against her tears and wipe them away.

"It's time to go home, Emma. It's okay. It'll be okay. I promise."

She cries then, big, racking sobs, and I pull her to me, memorizing the smell of her hair, her soft, full skin, her crooked fingernails I could never quite cut on a horizontal line.

We pull apart, our bodies sticky with tears. My eyes scan the street to make sure no one is watching, that no faces are peeking beyond parted curtains or upstairs windows. Yes, it is dark, but my new car is white. The license plate has been covered, but if anyone is looking hard enough, they could trace it to me and inevitably back to this night. To what I've done. I haven't come this far to mess it all up.

I press both hands to the sides of her face and squeeze. How can I live without this little person? My every day is designed around her, my every thought, my every action. But looking into these innocent eyes, I know ours would be a life on the run, a life of looking, watching, and worrying. She wouldn't, but I would. This was always the only answer. This was always the only choice.

She exits the car and clicks the door shut—quietly, like I showed her—and begins walking at a diagonal, sawing the street neatly with her timid walk. Though it is late, I still flinch at her walking in the middle of the street without me. I wipe the mascara smeared under my eyes and focus on Emma's back, which is now frozen in the middle of the road.

I grab the door handle and push it open. "Go," I whisper. "You have to go home, Emma." Somehow, my voice sounds massive in the absence of daylight. She alters her stance to look at me, her mouth open, her eyes sad. I can barely make out her features underneath the streetlamps, but I can still see her, *feel* her. Her left foot stands rooted toward home, but her right foot is poised to take off running back to me.

I pause, one leg out of the car, the other inside, both of us stuck between split actions. I whisper the word again—*go*—but she continues wavering, and the panic makes its ascent at the possibility of a speeding car careening around the corner and striking her. "Emma, you have to go now. Get out of the street."

Come back. Don't go. Please, we'll figure this out. Just come back to me.

Emma blinks and begins to come back to her body. Her eyes clear; her posture shifts. She shuffles her feet and wags her arms, as if shaking off excess water after a bath. Slowly, exquisitely, her lips pull up at the corners—a millimeter, maybe two—and she is taking small steps, then bigger ones. Left then right. Right then left. Movement.

And then she is off, her dress ruffling in the moonlight, her hair bouncing above her shoulders, her fuller thighs, frosted white, slicing into a full run.

Toward me. Away from me.

Back to me?

Back home.

amy

now

The phone rings, her cell. No one ever calls her anymore except Ronnie. Could there be something new with the case? She looks at the caller—blocked—but answers it anyway. She says hello, a burp lodged in her throat. She pushes *mute,* releases it, then unmutes herself. "Who is this?" She is so sick of being harassed, hassled, cajoled, and bullied. All she wants is to disappear into her new life, marginally scathed, and begin again.

There is a shuffle and then a voice, small and sure, that brings Amy to her knees. Everything she thought she knew unravels like a ball of kite string in a tornado. She hears the babble of young chatter, a rush of happy syllables and vowels interjected with giggling.

Her daughter is alive.

The line crackles and then there is a woman's voice in place of her daughter's. "I want you to know your daughter is safe. She's more than safe. She's happy."

There is silence, both women taking the other in. Testing. Baiting. Challenging. There are a million questions Amy could ask—*is Emma okay? was she taken? did she run away? did this woman find her? what has she been doing all this time?*—but she doesn't. "So, she's okay. She's not hurt." It is not a question, because she can tell from this woman's voice—warm, eager, reassuring—that she wouldn't hurt anyone. Though she has been wrong about so much, she knows she is not wrong about this.

"Hurt? No, absolutely not. I could never hurt her. She ran away, and I found her . . . but she doesn't want to come home."

The icy truth strangles her. Her daughter does not want to come home. The old Amy resurfaces, and her cheeks begin to steam and darken. *Who does this woman think she is? What right does she have?* "Why are you calling me, then?"

She hears a sigh—and Emma somewhere in the background, squealing and laughing about something. Amy plays the last few months over in her head: the investigation against her that was finally dropped; the new lead they are still chasing, all these months later; the freedom that she now has. It all clicks into place. This woman. The phone call. The options. She is breathless.

The woman again. "I need to ask you . . ."

Something unknots itself inside Amy and slithers from her gut to her toes. She struggles to silence her body. Her ears hum. Her head throbs. She waits.

"I want to keep Emma. I want to give her a good life."

The preposterousness of what this woman is suggesting threatens to unfurl all the anger she's worked so hard to bind. "How can you ask me that? Who do you think you are?"

"Because I brought her back home," the woman says. "And she came right back to me."

The silence swells around her. "Oh." It is all Amy can pull from the extensive vocabulary she owns. Two letters stuffed deep inside her throat: suffocation. This woman brought her daughter back. And her daughter chose a stranger over her own family.

She chews on the truth and swills it around until she is forced to speak. Her voice cracks as she clears her throat. The woman. She's waiting. Amy has a feeling she'd wait forever if she had to.

Amy falters and looks around her rental kitchen, at her quiet little apartment. Richard has custody of Robbie. He won't even remember his sister, or this crazy time in their lives. He has a chance to live a normal life. The house is under contract. She will soon have enough money to start over. This is her moment, her chance. Her new life has already been set in motion. All she has to do is stick to the plan.

She rustles around in the kitchen for a Hershey's Kiss—a stash she found when cleaning Emma's room—and brought with her, here. A memento. She plucks one from the glass bowl, unwraps the tiny foil, and pops the chocolate into her mouth. She sucks until the sugar and cocoa melt and stick to her teeth like mud.

She has a decision to make, and quick. Take her back or let her go? Move on or seize the second chance to become the mother she should have always been?

She stares at the phone in her hand, closes her eyes, opens them. The answer is startling in its swiftness, and there is an ease that settles into the flesh of her body, warm and restorative.

She exhales, perhaps for the first time in months.

She knows what she has to do.

"Keep her." She says it boldly, so much so that she can imagine the woman pulling the phone away from her ear, as if she's just been screamed at.

The woman's voice trembles: "What did you say?"

"I said you can keep her." She closes her eyes, feels those last ugly words she said to her daughter, the slap, the five years before the slap, the decades before her daughter even existed.

"Are you sure?"

Is she sure? "Yes."

Amy hears the click of the line, and she is surprised by the greediness of this woman. She thought they would talk more about it, maybe make an arrangement so she could know how Emma was doing, maybe even see her one day. She drops the phone and with it, releases the last few months, the investigation, the uncertainty, the divorce, the painful few years with her daughter, the pregnancies, the unhappiness, her whole life, really.

She just gave her daughter to a stranger.

Guilt trickles through her veins, then vanishes as quickly as it came. This is the right thing to do. She feels it in her marrow. She sucks the last bit of chocolate, wipes her mouth with her sleeve, pockets her phone, and moves on.

emma

epilogue

One year later . . .

Emma kicks the soccer ball, and it soars into the air. She hears cheering behind her—parents, friends, her coach, and the coach's little dog, Burlap, who is yapping while the kids play.

She runs as fast as she can when it lands, hoping to make it into the goal. She kicks again and brushes shoulders with Angela, another girl on her team. She lines it up but misses and feels the swell of disappointment like a punch. She keeps running, because that's what she's learned to do, and finishes the game. Her team wins. They win!

She jogs over to where the parents stand in a loose circle, congratulating their children. Emma searches for her face in the crowd. "We did it! We won! Did you see it? Did you?"

"Of course I saw it! You did such a good job!" She hugs Emma and says after lunch she's going to take her for ice cream. Emma waves goodbye to her friends—Jamie, Frannie, Claire, Alice—and wipes the sweat from her eyes.

She links hands and walks to the car, talking the whole

way. *Did you see how fast I ran? Did you see how I got so close to the goal? Did you hear Burlap and how loud he was? Look at my legs! They're getting so strong! This muscle here is called a quadracept. A quadriceps! No, that's what I said.*

She bounces all the way to the car, replaying every second of the game. She loves soccer. She loves the feeling of running after a ball, of trapping it between her feet and dancing with it until it whizzes past someone's ankles, legs, or head.

They get in, and she buckles into her booster seat. "What are we doing after ice cream?"

"I thought we could maybe go to a movie if you were up for it? How does that sound?"

Emma nods and squeezes her stuffed animal to her chest. She will never get too old for stuffed animals, she has decided. She will always carry one with her. She kicks her feet into the back of the front seat, an annoying habit she can't seem to break. The car starts, and they pull onto the open road, passing all the familiar houses and shops. She waves at a woman walking her dog, at another man who is watering his front yard. The radio flips on, stations scanned, until Emma yells *stop.*

This is their game, and today, Emma wants something upbeat. She mouths the lyrics, because she is good at memorizing songs after she first hears them. The volume cranks louder as the windows lower, her hair a tangled whip across her face. They are laughing and singing, and everything is just as it should be. There's no more yelling, saying mean things, being afraid, or getting so mad, she feels she could just hold her breath until she disappears.

Home is not far, and it is so hot today, she hopes she can go to the neighborhood pool and work on cannonballs. Her friend Amos taught her how to do a cannonball, and now she is obsessed, because making water explode out of a pool is a *powerful thing*. She learned about powerful things—how her body is powerful, how her voice is powerful, how she can do anything.

Lately, she has been spending more time in the backyard, because it is so warm out and she doesn't want to miss anything. After a day spent in the dirt, the grass, or up in the trees, she will come inside and sneakily iron her shorts, even though she's not supposed to use the iron. But she loves to listen to the dirt-smeared fabric hiss under the plumes of scalding water, the way they make steamy clouds in front of her face. Sometimes, there's a casualty if she doesn't shake out her shorts first, like the sizzle of the stray ladybug she forgot to brush away.

Just last week, she caught four butterflies in a jar and covered the top with a cloth and then poked holes in it so they could breathe. She watched them fly around for an entire hour before she started to feel bad and let them go. But she has decided she wants to know how to fly. She told Amos, and he suggested she climb up to the roof and jump off with an open umbrella. Emma told him she could break a leg doing something like that and then wouldn't be able to play soccer, so instead, she caught two flies and forced them inside her mouth and then puffed her cheeks out wide, just so she could feel them flying around, tickling her gums and teeth.

Amos said that every time a fly lands, it pukes, but they never really landed in her mouth, so she thinks she's fine. She swished mouthwash anyway for a full two minutes after, and it burned, made her eyes water, and her mouth sting.

At home, she jumps out of the car before it even makes a complete stop and heads to the tree house. The tree house was here when they moved in, and it is Emma's absolute favorite place in the whole wide world. She knows they might not stay here long, that they sometimes have to pick up and move without explanation. They have a code word when that happens—fairy—which means she has to pack her tiny suitcase, grab her favorite toys, and not ask questions. They have a story that they tell strangers, a script they stick to. This time though, she is hopeful they can stay. She has friends. And soccer. And the tree house.

She hears the back door open and close, and she climbs into the tree and looks out on the yard, most of the street, and then to the slivers of the neighborhood among the trees. She has decorated the tree house with a few special objects: her favorite books and trinkets, three red hair bows, pebbles, four stuffed animals in order of shortest to tallest. She rearranges them now—widest to smallest—and then rearranges them again. Dumbo is missing an ear and Fred's belly is covered in duct tape. Once, when she got really angry trying to tie her shoes, she pulled out his stuffing, but then felt bad and patched it.

A few minutes later, she hears, "Lunch!" but she's not ready to climb down yet. She does it anyway, because she's learned that listening gets her more things and is also the polite thing to do. After exactly two minutes—she knows, because she counts—she bounds from the bottom rung of the tree ladder and explodes through the back door.

"Go wash your hands, please."

"Okay!" She soaps her hands, changes clothes, and finally comes to the dining room.

"Hungry?"

"Starved," Emma moans as she tucks into her sandwich and fills her mouth with peanut butter, jelly, and a drizzle of honey that sticks to her fingernails. She is starting a new school next week, and she can hardly wait. She has already picked her first five outfits. She has all of her schoolbooks.

arranged in a colorful stack, and Sarah bought her a whole set of colored pencils, notebooks, and a beautiful butter-fly backpack.

"I wish school started tomorrow," she says through mouthfuls of bread.

"Yeah? Are you so excited?" Sarah asks.

"*So* excited." And she is. She can't wait for tomorrow, or the next day, or the day after that.

She can't wait to see what happens next.

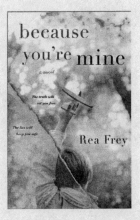